PRAISE FO

"Mike Thorn manages to find new and shocking ways to traumatize his readers, in the best sense. Even for a seasoned genre veteran, there are some truly scary and disturbing journeys to be taken in *Darkest Hours*. Mike is the real deal. A startlingly talented author with an imagination H. P. Lovecraft would have envied." - Jamie Blanks, director of *Urban Legend* and *Valentine*

"A collection of horror stories that are not only scary, but also intelligent, thoughtful, and carefully planned." - *iHorror*

"Take a dollop of Michael A. Arnzen and Brian Evenson's quirky styles, [...] add a pinch of Mark Twain, stir well and let bubble, and you have a sense of Mike Thorn's stories." - Marge Simon, Bram Stoker Award®-winning author of *Vampires, Zombies, and Wanton Souls*

"In these sharply compelling stories Mike Thorn intertwines the bizarre and the quotidian to form seamless chronicles of personal disaster. The protagonist may not know the precise nature of the catastrophe heading his way, but you get the feeling he's been anticipating something bad—and inexorable—for a long time. This rueful wisdom, a product of youthful disappointment and early trauma, informs each tale as it winds its way toward a natural yet surprising conclusion. The element of surprise is a tribute to Thorn's ingenuity; the assuredness of his prose is due to his extensive knowledge of the horror genre. Perfectly paced from the first sentence, these stories grab you by the collar with the urgency of mortal danger. Highly recommended." - S.P. Miskowski, Bram Stoker Award®-nominated author of *Strange is the Night*

"Everyone has their own mythology. Most people, however, don't recognize it as such. Mike Thorn gets it. His fiction seems to blur distinctions between horror and noir, between science fiction and fantasy. Between dream and reality. They're all here. Demons. Monsters. Big ones, little ones. (Sometimes the things done to them are worse than the things they do.) When you first encounter Thorn's writing, a number of qualities impress themselves: the macabre intelligence (brutal really), the chilling wit, the naturalness of the dialogue. Plus there's the skill and style of the prose. It may all play out like a nightmare, but a terrible logic remains inherent. His characters make bad choices, and it's those decisions that bring on calamity. At once, the reader recognizes this. Mike Thorn is inescapable, and he understands that most terrifying variety of monsters, the hidden ones, the inner ones. They're on display here. Savor the experience." – Robert Dunbar, author of *The Pines*

"*Darkest Hours* is for readers wishing to take a thrilling walk on the dark side. Mike Thorn has delivered a promising debut with this collection showing off his commitment to stories of nuance, heart, and of course... darkness." – Daniel Braum, author of *The Night Marchers and Other Strange Tales*

"Perhaps the central idea of this collection: Blessed are those cursed with the ability to see (meaning you and me and Thorn himself–all of us doomed and blessed to dwell upon the horrors of life so obsessively and with such pleasure)." – Philip Elliott, author of *Nobody Moves* (winner, Crime Writers of Canada's Arthur Ellis Awards for Best First Crime Novel)

"I've long been a fan of authors who can create a style and allow it to be as important as the story itself. Mike Thorn is a prime example of an author who builds off the baseline mechanics of prose on his own terms, and in the process writes witty and honest, dark literary stories, as is the case with *Darkest Hours*. Mike Thorn's debut story collection is not to be missed by those who enjoy an academic intellect with a potent flair for fiction." – Dustin LaValley, author of *A Soundless Dawn*

"Fast, fun and full of fear, *Darkest Hours* turns on a dime from a laugh to a scream. Terrifying and sly, Mike Thorn writes with refreshing originality and hides fangs behind a smile." – John C. Foster, author of *Mister White*

"Smart, strange, slanted, and chilling. This is a box of horror gems, polished to a dark lustre. If you like intelligent horror that rewards attentive reading, you do not want to miss this book." - Randy Nikkel Schroeder, author of *Arctic Smoke*

"I'm reminded not only of some of the best Stephen King from *Skeleton Crew* or *Night Shift*, but also of some of the more bizarre stories from Clive Barker's *Books of Blood*." - *Biff Bam Pop*

"An incredibly intelligent and insightful debut." - Erin Emily Ann Vance, author of *Advice for Taxidermists and Amateur Beekeepers*

"An amazing collection that felt like it took some of the loopier Junji Ito story hooks and the atmosphere of a good Stephen King story and made them its own thing." - Trevor Henderson, artist

"Dark, funny, entertaining, horrifying, clever, this book announces the arrival of a new frustratingly exceptional talent to the dark fiction scene." - Leo X. Robertson, author of *Bonespin Slipspace*

"Unique concepts meet a confident and fresh voice, with a good peppering of terror." - Daniel Barnett, author of *Poor Things*

"Mike Thorn is an author to watch. I think he's going to do great things in the world of horror and dark fiction, and I for one, will be there to watch it. Will you?" - *Char's Horror Corner*

"A superb collection of fantastic tales." - *Kendall Reviews*

"Beautiful mix of horror, comedy, sadism and pure gore." - *Horror Bound*

"One of the best and most rewarding feelings as a horror fan is reading a new author's work and being blown away by their talent and the awe of discovering something cool. That is the exact feeling I got when I first sat down to crack open Mike Thorn's debut story collection, *Darkest Hours*." - *The Horror Bookshelf*

"The most diverse selection of stories that I've ever read from a single author." - *Sci-Fi & Scary*

DARKEST HOURS

EXPANDED EDITION

MIKE THORN

JOURNALSTONE
YOUR LINK TO ARTIST TALENT

ISBN: 978-1-950305-81-0 (sc)
ISBN: 978-1-950305-81-0 (sc)
Library of Congress Control Number: 2021938215
First printing edition: June 11, 2021
Published by JournalStone Publishing in the United States of America.
Cover Design and Layout: Mikio Murakami
Edited by Sean Leonard
Proofreading and Interior Layout by Scarlett R. Algee

JournalStone Publishing
3205 Sassafras Trail
Carbondale, Illinois 62901

JournalStone books may be ordered through booksellers or by contacting:
JournalStone | www.journalstone.com

To all the editors and publishers who took a chance on me.

CONTENTS

II. CRITICISM

ACKNOWLEDGMENTS

ABOUT THE AUTHOR

FOREWORD

by Sadie Hartmann (Mother Horror)

LET'S SAY YOU and a friend are out at a new restaurant and it's time to order appetizers. Everything on the menu looks delicious and it seems like an impossible choice. Your friend suggests just ordering one appetizer you both can agree on but suddenly, you see the best option: The appetizer sampler. The menu points out in the description of this option that you can literally "try them all" for the price of one. Bingo.

Now let's apply this same scenario to an author. You're about to read a "new-to-you" author for the first time. The author has several novels and they are all appealing to you. But you only have enough money and time to try one. Then you see the best option: A short story collection. The synopsis points out in the description that there are 16 stories told by a versatile writer—each one uniquely special in its own way. Bingo.

An author's short story collection is like an appetizer sampler. A flight of beers in a brewery. The tiny sample scoop of ice cream before you choose one flavor for the cone. And the stories are satisfying in and of themselves but really serve as a way to whet your appetite for more.

When I'm reviewing a short story collection or anthology, I always make sure to talk up the importance of short fiction. For some reason, the novels get all the love among readers. But a novel is a pretty big investment, especially when you're reading an author for the first time. New authors appear on the scene every day. There are thousands of writers clamoring for a reader's attention. It's extremely difficult to make a good, lasting first impression and win readers over in a way that keeps them coming back for more.

The short story is different. The reader gets a full story from start to finish in just a few pages.

Through this complete story, a reader gets a sense of the author's storytelling voice, style, tone, and skill. And a collection of short stories piles on the benefits adding versatility, range, and subgenre to the checklist. It's important to note that short fiction requires discipline and finesse on the author's part in order to get an idea across to the reader quickly and effectively. Some authors can't do it, so it's worth noting the authors who can and are better than others.

In 2018, an unknown author to me, Mike Thorn, politely asked if I would be interested in reading his book. As a lover of short fiction collections and good cover design, I accepted. Upon the book's arrival, something on the back cover caught my eye, "For Unflinching Audiences Only."

Sounded like a personal dare.

The first line of the first story, "Hair," reads, "Tonight, Theodore voluntarily ingested hair for the first time."

I think my eyes bulged in their sockets a little as I wiggled down into my favorite reading position. I knew I would be invested for the long haul. That's it. One line. And this is the beauty of short fiction. That one, singular line:

Tonight? So what else will happen tonight?

Voluntarily? As in willingly? Willingly eating hair, Theodore?

For the first time? Will there be more times?

It's brilliant. All of this curiosity building within the first line of a story told in a manner of a few pages. It's instant reader gratification. I get what I showed up for with very little investment before moving on to the next tale.

"Mictian Diabolus." This story gave me nightmares. All I need to tell you is that one of the characters is named Paul *the Peeler* MacFarland.

This collection reveals that Mike Thorn is a real cinephile. Only true movie buffs could write stories this visually cinematic. As I was reading the words, they translated effortlessly onto that silver screen in my mind. I could, quite literally, "see" everything playing out in Technicolor graphic imagery and it was scaring me.

There's something for everyone here, no matter what your favorite sub-genre might be:

- Gross-out body horror

- Satirical/Black comedy
- Creature feature
- Drug addiction
- Human monsters
- Urban legends
- Slasher
- Satanic Panic
- Supernatural

"The Auteur" is one of my favorites, an homage to genre hounds and found-footage horror fans. I love how this story made me feel afterward—like it was a cautionary tale not to get too desensitized to everyday horrors...stop trying to turn up the volume—I might reach a threshold I can never come back from.

Apart from using classic horror tropes and putting his own unique spin on them, I also enjoyed getting familiar with Thorn's fingerprints all over the characters. Even though these stories are short, the fictional people seem developed and maybe even representative of people in the author's life or himself. They're not just cardboard cut-outs with names to feed through the grinder—they are easy to relate to, likable, and the reader can hope to invest (only to have your emotions exploited, so be warned!)

This is the appetizer you're looking for and once you sample the goods Mike Thorn has to offer, I promise you will look forward to an entire meal. I just hope you're hungry.

Sadie Hartmann
March 2021

DARKEST HOURS

EXPANDED EDITION

FICTION

HAIR

Originally published in *DarkFuse* (2016)

TONIGHT, THEODORE VOLUNTARILY ingested hair for the first time.

He hadn't seen a barber in years, and it showed, but he never made the effort to keep his locks from landing in his meals. He always let his bangs hang untethered as he tended to the pans on his stovetop; the decision to leave his mane untied while cooking had excited him for quite some time. Truth was he loved nothing more than gliding his utensils through a plate of hot food and uncovering a hair curled between the ingredients, or rising from the sauce like some illicit secret.

In the past, he'd always left it at that. The discovery of a hair was exciting in itself, even dangerous. Tonight, though, when he saw not one but several of his own hairs twined around a spear of asparagus, he made no move to pick them away. He felt the familiar physical reactions: accelerated heart rate, a warming face, the prickling alertness that seemed somehow to bring his every follicle to life.

And rather than cutting the sensation short, rather than riding the wave of excitement and then, post-climax, removing the hairs and going on with his meal, he smiled to himself and nodded. His life as the manager of a dirty, dead-end rock and metal T-shirt shop simply didn't afford him enough joy. What could be so wrong, then, with allowing himself such real elation when it presented itself? He pierced the asparagus and lifted it from his plate, watching as the hairs swayed slightly from its shaft. Then, careful to avoid allowing the greasy threads to drift uneaten from the vegetable, he plunged the fork into his mouth, closed his eyes, and chewed.

The fibrous morsel broke down and yielded to mastication, but the hairs twisted and slithered about inside his cheeks, as if consciously resistant. Theodore's pulse was a frenzied storm as he filled his mouth with saliva and sucked with his throat, a reflex forced into motion. Every moment of consumption was heightened, intensely tangible: the twining within the mouth, the slipping between the teeth, the tugging and slithering sensation as the hair went down, and the final, distant feeling that his throat was clogged with something forbidden.

In his ecstasy, Theodore could hardly continue eating. He tried to steady his quivering hands and eventually pushed through, gobbling every last crumb. Not a single bite came close to the orgasm of the hair-spun asparagus.

***

Some might refer to Theodore's hair obsession as "unnatural." He was under no delusions to the contrary; but any time he seriously questioned himself, any time the nagging undertow of his thoughts rose up to scream, *There's something wrong with you*, any time the guilt bubbled up from his unconscious, he levelled his brain with a coldly rational rebuttal: *What could possibly be* more *natural?*

Theodore understood his existence through only two comprehensible constants: life and death. Everything else, the chaos that came between the cradle and the grave, was unpredictable. What, then, could trump hair's utter completeness? Hair was both dead *and* alive—some said that even after human beings bit the dust, their hairs continued to sprout and extend. Others argued that this was an illusion, simply the result of flesh receding from a corpse's skull: as the skin disintegrated, the roots of the hair exposed themselves, thus providing the deceptive image of extended length.

To Theodore's mind, hair filled the tenebrous space between those two reliable poles, living and nonliving. Nothing set his body alight like discovering hair in unexpected places, nothing more thrilling than to consume the manifestation of existence's paradox.

***

Serene, Theodore disembarked his bus and strolled toward Magneta Metal Tees. He held his head high and smiled at the glowing sun. When a young woman passed by, he took a boldly sustained look at her luscious locks. Her face wrinkled into an expression of disgust and she promptly crossed the road.

Oh, it wasn't a matter of gender—Theodore was no more attracted to women than he was to men, or even to dogs, cats, or goats, for that matter. The fleshly bits were of no interest to him—when he thought of exposed bodies, male or female, he felt nothing. Now *hair*, on the other hand—male, female, and yes, even animal—that was the key to Theodore's proverbial heart.

He stepped into Magneta with a confident smile and waved at Jason, the jaded cashier-on-duty.

Jason lifted his bleary eyes from a true crime paperback and nodded. "Sup."

As the door closed behind him, Theodore watched a thinning sunbeam cast a glow on Jason's gel-slicked hair. The feelings of excitement were unusually intense today, almost unbearable. The hair-wrapped asparagus probed his thoughts with urgent force.

And in that moment, while gazing dumbfounded at the strands plastered against Jason's skull, Theodore made a choice.

Today, he would embrace it. He would learn just how far he could take this. Whatever *this* was, manifesting warm and insistent, like love in the pit of his stomach.

"Go home," he said. He wanted it to sound kind, like, *Hey kid, take the night off*, but his voice came out garbled and unsteady.

Jason set his fanned-out book on the counter. "The fuck?"

"I mean, take the rest of your shift off," Theodore said, making a conscious effort to level his tone. "I can handle the shop tonight."

Jason smirked and cocked his head. "I sort of need the money, Theo."

"The money won't be an issue." Theodore smiled. "You'll get paid out for the remainder of your shift. You've been pulling a lot of overtime lately, covering Lacy and Nick's sick days... you've earned it. Scram, skedaddle, go have some fun."

Jason, still smirking, arced an eyebrow in confusion. He looked at Theodore for several seconds, as if searching for the punchline.

"I'm serious," Theodore said.

Jason remained stationary, his face a mask of bafflement. By the looks of him, Theodore guessed he was even more stoned than usual.

After an agonizing minute, Jason finally appeared to register that the offer was real.

Theodore tried to smile good-naturedly. Made a shooing gesture.

Jason shrugged and scooped up his book. "All right, sweet." He slung his backpack over his shoulder and circled around the counter. "Thanks, Theo. I am feeling a little tired, actually, so this is cool." He reached out and fist-bumped Theodore's half-closed hand. With that, he crossed the sales floor and strutted through the glass door, chime tinkling in his wake.

Theodore waited a few moments and then took a quick scan around the shop. No customers whatsoever.

Perfect.

His heartbeat pummelled. His body came alive with the thrill of fantasy in motion.

He made his way behind the sales counter and found a container full of band patches. He dumped the logos, leaving a puddle of Burzum, Celtic Frost, and Venom behind the till. He'd put them away once he'd refilled the container with enough treasure.

Yes, once he'd combed a substantial portion of the store for the stray sheddings of customers and miscreants, he'd get straight to the work he was paid to do.

***

"You guys got any Godflesh hoodies in stock?" a young woman asked.

Theodore had been so caught up in his excavations that he hadn't even noticed the customer entering the shop. He'd now spent nearly an hour searching the store's corners and baseboards, greedily gathering locks and curls left behind by anonymous headbangers. He jolted in shock and upended the container, flinging tufts of dust-coated hair. He turned to look at the customer, his face split into the palsied imitation of a smile. "Godflesh," he said weakly. "Godflesh, let me think here..."

Too late. She'd seen the hair explode before him, surely an abject spectacle in her eyes, and she cried out in horror. "Ew, dude! What the hell? Is that even sanitary?"

"Sanitary, I..."

"What the hell are you *doing*?"

"Cleaning shop." Theodore trembled like a teenager caught masturbating.

The woman pivoted on her heels and burst out the door.

Flustered and more than a little distraught, Theodore collected his findings and crammed them back into the plastic box. He'd need to leave it be for the rest of the night. Too risky to continue.

Later that evening, the container made its way home quite effortlessly—no strange stares on the bus, thank you very much. Theodore had concealed the hairy treasure trove in one of Magneta's large black plastic bags. Nobody glancing at him would've suspected anything more unusual than, say, a new bong, or maybe a stack of records.

Or a Godflesh hoodie.

***

He was home. He could enjoy his findings in private. He steadied his excitedly quivering fingers as he slipped the bag from his secret gift. He opened the lid, and a thick plume of dust wafted into his face. He coughed fiercely. No matter; it was a natural consequence. This special experience was compensation for the inhalation of a little dirt.

The hairs, which had been forced into compression beneath the box's top, slowly rose and unfurled. It was almost as if they were lifting to get a look at Theodore—*Hey, sweetheart, how are you doing?* Like flowers reaching for sunlight.

Tears pricked the corners of Theodore's eyes. So many hairs, so many unknown origins: some nappy, some straight, and some miraculously clean, but most coated in oil and detritus and scum.

Theodore had a plan.

***

First, he let them soak in the tub for a while. He surfed YouTube to distract himself while he waited. When he came back, the bathwater was charcoal-gray, and the washroom was ripe with a smell not entirely unlike filthy gym socks.

Yes, a second soak would be in order; Theodore knew this rationally. His brain's calm and collected side was losing traction, though—it was soon buried by the loud and insistent voice of unreason.

He'd waited enough.

He undressed and dipped a foot in the mucky soup. Locks, like tentacles, swam and twisted around his toes. The water had cooled down to room temperature, but he wasn't dissuaded. His skin was flushed with the heat of ecstasy.

Any thoughts of restraint were gone. He pulled air into his lungs, a shuddering inhale, and he slid into the tub. The physical affect was overwhelming—the tepid water sloshed and redistributed, stirring the hairs into spirals, drifting in waves across his body. Eventually the hairs settled, nestling on his naked flesh, whispers of the undead, traces of unknown pasts that made this forbidden and intimate moment possible.

His body came alive.

***

Theodore awoke feeling cold, confused, and delirious. He raised his dripping, dehydrated arms. Hair clung and dangled. He shivered and jumped quickly from the mucky bath. He snatched a towel from the rack and promptly swaddled himself. He padded across the sticky linoleum and made his way toward his bedroom. He was, of course, still covered in hair—it stuck to the sweat and dirty water in beautiful clusters. Theodore didn't mind at all.

His eyes stung with fatigue; whatever short amount of sleep he'd caught in the bathtub, it must've been restless.

He entered his bedroom. He dropped the towel, shedding hairs across the carpet, and eased his quaking body beneath the bedcovers. He was slipping from consciousness and into darkness when he felt it: his mouth, going slack with sleepiness, developed an entirely new sensation. It felt thick, somehow full.

It felt almost as if his tongue was sprouting hair.

***

The feeling was still there when Theodore re-awoke. Groggy and perturbed, he entered the bathroom and looked in the mirror, extending his tongue like a child making a funny face.

His senses were not deceiving him. His tongue, that previously smooth pink muscle, was coated in ink-black hairs, slicked with saliva. What he hadn't expected was all the *other* hair. Strands grew from the cracks between his teeth, curled from the meat of his gums, rose in clumps from the insides of his lips.

Anyone else might've screamed, might've jumped back in shock.

Theodore did no such thing. Some kind of miracle had occurred, and he wasn't about to resist. He'd made the hair *his*, and now the hair was making him *its*. Yes, it was only natural. He would need to attend to the matter, no doubt about that, but he wasn't about to lose his composure.

It was time for a bit of unorthodox dental maintenance—the kind that would require a razor and clippers.

Theodore tried to whistle as he rummaged through his toiletries drawer, but he discovered that his vocal acoustics were incapacitated by the new growths. No matter. He unearthed his clippers, opened his mouth, and said *ahhhh* just like the doctor used to tell him.

He clipped away. The trimmings fell fast and heavy, forming a dark mountain in the sink basin. Once he'd satisfactorily shortened the length, he went searching for the next instrument.

Ah, there it was. *Gillette, the best a man can get!*

***

When the procedure was complete, Theodore ran his fingers along the finely stubbled flesh of his gums and tongue. It had been harder than expected; the wet, ridged surface of his gums proved much less amicable to shaving than the flesh on his face. He'd left some inelegant cuts, but nothing direr than the aftermath of a dentist's appointment. He fancied himself something like the flinty-jawed men in those stupid shaving foam commercials. *The best a man can get...indeed.* He chuckled.

He dressed in his finest clothes and exited the apartment. He didn't even lock the door behind himself; he had no fear.

He had time to kill before today's shift, and that was fine by him. He wandered for hours and trailed several strangers, staring intently at their scalps. In his travels he found a visibly unclean man passed out in the corner of an abandoned alley. The filthy sod appeared to be wasted on some nefarious drug.

Instinct clutched Theodore. Feeling bold, feeling reckless, he reached out with a trembling hand and grabbed a fistful of the man's matted bangs. The man, slurring and babbling, jerked in shock and took a defensive swing. His open palm connected with Theodore's forearm, hard enough to leave a stinging mark.

Theodore backed away and dashed from the alley, only slowing once he'd made safe distance.

That was enough excitement for now. While waiting for the bus, he eased his mind with the thought of all the comfort food awaiting him at home: he wasn't about to let a sink full of beautiful tongue-hair go to waste.

***

As Theodore entered Magneta, his guts clenched at the sight before him.

The Godflesh woman was chatting with Jason, and Theodore only needed to hear the tail-end of their exchange to catch the meaning.

"—honestly, dude," she said. "*Full* of hair."

Theodore saw Jason recoil, his wet-eyed babyface a caricature of horror. Yesterday, Theodore had fled the scene of a disturbing encounter. Today he was a different man. He'd woken up with more than a few surprising growths, and the discoveries only made him feel stronger. When he'd conducted a Google search about the possibility of hyper-speed oral hair growth, he'd found no evidence that anyone had ever experienced what he was now experiencing.

He was content to be an anomaly, and he was more than happy with the results. To calm down, he reminded himself again that none of this morning's clippings would go to waste.

But the solace of home would come later. Right now, all he saw was this judgmental, nosy metalhead. Who was she to condemn him in his place of work?

Dirty little rat.

He pounced. He wasn't a big man, but he had the element of surprise. He seized her shoulders and sank his teeth into the crown of her head. He tasted sweat and dandruff, but what he *felt* was the thing that mattered: her dye-damaged hair yielding to his spit, softening and tangling around his tongue.

She screamed, probably more from shock than pain, and she clubbed him in the neck with her fist. He heard Jason yelling in astonishment, a stunned repetition of, "Whoa, fuck, whoa, fuck," but Theodore wouldn't let go, no way, not yet; instead he bit down harder, and then even harder still, before finally tugging away, his mouth clogged with a clump of the woman's hair, torn right to the roots, blood speckling the countertop, and customers were exclaiming elsewhere in the store, here they came, clamoring like vultures to the ugly scene, cursing and shouting in protest, but this was *his* day, not theirs, and so he got out before they could reach him, bolting for the door like a soldier avoiding gunfire.

He got out safely, but he wasn't paying attention to the road.

Theodore died in a most sudden and undignified way—chased onto the street like a rabid dog, a bloody tuft of some metalhead's hair hanging from his mouth, and he looked up just a second too late as the Subaru tried to swerve but smashed into him anyway, three thousand pounds of speeding steel pulverizing his left side, mashing his ribs, snapping his spinal cord with a crack like a whip, ripping skin from muscle like the peeling of a potato, spinning his limp body into the storefront across the street in a vibrant flurry of gore.

In Magneta's open doorway, the Godflesh fan brought a hand to her mouth and said, "God."

***

The news reports were nasty. Theodore's parents, wherever they were, would likely weep at the headlines and interviews, if ever they read them.

"*He was a weirdo,*" *said Jason, Theodore's 21-year-old co-worker.* "*There was always something off about him, ever since he first hired me. When I heard about the hair thing, I just said 'of course.'*"

Turned out Theodore would've died within the week, if not later that same day, of natural causes (if one were to use the word "natural" loosely). The autopsy report revealed a medical aberration: a heart whose ventricles were sprouting hair at an impossibly accelerated rate, a brain whose cerebellum was beginning to sport some gruesome imitation of a mullet. There was nothing the man could've done to prevent it.

Death, the dependable opposite of life, would've come along sooner or later, just as it always does.

"Hair" – Author Notes

DID I WANT to gross my readers out? Yes, of course; but I also had other ambitions in mind.

When I set out to write "Hair," I was aiming to express something about addiction through a genre-specific lens. I was neck-deep in my master's thesis at the time, and I'd recently re-read Eugene Thacker's *Horror of Philosophy* trilogy (2011-15) and Dylan Trigg's *The Thing: A Phenomenology of Horror* (2014). I think these philosophers' reflections bled unconsciously into the fiction I was producing. "Hair" picks up on Dylan Trigg's study of alien anteriority within the human body.

Most of us tend to react with disgust and horror when we discover human hair in unexpected places; there is something abject, even alien, about these protein filaments that sprout from our own bodies. As a horror writer, this fascinates me, so I wanted to explore that affect.

Protagonist Theodore's fixation stems partially from hair's weird and seemingly paradoxical nature—something that reads as both dead and alive. His interest tilts quickly into the realm of madness. Indeed, this story is very much about the corrosive power of obsession, a topic I find myself returning to time and again. That probably comes in no small part from my love for fiction's ultimate study of monomania, Herman Melville's *Moby Dick* (1851).

MICTIAN DIABOLUS

MARY PUNCHED HER sweater-wrapped hand through the window. The break caused more of a click than a crash, the glass shards clattering into the classroom rather than out onto the moonlit tarmac. Clearly, she'd had practice. She unraveled the sweater and turned to face her friends, piercings glinting on her smiling lips. Her expression said, *Voila!*

Sean clapped his hands. "Oh man. We're in!"

Melody and Justin stood back about a meter. His heart fluttered with excitement, while hers thumped with uneasy resolve.

He whispered into her ear, "It's gonna be fine."

Sean cocked his head at Melody and threw his hands in the air. "Seriously?"

Melody scraped gravel under her boot. "What?" she asked, jamming a cigarette between her lips.

"Are you *still* worried?" Sean asked. "We've got this all planned out. Plus, this is *supposed* to be a celebration. You only get to drop out of your boring-ass business degree once. Right, Mary?"

Mary winked at him, then hoisted herself onto the window-ledge. She stuck a denim-clad leg into the opening and glanced over her shoulder. "You wanna finish your smoke first, Melody? We can wait."

Melody sniffed and lit up. "Let's just do this stupid thing."

Justin shot Melody a look of concern, which she pretended not to see. Meanwhile, Mary slithered through the window, her black Doc Martens sticking out cartoonishly. The moment she dropped inside, a thunderclap rolled across the night sky.

Sean laughed.

Justin crinkled his brow. "It's not even raining."

From inside, Mary called, "It's the ghost of Paul MacFarland!"

The guys laughed uneasily, while Melody dragged too deeply from her cigarette and coughed. She remembered the news stories as she watched Sean slip through the broken window. *Paul MacFarland.* Just the name sent crawling sensations up her spine. It also struck her brain with images too grotesque for even the most brutal horror films: human bodies sticky and wet and red, mutilated to resemble *things* rather than people...

"What the fuck are we doing?" she asked.

Ahead of her, Justin plunged headfirst into the classroom, then stood up and poked his head outside.

He flashed her an excessively cheery smile. "You know Mary loves this creepy shit. Dahmer, Gacy, Manson... She lives for this stuff."

"Damn straight!" yelled Mary from somewhere inside.

Melody's throat closed around the dregs of her Camel-smoke. She almost coughed again, but she trapped it inside. She tossed the butt and stepped closer to Justin. As she kissed him, she couldn't help but notice that he moved backward, just the slightest.

She gave him a look of false reassurance and nodded: *Okay, I'm coming in after you.* She hoisted herself through the opening, her lungs huffing in protest. Looking at Justin now, his arms crossed over a Carcass t-shirt and his shaved head reflecting pale moonlight, she remembered life before Mary and Sean. Damn, it had been good.

Their old friends had also been weirdos and dropouts, most of them antisocial and some of them petty criminals. But there'd been an understanding among the group—a shared, unspoken set of limitations. Like, for instance, that it was probably best not to break into recent crime scenes to smoke weed, snort coke, and drink hard liquor.

As Melody spilled inside, her hand squashing against a puddle of broken glass, she couldn't help but crave all the world's whiskey just the same. She rose shakily to her feet, wiping dots of blood from her palm, and noticed that the classroom was now empty save Justin.

The room smelled damp...like a sidewalk washed with rain. On the blackboard, two chalk-scrawled lines remained: "Murders in the Rue Morgue" and "Metaphor."

How fitting. Melody scoffed.

"You good?" Justin asked. He flicked his eyes across her face, like he was searching for her doubt.

She forced a smile. "Yeah."

He leaned in closer, and she rolled her eyes.

"Really," she said. "I'm all good."

"Okay, if you say so." He squeezed her shoulder gently, then crossed the room and exited into the shadowy hallway.

Melody hissed and glanced again at her hand; in the darkness, her blood looked like ink. She walked past the rows of desks, glancing cautiously at the broken window. She stepped into the hall and was greeted by the nasal whine of Sean sucking powder into his skull.

Christ, what have I gotten myself into?

Sean leaned away from his snorting surface (the webbing between Mary's thumb and forefinger) and asked earnestly, "Should we break out the weed?"

Mary chuckled and shook more coke onto her hand; she referred to that spot between thumb and pointer as "the powder pouch." She lifted her hand toward Melody with eyebrows raised.

"No," Melody said. "You know I don't snort that shit."

Mary shrugged and said, "Bottoms up." After she sucked up the coke, she shot Justin a smile that Melody didn't care for in the slightest. A quivery, stimulant smile.

Justin smiled back, then gave Melody a look that said, *Come on, just a little bit won't kill me.*

Melody had never told him what to do, and she *would* never. For the first year, she hadn't felt like she needed to, anyway. But things were different now. She distinctly remembered the expression on his face last summer, when he'd told her that his cousin Serena had died of an overdose the previous night.

He'd reported the news in a flat and distant voice, as if relaying a bad weather report. But Melody had hugged him close anyway, figuring the hurt must be buried somewhere deep inside.

"Twenty-five years old," he'd said. "And dead."

Earlier that night, before even telling her why he'd called her over in such a state, he'd snorted three lines from the arm of a lawn chair.

While she stood shivering in his backyard, he crouched teary-eyed over the ragged chair with an eagerness that suggested the coke was a respirator. As he drew the first line into his nostril, ants skittered across his wrists.

This shit will kill him, it dawned on her. *If he doesn't stop, this shit will kill him.*

And he *had* stopped—until now.

Melody stuck another cigarette in her mouth and turned around. "Knock yourselves out. I'm gonna go look around."

Part of her didn't want Justin to see her impossible-to-hide look of disappointment; but part of her badly ached for him to see it, for him to feel all the discomfort and anxiety and frustration that flooded her mind like a terrible flashback.

She lit her smoke and walked down the hall toward an open area lit by dim red light (probably the foyer leading to the gymnasium—the red light, Melody deduced, likely came from exit signs).

"Melody," called Mary. "You better be careful!"

"Watch out for the Peeler!" Sean added.

"Fucking idiots," Melody grumbled.

If there'd been any doubt earlier, it was now official: she was in no mood for this bullshit.

The Peeler. Her brain flashed the nickname in garish neon letters, like the title of an '80s slasher film. She crossed the foyer and opened the gymnasium doors. Her squeaky sneakers echoed across the lacquered wood floor. The gym scoreboard was her first clue that something was wrong—its bold, glowing red numbers announced 06:66.

***

Before the principal of Woodcrescent K-12 was exposed at the center of a hellish serial murder case, he was known to be gentle, unassuming, and even charming in his own quiet way. After the bloodbath of 2017 came to an end, the town's adolescents renamed the late Paul MacFarland "Principal Peeler." This nickname was grotesquely appropriate, seeing as the fifteen students he'd kidnapped had died by skinning. These had not been standard murders, even in a world where murders could possibly be described as such.

The Peeler had shackled the teenage victims in the boiler room of a recently closed factory on the town's outskirts. There, he subjected them to months of psychological and physical torture, often conducted in what newscasters described as a "ritualistic manner." One fateful night, MacFarland brought a truckload of candles and placed them in a ring around the dangling, emaciated teenage bodies. Again, newscasters deemed this arrangement part of some sordid "ceremony." After lighting the candles, MacFarland had used a hunting knife to strip the flesh from the still-living teens (eight boys and seven girls). Turned out that Principal "Peeler" MacFarland had been a skilled and prolific hunter in his day.

Nobody knew the ceremony's end goal for certain. Police consulted with occultists and ritualist scholars, but the details didn't adhere conveniently to any established religious code. One man, living in an isolated farm several miles from the factory, claimed he saw something "gigantic and inky black, with dozens of tentacles and a head like a skull" sailing over the torture site's roof on the night of the skinnings. His testimony was discredited due to reasons of substance abuse and possible insanity.

Maybe even more disturbing than the torture and murder of the students was the vigilante vengeance that the town's parents had exacted in return. Yes, MacFarland was the murderer, but before he was convicted, before he was even publicly named a suspect, a horde of fathers and mothers had broken into his picturesque suburban home and forced him away from a quiet dinner with his wife and two daughters.

They drugged him and then bound his arms and legs before driving him to the field outside Woodcrescent. They used one man's leather belt to suspend MacFarland by the neck from a swirly pole in the school's playground. The principal had been unconscious throughout this affair, but he woke up when the parents came at him the way he'd come at the flesh of his young victims; these outraged vigilantes were no trained hunters, though—mostly bankers, retail managers, accountants, and corporate assistants. Peeling Peeler proved a slow, crude, and brutal process: his skin came away in ragged, uneven strips under the frantic use of kitchen knives, wood saws, and even gardening instruments.

When police discovered his crimson, musculature-baring body suspended like a giant roast on the Woodcrescent playground, dripping blood onto a mangled lump of his own stripped-off flesh, they'd judged it necessary to close the school indefinitely.

***

And for good reason, Melody thought, remembering the horrific news stories. *All this so Mary can get her kicks, and now...666 on the scoreboard? It doesn't take a Sunday school regular to know what that means—*

A sound.

She froze so completely that she forgot the cigarette dangling from her mouth. She only came out of her shock when the Camel's retreating ember tickled her lip with heat. She cursed and tossed it to the floor, snuffing it under her boot.

Relax. It was probably just Mary and your idiot friends trying to scare you.

Only she knew it wasn't true. She knew the sound had, in fact, come from behind the closed door at the other end of the gymnasium. From inside the boys' locker room.

Boo!" Two hands grabbed her shoulders.

She jolted, then turned to a chorus of laughs. Sean was doubled over and gripping his guts, Mary was fighting to keep a mouthful of whiskey from spraying free. Justin, who'd grabbed her, already looked higher than high.

That was the last time Melody saw Mary and Sean alive—in a manner of speaking—both standing behind Justin, their bodies shaking with crazy laughter.

Behind Melody, the scoreboard announced the devil's favorite triple-digit combo.

***

The week before they'd planned their morbid nighttime party, Mary had told Melody something she'd never disclosed to any of the others.

They walked ahead down a downtown alleyway, as Sean and Justin trailed behind with their cigarettes.

Mary had wrapped an arm around Melody's shoulder and turned around to make sure the guys were out of earshot. Satisfied, she leaned in and asked, "Did I tell you about that kid who lives down the hall from me?"

"What kid?" Melody asked.

"Punk kid. Sometimes she comes over for a drink. Her name's Danielle. Ring a bell?"

"Not really, no."

"Doesn't matter." Mary turned around again.

"What are you staring at?" Sean called.

"Don't worry about it," Mary replied, and winked. She turned back to Melody. "So, Danielle was walking past Woodcrescent the other night. I guess she wanted to cut across the school grounds to get to a convenience store or something. Anyway, this is so fucked up, Mel—she glanced in the window as she passed, and guess what she saw?"

Oh gee, it couldn't be something absolutely terrifying, could it? Melody decided she'd let Mary entertain herself with her spooky story.

"What did she see?"

"A crowd of people, around fifteen or sixteen, she said...except they were *red* instead of pink. They were all standing still behind one of the windows, and she said even though it looked like they didn't have any skin, they still had *eyeballs*. They just watched her as she passed. You'd best bet my girl picked up the pace after that." Mary laughed at this, morbidly.

Right. I'm sure this story is one hundred percent true... Couldn't be that you're trying to scare me or anything, now could it?

"That's freaky," Melody said, without real fear in her heart.

"Weirdest thing about it, though," Mary said, slowing almost to a stop, "was the thing gliding over the roof—Danielle says it wasn't just a storm cloud, because it kept *moving*, and it had these long arms. No, that's not right—not arms... She said they were, like, tentacles."

***

The scoreboard emitted a buzz loud enough to rumble the floor, and a circle of candlelight erupted along the gymnasium's perimeter—in the darkness, Melody hadn't even noticed that the candles were there. The 06:66 had distracted her from noticing much else.

As the candles lit themselves, filling the vast space instantly with an eerie and somehow autumnal glow, Mary and Sean went from cackling ne'er-do-wells to Francis Bacon portraits in motion. Melody had once flipped through her art professor Aunt Gwen's Bacon book, and the images had never left her mind; but they were nothing compared to the real deal.

Cacophony. The buzzer blaring on and on, louder than the blazing feedback of any metal show Melody had ever attended; the sound of Justin screaming in a pitch she wouldn't have thought possible; and the hideous din of Mary and Sean's giggling as their clothing and flesh was shorn away in one single, swift, invisible motion. Some suctioning force seemed to be suspended above them, because everything tore away at once, fanning the floor with blood.

The worst part? Even after their artificial and natural layers were stripped away and dropped like dirty laundry, even as they stood before Melody with their bodies of vividly red and fleshless muscle—they continued laughing.

How? Melody's mind screamed uselessly. *How, how, how?*

Driven by impulse, she snatched Justin's arm and yanked him away from their skinless, cackling friends. Backing into the gym, she saw a figure emerging from the dim red light of the foyer.

The figure (*a man, definitely a man*) circled around Mary and Sean, raising its arms. It (*he*) was wearing a cheap wool suit, and his polished shoes glinted candlelight. Rising from the top of his shirt was a fleshless neck and a gooey, grinning face. His fingers, which looked like raw chorizo, gripped the handle of a hefty hunting knife.

I've never seen someone smile without lips before, Melody thought, madly.

Paul "the Peeler" MacFarland faced Mary and Sean, who were still laughing, and he brought a finger to his mouth: *Shhhhh.* They went silent, and so did the buzzer.

"Fuck," whispered Justin. "Oh fucking God."

Melody took his face in her hands and stared into his coke-reddened eyes. "There's an exit across the gym. Let's run for it."

As soon as they turned to do just that, the boys' locker room creaked open. The girls' room door eased open a moment later. Slowly, shapes trailed out from inside the rooms—fleshless people, obscenely crimson, staring with lidless eyes.

"It's them," Justin said, his voice shaking. "Eight boys and seven girls. They're MacFarland's victims."

The red teens' feet squelched on the gymnasium floor, like swimming flippers. They left damp, glistening footprints as they shambled toward Melody and Justin.

The couple wheeled back around to face MacFarland, Mary, and Sean.

"What do we do?" Justin asked. "What the fuck do we do?"

Trapped. Fucking trapped.

Justin released a coke-addled scream. "Stay away from us!" He bared his teeth at MacFarland. "Back off!"

MacFarland maintained his skinless smile and stepped forward. He raised his arms at his sides. His knife flicked red light, as if foreshadowing the blood it would soon draw.

Peeler's hand-spreading gesture reminded Melody of some Catholic sacrament from her obligatory childhood church visits. *Take this, all of you, and eat it...*

Ah, yes. Communion. The body of Christ. Only Melody had the distinct feeling that if Christ existed, if God existed, neither of them would be invited to this party.

MacFarland said something that sounded like, "Mictian Diabolus."

The skinless teenagers echoed him tonelessly.

Justin faced Melody, fury flushing his sweaty face. "Why are they listening to him?"

"This is some weird occult shit," Melody said, her jaw tensed. "They're back from the dead to do his bidding..."

The teens repeated the words again, and again, and again. Their deadened, synchronized voices brought Melody back again to her childhood church—hundreds of adults standing behind pews, speaking in empty harmony, their robed leader raising some icon or other before his placidly solemn face.

"Oh," Melody whispered. "Oh, it's coming now."

She intuited the awful thing on some primal level before she could even glimpse it. Something that glided through the corridor leading to the gym, vast and black and writhing with alien appendages.

Tentacles.

"What?" Justin said. "Do we run through the teens, make a break for the door?"

"No," Melody said. "That won't do any good."

"Then what do we do?" Justin protested.

His whining voice flipped something in Melody's horror-stricken mind, and when she turned to look at his swollen pupils and sweat-sheened face, it dawned on her with brutal clarity: *I don't think I love him anymore.*

The thought knotted her guts, brought a heavy feeling to the bottom of her throat. Watching his drug-blasted eyes register this dread, she felt pity, yes...but not love.

She said nothing.

"Justin," Mary called, and her voice was eerily unchanged by the skinning. "I have so much more coke. Trust me, man, you're seeing things, that's all. It's just a bad trip. There was some psychedelic stuff mixed in with the powder—I wanted to loosen you up."

Justin looked at Melody with a wet, pleading gaze—like a little boy begging Mommy to buy him a cool toy at the store.

Confusion and anger crowded Melody's fear-stricken mind. A shiver ran down her body, starting at her shoulders and working its way down, practically knocking her knees together.

"Are... you," she said, fighting to produce the words, "fucking insane?"

Justin implored her with a look that said, *Please, Mommy? Please?*

The undead teens chanted, and they shambled, and they chanted—"Mictian Diabolus... Mictian Diabolus... Mictian Diabolus..."

"Come on!" Mary called out, her lively voice bouncing off the walls.

"Yeah, Justin," Sean joined. "We've got *shopping bags* full of the shit!"

"Mictian Diabolus... Mictian Diabolus..." The chanting grew louder, the squishy skinless feet stepping nearer and nearer.

Melody snatched Justin by the shoulders and stared fiercely into his eyes—seemingly all pupils, no whites.

"You decide now, Justin," she said. "If you go to them, I have to leave this place."

"I know," Justin said, but all his expression said was, *Give me that coke.*

"They will fucking kill you," Melody snapped, through clenched teeth. "They will *peel* you."

The undead teens were now mere meters away, their red jaws moving in terrible synchronicity.

She took a long, agonizing look at Justin's dazed and hungry face. And though she felt pity, so strong it seemed to scorch the inside of her chest, she knew she could do nothing to pull him away from the promise of that scintillating white powder.

She glanced toward the skinless trio at the end of the gym, and then she saw it... The thing was here, slithering from the corridor into the entrance.

It seemed all tentacles, lashing and suctioning ropes of tissue whose undersides were pale and sticky. As it lurched onto the wood floor, Melody saw its head mounted atop the writhing mass of appendages, like some ghastly afterthought. The humanoid face was indeed skull-like, as reported by Mary's punk friend, but instead of bare bone it gleamed with purplish flesh. Its black eyes stared blindly ahead, seeming to perceive her in some horribly alien way.

Instinct took reign—she released Justin's arms, and she sprinted for the exit. The teens cast bloodshot looks in her direction, but they continued shuffling forward. Melody opened the exit door, and turning briefly, watched it happen like some terrible movie scene.

Justin ran toward the demonic figures, his willingness suggesting madness more than drug-lust. When he reached the group, one of the thing's tentacles extended like elastic and slipped around his neck. He clutched the suffocating appendage and gurgled something that might've been the word *no*.

The monstrosity lifted him into the air: this was some devilish, makeshift hanging. As the Peeler drifted toward Justin, knife outstretched, Melody knew there was nothing within the realm of human ability that she could do. The pity was still there, sickening and brutal, and her body was goose-fleshed with dread.

As she turned to run out into the darkness, she heard the wet and leathery noise of blade gliding through flesh. She heard screams, and tears pierced her eyes.

She ran aimlessly toward houses in the distance, screaming for help. Her voice seared like acid.

From inside the gymnasium, she thought she still heard that harmony of toneless voices: "Mictian Diabolus," they said. "Mictian Diabolus."

"Mictian Diabolus" – Author Notes

I LOVE SLASHER horror films—from the proto-slashers of the 1930s-1950s, to *Psycho* (1960) and *Peeping Tom* (1960), to *Black Christmas* (1974), *Halloween* (1978), and all the unholy offspring of the 1980s and onwards (*Friday the 13th* [1980], *The Burning* [1981], *The Slumber Party Massacre* [1982], *Scream* [1996], *Urban Legend* [1998], *Final Destination* [2000], etc.). With "Mictian Diabolus," I wanted to put my own occult twist on some of my favorite slasher frameworks and iconography. I aspired to translate some of the things I love about movies like *A Nightmare on Elm Street* (1984) and *The Funhouse* (1981) while also studying the relationship between drugs, horror, and heavy metal.

I lifted the title incantation from Anton Szandor LaVey's listing of "Infernal Names" in *The Satanic Bible*'s "Invocation to Satan" section. "Whether all or only some of the names are called," LaVey writes, "they must be taken out of the rigidly organized form in which they are listed here and arranged in a phonetically effective roster." Paul "The Peeler" MacFarland, this story's villain, picks up on LaVey's instructions in a warped, misguided, and profoundly evil way. By no means is this traditional Satanism at work; MacFarland is tapping into something cosmic and destructive.

A NEW KIND OF DRUG

"ARE YOU A KILLER?"

I was so dead with boredom that it took me a moment to realize the question had been directed at me. I turned to face Benjamin Bentham. We'd sat in the same classrooms for tenth grade social studies, eleventh grade math, and now we silently shared the drudgery of Mr. Thibault's twelfth-grade chemistry course. This was the first time he'd ever said a word to me.

As always, Benjamin slouched in his desk like he was too wasted to sit up straight—probably *was* too wasted, judging by the dark and acrid smell wafting from his body. I wasn't put off by his bedraggled hair, his eyebrow piercings, or by the pentagram adorning his shirtfront. But I was a little uncomfortable meeting the stare of somebody whose eyes were ringed by twin purplish-black bruises. Yes, if anything, it was the bruises that made me uneasy. This guy knew violence. I did not.

He moved his lips slightly. It might've been a smile.

"Did you say something?" I asked him.

"Your shirt," he said tonelessly, nodding down at my Jason Voorhees tee. "I asked if you're a killer."

"Oh." I laughed once. "No, I just like the movies."

"Freddy Krueger's better," Benjamin said. "He's tougher to kill."

The bell rang, and I gave him an awkward nod as I stumbled out of the room, half-zipped backpack flopping over my shoulder like something dead.

It wasn't that I disliked Benjamin. Honestly, I found him insufferably cool...so cool it was almost threatening. And yet, at the soonest opportunity I bolted for my exit, just like my life depended on it, my heart rat-a-tatting like an automatic weapon. It's easy to be that way when you've got no friends, but it's just as hard to explain why.

***

Only one week after I'd first met Benjamin, I found myself standing in his backyard storage shed, promising I'd never tell anybody about his secret "drug." It was musty and crowded in that shed—crooked shelves overflowed with crumpled tarp and power tools; three bicycles leaned lazily against the left wall; in the far right corner, a thin beam of sunlight glinted dully off a chainsaw's blade.

Somewhere in my mind, a timid voice said, *This doesn't seem normal, hanging out in the shed like this,* but a louder voice said, *Aren't you just sick and tired of being lonely all the time?*

I didn't wait for the timid voice to crank its dial. "Okay," I said. "I promise not to tell anybody about your...drug. But what is it, Ben? You say it's not an amphetamine, it's not a psychedelic? I mean, how did you find it?"

My experience with drugs was extremely limited. I'd only ever smoked weed once, with a group of boys who'd convinced me to skip seventh grade science class. It had left me dry-mouthed, panicked, and dizzy. I'd puked behind a tree. "It always happens the first time," the other kids had said, laughing. I hadn't yet had a second time. Nor had I ventured any further into the world of things that kids take to get fucked up.

"Cool, I knew you would promise," Benjamin said, ignoring my questions altogether. He stepped further into the shed, hands in pockets. Then, with a nod that seemed to signify a moment of decision, he crouched on his haunches and reached for something in the corner. He tucked his locks behind his ears and muttered, "Get outta there, you fuck."

There was a scuffling sound, followed by a fearful mewing. For a second, my mind was filled with the terrifying possibility that Benjamin was about to uncover some poor, trapped animal. I loved animals, always had, and that timid mental voice crept up again, reminding me that at the age of ten I'd cried for weeks after my pet hamster Laurel died. If Benjamin was about to do something...unkind...to an animal in my presence, what would I do? Would I have the courage to tell him to stop?

Maybe an animal would've scared me less than what I *did* see.

Benjamin yanked away a pile of blue tarp and tugged something out. He held it up and turned around to face me. His thin and oddly determined smile unnerved me, but I was mostly transfixed by the hairless black creature jerking weirdly in his fist, its mouth agape in a feeble cry of pain. It was vaguely humanoid, but with stumpy and malformed limbs—I would've assumed the creature to be mangled if not for the wriggling, twitching digits at the ends of its arms and legs. Its head was an oblong lump, with yellowish eyes that gleamed like something infected.

"Drug?" I said, my voice a distant half-whisper.

"The drug comes when I get it to do what I want it to do." Benjamin clapped it over the head with his free hand, almost absently. "Because what I want it to do, man... It's better than cocaine. It's better than *sex.*"

In this state of shock, it was hard enough to move my lips, let alone produce a verbal response. I said nothing.

"You're the watcher today, okay? It's like salvia. One guy takes it, and his buddy makes sure he doesn't jump out a window or anything," Benjamin said. The creature swung frantically in the air, its stumpy arms spinning. "Just make sure I don't take longer than half an hour. It's easy to lose track of time in there."

"In where?"

"Just do what I tell you, all right? It's your turn next." Benjamin gave me a smile, too full of teeth for my liking. Then, without pause, he crouched down with his back toward me, still imprisoning that miserable thing in the grip of his big hand. Muscles tensed in his broad back, and the creature's protesting mews escalated into an ungodly scream. Benjamin, tending to whatever force of coercion he was hiding from my sight, was eerily silent.

"How do I...let you know half an hour has passed?"

"You just make *him* stop it," Benjamin said. "You won't have to hurt him if he listens. Tell him once. Tell him again. If I'm not back here when you've told him three times, then we have a problem. He's small, so you don't have to worry about him fighting back. You can make him do it if you try hard enough."

My stomach swam at the thought of inflicting more pain upon this tiny, miserable thing. "Benjamin?"

"He'll do it if... He'll do it if he learns there's no sense in fighting it."

"Where did you find this...this—?"

"Only thing Dad left behind." Benjamin rotated his head for a brief but intense glance. "He told me about it, and *only* me. My brother

George found out, but not because I wanted him to. Dad always said to treat the little guy nicely, but to show him who's boss."

"Your dad died? Where's your mom? Is she—?"

It dawned on me that we hadn't talked about much of anything since we'd met. We'd learned each other's favorite entries in the *Nightmare on Elm Street* and *Friday the 13th* franchises, and we'd expressed mutual disinterest in school. Other than that, we'd probably only had one full conversation, and that was when Benjamin had taken the opportunity to invite me over. "You'll love this drug, man," he'd said. "*Truly* out of body. No hangover, either. You have to try it to believe it, though. Just wait."

I shivered and gripped my arms, self-conscious.

"Mom's gone, too," Benjamin said. "Not dead like my dad, I don't think, but...who knows? George takes care of the bills now, most of the time. When he's not throwing me down the stairs or banging my head against a wall. George is just pissed he can't figure out how to go where this little guy can take him." Benjamin's voice maintained a level of quietness, of calm. "No more questions now, okay? He's almost ready to show me now. It's in his eyes. You'll see what I mean. It's the way his eyes change."

The creature's howling reached a crescendo, so enormous in volume and pain that I thought I might actually break down and cry, or maybe just run for the door, leaving this horribly murky shed behind, but then it stopped, just like that. Benjamin's muscular arms stopped jerking and moving, and he expelled a sigh that sounded like the release after orgasm.

"Like I said, man," he said. "You're the watcher now."

His long hair swirled suddenly into the air, like an invisible vortex was suspended overhead, and he turned to face me with his weird and listless smile, and I wished he hadn't, because I actually saw the flesh of his cheek pulling toward the wooden wall, his skin drawing away from the bone like gooey pink elastic.

***

Mom was watching an old Cary Grant movie on TV when I got home. As I broke through the door, she gazed at me with bleary, red-ringed eyes, barely visible through the gray curtain of her hair. She called my name with all the strength of a dying woman, but I didn't respond. I went straight down the hallway and into my room.

When I collapsed into bed, I almost expected to break into a state of hysteria, to start sobbing, maybe even screaming. My mind and body allowed me to do nothing of the sort. After what I'd seen, the best I could do was stare at the wall and try to control my breathing.

This must be what medical professionals describe as "shock."

***

Benjamin's face pulled impossibly far from his skull, like flesh-toned cheese fondue, drawing a wet and blobby trail toward the wall. And there were sounds, horrible and guttural and savage, that were either coming from Benjamin or the creature, or maybe both, but even those grating cries were nearly drowned out by the unearthly tone that seemed to groan from within the fabric of the shed. I turned to face the wall, and I saw that its surface was reconstituting into something no longer solid, somehow swirling *into itself*, like a whirlpool of wood-pulp. It was opening at the center, and the ingress looked deeper and darker than any night I'd ever seen.

And maybe I was screaming, I don't know, but I'm quite sure I would've done something to stop this awful spectacle if I'd had the time, or the will, or even just a modicum of bravery.

It all stopped as quickly as it had started. There was a watery sucking sound, like a Garburator gobbling vegetable matter, and then the remainder of Benjamin's body followed the tugging length of his distended cheek. He disappeared into the wall. There's no other way to say it: one minute he was a human elastic suspended in space, body tugging toward that swirling energy, and then he was gone.

My entire body buzzed with shock. My ears rang. I trembled uncontrollably.

There was a period of silence; I can't say how long for sure. I looked down into the corner where that otherworldly thing lay in a tiny heap. Its limbs twitched spastically. Its tiny chest pumped like the gills of a fish drawn from water.

Benjamin's words echoed in my mind: *You're the watcher now.*

What else could I do? I followed his instructions. I drew my mobile phone to check the time—8:22—and I waited, nerve-shot, for the clock to announce 8:52.

***

That night, my dream carried a horrific sense of reality; there was no difference between my real bedroom and the version in my nightmare. No difference, save the imprint of Benjamin's face drooping down toward me, pushing its screaming features against the inside of my stucco ceiling. I couldn't make out his words, but I could hear his protesting moans. I thought that maybe he was saying my name, over and over again.

Come to think of it, I'm still not sure it was a dream after all.

***

8:52 did arrive, by which time the wall had stopped swirling like some gravity-defying mass of wooden soup. It was perfectly solid again, and the inside of the shed was mortuary quiet. Even the creature's breathing had returned to normal. It lay on its side, gooey yellow eyes staring into the blackness.

"Hey," I said. "Could you please let him out?"

My demand was met, unsurprisingly, with silence.

Tentative, I stepped toward the creature. No matter how small and unassuming this mutant was, the thought of touching it struck my brain with extraordinary dread.

Maybe it's because I'm a coward, or maybe it's because I knew, somehow *knew*, that this creature would never do what I asked it to do—whatever the reason, I made no attempt. Instead I stepped out of the shed, clicking the padlock back into place as I exited, and crossed the backyard toward Benjamin's place. George was home; Benjamin had told me so.

George sounded like nobody I ever wanted to meet, but the horror of whatever had happened inside the shed was greater than the fear of meeting my new friend's tyrannical brother.

He was only a person, after all. How bad could he be?

As I walked, the neighbor's Doberman took a running leap at the chain link fence dividing yards. The jangling noise startled me so badly that I jumped back a foot and screamed.

Stop being such a goddamn baby.

I looked into the yammering dog's fierce black eyes, widened my stance, and leaned in closer. "You don't scare me," I said.

The Dobie leaped higher, his snapping jaws nearly landing atop the fence. Spittle sprayed across the barrier and spritzed my cheeks. Deciding I'd made my point, I quickened my pace and made my way to the front door.

I paused on the doorstep, heart hammering against my chest. I sealed my eyes closed, made a mental count to five, and tried to pretend I couldn't hear the dog's outraged barking. Then, refusing myself the chance to second-guess, I rang the doorbell.

I heard something clang and thump, followed by a baritone cry of, "Fucking *shit!*"

Breathe. Just breathe. Calm down.

Heavy, angry footsteps moved toward the door. I looked over my shoulder, as if expecting on some abstract level to find a guardian awaiting me on the sidewalk. The streets were as empty as they were silent; night had fallen. I shivered.

The door swung open, and I found myself facing George. Well over six feet tall, and built like a linebacker. Vascular and heavily muscled arms jutted from a tight tank top. He had a neck tattoo, and while it was a little dark to make out the details, I could see that the tat included a skull.

"What?" he asked. "You one of those Mormon Bible sellers?"

"No, I'm... I'm Benjamin's friend."

What do I say? I should've thought this through before I got to the door.

"What do you want, permission to marry the faggot?" George smiled at this, as if we were both in on some joke.

I forced a shaky laugh and shook my head.

"It's actually kind of serious," I said, before adding uselessly, "You must be his brother."

"Yup. I'm kinda busy right now. What, did he drink too much whiskey and pass out again? He can drag his own ass home."

My mind blanked, and my eyes wandered over George's titanic shoulders. An impossibly weighted barbell lay on the hardwood. A woman's oiled buttocks wagged on the plasma TV screen. And only then did I become aware that some nü metal track was blaring from his stereo, broadcasting vicious endorsements of self-harm into the street.

"Are you guys taking mushrooms or some shit?" George snapped his meaty fingers in front of my eyes. "If he's hiding a stash of psychedelics without dishing some to big brother, he's got it coming."

"No, no," I said. *Focus! He's going to close the door on you.* "It's a different drug. A...secret drug. I think your brother is trapped."

George dropped his facetious smile. He set his big jaw into an expression that said, *Don't fuck with me.* We made sustained, uncomfortable eye contact. A low-tuned bass solo raged from the stereo.

"The shed?" George asked.

"Yeah."

***

I had many diagnoses and prescriptions. Mom and Dad made me change schools, twice. They took me to four different shrinks. Every time they suggested a new remedy, they gave me these chilly smiles that did nothing to mask their panic. Their eyes said, *My son is nuts*, even while their mouths said things like, "You're just stressed. We're going to figure this out together."

Because, although parents are supposed to be the most patient and caring people in the world, there comes a point when Mommy and Daddy can no longer handle their son pointing at cupboards or walls or ceilings midway through dinner and crying out in terror. Because apparently Mommy and Daddy can't see the face and hands that push agonizingly, insistently, desperately, against the insides of their home, and even if they did, they wouldn't recognize the horror-maddened shape of Benjamin the way that I can.

Yes, they've tried many antidotes, and I fear that very soon they'll send me away. It's not that I'd mind being sent away. It's that I know, no matter where I go, Benjamin will find his way into the bones of whatever building contains me—and locked in there, he'll plead endlessly for me to draw him back out.

Because the drugs and the therapy and the chamomile tea and the meditation and the reassuring words do nothing to help. And the police were no use, either. After conducting a full investigation, during which I mostly stared, dead-eyed, into space and repeatedly said, "I don't know," they eventually gave up and reduced the incident to a "Missing Person" report.

Missing, indeed.

***

George shoved past me like I was blocking his way to an oncoming quarterback. My breath whooshed from my lungs; I doubled over as I chased after him. He stalked into the backyard, turning his head to glare down the infuriated, barking Doberman as he moved.

"Shut the fuck up!" He kicked the chain link fence into the dog's outstretched abdomen. As his big foot clanged the metal rungs against the animal's ribs, Dobie bore down with a whimper, scampering back into his yard.

Without pause, George spat into the grass and stamped toward the shed. Veins pressed against his forehead. Sweat beaded on his brow. He breathed with the ferocity of a man prepared to kill.

"Fuck," he muttered to himself, pausing with his hand wrapped around the padlock. He turned to face me, pointing a thick finger at my face. "Wait here."

As stunned as I was horrified, I nodded my head. "Okay."

George jogged across the yard and burst back into his house. As the front door swung back open, I heard the faint sound of the nü metal vocalist howling, "*Whyyyyyyy?*"

My flesh prickled with goosebumps, either from fear or cold. Maybe both. I stared at the shed's closed door and my eyes welled with tears. Distantly, I became aware that the dog had begun yakking furiously again.

It wasn't long before I was snapped out of my morbid reverie by the brutal sound of George smashing Dobie with the fence, and then the squelching of his huge feet stomping across the yard.

"Move," he said.

I shifted out of his way. As he swooped in front of me, I saw what he'd returned to the house to collect: moonlight glinted off the pair of scissors clutched inside his fist.

He unlocked the shed and swung open the door, turning around to spit before stepping inside. Walking close behind him, I caught the saliva's wet mist on my cheeks. I said nothing as I wiped it away.

George stepped into the shed's blackness. "You little fuck."

His tone said violence. His tone said cruelty. Though I didn't know what else I might've done instead, I regretted going to George. This would get nasty. I knew this with a dark certainty, nausea coiling in the pit of my stomach.

George paused, his huge shoulders moving with hectic breath. He raised an arm, his bicep bulging. "Phone."

"Excuse me?" I asked.

"Give me your *fucking* phone."

My fingers quivered as I reached into my pocket and pulled out my Android.

"Flashlight app?" George asked. He was still turned away from me. His huge back was wet with perspiration.

"I...don't have one," I said dimly.

"Fucking *download* it, then."

I did as I was told, taking too long for this monstrous man's liking. More than once he urged me to hurry the fuck up.

When the app was downloaded, I handed back the cell. He slipped the scissors into his back pocket, then tapped on the flashlight and pointed it into the corner. I saw the creature scuttle and hide under the tarp, a blur of stumpy limbs. Behind it, the shed's wall throbbed like the breast of a breathing animal.

George hulked into the shed, looking too huge for this cramped space, and he tore away the tarp. The tiny creature jolted in surprise and tried to make a run for the door, but George pinned it under his foot.

The creature screamed, and I grimaced.

George didn't flinch. No, George smiled. His calf twitched as he applied more pressure, and the creature's protests grew louder.

"You're gonna let my brother out, aren't you?" George said. "And when he gets back out, he's going to get his ass whooped, isn't he?"

He turned to look at me after making this second remark, his eyes flashing in the phone's white light. He laughed once, a dumb and lifeless noise, then snatched the critter with his free hand.

He squeezed. His forearm's veins pulsed, thick blue cords against his flesh. "Phone," he said tonelessly, extending it toward me.

My face flushed with heat. The nausea bubbled up my stomach, making its way dangerously toward my throat. *Don't puke. Don't puke or he'll hurt you.*

I took the phone and pointed it dutifully at George. What else was I supposed to do?

And what was I supposed to do when the man yanked the scissors from his pocket, closed the blades on one of the creature's miniscule wrists, and snipped? When its grayish blood spurted from the wound and its alien eyes rolled back into its head, how was I to avoid collapsing into the corner and barfing all over my Converses?

"You fucking pussy," George said. "Get up. You asked me to help your little butt-lover, and that's what I'm going to do. Get up and shine that light before I give you a whooping, too."

Wobbling on my feet, I did as I was told. The strongest protest I could muster was a meek and almost silent question: "Do you have to hurt it so badly?"

"Don't mess with drugs, kid," George said. Then he leaned in close to the miserable thing's twitching face and slanted his eyebrows. "Let him the fuck out," he told it. "Now."

"Drug," I said. "That thing isn't a drug. It's *alive.*"

"So is weed," George said, vaguely. "So are mushrooms."

I said nothing.

The creature screamed and wiggled, twisting away from George's imposing glare. Looking back, it was probably the second snip that did it. When George closed the scissors around its other little arm, slicing through flesh and cartilage and bone, before sending its severed hand splatting, gore-spattered, onto the floor, it went silent.

And the flashlight app, rated five stars by other Android users, was all too efficient. I saw in vivid detail as its lolling eyes went dull and flat. I saw it die.

George yelled "fuck" into the night. The dim sounds of yet another machine-like guitar riff carried from the house, and I thought uselessly, distantly, that he must have left the door open.

George tossed the corpse into the corner and slammed the blood-splattered scissors back into his pants. Then he stood with his back to me. Silence descended, and I thought I saw him trembling.

"Not Ben, too," he said, nearly whispering. "First Dad, now my bro…"

Without thinking, I reached out my hand and let it hover inches from his shoulder. *If you touch him, he might just kill you.*

As if sensing my thoughts, he turned around. In his expression, I saw something that looked a lot like grief, but only for the briefest moment.

He pointed at me. "If the police come knocking, we don't know anything. Do you fucking understand?"

"But...where is Benjamin? Is he—?"

"I asked if you *fucking* understood." Tears glinted in the corners of his eyes, barely visible in the darkness.

I gulped, still pointing the flashlight app unnecessarily into the gloom. "Yes."

George did not say "good." George did not say "get out of here." George stormed past me. He re-entered his home and slammed the door, decisively closing off the world to the sounds of that anonymous nü metal group.

For a while, I simply stared at the unmoving body of that mysterious thing on the floor. I think I wept, but I'm not entirely sure. A lot of that night has retreated into some inaccessible corner of my subconscious. The doctors say things about "trauma" and "shock"... In this context, I'm more inclined to go with the term "horror."

Whatever *has* happened to my brain, I haven't been spared the most disturbing memory of all. As I took one step further into the shed, I saw the imprints of three faces bulge against the inside of the wall. To the left, I could make out a woman's angular features and long hair; in the middle was the distinct shape of Benjamin's face; and on the right pressed a taller figure, whose slender hooked nose looked a lot like Ben's.

One big happy family.

Except for George. Tonight, he'd been left to simultaneously power-lift, watch pornography, and listen to bad music all by his lonesome.

Looking again at the mangled shape on the floor, I thought nastily, *Looks like even the family pet has passed away.*

That's the last thing I remember, before I turned around and ran off into the night.

"A New Kind of Drug" – Author Notes

I HAD RECENTLY read Jack Ketchum's devastating novel *The Girl Next Door* (1989) when I dove into "A New Kind of Drug." Ketchum's book is a harsh, realist account of actual events involving the horror of social complicity and violent conditioning. By contrast, "A New Kind of Drug" depicts teenagers who discover creature-induced dimension-hopping as a method of getting high. Hardly realism. But still, this piece involves violent coercion of an innocent being, and I was influenced by Ketchum's empathy and painfully exacting descriptions. I also wanted to write in an abstract way about the ways that humans regularly and systematically exploit nonhuman animals. It's a dark, nasty, unpleasant piece of fiction, but that's where it took me, and I couldn't see it going any other way.

The story's speculative elements probably owe a great deal to H. P. Lovecraft. Lovecraft's work is always clattering around in my conscious or subconscious mind, and "A New Kind of Drug" certainly contains the residue of "The Dreams in the Witch House" (1933), "The Colour Out of Space" (1927), and "From Beyond" (1934).

PARTY TIME

STEVE WALKED WITH the kind of clumsy determination reserved only for the psychologically ill and the extraordinarily drunk. He liked to believe he didn't belong in the former category, but he couldn't deny his station in the latter. His head thrummed with whiskey and vodka and God knew what else. His shirt was wet with beer from the bottle he'd sent sailing across Suzette's kitchen. Or maybe the wetness was sweat, or perhaps even blood; the bottle had exploded against a cabinet, and some of its rebounding glass shards had sliced up his forearm. Perhaps that was what had caused all the screaming and commotion, even more than the noise of the bottle popping on the tile, even more than the damage dealt to Suzette's cupboards and walls. Blood always had this funny way of making people uncomfortable.

These were not the sorts of things Steve wanted to think about, not in the slightest. As he lumbered down the residential street, miserable and dripping and shivering in this cool April night, he only wanted to think about getting sober. This was so far beyond the first straw, he felt quite confident calling it the last. His thoughts drifted gracelessly from angry tirades targeted at his ex-girlfriend Katy to excruciating flashbacks of the scene he'd just made.

But how? his drunken mind barked at him. *How?*

How, indeed! How could Katy take even the faintest interest in a fucking nitwit like Robby Conner? She'd only just dumped Steve a few weeks ago, and yes, Steve could admit that he had his own share of problems that needed solving, but what on earth would possess the love of his life to go and share her affections with Robby *fucking* Conner? She was only twenty-five years old, for Christ's sake... What on God's green earth could've led her to settle for that empty-headed bore?

Katy could belabor all she wanted that Steve had "overreacted" when he'd learned of her new romance, but how could he not? Yes, he'd done a little bit of property damage, but it wasn't as if he'd *meant* to cause any harm. He'd just sort of gone blank, the way he sometimes did when anger got mixed up with booze. He admitted without hesitation that it had been inappropriate to put his foot through her living room wall...but he'd shown up the very next day and patched it up, hadn't he? Yes, he fucking well had. And even still, when he'd got down on his knees, his hands crumbly with Drydex, begging her to give him this last chance, she'd said only one word: "Leave."

Steve found himself suddenly tortured with the memory of seeing Katy and Robby at tonight's party, all tangled up in a mushy display of puppy love, while some song by Drake blared on the stereo (Steve *hated* Drake). The memory's details were somehow getting more and more painfully vivid by the second, when suddenly, he heard a crunch.

It was well past two in the morning, and in this little residential pocket of the world, everything was silent. The crunch was startling.

Steve whirled around. When he first saw what he saw, he had to squeeze his eyes shut and reopen them.

It can't be...

It *was.*

The figure stalked toward him down the sidewalk, arms jutting like weapons from the sockets of broad shoulders (and was that a knife glinting blue specks of moonlight inside one of those shadowy fists?). That figure conveyed possibilities that Steve could not at this moment even begin to deal with. Because the face...

Steve didn't take a moment to think, because that might just cause his brain to snap altogether, and what he needed right now was pure and sharp instinct. He didn't pause, didn't consider that maybe it was all the booze crowding out his logic, or that perhaps the weed he'd smoked tonight had been from the same batch of insidiously strong shit that had sent him into a paranoid craze merely two weeks ago. Even through the soupy daze of all the THC and alcohol, Steve knew.

This figure was real.

He whipped around with such panicked abandon that his sneaker snagged a crack in the sidewalk, sending him spilling onto someone's lawn. He fell fast and hard, tearing through his blue jeans and skinning his knees. He sputtered in panic through a face full of wet grass. The scabs along his forearm reopened, and now there was blood pouring from his legs, too. The pain was sharp and sudden, a hot sensation that cut through the crisp evening air.

"Fuck," Steve said. He trembled as he got to his feet.

The figure was drawing nearer.

Steve limped down the sidewalk, dripping and moaning, his mind concerned only with survival. He was heading back to Suzette's party, damn it all. Although the people there would be less than likely to celebrate his reappearance, he was more concerned with the closing distance between himself and that large, glistening blade.

His brain yammered idiotically as he moved: *You're seeing things.* He shook his head, plodded onward. *You're wasted.* No, the figure emerging from that splash of moonlight was too perfectly specific in its details, too particular in texture... He knew goddamn well what he'd witnessed.

He made his way to Suzette's street. Even from two houses away, he could hear the distinct sound of some fiercely infectious song by Kanye West. Suzette's house was positively rumbling; the party was still alive and well.

He clapped a palm against his gushing left kneecap—it was much too squishy for his liking. He turned to look over his shoulder.

The figure was stalking into a pocket of streetlight. And yes, that was indeed a knife in its (*his*) right hand.

Steve fought through the agony, staggering up Suzette's driveway, hissing through his teeth and huffing his smoker's lungs into near-submission. By the time he'd made it to the porch, he dispelled with anything that might resemble a social norm.

Sweat pasted his long bangs to his face. Spittle bubbled along his cracked lips. He tilted his head toward the sky and screamed, "Help! Fucking help me, for the love of Christ!"

He thundered his fist against the door, his wounded forearm leaving red splotches on the wood. He glanced over his shoulder, and he saw immediately that the figure was trudging up the curb, moving closer and closer to Suzette's driveway.

I've got fifteen seconds, thought Steve. *Fifteen seconds at best.*

He was drawing back his aching fist for one last desperate knock when, finally, the door opened. Steve charged inside. Under the bass-heavy tones of hip-hop rang an assortment of screams and shouts.

Steve sprawled across the entrance mat, landing nose-first inside someone's well-worn Nikes. "Close the *fucking* door!" he bellowed.

He heard the clicking of a lock. As he rose to his feet, trembling and panting, he became aware that he'd caused yet another disturbing, party-stopping scene. The music was bumping, loud as ever, but otherwise the room was grimly comic in its stillness. Groups of people stood gape-faced in the hallways and living room. Two men reached out toward Steve, slowly and resolutely. Their body language said, *Calm down.* Their mouths formed silent words: *Okay. Easy. Just. Easy.*

Steve had no time to consider his embarrassment. Right about now he was too busy with his threatened livelihood.

He tried to speak, but all that came out was, "My...my..."

He looked down at his knees. Both were tattered down to the bone, and the blood was flowing in rivers down his shins. His socks were painted red. *I'll need stitches,* he thought with crazed clarity.

He looked back up into the staring hordes and saw Katy. Another young woman was pulling her through the living room, nudging past those bizarrely frozen masses. Katy wore a look on her face that was close to unreadable. Steve thought the night must've been pretty shocking for her, too.

He turned back around, facing the door.

He must be awfully close now. He must—

Midway through his thought, the door rattled inside its frame. His pursuer was trying to break through.

Steve whirled back around with a helpless cry of, "Holy Jesus!"

The room remained horribly, ludicrously still. The Kanye track had finished, and the iPod shuffle had selected something even less fitting for the occasion—some ancient hit by The Beach Boys.

Steve ran for the stairs, nearly stomping on the lap of a stone-faced young man on the bottom step. As Steve ascended, leaping two painful steps at a time, the door quaked. Beneath the sound of thudding and shuddering came the more concerning noise of cracking wood.

He made his way to the top of the stairs. Three young men were huddled around a laptop; they'd paused whatever YouTube video they'd been watching. Steve charged through them and looked down from the landing at all those befuddled, dumbfounded faces. It seemed that shock had driven them all into complete submission. He couldn't let them stay this way. As the sound of the cracking door increased in volume and frequency, Steve lost what little shred of restraint he possessed.

He leapt for the banister and glared down at the stunned-stupid groups. "I'm going to be *murdered*, do you understand?" He paused. Their dumb silence told him that no, they didn't understand. And why should they? He was just a drunken fool ruining their party for the second time in one evening. To them, that ferocious pounding on the door was probably just some other dejected partygoer who'd had far too much to drink. If only they knew…

Steve tilted his head even further across the banister, nearly leaning his entire midsection over the edge. He was inches away from tumbling twenty feet onto the coffee table below. He yelled even louder this time: "Because I don't! *I* don't understand!"

The door sagged under another punishing slam.

"You're fucked," a man called from downstairs.

No time for debate, Steve decided. He waved his hand at those impassive groups—*to hell with all of you*—and turned around in search of a door. There was a room at the end of the hall. He'd make his way in there, lock and barricade, then call the police.

Hopefully one of the morons down there would have the good sense to put up a fight—SLAM, the door took yet another brutal knock—before the house's entrance finally gave up and came crashing down. Steve had no intention of standing around to see what might happen. He sprinted down the hall and into the room at the end, slamming the door with such force that a woman downstairs screamed in surprise.

He whirled around to survey the space. It was a standard bedroom setup: wardrobe, twin bed, a lamp glowing on the bedside table. He was also half-relieved to see the sturdily built man sprawled across the bed's mattress, a roach pinched between thumb and forefinger.

"Oh, thank Christ," Steve said. "Listen, we don't have much time. As soon as…as soon as someone tries to get through that door, we attack. Okay?" He rummaged through his pockets, searching for his phone. No such luck. He must've lost it somewhere in all the evening's mayhem. He looked with pleading eyes at the stoned man. "Would you call the police?"

The man ignored Steve's question. His broad face cracked into a grin of disbelief, and he took a wistful suck on the tiny roach.

Steve heard the house's entrance door exploding open.

"Please, for the love of fuck." Steve clicked the bedroom door's lock into place. "Take out your phone, please."

"You're Steve Delisle, aren't you?" asked the brute on the bed.

Steve brought his hands to his face, now nearly howling in terror. There were footsteps on the stairs, slowly ascending.

"I heard what you did," the man said. "Katy told me everything."

The footsteps were getting closer. Steve stepped closer to the man, his body tingling with pure dread.

"Everything," the man repeated. "She told me that you downed a whole bottle of mouthwash one night, glug-glug-glug, drinking it just like it was water, because she wouldn't let you leave the house to buy real booze. But we both know the *real* kicker of that little episode, right? The story goes that you lifted your shirt over your head, took out the kitchen scissors, and clipped off your nipples. The left one first, I heard—one guy says it landed in Katy's glass of milk. Plop." The man laughed once at this, humorlessly. "Then went the right one, you clipped it off and let it fall right onto the kitchen floor, and then the story goes that you went for Katy with the scissors, and you almost—"

"—*Enough!*" screamed Steve. This was not the last thing he would hear before his untimely demise. Not if he had any say in the matter.

WHAM. The bedroom door bent inward. The pursuer clearly had no intention of relenting any time soon.

Steve pounced onto the bed, wrapping his arms around the man's vast shoulders. The imbecile pushed him away, a sneer plastered across his ugly pink mug. Steve thudded against the wall, his head connecting with such force that comets danced across his vision. "Please," he said, dazed. "Please..."

His vision was blurring as the bedroom door crashed in, splintering down the middle and unhinging at the top. Even through his pain-fogged sight, Steve could now confirm in this bright and clear lamplight that his worst suspicions were true. Not that he'd ever *really* doubted his instincts; what he'd seen then, out on the dark street, could not be denied any more easily than what he saw now.

What he saw was *himself*, standing in that doorway with a kitchen knife in hand, heaving with strained and furious breath. And his double was indeed shirtless, revealing horribly puckered purple scars where his nipples should've been.

And Steve only had the chance to say "Please" once more, barely aware of the frantic screams coming from the man on the bed. The moment Steve allowed the word to slip from his lips, his horrid and undeniably tangible double stamped across the room, knife raised.

Steve's double thudded the knife into the soft hollow above Steve's collar bone. Blood spouted from Steve's wound and into the livid face of his double, drenching the walls, pooling on the carpet, and spritzing the bedsheets.

The man on the bed unleashed a noise of pure and unbridled despair, lunging for Steve's double with all the clumsy coordination of the irrevocably baked. Steve's double side-stepped the attack and slammed his knife downward, lodging it into the meat below the back of the man's skull. The man jittered as if electrocuted, emitting a cry that sounded like an absurdly perfect pronouncement of the word garble, before going limp and twitchy.

With great effort, Steve's double yanked the knife free and hurled the man's hefty corpse back onto the bed. The man's left shoulder squashed the simmering roach he'd left there. Gore poured across the floral patterning.

Before exiting the room to make his way back downstairs (how had nobody even noticed him entering the house?), Steve's double turned around and surveyed the room. There was a lot of blood, and he'd made a dent in the wall where the door had collapsed.

And there was also a single dead body, sprawled massively across those gaudily flowery bedsheets.

Steve nodded to nobody but himself, and he stepped back out into the hall. His knife left a pitter-pattering trail of red. Katy and Robby must be somewhere down there, and he promised himself he would get to them, even if it took a lot of slicing and dicing in the process. He would've shut the door behind himself, if it was still connected to its hinges.

"Party Time" – Author Notes

THIS STORY IS the product of a couple quick, hyper-focused writing sessions. I wanted to use indirect narrative discourse to write from a toxic protagonist's perspective, and I also wanted to reflect hyperbolically on the ways that parties can quickly become menacing, or even terrifying. I aimed to portray the demons that can arise from a concoction of lowered inhibitions, social anxiety, heightened emotions, and crowded space.

Whenever I'm tapping into scary or violent psyches, I think back to Hubert Selby Jr.'s techniques, especially the epic inner-monologue that comprises his horrifying novel *The Room* (1971). In terms of narrational style, I was also influenced by Don Robertson's *The Ideal, Genuine Man* (1987), Jim Thompson's *The Killer Inside Me* (1952), and Robert Bloch's *The Scarf* (1947). And, of course, like any diligent student of horror exploring the doppelgänger trope, I was inspired by Robert Louis Stevenson's classic *Strange Case of Dr Jekyll and Mr. Hyde* (1886).

MIRED

Originally published in *Double Feature Magazine* (2016)

THE BLIZZARD WHIPPED twisters of snow across Randolph's front lawn. Water bulged through his window's sealant, trickled down the wall, and pooled on the floor. On any other day, he might've worried about the hardwood swelling from the moisture.

On no other day, though, had he found himself standing gape-faced before his storage room, while his eyes reflected the neon greenness of a heaving blob.

Yes, there was a blob in his storage room.

As Randolph watched in horror-stricken silence, the creature opened its wet, central orifice and absorbed an entire box of his research material.

Randolph, who'd awoken to these tempestuous weather conditions and decided his storage room was finally due for a cleaning, screamed in dumb disbelief. He'd planned to comb through these boxes in hopes of mining old theoretical sources. He'd only just moved into this flat a month ago, and he hadn't yet sifted through the books to shelf what was important and stow away what wasn't.

The blob paused. The slimy body—if it could be considered a body—went eerily still, the domelike top (*Head?* Randolph thought wildly. *Does this thing have a head?*) shimmered with moisture. The creature's frozen position lent it the illusion of countenance: its mouth mirrored Randolph's own, a yawning expression of cluelessness that seemed to say, *Oh gee, I wasn't expecting this.*

It wobbled, bringing the unwelcome image of lime Jell-O to Randolph's mind. The monstrosity quivered, its form squelching and squishing, and it burped with startling volume. Gusting from its insides was the porky stench of dead things left sitting on a kitchen counter. Randolph tilted backward, his eyes watering and his stomach swimming.

He watched hopelessly as the sodden remains of Derrida's *The Gift of Death* eased their way from the blob's glistening lip, splatting slime across the hardwood.

Randolph remembered a notation he'd made in the text, some half-formed critique of the book's theological limitations—a point he'd intended to raise at the upcoming Post-Structuralizing Post-Structural Structures conference—and, for one lunatic moment, he almost reached down to collect the book.

Then the scene struck his mind with horribly palpable truth, like the sudden registering of a child's death; poor Randolph was, after all, still in the laborious process of waking up. There'd been a few too many glasses of port at the after-reception get-together last night, and the reception itself had offered a great deal of alcohol...

Randolph screamed a stream of nonsensical obscenity—"Bastards shitting on the idiots of fuck!"—and, with a single swing, he cracked the storage room door shut.

He stood, dazed and delirious. His head pounded. He ran a palm across his sweat-glossed scalp.

Call the police. The thought whizzed into his brain like a train's scheduled arrival: utterly necessitous. He snuffed it out quickly with cold, studied logic, imagining the unthinkable phone conversation that would result: *Hello, yes. This is going to sound preposterous, but please hear me out. You see, an apparently sentient mound of ooze has camped out in my storage room and is currently devouring my philosophy and theory texts... Yes, that's right, o-o-z-e. Ooze. You might describe it as "slime." You know, like from one of those old science fiction B-movies. Nuclear waste paranoia pictures. Right.*

No, that wouldn't do.

There was a slurping sound behind the door. What was it eating now? His Nietzsche? His Hegel? Nietzsche and Hegel could go, he could live with that, but it was the loss of post-1968 French intellectualism that worried him deeply. The conference next week was to feature a leading academic from New York, a tidily bearded man named Dr. Adam Langford, whose work studied the tenebrous politics of YouTube hairstyling-tip videos within the post-Foucaultian context of panoptical anti-power.

Truth be told, Randolph couldn't make tails of Langford's work any easier than he could make heads of it. Randolph had intended to begin a desperate retrospective search into his undergraduate theory readings before the conference arrived. He wanted to wow his colleagues with inspiring and affirming and maybe even incendiary responses to the panels, to the work of Dr. Langford himself. Randolph's output had been diminishing lately, and he'd heard mutterings and rumours: *Dolphy the dinosaur ... an unproductive representative of Ivory Tower oppressions ... hasn't written anything worthwhile since his PhD dissertation ...*

Yes, Dolphy had planned to start with the torturous Derrida, but that wasn't likely to happen, now was it?

He tugged his earlobes until the flesh stung in protest, paced a half-circle around the room, heard the grotesque noises increasing in volume.

Was the slimeball now moving onto box number three? Number four? Did its appetite know no end?

Alice Braun. The name dropped abruptly into his mind. Yes, Alice, the new member of the Natural Sciences department, whom Randolph had met by chance at the pre-reception cocktail gathering. They hadn't got along famously enough to exchange contact information or anything, but still—she might be able to offer some explanation as to what this thing *was*. What did she say her research focus was? Organic anti-matter? Material organisms? Anti-organic organs?

Whatever the answer, Randolph took no time to reflect. He made a quick, shaky-fingered Google search on his Android, soon found her phone number, and dialed.

One ring. *What am I doing?* Two rings. *What else am I supposed to do?* Three rings. *This is irrefutable goddamn insanity.*

Randolph ended the call and continued pulling at his earlobe, bobbing on his heels and hissing air between his teeth.

Kill it.

No, he couldn't very well do that, either. The blob hadn't exactly threatened him. No, it had only made exceptionally rude and presumptuous dinner plans.

He laughed once, shrilly, and the sound made him jolt. The scenario's madness was blotting his thought processes, making him feel airy-headed and drunk all over again. He massaged his temples, folding flesh under fingertips, and collected himself.

No, killing it was not an option. This thing might be some rare and unheard-of organism. Randolph might be unwittingly housing an entirely new, entirely alien specimen. How did it survive the climate? Or did it need to? Was it, perhaps, a pipe-dweller, something that had made its way through the house's guts and into its open body?

A sudden silence.

Randolph paused, closed his lips, and leaned in closer to the door. No more squishy noises. No rustling. No suction.

Gone? Already? His muscles depressurized in relief, and then, despite himself, he felt an unexpected sense of disappointment. *Already gone?*

The thought was almost, dare he say...anti-climactic.

There was only one way to confirm.

He raised his hand uneasily, closed it around the knob, and yanked the door open. He'd once heard from his uncle Bill, an avid hiker, that some animals backed away from humans if said humans made themselves appear "big," and so Randolph released a guttural cry and spread his arms as the door thudded against the wall.

Empty.

Scattered across the floor were the muck-shrivelled remnants of three Derrida books, and there was a wet imprint where the blob had been—unfathomably bright, comic book green.

But no slimeball.

Randolph turned and looked over his shoulder, as if the creature might've slipped between his splayed legs and reconstituted itself behind him, towering and ready for the kill.

His body eased further at the sight of his unmarred living room.

Gather the books that are left. After that, you can make another Google search—there must be some local organization that can attend to matters such as these. Right?

Yeah, right. Randolph wasn't so sure. Maybe some in-depth investigation would prove him wrong, but he felt safe in doubting that anyone would be able to give him an educated answer to this outlandish situation.

He sighed and stepped into the storage room. He crouched down, and he was about to reach for *The Gift of Death* when he heard a slushy, goopy noise, right above his head.

He raised his eyes slowly, hesitantly, toward the ceiling.

There it was: smeared like emerald milk-skin across the stucco, its vast ingress dribbling strands of liquid.

Randolph opened his own mouth to scream, but he was cut short as the thing swelled and drooped like a raindrop, detached itself from the ceiling, and—

***

—Randolph is standing in a viridescent void. He's awash in green. He looks down at his body to ensure that everything is still intact, and he notes that his skin appears to have taken on the same sickly bright shade of the storage-dweller's flesh.

Have I been eaten? The thought strikes Randolph with fear, deep in his guts, and his entire body stiffens with goose pimples.

But he can move. He can spread his arms, and does, and they make no contact with anything.

What in the good goddamn—

He has no time to process, no time to reflect. An echoey, reverberating gallop rings across this neon chasm, and he notes immediately that it's increasing in volume.

That it's getting closer.

He spins around, and he feels a weightless sensation, like he's underwater, with all the lightness and none of the pressure enforced by liquid. He looks down and sees nothing of substance beneath his slippered feet. There's only what seems to be an endless greenness, spanning the entirety of his vision: up and down, side to side, above and beyond...

Nowhere to run, Randolph. His pulse ascends with the closing distance of that galloping sound. *Nowhere to hide.*

He stares ahead, fear-numbed and lacking substance.

What he sees is somehow, impossibly, even more outrageous than the monstrosity that turned up in his storage room, that gulped him down like he was just another theory volume.

He faces a thin and humanoid figure with bleach-white flesh and a bulbous, yellow-eyed head resting atop its swaying stalk of a neck. Its spindly white legs are stretched across the back of its steed: a heavy beast, plated like a rhinoceros, with a neck as long as its rider's. The steed's reptilian skull reveals more teeth than Randolph cares to count.

The rider lowers a staff toward Randolph; the weapon's tip glows with an opalescent gem, and Randolph retreats a step.

Tell us what you've learned, and you may go freely. Its voice sounds like a fading transmission, like a radio tuned halfway between two stations.

"I beg your pardon," Randolph says, "but...what?"

Tell us.

"Us."

The rider swings its left leg upward, nearly to neck-level, and slides off the beast onto its right leg. It stands in this impossible contortionist pose for what feels like a minute, then brings its left leg slowly to the groundless ground.

Tell. Us. What. You've. Learned.

"...and I can go, right. I heard that part. I suppose I'm just not quite understanding what it is you *mean*, precisely," Randolph says. *This is the maddest fever dream of all time. More intense than the night you experimented with LSD in the '60s at a symposium on Timothy Leary's radical thought.*

The rider steps forward and points its luminous gem at Randolph's chest. *You understand. So tell.* It holds out its free hand, fingers twitching, and a book materializes into its palm: *Process and Reality*, by Alfred North Whitehead.

It holds out the book, and Randolph pauses. "You want me to...read Whitehead to you?"

The beastly steed stamps its front hoofs and huffs obdurately. The rider turns to it, raises *Process and Reality* as if it's some transcendent peace offering, then rotates to face Randolph again.

Tell us.

Randolph laughs at the lunacy of the scene before him. "For God's sake, we're really not getting anywhere, now are we?"

The rider stares.

"I mean, I haven't even read Whitehead," Randolph says honestly. "I've always meant to, but I couldn't find any way to incorporate his thought into my own research questions." *Right. Because you've had so many vital "research questions" in the last, what—two decades? Three?* Randolph ignores his nagging inner voice and stares straight into those nonresponsive yellow eyes.

The rider holds the book toward the green infinity above. *This is The Whitehead?*

"Uh...yes, that's probably Alfred North Whitehead's most famous text. See, Whitehead was a mathematician to begin with, by trade I guess you might say, but..." Randolph's brain sells his mouth short, and the sentence drops off before he's sure where he wanted to go with it.

Tell us of The Whitehead.

Randolph stops and thinks. During his master's degree, he met briefly with an accomplished professor in the Philosophy department, a man named Frank Cadigan. Frank spoke from the side of his mouth, his hair a tattered and snowy cloud over the weathered globe of his head. Frank, if Randolph remembers correctly, had whispered, "Thoughts are dead, but the world is alive." Dear old Dr. Cadigan's relation to *Process and Reality?* Randolph seems to recall that one of his instructors had once referred to Frank as "the only true Whitehead scholar."

Randolph opens his mouth to speak and, in a fit of desperation, says the only thing he can muster: "Thoughts are dead, but the world is alive."

He expects to tumble face-first into the congealing slime pooled on his storage room floor. Expects this nightmare's overstayed welcome to come to a stop. He expects, at least, for the rider to nod in appreciation.

He does not expect what *does* happen.

Impostor. He's given us all we need. The rider faces his steed. *You may feed.*

"Feed?" Randolph's heart throbs somewhere in the neighborhood of his esophagus. "Impostor?"

The beast grunts deep in its long, pasta-like throat, scrapes its hooves and plunges forward, jaws snapping.

Randolph turns to run, and something clips him on the skull. He looks down to see his own dog-eared copy of Kant's *Critique of Pure Reason*, its corner scuffed where it connected with his bald head. He sprints, and another book drops down to whack him on the shoulder. He continues running, and the books come down in torrents. Bataille, de Beauvoir, Foucault, Heidegger, Kierkegaard, Sartre—theorists disparate and tedious, read and unread by Randolph in equal measure, their textual physicality hammering his horrified, exposed, fleeing body.

The beast charges ahead, gaining speed, its hot and ravenous breath pushing through the books, blowing against Randolph's neck.

Randolph falls, landing on nothing, screaming into the luminously lime-colored void, and he braces himself for the sensation of those countless pointed teeth puncturing his flesh and splitting his bones, when—

***

—Randolph's hand clattered, palm-up, against the floor. He yelped. He leapt to his feet, body churning adrenaline, skull aching. He whipped around to survey his surroundings.

His own storage room. Poor lighting, colorless and decidedly non-green walls, a stucco ceiling that now looked stained with a gallon of liberally distributed mucous, *The Gift of Death* squelching under his slipper.

The mark on the ceiling. The gluey, slimy substance clinging to his slippers. The three regurgitated books on the floor. These were all confirmations that what he'd just experienced had, in fact, happened.

"Randolph?"

A woman's voice.

He whirled around, half-expecting in his panic and delirium to see that stringy and coldly demanding rider standing beside his ottoman.

He was deeply relieved to see instead that Ann Braun was reaching to him from outside the storage room, her face lined with concern.

"What are you doing in your storage room?" she asked.

Randolph froze. How did she get here? Had she received his call?

"I, uh...I don't know." His voice came out flat. "How did you get in?"

Ann chuckled and gave him a playful look of consternation. When Randolph responded with a genuinely dumbfounded expression, she crossed her arms pertly.

"Oh, come on, get real," she said. "You weren't *that* drunk, were you?"

"I... Drunk...? I called you..."

"Pffft, there was no need to call me. We came from there to here, and thankfully you weren't too drunk to...well...you know." Ann laughed again. She stepped forward and took hold of his hand. "Come on, get out of there, you eccentric Liberal Arts maniac. Goodness me."

She can't see the slimy, gooey mess all over this room? She can't see the befouled Derrida books at my feet?

Randolph found himself unable to speak. Ann pulled him gently toward the sofa and lowered him to sit beside her.

"Is everything all right?" She flicked her eyes across his sweaty face. "You seem really stressed out."

Randolph looked down into his lap and shook his head in disbelief.

"Don't worry about it. Let's talk about something else." Ann tucked a fingernail under Randolph's chin and tilted his face toward hers. "Tell me what you learned at the conference."

Tell us what you've learned.

Randolph looked at her with the despaired expression of a man who has gone suddenly, completely mute. His eyebrows drooped. His frown deepened.

"Come on, Randolph," Ann said. "Tell us."

Good God, what is happening.

There was a trickle, slow and warm, where Ann's fingernail had touched, and he dabbed at the flesh there: his fingers came away wet with luminescent greenness.

He stared at Ann with escalating hysteria. *Good God it isn't over just make it stop please God please.*

Ann grabbed her hair and collected it to fall across one side of her face. Her exposed neck excreted a wave of slime that spilled over her collar and onto the sofa cushions.

Tell us. Tell us what you've learned.

"God," Randolph said, his lower jaw dropping until he thought it might just unhinge. "God, no."

The ooze puddled before Ann's unmoving form. It reassembled itself as a great, grotesquely moist mound, and it lurched up, then down, to swallow him again. He raised his arms to shield his panic-frozen face and—

***

—He's back. Back where it's so green and infinite and formless.

Now, that cold voice declares. *Tell us.* It's wielding a copy of *The Uncanny,* by Sigmund Freud.

Never did get around to reading that, Randolph thinks, and giggles.

His giggles turn to laughter, until the merriment twists his insides, until he thinks he might vomit all over the bright endlessness below.

Even under the din of his laughter, he can hear the question repeated: *Tell us... Tell us...*

And the sound of those hooves, plodding forward with slow urgency.

Randolph tilts his head skyward and bellows the phrase until his voice shreds: "Thoughts are dead! The world is alive!"

The books begin raining again. First, a Frege volume. Next, Lacan. The papery torrent thickens, clobbering his head and shoulders. He won't run this time. He grits his teeth and allows it to happen: a slow and philosophical burial.

"Mired" – Author Notes

AFTER I'D PRODUCED several consecutive horror stories, all of them nasty and pessimistic, "Mired" was my deliberate effort to write something funny. I don't know if it's funny, but it *is* pessimistic, so I'm not sure how successful I was in achieving my goals.

I was just beginning my graduate degree in English literature, and I was already suffering from a bad case of impostor's syndrome, which was exacerbated by perpetually increasing struggles with anxiety (a lifelong challenge). I can't say with all honesty that the anxiety has passed, but at least this story provided me with some genre-codified release. So, yes, this is a horror story of sorts, but it's mostly an attempt to have a laugh.

What are its influences? Probably the countless philosophy and theory texts that I've failed to understand, or the endless seminar discussions that have left me feeling nervous and alienated. It's supposed to be a humorous and exaggerated reflection of actual fears. I hope that it does its job.

THE AUTEUR

Originally published in *Turn to Ash Magazine* (2016)

CATE CLUTCHED SIMON'S wrist, so hard that he jerked back in shock. She snatched the *Cannibal Holocaust* tape from his hand before he could shelf it, and she held it up like a religious icon.

"You've been asking me all month for some 'real horror' recommendations," she said. She was trying to give him one of her serious cinephile gazes, but she looked more like she was fuming behind her bangs, charcoal-toned from stale dye. "Okay, here's your answer. *Cannibal Holocaust* is a peerless work of transgressive cinema...debatably matched only by Jörg Buttgereit's *Nekromantik* films. For my money, though...it's *Cannibal Holocaust* all the way. The horror of the flesh, dude. Real shit. Don't put it away. Rent it."

"Edwin said I'm all out of free rentals until next pay period."

"So pay for it. Rent it, trust me."

Edwin, their manager, rose from his stool behind the cash desk. He pressed his glasses up his sizable nose and raised his arms in exasperation. He paused the *Rudy* tape he'd been watching; last month, he'd stationed a miniature TV set behind the desk, and it kept him agreeably distracted throughout most shifts. "Hey, weirdos," he called. "You putting those horror returns away like I asked, or are you havin' a little pow-wow?"

Simon returned to the cart and quickly shelved a copy of *Carrie*.

Cate turned to flash Edwin a joking-but-not-joking scowl. "Watch your football movie, Ed." Her voice was a cynical monotone. "Get inspired."

Edwin chuckled a humorless chuckle. He shook his head, and his neck folds rippled. "Remind me why I ain't fired you yet."

"Will do, as soon as I finish demonstrating *why* I am your in-house horror specialist to my lovely co-worker Simon."

Simon plucked a wad of crusty gum from the shelf and set down John Carpenter's *Christine*. He'd learned to keep his eyes on the job. Cate was the back-talker, he was the shut-up-and-walk-away type.

Cate glanced at the cassette. "*Christine*'s not bad," she continued, as if nothing had happened. "Beautifully composed shots. Lens flares like the most gorgeous nightmares. Kind of a surface-level adaptation of the novel, though."

Simon shot a glance back toward the cash desk. Edwin had returned to the TV set, leaning in close as if he was witnessing the birth of Christ.

Simon turned to face Cate. "Listen, when can I borrow *your* movies? I mean, all this old horror stuff is good, but you keep promising to let me watch your films. Can you bring them tomorrow?"

Cate clutched a fistful of her bangs and exhaled with unnecessary volume. "Simon, dear Simon. I keep telling you... You're not *ready* yet." She grabbed *Bride of Chucky* from the cart and sneered at the cover. "Now *this* is garbage."

"What do you mean, 'not ready'?" Simon pressed. "I've watched everything you've recommended. Got through *Maniac* without a problem. Watched *I Spit on Your Grave* without even flinching. You think I'm a lightweight?"

"No."

"You think your films are just *too good* for me? What? What is it?"

Edwin's eyes, now bleary with artfully restrained tears, floated over the TV. He glared at them and offered a second warning: "Not gonna tell you two again."

Cate hissed between her teeth and gnawed on her knuckles. "Okay, fine," she whispered to Simon. "You win. But if you find that you're never able to sleep again, don't come crying to me. I'm telling you—I'm the next Ruggero Deodato. No, I'm *worse* than that."

"Roogairoh *who?*" Simon said.

"Director of *Cannibal Holocaust*." Cate shot her eyes back toward the desk. "My shift finishes an hour after yours. Wait for me."

Simon's chest swelled, like he'd achieved something monumental. Ever since Cate had declared herself a "world-changing auteur of *pure* horror," he'd been begging her to share her work.

"Goddamn *Rudy*," Edwin said, his voice carrying across the store. "Best goddamn movie ever made."

***

Cate lived in a dingy basement suite—sparse furniture, a dim lamp glow, blacklights drawing bluish surfaces across the gallery of garish posters adorning the walls: *Tenebre, Beyond the Darkness, The Driller Killer, The Devils...*

Despite their shared interests, Simon and Cate had never actually spent any time together outside the video store. He was as unsurprised by her creepy pad as he was excited to see her creepy films.

Cate threw her coat on the floor. "Want a drink? Coors? Jack Daniel's? If you're feeling anything else, there's a liquor store just down the street."

"No, thank you," Simon said. "I have to work in the morning." He watched Cate pour herself six fingers of whiskey and added, not unkindly, "So do you."

"Coffee, then?" she asked, as if he hadn't spoken at all.

He sighed and slouched into her liquor-sticky couch. "Coffee would be fine."

Cate disappeared into her bedroom, slurping from the glass of Jack. There was a rummaging, then a dim crash, and a creative assembly of mumbled obscenities.

"You all right in there?" Simon called.

Silence. Cate emerged a minute later, clutching two tapes in her fist. She tripped over a lump of laundry and sloshed booze all over the carpet. "Fuck," she said, popping one of the cassettes into her VCR.

She sat beside Simon, close enough for the whiskey fumes to make his eyes water. She belched, and he regretted opening his mouth to yawn.

She leveled her dark eyes on his. "Ready?"

Simon fanned the burp away from his nose. "I will die ready, Cate."

"Good one."

She switched on the television, pressed PLAY, and gulped the dregs of her drink.

Simon expected to see amateurish opening credits, some try-hard red font, maybe accompanied by cringe-worthy MIDI scoring. What he saw was nothing of the sort.

A static shot: a wall, dimly lit, filling the entire frame, unaccompanied by music. The image was stagnant, lingering, and for a moment Simon wondered if Cate was simply shooting wannabe minimalist garbage on her Camcorder and labelling it "horror."

But the shot changed. The camera might've been zooming, or Cate might've implemented some subtle cross-fades, but the wall seemed to be getting closer. And then the sound of a voice drifted into the scene. It was a man speaking, husky and weary sounding.

"...Cerebral peduncle," the voice said. "Optic chiasm... Thalamus... Septum pellucidum..."

The voice sounded cluttered, as if two people were attempting to speak from the same mouth. The effect made Simon's skin tingle.

The camera moved in closer and closer, until the wall's paint was visible in vivid detail. The shot appeared to change with impossible speed, transforming from wide shot to extreme close-up in the space of a sneeze. No movement or edits were the slightest bit apparent.

"...Great cerebral vein... Anterior commissure..."

The shot became *too* close, so that the lens appeared to bury itself inside the wall...but the frame was not submerged in blackness. Instead, Simon had the unnerving sensation that he was being drawn closer into its surface. The flaking paint was developing grotesque, textural detail: there were animal hairs twined within, and the half-decayed exoskeleton of some wall-dwelling insect.

"...Superior medullary velum... Fomix... Paracentral lobule..."

And still it got closer. Simon registered that he was now seeing the atomic structure of the wall. To conceptualize atoms, his high school science classes had given him neatly geometric patterns. What he saw now was anything but "neat," anything but clean. There were misshapen globules, which clung to one another in revolving clumps; their porous, puckered linings were fuzzed with red tissue. And the off-screen voice was now muffled and distanced, its tone fraught with frantic and miserable intonations.

The shot delved not closer now, but *deeper*, and Simon thought for one maddening second that he might scream, when finally...

The shot changed.

Medium wide shot, black-and-white. A human cadaver, split wide open, was sprawled across a kitchen table. A man wearing a double-breasted suit stood over the corpse, reaching into its gooey abscess with tweezers and a scalpel.

The scene was unnerving in its silence, and hyper-real in its anatomical details...but Simon took comfort in the fact that he'd seen such lifelike atrocities regularly, thanks to the make-up artistry of Tom Savini.

That's what he kept telling himself, anyway, but he couldn't quite ignore the sense that he was watching something not meant to be watched. That this operation was more documentary than fiction.

The suited man dropped his instruments beside the body with a clang and expelled a cry of frustration. He plunged his arms, elbow-deep, into the bloody fissure. His shoulders twitched and jolted, as if he was struggling with something that didn't want to leave the corpse.

"This reminds me of *Begotten*, a little bit," Simon said, a desperate effort to break the silence.

Cate slapped his forearm, hard. "Shhhh."

Simon would've got up and left if he wasn't so utterly mesmerized by the images onscreen. And so, he complied: he shut up, and he watched.

The suited man moved away from the slab, holding what he'd sought to remove: an inky black spinal cord, lashing in his hands like a threatened animal, spattering ichor. He held the bottom half in his trembling fists, but the top half remained deeply entrenched in the cadaver, suctioned to the necrotic flesh.

The man screamed once, then continued pulling. He squeezed his lips shut and shook his head, then screamed again. The shot moved closer, and closer...

And the tape ended.

A palpable silence fell immediately on the room.

"So?" Cate gave him an expectant smile. "That was fucked up, right?"

***

When Simon got home, he decided to cleanse his palate with the comfort of an old movie: *The Wolf Man.* Normally he chuckled fondly when Lon Chaney Jr.'s beastly mutation finally revealed itself onscreen.

Tonight, every scene struck him with unwelcome dread. When he watched Chaney, framed by black tree branches, bludgeoning the off-screen animal that would eventually seal his fate, Simon took no comfort in the dated score and sanitized violence.

Nausea compelled him to switch it off.

And even though it was past two in the morning by the time he finally went to bed, he didn't sleep at all. He thought about that yellow wall, and that persistent voice, and along with his unease came the nasty and persistent urge to see more.

***

Simon's eyes stung with fatigue as he scanned the remainders of yesterday's late returns. He'd spent most of the morning's early hours talking himself down, and he'd eventually resolved to allow last night to be what it was: a thing of the past.

If he ever wanted to sleep again, he figured it'd be best to avoid any more of Cate's aspirational works.

And yet, when she stepped behind the counter, two hours late for her shift, hissing angrily at the title of a movie in the drop-box, he faced her and said exactly what he'd promised himself not to say: "Is there a second part to the film?"

Cate's face cracked into a smile. "You know it, boss." After a pause, she added, "Horror is *the truth.*"

***

This time, Simon took up Cate's offer for whiskey. He guzzled a liberal amount before sinking into the fetid couch, preparing himself for the experience of Cate's promise. Preparing for *the truth.*

Part two reintroduced the same voice, but there was no variation in its utterances this time. Now, there was only one repeated pronouncement, stated with the firm tone of a criminal prosecutor: "Medulla oblongata... Medulla oblongata... Medulla oblongata..."

And the film began with an extreme close-up of that sentient spinal cord, wet and darker than shadow, excised finally from its host with a nauseating squelch. The wretched cord lashed and flapped, flicking droplets onto the wall, the suited man, the floor, the lens.

Cut. From behind, a medium shot of a woman. That untraceable camera movement began again.

"...Medulla oblongata... Medulla oblongata..."

Simon had never felt *closer* to hair follicles before, never been so uncomfortably near to the drying flakes of flesh, the soap scum and detritus that lingered on a human scalp. Just when he thought the microscopic detail might intensify, the shot went black.

Even within the darkness, though, he perceived movement. The camera was always moving, always drawing closer.

...But closer to what?

Suddenly the shot focused on the yolk-coloured wall from last night's film, this time from a distance. As soon as Simon saw that mortifying yellow surface, he worried he'd be forced to see its own disturbing brand of "truth" again.

He gulped and braced himself.

The shot changed. The camera rotated to frame the woman's face in close-up; her eyes were closed, her lips fused shut. Simon thought for a brief moment that this woman might be Cate, but her expression was too vacant, her pallor too deathly. The shot was static for a long time, so long that he started to wonder whether he was now watching yet more footage of a corpse.

Then the woman's eyelids opened, and he jolted with shock.

Sprouting from her eyes were wiry clumps of hair; they'd been folded up behind her eyelids, it seemed, and now they unfurled and dangled across her cheeks. In the shot's closeness, he could see that the hairs were growing from her corneas, her retinas, her pupils. The woman raised quivering hands to cover her horrible aberrations, but that judicial voice cried out from behind the camera: "Medulla oblongata!"

She lowered her hands, and the shot drew closer. The surface of her eyeballs had developed visibly painful follicles.

Simon had seen enough.

He moved to stand up, but Cate thwacked him across the chest with her forearm. "It's a cinema of transgression," she said, her voice raised. "This isn't Freddy Krueger spitting jokes. This is no fucking Boris Karloff in face-paint bullshit. This is *the truth,* and you need to see it. *You* asked for it, man."

"...Medulla oblongata!" the voice spat, as if cursing the miserable woman with the foulest of profanity. "Me! Dull! A!"

Simon pushed against Cate's arm with force, and he broke free. In horrified delirium, he ran toward the bathroom.

"Transgression, you bastard!" Cate screamed after him. "Jason Voorhees can go straight to sanitized mainstream *hell!*"

Simon slammed the bathroom door behind himself, clicking the lock. He flicked the light switch and a single bulb guttered dully to life. He paced across the half-metre of linoleum, trying to steady his breath. His eyes landed on a clump of Cate's hair, tangled through the slats of the heat register, and he turned away in fright.

He whirled around toward the sink. He gripped its sides and looked into the grimy basin, collecting himself.

Calm. Down, he told himself. *It's a scary movie. Cate's done her job. You love scary movies. Just go out there and apologize. You still need to work with this woman.*

He inhaled deeply and squeezed his eyes shut.

Cate rapped on the door. "Hey!" she called. "I thought you were serious about this...about horror. I'm sorry if I misunderstood. I'll walk you to the bus stop, okay? We don't have to watch any more."

"Just give me a minute," Simon replied automatically.

He heard a stirring, a mumbled curse, and then the sound of Cate padding back down the hall.

Just a scary movie.

She was right. He wasn't as committed to this stuff as she was, and he never would be. That was okay. He could live with that. He'd wash his face, and they'd share a cigarette on the way to the bus stop, and they'd say good night and forget about the whole thing. No harm done.

He looked up into the mirror.

His own eyes didn't look back at him.

The familiar eyes that he perceived with, the same gray-blue shade as his late father's, were not reflected on that surface. Staring at him from the scuffed and water-stained glass were two black orbs, as slick and damp as the thing that had been removed from the man's body.

Simon did not calm down. He fell back against the wall, and despite himself, he cried out.

He heard the rapid approach of Cate's return.

She knocked again, violently. "Let me in."

Another voice spoke behind her, soft and persistent: "...Pineal body... Precuneous..."

"What have you done?" Simon shouted.

She pounded harder. The door bowed in its feeble frame. Simon's heart jack-hammered, and he clapped sweaty palms over his deformed eyes.

Cate whacked her fist against the door. There was a pause for a moment, and Simon thought she might've given up.

And yet he couldn't ignore that urging voice. "...Cerebral aqueduct... Choroid plexus..."

The bottom of the door cracked inward, revealing Cate's bare foot. Simon curled into the corner, retreating against the shower curtain.

Cate broke through. Her face was flushed, feverish with excitement. She held a Camcorder in her hand, pointed it straight at Simon's face.

She opened her mouth to speak, and it was not her voice at all: "Medulla oblongata," she said. "Medulla oblongata..."

Simon collapsed back further and pressed his face against the wall. When it dawned on him that he was touching the very same yellow surface from the films, he cried out in terror.

He continued screaming as she advanced, and he found no solace in his own thoughts. Nothing could shut out that insistent and menacing utterance.

"Medulla oblongata... Medulla oblongata..."

Panic took hold. He leapt forward, headbutting Cate in the midsection. Her back connected with the sink and she exclaimed in shock.

Simon didn't stop to think. He ran for the door, clattered up the stairs and out of the house. He sprinted for one block, two blocks, four, sprinted until he finally lost count, until his smoker's lungs burned like they were filling with blood.

He lost his energy and hunched over at a bus stop, hands on knees, the act of breathing a gruelling task.

He lit up. He smoked in feverish gulps, burning a cigarette down to the filter in less than two minutes.

When he boarded the first bus that arrived, he cast his eyes toward the floor. His hand quivered violently as he showed his pass to the driver.

"You all right, mister?" the driver asked.

Simon ignored him and moved to the backseat, as far from the other riders as he could manage. He spent the trip looking out the window. Nobody should have to see what he saw in the mirror tonight.

Ever.

***

Simon didn't answer his phone when it rang early the next morning. He heard Cate's message, though, and his horror-struck mind replayed last night's incidents in vivid detail.

"Listen, Simon," she said. "There must've been a misunderstanding. I'm a horror filmmaker, and my duty is to shock. I'm not coming in to work today...or ever again, actually. I'll see you around, I guess. Keep on living the good life."

Click.

Simon remained in bed.

I won't be going to work, either, with my eyes looking like the deepest, blackest pits of hell. What has she done to me?

***

Simon's phone rang a great deal over the next couple days. He never picked up. He kept his shades drawn, exiting his bedroom only to rummage for food in the cupboards and refrigerator.

It might've been a week later when someone knocked at his door. He crept across his darkened living room to peer through the peephole. A deliverywoman stood on the doorstep, parcel in hand.

Simon waited until the woman was long gone, then reached outside with a trembling hand. He snatched the box and brought it inside.

He knew the truth before he even glanced at the address: the package was from Cate.

And despite himself, despite the unthinkable disgust and terror wracking his brain, he slit the box open.

A sheet of paper was folded across the top, inscribed with a bold and simple command: *READ BEFORE OPENING.*

As Simon unfolded the sheet, he tried to ignore the rattling of his fingers. He inhaled deeply, looked up toward the ceiling, and forced himself to read.

Dear Simon,

I would say I was sorry if I sincerely felt apologetic. Truth is, you asked for it. You could've lived with the simple stuff, could've just watched the odd Universal monster movie, caught the occasional Michael Myers sequel on cable.

But that wasn't enough for you. You signed the pact long before I invited you to see the truth (and don't try to fight it—you know as well as I do that my films are the fucking truth). You invited horror into your life, Simon. Now it's your chance to really embrace it.

This thing you have—these black eyes—it's really a kind of magic. Your eyes will only look this way when you're close to a lens, a mirror, a reflective surface. They're a product of reflection.

Now that you're so deeply ingrained in my work, I should fill you in on the details. My films have been intensely collaborative projects. That man in the film, Dr. McBride—he's been forced into unemployment by the city university. He was supposed to be teaching nihilistic philosophy, and he wanted more. He wanted the truth. He studied biological science, advanced physics, and luckily for me, he also learned everything there is to know about black magic. When I finally met this man, I knew that film was the way, the only way, to make the truth real.

You've been filmed by a necromantic device, Simon. Your eyes won't look this way, so long as you stay away from your reflection.

Sorry, but not sorry. You kept asking...and Dr. McBride and I really don't do this unless we know the subject wants it.

Cate

P.S. Don't bother trying to report me, or whatever. Dr. McBride has protected all of us (no, I'm not the only filmmaker he's brought under his wing), and you can now consider me totally M.I.A. Embrace the horror. It's all that's real.

Simon stood unsteadily in the center of his living room, his mind blank. The concept was brilliant; ingenious, even. How could he know what his eyes looked like without using some kind of reflection? Mirrors and recording devices showed this "truth," and he had no reason to believe that it went away otherwise.

Where in the world did reflections cease to exist, anyway?

Rage took hold, a physical tide making his muscles tense and his temples thrum. She'd got him. She'd fucked him over for good.

Impulsively, he reached into the box and removed the parchment from the item inside. With the blackest of comic realization, he looked at the item in his hand.

It was a videotape. Inked on the label in permanent marker was the title. *True Horror, Volume 3. To Simon. Love Cate.*

He moved across the room and slipped the cassette into his VCR. He sat down on his couch and searched for the remote control.

"The Auteur" – Author Notes

I WORKED AS a video store clerk for a period in my mid-teens (back when video stores still existed). I loved that job—the environment, the free rentals, the whole experience. I wanted this story to function as an ode to that time while also serving as a kind of love letter to horror cinema. For the record, I adore *Bride of Chucky*.

As with many of the pieces in *Darkest Hours*, this was influenced by several stories in Thomas Ligotti's *Songs of a Dead Dreamer* (1989) and *Grimscribe: His Lives and Works* (1991)—specifically, Cate was inspired to some degree by a character in Ligotti's "The Night School." Without a doubt, "The Auteur" also serves as an homage to Kathe Koja's *The Cipher* (1991), which is not only one of my favorite horror novels but one of my favorite books, full stop.

CHOO-CHOO

Originally published in *Polar Borealis Magazine* (2017)

"WHAT TIME IS it?" Charles asked.

Dex turned around and kicked a spray of tree-shavings at him. "Baby, it's the *right* time!" He flashed a dopey grin, whirled around and plunged into the shadow-painted foliage ahead.

Charles laughed despite himself. That was just the effect Dex had. It was something about that crooked smile. It was like Dex was in on something. Like he'd always understood the bulk of his life to be a great joke, and he was just waiting for everybody else to catch up and get the punchline.

Dex was fun, no doubt, but Charles still questioned himself: Why had he agreed to go for this late-night walk through Birch Grove Park in the first place? Dex didn't like being told no, it was true, but hadn't the two of them reached a point in their friendship where Charles could appeal to Dex's conscience?

Dex did have a conscience...didn't he?

Charles couldn't answer the question as quickly or as easily as he might've liked. Sure, Dex showed remorse on occasion. Once, after deliberately flooding the boys' washroom with foul sewage backup, he'd turned to Charles with a half-smile and said, "I didn't think about anyone having to clean it up until just now."

Charles produced another cigarette.

"Like I said—you shoulda charged your phone if you wanted to keep track of the time, man," Dex said. "What do I look like, a human timepiece?"

Charles plodded on without responding. *I would've charged it if you'd given me the goddamn time, hadn't rushed me outside in the middle of the night,* he thought. He sparked his smoke to life, sucked nicotine into his lungs, blew a slow and nonchalant stream, as if he couldn't care less.

Truth was, he cared a great deal. Even the moonlight was now beginning to lose its influence in this place, blocked out by the increasingly thick overhang. Any trace of light was dimming to infrequent splashes of blue; the faint glow of Dex's silhouette was giving Charles the creeps.

"No need to hurry back." Dex pulled out his phone to consult the time and nodded, but neglected to fill Charles in. "You'll wanna walk off the scent of that new ciggy, anyhow, right? I mean, if we head back now and your mom's wandering around in search of a midnight snack, she'll smell the smoke all over you."

Charles silently agreed. His mom had never liked Dex in the first place, and he didn't want to give her any more ammunition for her distrust. He'd certainly never enjoyed a cigarette before he'd met Dex. Mom had had bad feelings about Dex ever since Charles had first relayed stories about his outrageous outbursts at school. The first example: in Mr. Connor's math class, third period, Dex once filled his mouth with Alka-Seltzer tablets and, just as the foam began bursting through his lips, he collapsed and twitched on the floor in a mock seizure. Charles had found the scene hysterically funny.

When he described the events to his mom, she didn't even break a smile.

Charles figured the only reason Mom let Dex sleep over was because he "came from a bad home." Charles didn't know about that, really—the "bad home" part. In fact, Charles sort of liked Dex's dad, a man who didn't talk down to Charles the way other parents did. Dex's dad was prone to telling Charles the dirtiest jokes, recommending the most messed-up movies, and he was an unfailing source of cigarettes, booze, and even (on one special occasion) a bag of really good weed (well, since it was the only weed Charles had ever smoked, he couldn't *really* testify to its high quality, but still—it had done the trick).

"Hey," Dex called. "Come check this out."

Charles only now realized that he was falling behind. He'd slowed to a leisurely pace to enjoy his cigarette, and Dex's shadowy figure was perched on a hilltop several yards away. Even at this relatively small distance, it was difficult to make him out.

Charles took a final drag and flicked his smoldering half-cigarette into the shrubs. *Good way to set the place ablaze*, he thought, but quickly dismissed the concern from his mind. Right now he had bigger concerns than starting a forest fire.

Like not getting shit from his parents.

"What?" he called back. Then, after a pause, "What time is it, for Christ's sake?"

Dex didn't answer.

As Charles approached the hill, a protruding root snagged his Converse. He tumbled hard, and gravel rolled abrasively along his knee, breaking flesh.

"God fucking dammit."

Dex laughed. "Take it easy down there, willya?"

"Look, Dex, I just scraped my leg open. Can we please just head back?" Charles trudged up the hill, his scrape stinging.

He saw the momentary flash of Dex's cellphone, a halo of electric light in the blackness.

"It's 3:30," Dex said.

Charles dabbed his fingertips into the tender wetness on his kneecap. He winced. For the fourth time tonight, he pulled his Android from his pocket and pressed the power button. To his total lack of surprise, no miracle had yet occurred: the phone was still dead.

"You coming up here or what?" Dex cried out.

Charles broke into an uneasy jog, his injured leg protesting. Blood poured down his shin, soaking into his socks. *This is no small scrape. Might need stitches.* If that was in fact the case, he thought while climbing the hill, how on earth would he be able to keep the truth from Mom?

He stood beside Dex. His friend extended his arms, a grandiose presentation of the vista before them. They were staring at what appeared to be a moon-bathed train yard: chain-link fence surrounding metal hulks, unmoving railcars that looked from this distance like sleeping prehistoric beasts.

"How the hell—they can't have built a train yard on the edge of Birch Grove..." Charles said.

"They can!" Dex screamed, rather unnecessarily. He pointed at the yard. As he turned to Charles, his face cracked into an unhinged smirk. "They *did!*"

"Okay, so we saw it. Real crazy, Dex. Can we go back now?"

Charles turned on his heels. For a moment, he thought he saw one of the railcars lurch forward, *crunch*, a subtle crawl across the inky dirt. *You're just tired. An illusion, that's all. You're just really goddamn tired.*

He began descending the hill, his knee sharp with pain, when he heard the click of Dex's wakened Zippo. Moments later, the air was filled with the pungent, familiar smell of marijuana.

He turned to see Dex pinching a cigar-sized blunt between his fingers, eyes dozy, mouth popped open into a smoky O.

"Whaddya say we pass, piss, puff first—or however the saying goes?" Dex asked, before erupting into squeaky hysterics and taking another long drag from the joint.

That thing's too fat to be called a "joint." The word's just too measly. Too, well...small. If I let Dex smoke the whole thing himself, which he definitely will if given the chance, he might get lost and never find his way back out. Charles looked down at his banged-up leg. *Maybe the weed will take the edge off the pain...make the walk back home a little easier.*

"All right, you maniac." Charles walked back up. "Fuck it. Give me a hit."

He took the blunt from Dex's already rubbery grasp, wrapped his lips around the makeshift filter and dragged. The smoke came hot, thick, and heavy. It seemed to rush into his nasal passages, esophagus, lungs, ears, and eyeballs all at once, his body quickly alight with the first-puff tingles. He coughed—he always coughed so hard—his body doubling over.

As they took turns on the blunt (Dex doing a lot more than half the work, Charles was happy to see), the trees took on a vaguely sinister appearance: branches curled like gnarled fingers, leaves rattling a papery, foreboding ambience. Charles also began to find the sight of Dex's scarlet-ringed eyes unnerving, a primal gaze that looked unfit for his drooping, guffawing mouth.

"Let's go, man." Charles' words clogged at the base of his tongue before rolling, clumsy, out of his mouth. "It's too dark. Let's head back."

"Gonna go for a train ride first." Dex killed the roach with a powerful, lung-filling hit. "Choo-choo, baby. Choooo-chooooooooooo."

"No way, Dex. I'm putting my foot down. That's trespassing."

Dex only looked at him for a second, rolling the filter between his fingertips, raining charred resin on the grass. Then he snickered once, "Ha," and turned to gallop down the hill. "Choo-chooooooooooooo," he howled. "Choo-chooooooo, biiiiiiiiiiiiiiiitch!"

That's it. Leave him. Let him learn his lesson, Charles thought, but then he saw it again: the car urging forward, like a dormant monster stirred from its slumber. It stopped as quickly as it had started, but Charles wasn't so sure he'd imagined it this time. *Weed can't make you hallucinate, can it?*

"Dex!" He was surprised by the shaky, panicked sound of his own voice. "Dex, don't do it!"

Too late. Dex was already climbing the chain-link, spider monkey fast.

Charles had no other choice that he could see: he ran to meet up with his friend. As he pounced on the fence, he saw barbed wire curled across the top, tatters of something waving from its points. *Is that cloth?* Charles thought, dropping down and backing away. *Or is it flesh?* He shuddered.

Dex was now hobbling across the train yard, moonlight glancing off what appeared to be bloody rivulets trailing his exposed forearms.

"Dex!" Charles screamed. "Dex, for God's sake stop!"

Dex stood on a section of rusty tracks in front of a massive railcar and held his bloodied arms akimbo, cellphone glowing in the blackness.

"Guess what time it is?" Dex called back.

Don't encourage him. Just turn around and walk away. Charles didn't move, but he also didn't speak.

"It's not 4:20, but it would be funny if it was!" Dex shouted.

Har-de-fucking-har. Charles had finally resolved to leave when he saw it happen again: the car sliding forward, its nose settling mere feet away from Dex. Dex yelped in shock. Charles screamed.

It happened. Charles' heart thwacked against his chest. *It really happened.*

"Malfunction, Charles," Dex called. "Just a little malfunction. Chill the hell ou—"

His sentiment was cut short as the train went into blinding motion, blasting into him like a monstrous bullet, crashing through his body as if it was no more cumbersome than a shrub, viscera and boney remnants bursting across the yard. The sound was excruciating. The noise of strained train brakes played in reverse, piercing Charles' brain.

The din stopped and was quickly replaced with the dim thump of Dex-pieces hitting the ground, a slow and scattered rainfall of blood. Charles collapsed to his knees, forgetting his own wound in the terror of the moment. He pressed his fingertips against his eyes. His mouth dropped open in a silent wail.

Moments later, a buzzing in his pocket.

My phone is dead, he thought.

Impulsively, he reached for it. The green Android logo blazed on the screen. Incoming call from Dex Morton.

What the fuck?

He stared at the train yard, looking for the glow of Dex's iPhone. *I must be seeing things. He's okay. He's calling me to tell me he's okay.* He laughed without knowing why, and he tapped the Answer button with a shaking finger.

He pressed the phone to his ear, and what he heard tilted him over the edge of panic into the realm of all-consuming horror. "Choo-choo, Charles." Dex's voice spoke through a staticky rumbling, a sound that was vaguely taunting and faraway. "*It's dark in here. No moonlight now. Just dark and hot. So, so hot. Come take a train ride. Choo-choooooooooooooo...*" and then Dex's voice was washed out in that screaming, screeching tumult of gears under pressure, a train trying but unable to stop, and Charles swore he heard a legion of human cries beneath that awful sound.

He jabbed the End Call button, but to no avail. The sound only continued, and he could hear it even as he dropped the phone in the grass and turned to run.

He didn't stop hearing it until he was miles away.

For years afterward, the sound disappeared only occasionally...while he was awake.

As for his nightmares: that was another story.

"Choo-Choo" – Author Notes

I LOVE THE final, often terrifying revelations that close so many episodes of *The Twilight Zone*. I also love how R. L. Stine has updated that tradition for young readers in his *Goosebumps* books. With "Choo-Choo," I intended to write a considerably darker *Goosebumps*-inspired story about adolescents in peril. I aimed to produce something fast and narratively concise with a gut-punch of a spooky ending. As brutal as it is, I also wanted this to be a fun read. Think *Say Cheese and Die!* (1992), the R-rated version.

FEAR AND GRACE

JUSTINE NEVER SET foot in places like the Beaver Tooth Bar, even in her undergrad years. Now a blazer-wearing scholar in her mid-thirties, she felt something like an undercover cop in a criminal hotspot. Somewhere behind her, pool balls cracked across a billiard table's surface. A man in the corner bellowed "Yee-haw" three consecutive times, and the woman beside him barked a syllable-by-syllable "Ha-ha-ha" in response.

The sounds seemed altogether distant, someplace else. Apprehension knotted Justine's stomach as she sipped her Keith's. What was her partner, Joyce, doing tonight? Was the Lauren Berlant paper finally, mercifully taking form, or was Joyce succumbing again to the temptation of red wine and another *True Detective* marathon? Were Justine's students whispering harshly about her Gothic Femininities course, at this very moment, in the college pub? Did her students even care enough to discuss her course at all?

And Herbert, Justine. Lest you forget why you're here. Dear, dear Herbert. He's somewhere in your thoughts, too, isn't he?

As if cued instantly by Justine's pesky inner voice, Herbert entered the bar: sudden, anticlimactic, a strutting entrance that brought with it a gust of February air.

Herbert came with a smile, and Justine quickly observed that, indeed, his smile had stayed the same after all these years: upper lip tucked beneath the lower lip, blue eyes widening subtly, as if he was watching naughty zoo chimps. As a teenager, Herb had been graced with unusually mature handsomeness, and his features had only sharpened and become more strikingly attractive over time. Even in that dopey smile, there was an unbearable charm.

Justine used to find the smile as winning as everyone else did. Now, she thought not of a silly boy veiled by an Adonis. Instead, she saw some

'30s character actor hamming up the role of a psych ward patient. Maybe Dwight Frye, playing Renfield in Tod Browning's *Dracula*.

It had been twenty years since Justine last saw Herbert smile, and it took her several moments to notice that the flesh around his features had aged from years of heavy reading and light sleeping, that the wrinkles webbing those bulgy eyes had deepened.

In one instant, the early teenage memories came back strong—Herbert and Justine chattering at the tops of their voices, while cassettes by Mayhem and Darkthrone filled their dimly lit basements with menacing and welcome noise. Sneaking outside at two in the morning for no other reason than to prowl the streets and chatter under streetlights, Herbert the talker and Justine the eternal listener. Herbert smirking in the gymnasium during lunch break, betting Justine he could persuade this gorgeous girl over here or that elusive girl over there to go on a date with him, and winning the bet every time. In that instant the memories were so strong, so overwhelming, that Justine nearly forgot why she'd ever severed contact with this grinning, beautiful man in the first place. That was the power of erudite, virile Herbert: with one expression, with the subtlest of body language, he could make you forget anything.

She twisted awkwardly in her barstool and wrapped an arm around Herbert's bulky shoulders. Boston's "More Than a Feeling" blared from the jukebox, lending a surreal theatricality to the moment. A bulky man in a parka vest glanced at them from the end of the bar, gathered mucous in the bottom of his throat, and downed a shot of whiskey.

"Good to see you," Justine said, and she meant it. When it came down to it, she'd agreed to meet for a reason. Buried somewhere beneath her deep and studied cynicism was the under-nurtured belief that people *could* change.

And yet still...she noted the manicured fingernails; the lotion-sheened skin; the hair plastered neatly to the skull, Herbert's only secret imperfection—on the few occasions that Justine had gotten close enough, she'd seen flakes of unscrubbed flesh gathered at his crown. "Natural grease is the only product that keeps my hairstyle *perfect*," he'd once told her, grinning too wide.

She'd always brushed it off as another Herbie quirk. But she couldn't ignore the fact that the flakes were still there, his follicles secreting something dirty.

"Justine," Herbert said. He glanced around at the sports bar décor, the classic rock jukebox, the miniskirt-donning servers, and he gave Justine a knowing look: *This is your idea of culture?*

The truth was that it was the only bar Justine knew in the area. She hadn't been to Edmonton in over a decade, and her first and only priority tonight had been to meet Herbert someplace public. Not private; no, there was definitely no chance of that. She was willing to entertain the notion that people who did bad things were not necessarily bad *people*, but no matter how hard she tried, it seemed she just could not forget some bad things.

Some bad things, Justine had learned, stayed with her for life.

She waited for Herbert to speak more, but he just kept smiling.

"You'll be needing a drink, I imagine," Justine said. "Did you present today?"

Herbert tucked a blonde lock behind his ear. "No, I'll be presenting tomorrow. I'll be participating in the morning panel: Affect and Otherness in Late-Capitalist Markets."

"Oh, that's right. You're presenting with Helena Danielewski—Camille Farris's student, correct?"

Herbert's face slipped into a sober mask of humility, and he nodded. "Yes, I was very lucky. Camille Farris graciously cited the paper that I published in *Philosophical Review*, and it's the strangest thing... Helena's thesis addressed a lot of the material in that paper—in my paper, that is. In fact, I believe I might've been her primary source. Really, very gracious..."

The academic elevator talk. Who's reading whom? Who's getting published? I'm tapped right into the scholarly zeitgeist—how about *you*? Justine found the whole procedure tiresome. Grotesquely capitalist, almost. Or worse, downright masculinist (*my scholastic cock outsizes everyone else's*, said Herbert's braggart smirk).

Justine turned to the bartender, a young woman who looked about as excited about their reunion as Justine was starting to feel. "My friend would like... Uh, what *would* you like, Herbert?"

"Are you offering any specials tonight?" Herbert asked the bartender's breasts.

"Pints of Keith's—"

"—Keith's sounds lovely, I'll have that."

The unsmiling bartender nodded and turned around to pour. Herbert, unaccustomed to women turning away before staring for at least a moment, leaned heavily on the bar. Feigning a look of pity, he turned to Justine and said, loudly, "I wonder if servers work very late on such slow Saturdays."

The bartender smiled without her eyes and set down the beers, maybe-accidentally slopping some suds onto Herbert's coaster.

Herbert said "thank you" in a tone of predatory suggestion that would escape any casual passersby. A tone saved especially for the bartender, which Justine couldn't help but hear as well.

You remember old Herbert now, don't you? she thought, reclaiming her seat. *Regretting it yet?*

Herbert sank down beside her. For a moment, they stared together, in mutual silence, at the line of liquor bottles behind the bar. Justine nodded for no particular reason.

"It's lovely to see you, Justine. When will you be presenting, then? I've forgotten..." Herbert buried his mouth in beer foam, surfaced quickly, and ran a finger across his mustache.

"I presented last night," Justine said; then, in response to Herbert's expression of pure faux-regret—*Oh my, how could I have missed it!*—she added, "It's okay, Herbert. It went fine. I'll be leaving tomorrow evening."

"My, how could I have forgotten?" Herbert asked earnestly. His flickering smile insinuated the truth: *I forgot because you're presenting bland bullshit to an utterly despondent audience.*

He was right. Justine's paper on Matthew Gregory Lewis had fallen on three sets of visibly nonresponsive ears. One man sitting in the back of the room had looked like he was coming down with a sudden migraine and needed a quiet space to nurse the pain.

"It's okay. It's just strange that we ended up presenting at the same conference. I mean, our research areas are so far apart," Justine said.

What she didn't add was that she was a struggling sessional instructor in a community college, whereas Herbert was a top scholar teaching interdisciplinary doctoral seminars. Said seminars focused heavily on gender politics and critical race theory. Humble, handsome Herb was also married to one of his past students, a woman nearly half his age.

Herbert stared at the bartender's backside and tried to look instead like he was staring pensively at the beer fridge. "Yes, it's strange, isn't it? It's almost as if we've been—I don't want to say ushered, as if to imagine some bizarre sort of nonsecular belief—no, not ushered, but...*brought together*. Is that a weird thing to say?"

Brought together? It was an unusually banal, un-theoretical conclusion for Herbert to arrive upon. Justine finished nearly a third of her beer as she waited for him to expand.

They hadn't been "brought together" at all; they'd both submitted papers to the same conference, a far-reaching and multi-faceted academic gathering on Violence and Visibility. When Herbert had spotted Justine's name on the program, he'd sent an email and Justine had made the impulsive decision to reply.

It *had* been nearly two decades, after all; maybe the young, ambitious metalhead Herbert and the older, academic superstar Herbert weren't the same person, after all. It made sense in a quick, uncritical sort of way. *Teenagers do strange things all the time*, Justine had told herself. *I probably just overreacted. I was a kid, for God's sake. I didn't know anything.*

Herbert didn't continue speaking; instead, he sealed his lips in that strange Herbie way, bottom over top, and he tapped his fingers on the sticky bar: *click-click, click-click...*

He leaned in to whisper some scandalous critique of a popular theorist, and Justine saw a single skin-flake, finer than snow, drifting to rest on the top of his beer.

She said nothing.

Her mind drifted suddenly, inevitably, unwantedly back. Back to a cold garage in suburban Calgary, nineteen years ago.

***

Click-click. Justine hears the sound as she crunches up the driveway, and she wonders vaguely about its source. It's a rhythmic sound. Hollow and insistent.

She steps into Herbert's open garage and drops her hood, shedding snowflakes. She shakes her head vigorously, flinging big drops of water from her short hair.

She pants breath from her ice-lined lungs. "What's up?"

Click-click, click-click, click-click...

It's only then, once she's emerged from the unbearable cold of outside to the marginally-more-bearable cold of the garage, that she spots the source of the sound: Herb's slender fingers drumming against his mother's deep freezer.

In the same instant, she notices how strange Herbert looks. He stands facing her, framed by the closed door that leads into his house. His golden hair, usually side-swept with great care and attention, looks tousled and ungroomed. "I told you about this problem with mice, didn't I?" With his right hand curled into a fist and his left hand drumming the freezer, his grin develops an unnerving dementedness.

"Uh, I don't know." Justine unshoulders her bass guitar and leans it against the tool shelf on the wall. "Maybe?"

The wind makes swirling twisters of fresh snow outside. With the wind chill, the weatherwoman told her this morning, it's minus forty degrees Celsius. She can feel every icy degree of it in this wide-open garage. Her fingers are going numb. There's a palpable silence, though, that serves even more discomfort than the frigid air. Between every word, it seems, a heavy quiet descends. It's dismal, morbid—like being in a funeral parlor.

"Mouse problem in the house," Herbert says. "Dad says he sees them run across the entertainment room. He'll be watching the game, all caught up in the final period and then—*scurry scurry scurry!*—they go running across the carpet in a neat line." He pauses. *Click-click*, go his fingers. *Click-click*.

"Um, okay..." Justine says.

Normally, Justine walks straight through Herbert's garage and into his living room, and then downstairs into the basement, where they thrash out metal-influenced jam sessions. Brian on drums. Robby on lead guitar. Herbert the howling, raging vocalist. Justine the only girl, but that's okay. She's never been lucky enough to meet another girl who's into old-school Scandinavian black metal, and she's pretty much resigned to the fact that she never will.

But today, there's only her and Herbert, and the cold and the stillness and that horribly palpable silence. The very walls and floors seem to radiate with the chill.

Herbert is visibly shaking beneath his Burzum t-shirt. No jacket. Not even a sweater.

"Why don't we go inside and practice? It's frozen out here," Justine says. After a pause, she hesitantly adds, "You all right?"

Herbert smiles that unceasing, bug-eyed smile. "Mouse problem in the house." He turns around and crouches to grab something from behind the freezer.

"Jesus, Herbert, can't we just go inside?"

Herbert doesn't respond. A Ziploc bag dangles from his hand as he rotates to face Justine. For the briefest of moments, Justine assumes the bag to be filled with drugs of some kind, and in that moment she's mildly surprised. Herbert has never expressed any interest in intoxicants of any sort, and neither has she.

That brief moment ends when Justine sees that the bag is moving. That the thin plastic is fogging with little puffs of steam.

Mouse breath.

"How many mice do you have in there?" she nearly shouts in surprise. "They'll suffocate!"

Herbert's mouth smooths into a grim line. He stares her straight in the eyes.

Justine feels inexplicably embarrassed—why should she care about a bunch of mice? What is she, a little kid? No, she's a tough teenager, a tough young *woman* in a tough-as-fuck metal band with the toughest, most popular kid in school, Herbert Delano.

She covers her tracks. "I mean, not that I care. Let's go practice. Are Brian and Robby here yet? Where are they?"

Herbert brings his fist forward, and then swings backward to whack the wall. The noise is startling. His face flushes, and he does it again. His knuckles purple and split from the impact.

Justine's hands fly to her ears. "Jesus, Herb!"

Herbert smiles, and for the first time since Justine met him, she thinks he's about as far from handsome as a person can be. There is a blankness in his expression, like he's trying to comprehend her from a great distance, and for a moment she feels just like that void in his eyes, like a shaft of air that he's peering straight through.

There's a sense of offness, something Justine will never find a way to describe. It's a feeling beyond words. It dwells first in her guts: a clenching sensation, like she's just eaten something expired. "Herbert," she says. "I'm leaving."

She doesn't turn around, though, and for the next twenty years, her brain nags periodically: *What if you had? What if you'd just left at that moment? Where would you be now? Herbert was always bound for success; nothing could change that—but you? What did that day do to you?*

She notices now that Herbert has muscled at an extraordinary rate in this past year. His biceps and pectoral muscles press through the fabric of his too-small shirt, stretching the letters of *Burzum* to their thresholds.

Justine's never had cause to think about it—never seen Herbert as sexually attractive in any tangible way, really—but now, a nasty thought surfaces: *I don't think I could fight him off if I tried...*

Herbert sets the squirming, rustling bag on top of the freezer, and the garage door squeals shut.

A ludicrous thought whizzes into Justine's brain (*He's closing it with his mind*), but Herbert reaches into the pocket of his tight jeans and reveals the door's remote.

"Mouse problem," he says again, and a strange expression crosses his face: like a boy who's just emerged from a deep, overlong sleep, only to realize he's in a stranger's house.

"Herbert—"

Justine is cut off by the first strike of his fist, a stiff and mechanized motion that fills the garage with an explosion of noise: rupturing air as the Ziploc bursts, the crack of knucklebones as they connect with the freezer lid, and the horrendously loud squeal of a mouse left presumably half-alive, a sound like a bird whose foot has been caught in a door, and Justine knows that she would scream, too, if she could, but she can only stand motionless, forgetting about the cold, and the sickness inside her tightens, and she watches with unwanted fascination as Herbert's fist *thud thud thuds* three times, four times, five, the bag filling with pulpy and vibrant red, and her vision sharpens somehow, trauma honing her senses, and she can see every detail even from this relative distance, yes, she can see spinal cords and little bones jittering and jolting with the force of the blows, clicking and clattering against the top of the tattered plastic, and blood and liquefied innards spatter Herbert's forearm, flecking the now-dented freezer, and Justine still wants only to scream, but can't for the love of God make a single sound, and her brain begins impulsively to rattle off a silent prayer, when finally...

It stops.

Herbert's bangs have flopped into his eyes, and he wipes them away with his wrist, leaving a scarlet smudge on his forehead. "Problem solved."

"Herbert..." Justine says, but something about Herbert's delirious grin disarms her, and she finds herself unable to continue.

Herbert rests his palm on the battered lid.

Justine's mind circulates questions at hyper-speed, like a crowd fleeing a burning building, only to clamor at the exit. *How the hell is he going to explain that to his parents? How did he catch all those mice?* Then, perhaps the most disturbing question: *Was he waiting to show me?*

Herbert leans back, facing her, and his smile smooths into a neutral expression.

Say something, she thinks. *Do something.*

Herbert dips his fingers into the soupy mess of fur, fluid, and viscera, and he holds them out for a second. Little drops fall off, pitter-patter on the floor.

This is not something people do, Justine's mind whispers. Her trembling mouth produces words, but they're not the words she needs, they're not enough. "Herbert... You..."

Herbert stares ahead, his gaze landing somewhere between the ceiling and the top of Justine's head. "God?"

His mouth keeps moving after he speaks—open, then closed, a slow and automatic motion. He steps forward, eyes staring without seeing, and Justine's shock-numbed mind summons up the zombies from *Night of the Living Dead.*

She backs away, but she doesn't turn her back to Herbert. She's going to get out of here, one way or another. She tries to look him in the eyes, but she can't. Her gaze keeps drifting back to that mess of cartilage and blood and torn plastic. She shakes her head and looks down at the floor.

Suddenly, Herbert's expression shifts. His body relaxes, his muscles untightening beneath that painted-on band shirt. He laughs mildly. "I'm just messing with you, Justine. Geez! Relax!"

Justine takes another step backward, eyes still cast downward. She connects with the garage door, and it rattles noisily. "Let me go, Herbert."

Herbert reaches out with his big, dripping hand, and he brushes her cheek with his fingertip. "Are you a dyke, Justine?"

"Let. Me. Go."

She can smell the gore, earthy with the all-too-human scent of blood. It trails down her flesh, a fat bead trickling to her lip. A stream slips through. Her tongue coats instantly with the taste of filth and death.

"Dykes don't like boys, do they?"

Tell him one more time, and then... Her heart is a piston. *...And then what, Justine? You're going to fight off this sensitive bench-presser?*

"Herbert. If you don't let me go, people will *know*." She tries to look him in the eyes, but his vision is someplace else. Someplace with unseen corners where, Justine knows, she'd be bound to find skeletons if she dared venture any further.

Herbert's hand drifts away. He clicks the door remote, smirking with one side of his mouth. "No problem."

Justine forgets about her bass guitar, doesn't even think about it, stumbles forward with such eagerness that she trips on the uneven level between driveway and garage, landing face-first in the snow. It's viciously icy, and it stings her flesh. She spits obscenity.

Herbert walks toward her. "Whoa, chill out! You okay?"

Justine doesn't respond. Hoists herself to her feet and runs out of the cul-de-sac as fast as her heavily booted feet will carry her.

As she disappears around the corner, plunging through the curtains of blizzard, she hears Herbert calling, "See you on Monday, dude!"

***

"—and it's almost as if, strangely enough, Massumi deviates in that moment from the innately feminist politics of this strain of affect theory, succumbing instead to... Justine, are you okay?"

Justine jerked to alertness. She must've slipped away...slipped *back* into memory, into trauma. From the corner of her eye, she caught the bartender shooting her a quizzical look. Justine raised her pint glass awkwardly and forced a smile, then turned to face Herbert.

Yeah, that kid in the garage was still here.

She could see him in that glassy Herbert stare, the features twisted too meticulously into a façade of concern, and she could see very well that the impersonation of empathy looked nothing like the real article. It was in the eyes, yes—the sense that the watcher saw a task, not a conversation, saw potential opportunity rather than reunion, saw a cipher rather than a person.

No matter how tidily he plastered the hair to his skull, his flesh still peeled and came free.

"I'm fine, Herbert," Justine said. "It's been a long couple of days. Tell you what, I'm going to need to leave after this drink, but I'll come see you deliver your paper tomorrow, okay?"

"I understand." Herbert's lower lip trembled for a few moments, before he found it within himself to force it still. "It's been really terrific catching up with you. Before you leave, I wonder if I might be able to ask you for a quick favor."

Always a quick favor. Herbert had never failed to find a way to get something out of somebody. And that meant *everybody*. In junior high school, he'd even persuaded the school janitor to forge leave-of-absence permits on his parents' behalf. He'd single-handedly convinced the principal to extend the final school dance by three hours so that his band could play.

A black metal concert in a junior high school gymnasium. Imagine that.

Herbert understood economies of exchange, but it wasn't his understanding that was frightening; it was the fact that he *only saw* those economies. He knew when to push buttons, and how. Even when to give back, because that was a part of it, too—but only when necessary, and never too much. Always just enough.

For Herbert, human life was organized around a resolvable dualism: debtor and creditor.

"A favor?" Justine asked. "What do you need?"

"Well, since you'll be in attendance, I wonder if perhaps you might find a point-of-entry with Liz Park in the post-discussion session... For me, that is. Her work, after all, offers some intersection between yours and mine, believe it or not," Herbert said.

A point-of-entry? So, what does that mean? Is your ex-student wife no longer giving you what you want in the department of sexuality, or does Park know of a professional "in" that you want to see about slipping your way into?

"I've never met her either, Herbert," Justine said honestly.

Herbert's lower lip twitched again, sending a spasm up the left side of his face that caused him to wink once—a strained and ugly expression.

He reconfigured his features, smiled—bottom lip over top—and clapped Justine on the shoulder.

"Well, it'll be lovely to see you tomorrow in any event, and it's good to see how your work has progressed." He allowed the sarcasm, hardly veiled at all, to set in. "It's great that you're reaching a bigger audience."

Justine ignored the comment and nodded. "See you tomorrow, Herbert."

***

Halfway through Herbert's presentation, Justine thought, *Just as expected.* His paper was the last, the longest, and the most hungrily received.

The room was filled with awestruck academics sharing silence, taking notes, nodding soberly, offering brief, hushed exchanges. The man beside Justine kept murmuring, "mm-hmm, mm-hmm," in a tone of grim affirmation.

Herbert spoke in a voice much older than his face—the voice of a CEO, the voice of an activist, the voice of a king: "...in this moment, that is, in this *new* moment, whether future or present—for the politics we must embody is, by its essence, a pre-emptive politics—I urge us to usher the promise of alternate optimisms, the newness that denudes neocolonial, neoconservative, and neo-fascist models of 'progress'..."

His posture was impeccable: broad shoulders arching over the podium, handsome brow knitted into a scrupulous frown, undersized button-down straining against still-maintained musculature. The emphases were understated but direct, the pauses rehearsed and precise, the voice measured and smooth.

He glanced up before prefacing a quote by Judith Butler, and his eyes, even from this distance, instantly met Justine's.

And even from this distance, Justine saw the imprint of sockets beneath his baby blues. Something deep and black below the fatigue-purpled flesh.

Mouse problems everywhere.

"Fear and Grace" – Author Notes

IF YOU ASK me, this might be the scariest thing I've ever written. Herbert terrifies me, because I know him. I recognize him.

"Fear and Grace" is an enclosed, intimate story about a traumatized woman who reluctantly reunites with her success-laden, sociopathic friend, a man who has left a trail of destruction in his wake. While it's a very particular, insular, and character-focused piece, I was working with bigger ideas about power, hierarchies, and the corporatization of radical thought. So many of the things that scare me can be traced back to human negotiations with power—the psychological, emotional, and physical violence that many members of our species enact in the name of obtaining prestige, money, status, sex, and material goods. Most disturbing to witness is how the brutal machinations of capitalism reconfigure themselves within nominally progressive environments.

Conceptually, I was intrigued by the challenge of writing a public exchange that carried intensely private connotations between the parties involved. It's all in the gestures and undercurrents.

I wasn't conscious of any specific influences, but I was probably inspired to varying degrees by Stephen King's 1982 novella *Apt Pupil* (from the collection *Different Seasons*), Joyce Carol Oates's *Daddy Love* (2013), Simone de Beauvoir's *A Woman Destroyed* (1967), and excerpts from Eden Robinson's *Traplines* (1996).

LONG MAN

Originally published in *Creepy Campfire Stories (for Grownups)*
(2015)

IT MUST'VE BEEN the sound that woke me up. That wet slurping, like a saucy noodle slithering its way into a mouth.

I rolled over and saw something that shocked my groggy senses.

There was a shape like a man in the mirror. Not in front of the mirror, but *in* the mirror. In front of the mirror was the impression of empty space, but the carpet was rustling, as if something was stirring there, and there was a steady snowfall and buildup of detritus.

Terror incited paralysis. I could only stare with my mouth stretched open, a failing effort to cry out, to produce any sound at all.

And he watched. He watched me with eyes that were not like eyes, gazing without seeing, an unblinking and unearthly sentinel. Deathly skin ringed his pinpoint eyes, skin too thin for eyelids, and his mouth gnawed and chewed, forming infected holes lined redly with flesh that dangled, wet and raw, hanging in strips from its—not its, from *his*—face. His fingers picked at a naked torso, no genitals, but I knew it was a he, and flakes of tummy-flesh came off, drifting to form ashen puddles on the carpet.

I told myself that it was a nightmare, and I tried again to scream, but I could not find the strength. I rolled over to face the wall, and I cried, and I tried to sleep.

I was only six years old, after all. How was I supposed to deal with something like that?

***

The Long Man showed up every night for a month, and even when I turned away, I could hear his ragged breath, the meaty sound of teeth tugging flesh.

Every morning, I'd sit dead-eyed at the table, and my father would urge me to hurry up or I'd miss the bus.

I often considered telling him about my nightly visitor.

Eventually, after thirty nights—or maybe more, at some point the weeks started to bleed into each other—I told my parents. They didn't laugh. They calmly talked to me about nightmares, and the power of imagination, and they told me that monsters weren't real, that monsters would go away if I just didn't believe in them.

I tried so hard not to believe, but this monster had no intention of leaving.

I couldn't rest until a year later, when my parents—by now exasperated with my hysterical rantings about the man in the mirror, and even more exasperated by the ballooning cost of child psychiatrists—finally took action. My bedroom mirror was a family heirloom, and they had no intention of disposing of it, no matter *what* I saw. First, they moved it to another room and replaced it with a new, inexpensive model.

The new mirror brought the same nighttime visitations.

One exhausted summer morning, my mother finally tore the new mirror from its wall mount, slammed it into the backseat of her car, and drove it to the landfill. I went with her, and I still remember the sensation of cold and papery fingertips on the back of my neck as we sped away. I whipped my head around to make sure the mirror was gone, and I saw it tilted atop a pile of rubbish, emaciated gulls circling its cracked and dimly shimmering face.

He was gone.

By then, my child-mind had given him a name.

***

It took me two decades and a lot of whiskey to tell my best friend, Donny, about the shape that had haunted my childhood. I expected him to shake his head and say something along the lines of, "That's real fucked up, man—nothing like a kid's imagination, right?" Donny said no such thing. Instead, he seemed to forget he was in the process of pouring another shot. He just poured and poured, his eyes fixed on some spot on the wall, the whiskey spilling across the tabletop and dribbling off to pool on the carpet.

"No," he said. "Jesus fucking Christ, no."

"Donny." I grabbed his forearm.

To say he was shaking would be like saying he enjoyed a drink on occasion, and Donny was a full-on, bona-fucking-fide alcoholic. His arm spasmed under my fingers, his entire body violently rattling.

"*Donny*," I repeated, and he hollered with shock as if awoken from a hyper-realistic nightmare. He jerked, and the bottle sailed from his hand, smashing against the wall behind him.

He turned to face me, seeming to forget that he had marinated my living room with Maker's Mark mere seconds ago.

"Long, that's right," he said. "Not tall, but *long*. Yes, I remember him. The *Long Man*."

"Yeah, he looked sort of...stretched," I added.

"Like the skin was being pulled tight across his bones. Like he only grew up and up and up, like the shadow of a person."

"Yes," I said, and then, after a pause, "Only... How do you know?"

"Because he lived in my mirror, too." A manic, humorless smile flickered on his face.

"But, how? How could he—"

"—Be in two places at once? No. No, he couldn't," Donny said. "He only showed up when my parents moved me into the basement bedroom. They wanted to convert my old room into a guest suite, and guess what? There was a mirror in the basement room."

My whole body was goose-fleshed. I'd already forgotten about the booze now soaking into the white carpet and staining the walls. I could only focus on Donny's faraway stare, and the fact that I could almost *see* the Long Man haunting his eyes.

"For me, it started with the sound," Donny said. "Squelching. Like a dog pulling gristle from a bone. I thought maybe it was mice living in the walls, or bad plumbing... What the hell does a seven-year-old kid know, right?"

"Seven," I said.

Of course. It made sense. Donny was a year older than me. It seemed that the Long Man couldn't have more than one host at a time—

if we could be called *hosts*—and he also seemed to have a fondness for young boys, a fondness for watching them in their bedrooms.

Alone. At night.

"Did you ever see him disappear?" I knew the answer before I even put the question forward.

"No. There was always a blackness...like a rush of forced sleep...so quick. And I'd wake up—fuck, this is embarrassing—but, I'd wake up in a puddle of my piss. Usually crying, but not always. Nosebleeds too, most of the time. Just lying there in my piss and blood. And my dad would come in, you know, and he'd see the pile of skin on the floor and he'd see the mess in my bed and he'd just say, 'For Christ's sake, not again,' like the whole thing was my fault, right? And I'd say, 'Dad, how could I make that mess on the floor while I'm here in bed?' The theories my parents came up with were endless."

"Bad ventilation," I said, and it was only just then that I remembered my own parents' half-baked rationalization for the perpetual, ashy stain in front of the mirror. "Build-up in the furnace vents."

"I heard that one, too." Donny laughed once. "Moisture in the walls. Flaking paint."

"Rotting stucco."

"Now *that one* I never heard."

I learned that night for certain that the Long Man *was* real, no matter what my army of childhood psychiatrists might've insisted to the contrary. But the discovery was far from comforting. Instead, it gave me the sense that the Long Man might still be out there, waiting for the right time. Waiting for a mirror.

***

He'd never actually *done* anything—I'd long since reasoned away the bedwetting, the nosebleeds, and the blackouts as the products of powerful fits, although I was starting to doubt that now.

It seemed fair to assume that the Long Man was hungry. Why else was he watching? Why else that constant gnawing and tearing at his own face, and that heavy, awful breathing?

Donny slept on my sofa that night. I pretended to pass out on the armchair beside him. I didn't sleep at all.

I just didn't want to go into my bedroom alone. Never mind the fact that I didn't, and would never again, have a mirror.

It might sound unbelievable, but the topic never again arose between Donny and me. Not until the night it all happened, at least...but I'll get to that soon.

It was almost as if Donny and I believed that we could will the Long Man into nonexistence, simply by ignoring the memories. By avoiding them. By repressing them.

The nasty thing about memories is, as the tried-and-true cliché says, they can come back to haunt you.

And sometimes memories have teeth.

***

One night in December, our friend Cody drove us to a dingy but cheap nightclub called Studio 73. It was one of those nights when the cold wind seems to cut through your flesh and coil your bones. We thought a drink (or two, or three, or more) would be as good a way as any to warm up.

We pulled into the parking lot and Donny, in the back seat, leaned toward Cody and me.

"Did we ever tell you about the *thing*?" he asked Cody. "The fucking man-*thing* that used to show up in our mirrors in the darkness? That would stare at us, night after night after night, and *chew* its fucking face open? Did we ever tell you about that?"

His voice sounded so flat, so unbalanced, and it wasn't just from the weed we'd been smoking. The memories of the Long Man haunted both Donny and me, constantly, but tonight—the haunting was on Donny, big time.

Cody turned to me, sitting in the passenger seat. I avoided his eyes and rotated to look at Donny.

"Donny, come on, man," I said. "Let's not talk about this. It's weird. Let's just go have fun, all right?"

"Did we *tell* you, Cody?" Donny asked, louder this time.

"Uh, no...I don't believe you did." Cody released a stilted chuckle, shifting in his seat.

"I could hear it breathing, and you could, too. Couldn't you?" Donny looked at me.

I never wanted to think about the Long Man again, least of all when my mind was toasted from too much THC and alcohol.

"*Couldn't you?*"

"Yes," I said. "Yes, I could hear him."

"And this thing, this...*man-thing* was pale white, like ashes, wasn't he?" Donny continued. "Yes," (he answered for me), "and it would just *stare* and rip at its own cheeks with its teeth, and I could see the discolored infections spreading across its face. And its eyes were blank. Totally blank."

"His," I said. Nobody spoke, and so I said it again. "*His*. The Long Man is a *he*."

Cody glanced at me, and then at Donny. "Why are you guys talking about this right now? Is this some kind of fucked up joke? You're freaking the living hell out of me, man. Jesus."

Donny stared ahead, his eyes wide and wet, like a scolded puppy's, and he said something almost inaudible that I think might've been, "*Here.*"

"What?" Cody asked.

"*Because he's here right now.*" Donny quivered. Tears rolled down his cheeks. "He's sitting right beside me."

I twisted to see the empty space beside him, and I thought, *Good God, Donny has lost it. The Long Man has taken his mind and fucked it up for good. Donny's gone.*

It didn't take long for the thought to dawn on me, though, and I said it aloud: "The mirror."

Cody and I cast our eyes to the rear-view mirror, and I saw exactly what I knew I would see.

I saw *him*.

I saw his naked, mottled body. His ribs poked through a veil of tissue. Tattered skin-strips drooped from the gashes chewed into his cheeks. His facial lesions rained blood, splattering the floor of Cody's van.

There was an eerie pause, a moment of utter silence, and then I realized that the radio was still playing–"Believe," by Cher. It was just about to hit the chorus.

Donny started screaming, not yelling or crying, just flat-out fucking *screaming*.

I turned away from the mirror to look at him. His neck was being pulled toward the roof—pulled so far that it looked like some kind of gruesome taffy—until his head popped free with a nauseating squelch, his scream cutting short with the sound. His head swung in midair over the spouting stump of his neck, spewing blood. Then his chest pulled open, and his ribs were pried apart. His heart was visible, all wet and red, and I became suddenly aware that Cody was watching with a vacant face. He couldn't seem to register the scene with any degree of emotion or understanding.

I was frozen as well, watching Donny—my friend—pull apart. Watching him being *pulled apart*.

The parts that came off were suspended. I could only bear one more glance in the mirror, that was it. The Long Man was *chewing* on him. He was finally getting the meal he'd awaited for so long, and there was blood smeared all over his face.

I snapped. I mean, I completely lost it. I unbuckled my seatbelt, and with fumbling fingers, I yanked open the back door and threw Donny—Donny's remains, more like—out into the parking lot.

Cody floored it. He peeled out of there, and the radio was playing so loudly that I couldn't tell whether he was screaming or laughing, but judging by his face, he could've been doing either. Or both.

***

When Cody drove me home that night, I'd already made the decision to leave. I won't tell you where I came from, and I won't tell you where I've gone. The investigation must be well underway by now...or maybe they're already searching for me. Maybe they've been searching for a long time. I hope that Cody got away safe, but I couldn't stick around to find out. It was too much of a risk.

You might think I'm a real bastard for doing what I did, for running away, and maybe I am—but I doubt that any of you would've known what else to do.

Don't ask me what's happened since then. I don't read the papers. I don't even use the Internet anymore.

All I know is that no police officer in the world would believe that sometimes a thing called the Long Man decides to show up in a little boy's bedroom mirror, that he waits for the right moment until finally...he *feeds*.

The Long Man must've found a new host by now. If not, I imagine he's getting pretty hungry. I don't know how much I've aged since all of this happened.

I cannot, after all, look at my own reflection. No, I don't believe I'll ever do that again.

"Long Man" – Author Notes

THIS WAS MY first professional short story sale. It was included in a 2015 anthology called *Creepy Campfire Stories (for Grownups)*.

"Long Man" looked a lot different when I first submitted it under the title "In the Locust Furnace." Along with this section's final entry, "Remembering Absence," this piece originated as part of a road novel I was writing from the perspective of a sleuthing ghost. Ultimately, I abandoned that novel, but at least I got two stories out of it.

In the first draft of "Long Man," the incorporeal protagonist surveyed several interactions between a group of nefarious characters he suspected of guilt in his cousin's untimely death. The Long Man was the abandoned novel's main antagonist, but he was much less prominently featured in the first draft I submitted to *Creepy Campfire Stories (for Grownups)*. The editor wrote back, saying that she liked my prose style, but that the piece felt a little unfocused—she asked if I would be interested in resubmitting a sort of "origin story" about the Long Man, and I obliged.

While dealing with the part of this narrative that finds two friends connecting over childhood trauma, I was definitely conscious of Gregg Araki's 2004 film adaptation of *Mysterious Skin*, a 1995 novel by Scott Heim. For whatever reason, Cher's "Believe" was looping in my head while I wrote the horrific climax, so I worked it in.

Sorry, Cher.

ECONOMY THESE DAYS

JOHN ARRIVED AT the interview location, a stunning new condo development nestled comfortably between the downtown core and a beautiful public park. People lounged in the surrounding green space—holding hands, playing guitar, laughing, singing.

John tried his best to absorb some of their positive energy, but like some unwanted specter, Pop's voice invaded his peace.

John tried to avoid thinking about Pop whenever possible, but in this moment his father's advice came through like the word of God: *Don't work soft, Johnny. Work like you want to work, and it'll all play out just fine.*

Work like you want to work. John supposed Pop had been doing just that his whole life, long enough that by this point he really didn't *need* to work. Too bad John could no longer call up his father and ask for professional suggestions...or for financial help. Ever since that fateful dinner debate about gay marriage had evolved into a screaming match—

Don't think about it. John smiled at the sound of a chirruping bird, enjoyed the scent of a nearby lilac tree. *Maybe you can call Pop later, if this all works out.*

He had never attended an interview in a domestic space, but then, he'd never responded to an e-mail like this one, either. When he'd first glanced at the message three months ago, he'd dismissed it immediately as junk. It was exactly the kind of message that rang false: the subject line read, *Make $450 a day, NOT A SCAM.* Yes, John was well-informed enough to realize that emails and advertisements screaming *NOT A SCAM* were almost always scams.

And yet, three months later, things were looking different. He had defended his thesis nearly half a year ago, and the university's funding had long since stopped its pleasant trickle into his account. He'd submitted résumés and cover letters to no less than two hundred openings. He had been called in for a total of three interviews. No call-backs.

And so, although the message was bizarrely ambiguous (the body of the email never truly touched upon the subject line's $450 promise), and although John knew intuitively that it seemed too good to land anywhere near the realm of truth, despair eventually led him to fitting measures. He picked up his phone, and he dialed the number provided in the last line of the message.

So here he was. He took in a shaky breath, straightened his washer-dulled shirt, and buzzed the room number he'd been provided. He stood on the stoop and stared up at the cloudless blue sky, allowing himself another little smile. Things would be all right.

Almost as if it had heard John's positive thoughts, the buzzer remained spitefully silent and nonresponsive.

John consulted his phone for the time: 1:30 pm, as scheduled. He unfolded the piece of paper on which he'd written the condominium number. Yes, 807 was the one. Maybe the owner had stepped out onto his porch for a phone call or a cigarette. No need to fret.

John was unconvinced by his own faux-positive self-talk. He pressed the buzzer again, cursing mildly under his breath. He waited ten seconds. Twenty. After a minute passed, he shook his head and turned to walk away.

That was when he heard a voice hissing from behind: "*Pssst!*"

John rotated.

A tall, strikingly handsome man emerged from behind the shrubbery lining the condo. He wore skinny jeans, a blazer, and a tight black t-shirt that said *BELIEVE*. His face creased into a smile, and he extended a sun-pampered hand. "You must be John."

"Yes." John took the hand and shook it. Firm, but not aggressive.

The man swiped a well-groomed lock of brown hair from his forehead and gestured toward downtown. "Cole Jorgenson here, John. Our car's this way."

"Your—"

"Yes." Cole chuckled. "Yes, we'll be hosting our interview in the car. It really shouldn't take long at all."

John's mind asked him what the fuck he was thinking. John's mind told him this didn't seem right.

John's mouth said, "Very good."

He trailed after Mr. Jorgenson, until they arrived at a stretch limo parked on Third Avenue. Mr. Jorgenson opened the back door. John peered momentarily into the darkness of the vehicle and noted to his relief an absence of balaclava-donning men lurking within. Really, what was the worst that could happen? They'd mug him and steal his empty wallet? Kill him, maybe? At this moment in time, the thought was almost comforting.

And so, John slipped into the vehicle and nodded at the driver, a hairy-shouldered fellow wearing a white tank top and aviator sunglasses.

Cole slid in beside John, the leather straining beneath him with an awkwardly flatulent sound. He patted the driver's woolly arm. "Interview."

The driver flicked his signal and entered the lane leading toward Fourth Avenue.

"Well, John, I'm glad you gave us a call," Cole said. "Very glad. Our company offers cutting edge opportunities for a diverse client base. We thrive on innovative strategies that allow us to mobilize business development on a national scale."

John tried to maintain eye contact with Cole's baby blues. "Sounds great. So what exactly is this position?"

Cole clapped his own thigh and smiled at the driver. "Wow, I am so glad you asked, John. Well, I know I said 'national scale' just now, but really what we're after is *international* relations for new communications programs."

John waited, alternating glances between the driver's rear-view and Cole's coolly smirking face. After a couple minutes, he cleared his throat. "I don't mean to be rude," he said, "but going in, it's really important for me to know what it is I would be doing."

Cole barked a laugh that sounded more like an expression of pain than humor. Then, abruptly, he leaned across the backseat and pinched Cole's cheek between his thumb and forefinger. Hard.

John cried out in shock. Oh fuck, this really was a violent setup. Now that the terrifying reality was transpiring, he wasn't so sure he was ready to die.

Just as quickly as he'd pinched, though, Cole withdrew. He leaned away and held up his palms in a placating gesture. "Now, how did that make you feel, John?"

"It made me feel like I want you to let me out." John's voice wavered. "*Now*."

"We would be happy to do that." Mr. Jorgensen flicked a salute toward the driver's rear-view glancing eyes. "Before I let you out, though, please allow me to inform you that this job would entail nothing much more painful than that little pinch you just received. $450 a day, cash."

John rubbed his throbbing cheek and shrank away. "I'm not going in for a porno movie. Forget it."

"A porno!" Cole laughed. "A *porno*."

John's nagging mind kept urging him to get out of the vehicle, to go apply for a food service or retail position and wait things out until economic conditions improved. And yet, another mental voice screamed louder, calculating with feverish greed: *$450 a day, $2,250 a week, $9,000 a month...*

"I'm serious. If it's a porno, then you can let me out right now. I won't do any weird sex stuff, and I won't hurt anyone. If this job includes none of these things, and it pays as much as you say it does—"

"Sometimes more," Cole interjected coolly.

"—then we can talk."

"You won't be hurting anyone," Cole said. "You might get a little roughed up yourself, but no...you won't be hurting anyone."

***

They arrived at their destination, after many questions from John and vague half-answers from Cole. It was a small building in the city's northeast industrial sector. A weather-faded sign hung over the door, reading *Hugh's Wheel Replacements*.

Would John need access to transportation? No, he would be driven to and from this location five days a week.

What were the hours? Monday to Friday, less than five hours per shift, and he would have his weekends free.

How would he be paid? $450 in large bills would be provided in a sealed envelope at the end of every shift.

"What *is* this job?" John asked one final time, as Mr. Jorgensen unlocked the door and stepped into the fluorescent-lit interior.

"You're a human punching bag." Cole turned to face him, extending his arms in a gesture that said, *So what's the big deal?*

John laughed. He waited for Cole to follow up with either an explanation or a punchline. When neither came, he raised an eyebrow.

"A human—?"

"Punching bag, yeah. I mean, you won't actually be *punched* very often, and never in the face. There are all kinds of regulations, and our clients are respectful of the boundaries. If anyone goes against the rules as stipulated in the contract, there are strict financial repercussions. You would benefit from such repercussions, I might add."

"I—"

"You wanted an answer, and I'll give you an answer. Is this a legal operation? Simply put, no. But we have a front, and it's all been carefully accounted for. We have been growing our client base since 1985, and we now have upwards of six hundred customers. Our personal communications associates...uh, that would be *you*, John, if you choose to take this job...are in high demand. There's a little arena in the back, carefully padded and maintained. Throughout the duration of your shift, you would be enclosed within that arena with three of our clients...one at a time, just so we're clear. Said clients are allowed to, uh, 'blow off steam,' if you will, using you as their outlet, and at the end of your three daily sessions, you're taken home in one of our cozy limousines."

"So you set me loose in a room with your...uh, *clients*, and they, what? Beat the shit out of me for an hour and change?"

"Uh, yes." Cole handsomely crumpled his face and clapped his hands. "Very well put, John. Yes, within reason. Our contract plainly states, though—only hands-based steam-blowing. That means no kicking, no head-butting, no elbows or knees. Their attacks may only be directed at your abdomen, arms, and lower legs. We don't want to risk concussions or, God forbid, sore balls." He laughed at this, as if sharing a joke with a pal at the pub.

Words poured from John's mind, like water down a drain. His thoughts were stuck in some bare, gray space, unable to make sense of this ludicrous scenario.

"Why?" He was unable to come up with anything else.

"We like to think of this as a way to mitigate violent crime rates, John," Cole said. "Really, you're a public service employee. Many of our clients are confirmed to be recovered addicts, ex-domestic abusers, even murderers—"

Cued by the phrase "domestic abusers," Pop's face floated through John's mind. He gulped and waited for Cole to continue. This couldn't be any worse than anything he'd already been through.

"This is all regulated. I personally observe every one of these sessions to ensure that no conditions are breached." Cole leaned on a wall and crossed his arms over his chest. "So what do you say? It really is as simple as it sounds. Will you give it a go? You can start as early as..."—he consulted his cellphone for the date—"as early as tomorrow, I guess. What do you say?"

John had $1.69 to his name, and he saw no sign of financial hope anywhere in his near future. What *could* he say?

Don't work soft, Johnny. Pop's voice again, loud and clear. Yes, as a youth, Pop had worked anything but soft. John never expected himself to end up doing the same. At the very least, he wasn't the one doing the hitting. Young Pop couldn't have honestly said the same.

***

The first client was a lithe, scrappy-looking fucker whose eyes bulged so far from their sockets that John kept expecting them to drop right out and roll across the rug.

John was urged not to make eye contact with the customers, and certainly to never engage in linguistically coherent exchanges. He could scream, yell, or moan, but he was advised against using words like *ouch*, *shit*, and especially blasphemous exclamations like *God* or *Jesus Christ*. It was crucial that the clients leave feeling relieved, satiated, and unoffended. It was all outlined so neatly in his contract. He was permitted to scamper back and forth in an attempt to avoid the attacks, but he was *under no circumstances* to turn his back on the clients, or to make any attempts at self-defence. The "arena" was a room no larger than his first bachelor suite apartment, adorned with padded walls and clinical white lighting.

His sinewy attacker seemed to possess arms twice as long as he was tall (and John judged the man to be somewhere in the neighborhood of seven feet). The stretchy bastard didn't miss often, but when he did, he fluttered his almost nonexistent upper lip across his teeth in an expression of annoyance. The sound was like a deflating balloon.

The first blow to John's stomach made him cry out in pure, brute shock, and so did the first solid jab to his shin. By hit number five or six, though, he'd resigned to quiet grunts of displeasure. His body quickly became a mass of bruisy and achy sensations; his heart soon beat with alarming violence.

The session clocked in at ninety minutes, at which point the lanky creep exited with a wet inhale and a final rubbery flutter of his lip.

John stood throbbing and stinging, waiting for the next step. Sure enough, Cole entered the arena within a few minutes, rifling a stack of bills in his hand and whistling the synth line from Van Halen's "Jump."

"$150 for you, John," he said. "Would you like the payment now or after your next two sessions?"

John paused for a moment. "After my next sessions."

***

John's second appointment was even more brutal than the first. The arena door slapped against the padded wall with all the subtlety of a nuclear bomb; a muscle-bound man wearing athletic gear strutted into the room, his angular face expressing a warrior's intent.

John bobbed nervously and watched the man's paddle-like feet approaching. When the guy was a few inches away, John attempted to slide away from the first blow.

No such luck.

A fist like a boulder crunched into his ribcage, splitting bone.

John exclaimed toward the ceiling. "Time out, I've broken something!"

An air horn sounded from a speaker in the room's top right corner. As Cole strode in through the door, the man took a swing at John's chest. John felt something snap and cave, and he squealed in humiliating high pitch.

Cole wore a whistle around his neck, which he blew with all the conviction of a stern referee. The man ignored him, kicking John's shin with full force.

"Make it stop!" screamed John.

The next hit landed on his temple. Everything went fuzzy and dim before going black.

***

While unconscious, his concussed brain summoned images of Pop.

John's dreaming mind convinced him that he was five years old again, pedaling fast down the neighborhood sidewalk in a desperate effort to escape his father's wrath; but who was he kidding? There was no escape. Sure, Pop was carrying extra weight, but his rage propelled him forward at an alarming speed.

Dream John's bike seemed to spin without moving—the sidewalk yawned ahead and ahead like some perverse illusion, and before long Pop caught up. Pop *always* caught up. The feeling of the man's huge hand clamping John's collarbone was all too familiar—

"John," said a man's voice, too soft and gentle to be Pop's. "Wake up."

John looked up into the unassuming features of a medical professional, a man with cherubic features and cool green eyes.

While John awaited his diagnosis, Cole paced in the corner, gnawing his thumb like a father in the birthing room.

John heard the doctor speaking, in some dim part of his awareness (*Minor concussion ... Fractured rib ... Take some rest ...*), but his mind was still fixated on that vivid dream-memory of Pop. A punching bag in childhood; a punching bag in manhood.

After all that time in school.

***

Yes, the second session had resulted in minor injuries (a fractured rib, a concussion, and some severe bruising), but John was compensated for the inconvenience, just as promised. By the end of the first month he'd already paid off all his debts, replaced his outdated cellphone, and even began surfing the web for more appealing apartment options.

On the first day of month two, he eased his aching body into the limo, fully expecting to be driven to his worksite for a typical handful of beatings. Normally, the furry driver showed up alone. These days, John never saw Jorgensen until after his shifts ended.

Today, though, Cole waited in the backseat.

John eased into the vehicle, groaning a little at the stings and throbs that now ran continuously through his body, and nodded congenially at his boss.

"Wanted to come along for the ride today?" he asked.

"'Come along for the ride,'" Cole echoed. He exploded into a brief bout of laughter. "Well, yes, John, I guess I kind of did...only my real reason for joining you this afternoon is—oh, you can go ahead, driver— excuse me, John...my *real* reason is that I'd like to discuss a new opportunity for professional advancement."

The word "advancement" spiked through John's pre-shift bleariness. He waited for Cole to continue.

"Our company prides itself on providing its employees with opportunities for upward mobility, and normally I wouldn't offer this kind of placement to anyone other than a senior staff member," Cole said.

"I don't imagine you have many senior staff members, though, do you?" John smirked. "They probably die or quit before they make it to seniority."

Cole wore the expression of a man facing his beloved pet's murderer.

John opened his mouth to say, "I'm joking" (although he wasn't, not really), but Cole silenced him with a raised hand.

"I suppose I haven't made it clear to you yet, John, that termination is always a very real possibility."

John stared down into his lap. Although he'd paid off his debts and began making positive changes toward real financial autonomy, he was a long way off from being where he'd like to be. He remembered his spacious childhood bedroom and all the annual vacations, the extravagant family outings, Ma and Pop's three-car garage... He'd be lying if he denied the existence of some mini-John hunkering in his mind, a noisy little bastard who too often dragged up those memories and whispered, *Wouldn't it be nice? Wouldn't it be nice to have those things again?*

"I take it by your silence that termination is not in your short-term plan," Cole said. "Would you like to hear more about the possibilities for advancement within our group, or would you rather we drive you back home and call it a day?"

"Tell me," John said. "I want to hear all about it."

***

John remembered his feelings after the initial job interview—the unpleasant tightness in his gut, the anxiety and guilt. And yet a combination of desperation and the promise of true financial freedom had crushed those reservations rather quickly and efficiently.

Now, even though he continued rehearsing the phrase in his mind (*double pay, double pay, double pay*), the "Premium Package Service Associate" contract would not settle neatly.

And yet he'd signed.

Here he was, standing in the corner of a smaller and more brightly lit arena, sweat collecting in his armpits and hairline. When the door creaked open to reveal a bulky man in a button-down and dress pants, John tried his best to find solace in thoughts of cash.

But in this moment, money seemed like some grotesque abstraction; the process of reaching its ends were dwarfed by these terrible means. Because the man plodding across the cushy flooring looked altogether *too much* like John's brutal Pop. If it weren't for the guy's youthful face and naturally blonde hair, John might've actually mistaken him for the black-mopped brute who'd beaten him through childhood.

Dazed, John said, "Daddy," aloud, knowing very well that his new contract also forbade verbal exchanges.

The heavyset man marching toward him didn't seem to mind. In fact, a prurient little smile twitched the guy's lips. He reached into his pocket, pulling out the item allowed by his premium package payment: a small handheld Taser.

Don't work soft, said John's trusty mental-Pop.

John opened his mouth to repeat the word "Daddy," but that was when the customer lunged with the electroshock weapon.

John screamed as his muscles composed a symphony of awful contractions. Before he hit the floor, some part of his agony-gripped consciousness wondered what the next promotion might look like.

He stared up, rigid from neuromuscular incapacitation, and at a second glance he thought that maybe Pop had found his way to his son again, after all. Then the blonde hair flopped down across the man's lascivious, tooth-gritting face and John thought, *No...this is someone else's daddy.*

Before pain drove him to unconsciousness, he thought of money. His client might've mistaken his pain-stricken rictus for an expression of ecstasy.

"Economy These Days" – Author Notes

I WROTE THIS story as a deliberate counterpoint to the book's persisting darkness...which is not to say that it doesn't feature its share of pessimism, but it's certainly wrapped up in black humor. This is a satirical and deliberately blunt comment on the exploitation and artificial job scarcity of late capitalism, which takes cues from the sort of tonal acrobatics that Eli Roth puts to work in his *Hostel* films (2005/7).

I don't read much overtly humorous fiction, certainly not within the horror genre, so it's difficult for me to pin down the influences for something like "Economy These Days." I admire the balance between humour and profound insight in books like Zadie Smith's *White Teeth* (1999), Hari Kunzru's *Transmission* (2004), and John Irving's *The World According to Garp* (1978), but I can't see any explicit connections between those novels' uses of comedy and mine.

SABBATICAL

Originally published in *Dark Moon Digest* (2017)

THAD GESTURED OUT the windshield as he brought his Corolla to a stop. "Here it is, Gage."

And indeed, here it was. The cabin was much larger than Gage had expected. Truthfully, he didn't know what *exactly* he'd expected—maybe some tiny, hand-crafted structure nestled in the idyllic heart of the wild? Something worthy of Thoreau or Whitman? At the very least, he'd expected something that would typically qualify as a "cabin." Yes, the enormous and gorgeously maintained house before them was made of wood, and yes, it was surrounded on three sides by thickets of coniferous trees. But Gage was more than a little taken aback by its two-vehicle driveway, its spacious front porch, and the glinting satellite dish, which looked somehow arrogant from its rooftop perch.

"Wow." Gage laughed once. "Some cabin."

Thad pulled the key from the ignition and rolled his shoulders. "What can I say? My dad pulls in a lot of dough."

"I was expecting some little isolated nook," Gage said. "A sabbatical nook."

"It's a sabbatical nook, don't worry. Just a very luxurious sabbatical nook." Thad stepped out of the car and stretched. He waved at a hefty man who trundled up the neighboring driveway with a Corona in his fist.

Yes, there were equally extravagant "cabins" on both sides of this place, but the walls of pine trees made for very effective fences.

Gage certainly had no complaints. There was nothing wrong with finding some comfort in their academic getaway. He'd never been to Whitefish, Montana, had never actually made it out of the province of

Alberta. He would take any excuse to get away from his cluttered and poorly heated Calgary flat, even if the excuse was to take on a task more arduous than that of his usual day-to-day duties. The task, they'd agreed, was to finish drafting their first dissertation chapters before "sabbatical week" was up.

And yes, if he was to be completely honest with himself, there was an element of competition involved, too. If he was to be really, *uncomfortably* honest with himself, he wanted to see his braggart friend learn something about the value of hard work. Just last week they'd gone together to a party at a new graduate student's condo, and after five or six drinks Gage had heard Thad enter full boasting mode (*The trick is to do as little work as possible ... I haven't even started my dissertation yet, but I'll write it in a month, easy, and I guaran-fuckin-tee it'll be a success*). That was when Gage had said some unkind words...something about his friend being the worst example of unchecked privilege, an alpha male, an intellectual bully without an original thought in his head.

Yeah, something along those lines. The next day, they'd chalked it up to drunken nonsense. A week later, they'd scheduled the sabbatical.

"Hey, Earth to Gage," Thad said.

Gage blinked heavily and quickly realized he'd drifted off into the ugly details of memory, still leaning absent-mindedly on Thad's car.

"Smoke?" Thad offered, a cigarette wagging between his teeth.

Gage accepted a Camel, sparked up, and dragged. He cast his eyes toward the crayon-blue sky, blinking at the sun. A bird chittered from the treetops. It was a cigarette moment. "Have you decided whether or not you're going to ditch this chapter's Lacanian framework?" he asked Thad.

It seemed like Thad's dissertation shifted its framework every week. Gage usually tried to avoid discouraging his friend, he really did, but sometimes he doubted Thad would ever complete the project at all. One day the dissertation was a postcolonial reading of contemporary American genre fiction, and the next it was a critical engagement with Philip Roth through Kierkegaard.

Maybe this week-long retreat would produce something coherent, or even cohesive. Maybe miracles were possible.

"Lacanian framework... Yeah, something along those lines," Thad said, in typically vague Thad fashion. "I'm working it all out." He pushed a plume of smoke through his rolled-up tongue. "And you?"

Gage thought about the stack of Ligotti, Bataille, Zappfe, and Kristeva waiting like a stack of omens in the trunk of Thad's car. He flicked ashes onto the gravel, and he smiled at the sounds of birdsong.

"It's coming along," he said.

***

By the time they'd hauled their many boxes of books into the vast, expensively carpeted foyer, they were both exhausted. Gage wanted to collapse into the soapy-smelling linens of the guest suite's queen-sized bed. Thad wanted to drink.

It was Thad's dad's cabin, and so it was Thad's choice.

Alcohol it was.

They sat on the porch for many hours, and time passed with impossible speed, as drinking-time does. Once the sun had melted to a crimson wedge on the skyline, their full bottle of Glenfiddich had dwindled to nothing.

Their conversations meandered through shared undergrad memories, debates about recent films, interpretations of favorite novels, and whiskey-slicked takedowns of their English department's faculty members.

Eventually, Gage's nerve succumbed completely to drunkenness, and he spoke frankly. "Thad...you're never going to finish your dissertation, are you?"

Thad smirked. He hooded a cigarette with his hand and lit. "End of this week, I'll have completed a first draft. A *clean* first draft."

"Of the first chapter, you mean?"

"No," Thad said flatly. "Of the entire dissertation."

The scotch still had a stranglehold on Gage's manners, and so he reacted with unrestrained instinct: he exploded with laughter, spraying liquor all over his pants. It was a tenacious, drunken laugh that wouldn't let go, that kept pushing and pushing until he thought his gut might just seize.

Thad stood silently over him, looking so effortlessly cool in his designer sweater and fitted jeans, still smirking around his mouthful of Camel. He waited for the laughter to subside, and then he spoke again: "You can read it on the way home if you'd like."

And then Gage totally gave up—he started howling again, and that was the last thing he'd remember the next headachey morning: hysterical, rude laughter at his old buddy's expense, and Thad's expression of patient calm.

***

Gage started writing before he'd even been fortified with coffee. Hangover wracked his body like the curse of guilt, but he forced himself to ignore the nausea and fatigue, and he began toiling hazily at his laptop.

He was reworking an unwieldy sentence about the horror of alien subjectivity when he first heard the sound.

It was something like a voice, deep and insistent, that travelled through the wall between his room and Thad's. It sounded like a stereo tuned between channels, garbled and noisy. He assumed Thad's father had left an old alarm clock radio in Thad's room, and he tried to ignore the sound.

He spent nearly five minutes revising a parenthetical phrase, blinking against the pain of his whiskey migraine.

The noise persisted.

Finally, he rose to his feet and thumped his palm playfully against the wall. "Turn off the alarm," he barked. "Make me some goddamn coffee!"

Almost before he'd finished speaking, the sound cut short. He brought his ear to the wall, expecting to hear Thad call back with obscene protest. What he heard instead was the whirring of a printer, followed by steady footsteps.

A moment later, Thad stepped into Gage's room without knocking. He looked as far from Gage's unshaven, half-dressed state of disarray as imaginable. Thad was the image of success, poured into a form-fitting button-down, his unruly brown hair already styled into a pompadour. He held a formidably thick stack of paper.

"Morning, Gage," he said. "Would you like to read the first two chapters? They might need some minor revisions."

"What?" Gage blinked. "Uh...coffee and Advil first?"

***

Halfway through scanning the first chapter, Gage grudgingly accepted that Thad's project was completely polished. Not just promising, but expertly constructed, threaded throughout with theoretical nuance and invention.

He set the papers on the oak breakfast table and stared across the steaming coffee carafe at Thad.

"How?" he asked, his voice flat.

Thad ran fingers through his finely groomed mane. "Fit of inspiration," he said. He stared past Gage, his eyes fixed on the large living room behind his friend. It was the only tacky-looking room in this cabin-mansion. The walls were crammed with taxidermied animal heads; a preserved deer skull leered, dead-eyed, above the fireplace.

Gage shook his head and downed the dregs of his fourth coffee. He changed the topic. "Did your dad leave any food here?"

"Non-perishables. There's a lot of beef and venison in the freezer, too. You're thinking breakfast?"

"Yeah," Gage said. "Breakfast sounds glorious right about now."

But he was really thinking about the astonishing boldness and architecture of Thad's work. He twisted in his seat and made eye contact with the unstaring sockets of the mantelpiece animal skull. He wasted no time turning back around.

Thad was buried up to his shoulders in the freezer, gathering Ziploc bags of frozen meat.

"Thad? Could you do me a favour and turn your alarm way the fuck down tomorrow morning?"

Thad turned to face him, one frosty red bag in each hand. "What alarm?"

"I could've sworn..." Gage paused, stared down into his empty mug. "Never mind."

Thad turned back around to face the microwave. "I think you're imagining things."

Gage decided not to push the matter any further.

***

The next time Gage heard the noise, it was much too late (or too early) for any reasonable person to be making such a ruckus.

This time, he could swear he heard two voices through the wall—one was unmistakably his friend's, speaking low but very quickly; the other was...what? A voice recording? Two machines playing the same speech at different speeds?

Hairs stood on the back of his neck. He peeled away his sheets, pressed palms against his sleep-stinging eyes, and consulted his recharging iPhone for the time.

4:53 am.

He padded across the room, picked his Levi's off the floor and slipped into them.

He opened the door and stepped into the hallway. He was about to knock on Thad's door when he heard half a phrase that stopped him in his tracks:

"...we will deal with the body when we're through."

The words were crystal clear, delivered in a voice that was absolutely *not* Thad's. It was too slick, too mannered, too old.

Gage stepped back into the hall and pinched his own arm, administering the same test he had used as a child. The flesh stung in confirmation: no, he was not dreaming.

He turned around and retreated toward his room when Thad's door suddenly swung open.

Thad stood erect, like a man about to address a crowd of thousands. Lamplight flooded from his room, haloing around him. His hair was immaculately styled, his shirt clean and neatly ironed. If he was wearing shoes, Gage imagined they'd be polished to shine like mirrors. The stack of paper in his hand was even thicker than yesterday's.

"I don't know whether you'd like to look at this now, but I'm about three-quarters of the way through," Thad said.

Gage stared at him with utter bewilderment. "Three quarters...?"

"Yes." Thad's lips wormed into an arrogant smile. "That *is* why you're standing outside my door at nearly five in the morning, right? Checking on my progress?"

Gage looked down at his feet. He imagined his own thoughts as scattered paratroopers descending into a thick fog. Words backed up, half-formed, behind his tongue.

Without speaking, he absently patted Thad on the shoulder and turned back toward his own room.

Before stepping inside for another couple hours of much-needed sleep, he said what he'd been waiting to say: "Thad—who were you talking to in there?"

Thad's smile spread. Gage thought loopily of the Grinch, that famous green thief of Christmas.

"Thad?" he said. "Earth to Thad?"

Thad clutched his dissertation draft, so hard that it rattled in his hand. His knuckles whitened. "Get some *fucking* sleep," he said, pushing his words through the strain of that awful grin.

Then, without further comment, he whipped around and plunged back into his room. He slammed the door behind him, so hard that it shook like something frightened in its frame.

***

Gage awoke feeling heavy and warm, sunlight streaming through the slats of his blinds. He rotated slowly in the sheets and cast a glance toward his iPhone.

It was almost noon.

"Fuck," he said, kicking the blankets away.

He collected his crumpled jeans from the floor and pulled them on, his brain needling him with unwanted thoughts: *There goes your morning. Thad's dissertation is going beautifully, Gage—how about yours?*

"Shut up," he said aloud.

He paused, his pants still unzipped, his heart beating like a metronome on hyper-speed.

The room was silent.

Normally he would assume nothing of it, would probably shuffle up the stairs to brew coffee and get promptly to his writing. Normally, though, he wasn't prone to witnessing his friend grinning like some doped-up lunatic at ungodly hours and wielding a radical tome that he'd produced with the ease of a smooth bowel movement.

Normal might very well be the last word he would use to describe this sabbatical.

He crept toward the wall between his room and Thad's, and he rested his ear against it, fully expecting to hear something strange. Expecting that ghastly and somehow aged voice. Expecting, at the very least, to hear stirring or typing.

Instead he heard nothing whatsoever. He felt increasingly nervous, his shirtless abdomen tightening with gooseflesh.

His mind stepped in with a cool intervention of reason: *Thad was up just as late as you were, probably even later. Maybe he's still angry about your cruel words at that graduate student's party. Maybe he's still asleep, for Christ's sake. So why don't you behave like a rational adult, go upstairs, and fix breakfast for two?*

He pried himself from the wall and shook his head. What was his problem? Maybe *he* was the one with the issues—he was, after all, the guy who studied disturbingly nihilistic philosophy with such devotion.

Ligotti goes in, paranoia comes out.

He grabbed a t-shirt and pulled it over his head. Without a second thought, he ascended the stairs and made his way into the kitchen.

By the time the water had boiled and the coffee was brewing, it was quarter past noon. The cabin was still as quiet as a tomb.

Irrational thought flashed back into his brain like a neon sign: *something's wrong, something's wrong, something's definitely fucking wrong.*

"Screw it," he said before descending the stairs, refusing his fear the chance to fester any longer.

He rapped his knuckles against Thad's door. "Coffee?"

There was a long pause, and then a deep, moaning sound. The voice was low, frayed, and nothing like Thad's, and—

Will you stop scaring yourself already?

Gage tried to smirk. "You up, jackass?"

The moaning stopped abruptly. Gage stood poised outside his friend's room. He remained that way for what felt like minutes on end, and then finally he knocked again.

"Thad?"

Nothing.

If that was you in there, you'd probably want to be woken up, Gage thought. Then, his self-bullying mind added, *But if that was you, you wouldn't have so much beautiful work written already.*

Gage clutched the doorknob and pushed the door open. "Wakey, wakey, eggs and—"

The sight before him killed the sing-song chant midway through. His voice evaded him as his eyes took in the horrific scene, sending unthinkable images to a brain that didn't want to believe.

Thad sat upright at his desk, his scalp peeled back to reveal the glistening red top of his skull. Behind him stood a nude man who looked so ancient as to be defying death itself; his emaciated arms hung in the air, his bony fingers stroking Thad's exposed skull with feverish persistence. Thad's own fingers flew across his laptop keyboard, and he began speaking. The aged and naked man muttered along, his larynx bobbing visibly under paper-thin skin. As the two men spoke, Thad's typing accelerated. They both uttered phrases that sounded distantly familiar to Gage, quotes by philosophers ranging from Socrates to Deleuze, delivered in chilling monotones that would better suit a severe judicial setting.

Silent with terror, Gage watched as Thad filled a page, two pages, six, ten, composing multiple paragraphs in mere seconds. The pads of the old man's fingers continued massaging the blood-sheened bone of his skull, both of their voices maintaining that awful and inhuman rhythm.

"Thad?" Gage finally said. "Oh, good fucking Lord, Thad..."

Neither of the men responded.

Gage became aware that he was privy to some kind of waking dream, an induced trance. He stepped further into the room, his muscles stiffening with animal fear.

He moved to stand behind the old man (*Oh God, I can see the knobs of his spine coming through*) and looked at the screen.

Thad was almost two hundred pages into his dissertation, and Gage could only watch in dumbfounded silence as beautiful sentences flitted across the document-in-progress with machine-gun proficiency, and he thought that maybe he'd stand here watching this horrible and unnatural process until his mind finally just snapped, in which case he would cry out until all air escaped his body, but before the aberrant process could lead him there...it ceased.

Thad jerked like a marionette unstringed, his arms flapping to rest noodle-like at his sides. The old man twisted to face Gage and opened his puckered mouth to smile, revealing sickly gray gums and a tongue reddened with sores.

"Say the word," the man said, enunciating with impossible clarity for someone without teeth.

Gage watched as the old man's fingers formed pincers on the edges of Thad's detached scalp, pressing the flap back down against the skull.

"You'll lose this body, yes, of course you'll lose this body," the man said. "But there's always another."

Horror seized Gage's mind, crowding his thoughts with lunatic screams. No matter how badly he wanted to run out of this room, his body wouldn't allow itself to move.

He tried to speak: "I—"

Suddenly, Thad revolved in his writing chair, gracing Gage with an awful and joyless smile. Dark blood oozed from the seam in his head, pooling in the bottoms of his eye sockets. "All he needs are more bodies. Just a few more bodies, that's all."

His gentle tone struck Gage with incomprehensible dread, and the phrase repeated nastily in his mind: *Just a few more bodies, that's all...*

Gage tried again: "Thad—"

"Wait, before you continue." Thad raised his hand in a gesture that said *stop.*

The old man wheezed a moist laugh, posing like some nightmarish sculpture. "Show him."

Thad rose to his feet in that unnervingly puppet-like fashion, his mannerisms jerky and awkward. He jolted across the room until he'd reached the closet. "Are you ready, Gage?"

Gage opened his mouth wordlessly.

Thad took this as affirmation and opened the closet door. A body tilted forward from inside and dropped messily on the floor, spraying gouts of pinkish fluid across the hardwood. Another leaned lifelessly behind it, wavered, and collapsed on top. Gage saw the incisions even from this relative distance, wet and messy gashes where the scalps had been pried loose.

The bodies were Thad's. Somehow, impossibly, Thad was standing doll-like with the closet doorknob in his hand, but also lying dead on the floor...twice.

Gage looked into Standing Thad's eyes, now crinkled into slits by that disturbingly Grinch-like smile, and Gage did what he'd been wanting, no, what he'd been positively *aching* to do for minutes: he screamed in terror.

The old man stepped toward him, his eyes alight with strange and palpable empathy. "Screaming doesn't help," he said, speaking barely above a whisper. "Whether you're a young child yowling for candy or you're among the hordes of slaughterhouse cattle swimming in their shit, whether you're one of the uncountable many awaiting the machetes of genocide, or you're chained up in the basement of a killer, it's always the same. Stars will collapse, and new lights will prick through the sky, and screaming *will not* help."

Gage's cry thinned out, then frayed, before finally disintegrating into silence. He fell back against the wall. "What the fucking hell?" he said, his voice weak.

"Hell," the old man repeated. "Yes, hell."

Behind Gage, the door eased open further.

"Earth to Gage," someone said, and he couldn't mistake that voice for anyone else's, no matter how badly he might want.

He rose to his feet in quivering increments. His muscles felt somehow watery. He knew that as soon as he turned around, he would never be able to unsee what he was about to see.

And yet he turned.

Yes, Gage was looking at himself, right down to the wash-faded t-shirt and Levi's, the acne-scarred chin and the stubbly cheeks. And the Gage before him was holding a third Gage, this one limp and pallid-faced, blood drying in a blackish crescent along the ruin of his hairline.

Gage Two made a swift motion that jerked Dead Gage like a hollowed dummy. He plunged his hands into the gaping mouth with surprising aggression, and he pried the jaws apart with a crunch that made Gage's guts broil in disgust. Dead Gage's lower jaw came unhinged, swinging slack and loose from the head's upper half.

Gage Two dropped the body like a bag of laundry. Then he reached behind his back and removed something from the back of his jeans: a thick stack of paper, folded lengthwise. "We're catching up."

Gage scrambled into the corner, his pulse thrumming through his body like the worst drug trip gone rampant.

The old man crouched before him. As he bent toward Gage, his ribcage pressed outward. "Hell," he said again, his voice flat. "Hell is the body."

Gage looked into the old man's red-veined eyes, and he nodded.

From the corner of the room, Thad spoke: "I swear I didn't know it would be like this. You have to believe me, Gage."

Before Gage could open his mouth to speak, the old man slipped up behind him. Ten long and surgically precise fingers plunged into the back of his head, burrowing through the meat beneath his hair and finding their way to the thoughts that made him *him*. Before he got the chance to refuse the operation, the old man was locked into the meat of his consciousness.

In Gage's waning mind, an awful voice whispered, *You're about to compose your masterpiece.*

"Sabbatical" – Author Notes

HERE, AS ELSEWHERE, I was influenced by Thomas Ligotti's fiction and philosophy... while drafting "Sabbatical," I was working through the most unsettling and antihuman revelations in *The Conspiracy Against the Human Race* (2010). I was also reading a lot of cyberpunk fiction at the time, which is way outside of my usual genre wheelhouse... Some of the more conceptual and less plot-specific stuff in William Gibson's *Neuromancer* (1984) probably had some effect on this story, even if I'm not completely sure how. I was intrigued by cyberpunk fiction's capacity for imagining forms of embodiment and disembodiment. Of course, my interest in body horror bleeds into this piece, too (heavy hitters like John Carpenter, Clive Barker, Poppy Z. Brite, and David Cronenberg come to mind). Constant readers might have already picked up on my nod to Stephen King here: Thad is named after the protagonist of King's 1989 doppelgänger novel, *The Dark Half*, and Gage is named after Gage Creed, from *Pet Sematary* (1983). King's influence is obviously omnipresent, but I think those two novels, in particular, left an evident imprint on this yarn   .

SATANIC PANIC

AS JARAD STEPPED through the front door, he heard the words "another dead cat" coming from the living room TV set.

Fuck, he thought.

Last night he'd lain in bed hoping that this would be the last of it. He'd even toyed with the childish possibility that maybe he'd wake up in the morning to discover the killings had never happened, sigh, and say, "Oh man, what a *nightmare*."

His dad was too absorbed in the news report to acknowledge his son's entrance. Papa Charles worked long construction hours, and usually came home dragging his arms like fifty-pound weights. Tonight, he'd probably gone straight to the recliner after dinner. His big body moved with tired and smoky breath, eyes glassy from pilsner or exhaustion or both.

All the better. Jarad tried to sneak past unnoticed.

"Jarad, that you?"

Jarad stopped in the hallway, eyes fixed on his bedroom door. "Yeah."

"Someone killed another kitty," Charles called. Then, after a drunken pause, "I'm having that hot babe from Chili's over on Sunday. You know, the waitress?"

Jarad had grown more than a little tired of these stories. Charles spent his Saturday nights guzzling drink specials at the local Chili's restaurant, and last weekend he came home to report that he'd finally found "the special bitch to replace Mama" in his heart.

Don't engage. "Yeah," Jarad said, tonelessly. "You told me about her."

"Okay, well, don't be around here smoking your drugs and playing your weird rock and roll. Go find a honey of your own."

Jarad didn't entertain this with a response. He crossed the hallway without saying another word, shutting his door behind himself.

What was on his mind was not Charles' newfound object of affection, but rather the snippet he'd just heard from the news report. Every other night he glanced at the horror posters covering his walls with indifferent fondness. Tonight, the *Nightmare on Elm Street* and *Dèmoni* one-sheets gave him a moment of pause. The voice of local news reporter Cindy Dawson echoed in his mind, cutting through his thoughts like a strict teacher interrupting a desk-pillowed nap. "Reporters say the cat's neck was twisted and broken before the animal was *skinned alive* and thrown against a nearby brick wall," Jarad's mental Dawson said.

Exactly like the real Dawson had said last night, before Jarad was called down to the local station. Jarad was lucky he'd been the one to pick up the phone on the kitchen counter.

"Is Jarad Cross available?" a hoarse voice had asked.

"Who's that?" Charles had asked noncommittally, frying something fatty on the stove.

"Friend," Jarad had said, before returning discreetly to the call.

The hoarse voice had identified itself as belonging to a police official, requesting that Jarad come down to the station to answer a "couple quick questions."

"Yeah, sure," Jarad said quietly, before hanging up.

"Who's that?" Charles asked again, raising his voice over the sound of sizzling pig.

"I told you," Jarad said. "A friend."

Then he'd left the house to avoid further questioning, rushing out the door to catch the soonest bus. What other choice did he have?

Officer Shelley's "couple quick questions" actually translated to three hours of aggressive interrogation, Jarad looking inconveniently evil with his long hair, patchy beard, torn denim jacket, and heavy metal patches. For the past weeks, someone had been wandering the streets, brutalizing stray animals and house pets. The God-fearing cops had no doubt in their minds that these repeat killings were the crimes of requisite town weirdo, Jarad Cross. They'd watched the Geraldo Rivera special on the Satanic epidemic currently sweeping their Christian nation; they'd heard the chilling reports of daycare centers run by Lucifer-praising child molesters; they'd seen televised warnings about the bands and album covers that Jarad festooned across his jacket like demonic badges of pride.

"The proof," Officer Shelley had said, "really does seem to be in the pudding."

However, the truth was that Jarad loved animals a lot more than he loved all the judgmental fuckers populating this bum-ass town. Although he zoned out daily to the likes of Morbid Angel, Possessed, Death, Venom, and Slayer, and although he frequently rented gruesomely violent horror videos, he was no Satanist.

He also wasn't much of a reader, but sure, he'd checked out *The Satanic Bible*. Mostly he'd found it boring, frankly preferring to watch Mario Bava or John Carpenter movies than to read all that phony shit about powerful egos and casting spells.

This town's run by paranoid hypocrite bum-ass fuckers.

He pulled a baggie of fresh weed from his jacket pocket and tossed it on the bedside table, then stuck a Camel in his mouth and lit up. The smoke rolled down his throat, calming him. He pulled his newly purchased record from his bag—*Deathcrush*, the first EP by some weird new band called Mayhem—and placed it on the turntable.

Hey, Dad, you thought Kreator was bad? Wait 'til you hear this shit.

He dropped the needle, cranked the volume, and sat on the edge of his bed to complete the task at hand: rolling a fat, soothing blunt.

***

It wasn't that Jarad *wanted* to be scapegoated, but he also didn't much like the idea of sitting in class while meatheads like Frank Rafferty and Bonnie Carpenter whispered "cat killer" and "Richard Ramirez" in his ear.

And so, he did what seemed most appealing on Thursday afternoon: he ditched Ms. Holmgren's bland social studies class to go weed-smoking and video-browsing.

He knew he was in shit when he entered the alley behind Verne's Video, cradling his freshly rented *Friday the 13th 3-D* and *Night of the Demon* tapes. This was serious; the dog sprawled across the gravel was not just taking a nap. No, this poor retriever's jaws were pried open in an impossibly jagged and bloodstained yawn, the coat on its side peeled back to reveal scarlet muscle. Even more horrific was the state of its stomach—slashed open from jaw to scrotum, intestines spilling out in a pink crescent. Buzzing flies hovered over the exposed organs.

Last summer, Jarad had gone camping with this cute metalhead named Jennifer. When he'd returned home, he'd found his dad in a catatonic, boozy stupor, and the smell that had wafted from the kitchen garbage was like a sewage militia: aggressive, foul, like a mountain of slow-cooked shit.

The smell of this brutalized animal was something like that stench, only worse. At least the remnants of dead animals rotting in Charles' kitchen garbage had come from something meant to be eaten. This alley-murdered pup had been savaged for no other reason than to satiate human bloodlust.

Jarad heaved and pressed his wrist against his mouth. *Only, what kind of human could pry open its jaws like that?*

That was the last thought he had before he heard the sirens. He didn't run; instead, he jammed a cigarette between his lips, sparked, and sucked hard on the filter.

When the cops yelled "freeze," he did just that—hands raised over his shaggy head, cig hanging limply from his mouth.

"I didn't do it," he said.

"I said *don't move*," someone growled.

Two cops crunched across the gravel, following their drawn guns to circle around him. They looked like some perfectly paired comic duo—the guy on the left was tall, with a chiseled jaw and a smoothly shaved head, and the other was stout, with a puffy blowfish build.

"Kid smells like marijuana," said the tall one.

The puffy man stepped over the dog's wrecked body with surprising demureness. "Oh, good Christ, Chuck, would you look at this."

The brawny cop called Chuck cast his sunglassed eyes down at the animal's body and sniffed once, like a man sitting at a campfire. "I said the kid smells like he's been smoking marijuana cigarettes, Harv."

"These Satanists use drugs during their ritual sacrifices," replied the puffy cop named Harv.

Chuck turned around and mumbled something into his radio, then rotated to glare at Jarad through his shades. "Is this what you do for kicks? Torture innocent animals?"

"I didn't," Jarad spoke around the Camel.

"Put out your cigarette, kid," Harv said. "You're not even old enough to smoke, I bet."

"Doesn't matter if he's old enough, Harv. Kid's on dope, amphetamines, you name it. Look at his eyes."

Jarad's eyes were wet, no doubt, and they stung a little, but that was just from the weed. He'd tried other shit in his time—glue and pills, mostly—but he couldn't often afford that stuff. Today he was riding only on nicotine and THC, and that was Satan's honest truth.

"Oh, I see 'im, Chuck," Harv said. "He's been getting *all kinds* of thrills today. Haven't you, kid?"

Jarad looked down at the gory mess. This grotesque *thing* had once lived; maybe even as recent as this morning, this dog had run and barked and licked people's hands. The thought twisted Jarad's stomach with even more immediacy than the grisly sight itself.

Chuck again brought his radio to his mouth and parted his lips to speak, when a miserably agonized yowl rang from somewhere nearby. He removed his hand from the radio to double grip his pistol, pointing it at Jarad's chest.

"Have you got other devil worshippers doing the deeds for you, or what?"

"I'm telling you, I didn't do anything."

"Bring him in, Harv."

Harv shuffled forward, unclipping a pair of handcuffs from his belt. He clapped them on Jarad's wrists and snapped them shut.

The cuffs were cold and tight against Jarad's skin, and his videotapes squeezed hard against his armpit. He grimaced mildly as Harv wrestled him into the squad car's backseat, but he didn't resist. He felt baffled rather than outraged, disarmed by the weed, the morbid fumes, and terrible confusion.

Chuck slammed into the driver's seat like an action star, gunning the ignition. Harv plopped into the passenger's seat and they were off, siren wailing.

Even despite the siren-song and the closed windows, another of those ghastly sounds reached them, loud enough to fill the car's interior. It was like the death-cry of a thousand tortured souls, channelled into a single voice.

It was in that moment that Jarad's brain finally tore down the curtain of warm, weedy wooziness. *Someone's getting fucking slaughtered.*

He stared ahead, squinting at the sunlight blazing between the cops' big heads.

The car careened around a corner to merge into the rundown residential area, and Jarad saw something scarier than Freddy Krueger, Michael Myers, Jason Voorhees, and Geraldo Rivera combined.

For a moment he thought that maybe all the dread had driven him insane; that resulting from the ungodly combination of marijuana, twisted horror movies, and wrongful accusations, he'd finally flat-out lost it.

The moment didn't last long, though, because the figure stepping out from behind a trash bin and into the sun-flooded street bore all the weight and texture of something real. It paused between two sycamore trees, and its *actuality* hit Jarad's stoned mind as a hellish epiphany.

Its sinewy body was inhumanly white, paler than the untouched skin of a farmer's tan. The muscles bobbing inside its long limbs were too close to the skin's surface, bulging and glistening like butchered chicken breasts. An erect double-pronged cock rose brazenly from its groin, and between its muscular buttocks swung a spiny tail, tipped with a spade-shaped chunk of bone. Resting atop its vein-corded neck was a large and angular head, with something like a duck's bill in the center. Below its twitching feline ears, it gazed with eyes darker than the space between stars. It stared into the squad car, straight past the police officers, to focus on Jarad.

"What is that in its hand, Harv?"

"That's not an animal."

"Harv, what is that in the thing's *hand?*"

"That's no pet this time."

"They say they need human sacrifices for some of these ceremonies."

"Chuck, where is that little baby's skin? Oh, good God, where's its skin gone?"

Jarad pictured Ms. Holmgren raising judgmental eyebrows at the *Reign in Blood* patch stitched on the back of his vest; he pictured every wild-eyed televangelist and ultra-conservative TV personality that filled his living room with nightly fear; he pictured the station's roomful of cops—their interrogative stares, their mouths spouting unspeakable accusations. He thought of all this, and he screamed with lunatic triumph: "*I told you it wasn't me!*"

This small victory could only give him so much relief, though, because what he saw could never be unseen. The tiny, crimson human baby dropped from the creature's hand and rolled lifelessly onto a manhole cover. Then the creature contorted its blood-soaked hand into the symbol for devil's horns, as if making some tastelessly satiric gesture. With that, it turned around to reveal a pair of veined wings folded across its back.

"Jesus," Chuck said.

"Chuck," Harv said.

The gigantic wings unfolded with an audible *whoosh,* and the beast lifted into the air like a demonic pterodactyl, opening its beak to unleash some terrible approximation of a death metal growl.

It soared low across the street and glided over the squad car, scraping its clawed fingers along the roof. Jarad shouted in fear at the screeching sound, turning in his seat to trace the beast's movement.

It hovered for a moment over Verne's Video, knees bent and ankles touching. It closed the thumbs, middle and third fingers on both of its hands, repeating the famous gesture: *Hail Satan!* Then it lifted higher into the cloudless sky, until finally it flapped itself out of sight.

For what seemed a full minute, the squad car was silent.

When Jarad's heartbeat had slowed to a less frantic pace, he leaned between the two officers and said it once more, for good measure: "I told you it wasn't me."

Neither of the officers spoke for a moment, until Chuck turned to Harv and asked, "Do you think you got a good enough look for a description?"

"Yes," Harv said, in a tone of quiet awe. "Yes, Chuck, I do believe I did."

"Satanic Panic" – Author Notes

THIS STORY STEMS in large part from my fascination with the anti-Satanist Christian propaganda films of the titular era. I'm talking about the *Geraldo Rivera Show*'s floodgate 1988 special, "Exposing Satan's Underground," but also *Cults and Ritual Crime* (1990), *Devil Worship: The Rise of Satanism* (1989), *Exposing the Satanic Web* (1990), *Your Child and the*

Occult: The Games Children Play (1990), and *Law Enforcement Guide to Satanic Cults* (1994), to name a small handful.

Even more than "Mictian Diabolus," this story is very clearly about the ties between heavy metal and horror films; as a fan of both, the mostly normal and innocent protagonist personifies a perceived Satanic threat. I took inspiration from specific moments in the aforementioned propaganda documents; for example, *Exposing the Satanic Web* features a long and paranoiac analysis of the Satanic messages imbedded in Slayer's *Reign in Blood* (1986) album cover. So yes, I listened to some old Slayer records while writing this, and I also played the Possessed album *Seven Churches* (1985) on repeat. There's a lot of straight-up horror here, but I hope that the dark humor also finds its way through.

SPEAKING OF GHOSTS

Originally published in *Vague Visages* (2017)

JEM WASN'T SURE how long he'd been gazing into his scotch glass, but he came back to reality at the sound of Raymond's cough.

According to Jem's educated guess, Raymond was at least twice his age, but tonight the man looked even older. The aged academic's vast torso heaved under a shirt and dinner jacket, his bloated face gleaming red over a bowtie. Occasionally Raymond ran an arthritis-knotted hand through the gray strands floating on his skull; his reach extended just as often toward the dwindling bottle of whiskey, which he'd kept within close proximity for the majority of the evening.

Jem's living room was a space of uncertainty: diamond orbs without visible purpose collected dust on the coffee table, a rare Edvard Munch shared wall space with discount wall art purchased at the nearest shopping mall. Raymond glanced listlessly at one particularly horrid sea turtle print, coughed his bookish cough, and swilled scotch in his cheeks.

Jem broke the silence, finally broaching the topic that had inspired this visit in the first place. By now, they'd consumed enough whiskey; yes, he decided, now was the time.

"What if I told you there's a ghost living in my storage room? What would you say?" he asked.

The truth: he *did* have a ghost living in his storage room. Last Saturday, he'd gone in there to retrieve a jar of pickled beets (stone sober, if you must know), and a hideous apparition had drifted from the dark corner, seized a handful of his hair, and thrown him at the shelf. He'd knocked nearly every jar of perishables onto the laminate floor, his ass splatting in a puddle of vinegar and glass shards.

Later that week, he resolved to consult his past colleague and good friend Dr. Raymond Block about the matter. Raymond was a double PhD (Philosophy and English Literature) with a specialty in 18th-19th century Gothic fiction. Jem figured once he'd poured enough whiskey into the man, the man would talk...and talk...and then talk some more.

Yes, Raymond would get impossibly loquacious. What Jem hoped for, though, was a lowering of Raymond's guard, an opening of his mind.

Jem hadn't re-entered the storage room since his encounter with the poltergeist (for it *was* a poltergeist; his limited Internet research had taught him that much), and he badly wanted to clean the mess of pickle juice, shattered glass, and splintered shelving. Someone was bound to get hurt in there.

Raymond made two smooth blowfishes of his cheeks and harrumphed. "Before I respond to the basis, as it were, of your query," he said, "I might urge you to verify that you did in fact state your storage room as the location, the residence, as such, of this ghost, so to speak."

Jem stared into the man's eyes: watery beads set into a massive, doughy face.

"Who cares about the goddamn room, especially considering the fact that I've just now confessed my belief in life beyond the grave—don't you think you might be focusing on the wrong thing?" Jem said.

Just like Raymond to zone in on the most inane details. To redirect. To reframe.

Raymond looked toward the ceiling and smirked, as if Jem had said the funniest thing he could possibly imagine. "While you might be inclined to pose such a rebuttal, I should like to believe that the room itself does make a difference, especially if we are to acknowledge the fact that I have come to know this house very well over the perpetuating annum, if one can know a house as such, and, ostensibly, I have come to know all of the rooms within it, if one can know a room as such, which, I should think, leads me to develop entirely contrastive, varying, and altogether disparate relationships and associations depending on my position within the house, that is to say that so much depends upon my physical orientation, as it were, which is to say that I might feel something, an aura if you will, an ambience, a certain sense, in one room, let us say the storage room in this case, that I might not be inclined to feel while simply savouring a glass of fifteen-year single malt in your living room, which, at this moment, I am doing, and it is truly lovely scotch, by the way, truly lovely, I have no qualms with this vintage a-tall, and I feel quite confident at this particular juncture, physically, spatially, intuitively, and otherwise, in my assumption that there is no apparition sipping invisible whiskey beside me, to put it rather crudely."

So the room might make some kind of difference, Jem determined. *A fleeting thought expanded into an essay; thank you, Raymond. Typical.*

Jem leaned forward in his chair and set his glass on the table. "What you're suggesting, uh, is that the goddamn viability of supernatural existence depends on a certain sort of, like, geographically organized set of criteria, right?"

"No, I do not believe that that is necessarily what I am intending to say, although I conjecture that you might be gesturing toward my sentiment in a vague sort of way, that is to say, I think that you might be on the right track, as it were."

"Not geographical, then, but, uh, what's the goddamn word, uh, spatial—is that right?"

"I should like to imagine that what I am suggesting is something else entirely and, moreover, that your inquiry requires a certain amount of rephrasing, or, as it were, a certain amount of clarifying, that is to say, I do not believe that you have arrived at the basis of my reflection a-tall."

"Okay, let me ask you if what you're referring to is a certain sense of, uh, absence...or presence, depending on environmental specifics at any given moment—is that what you're referring to?"

On Saturday, Jem had felt neither a vacuous, chilly sense of absence nor a foreboding sense of presence. He'd entered the storage room and been promptly clouted on the head. When he'd stared up from the floor, his butt cheeks soaking in pickle juice, he'd seen the translucent and relentlessly staring face of a woman he'd never known in his life, and in that instant he'd intuited, somehow immediately, that she was a ghost. Maybe it'd been the abyssal look in her staring eyes, or the impossible way she shone, as if a powerful light was housed inside her body.

Raymond cleared his throat. "I think what you are now gesturing toward is an understanding of the ghost, the ghoul, the specter, the spirit, the spook, what have you, as an embodiment of either presence or absence, or perhaps as a paradoxical braiding of both."

Jem thought that maybe he could rope Raymond into a more detailed discussion if he could incorporate some philosophy. Deciding the French post-structuralists were as good a place to start as any, he asked, "What would our old friend Derrida have to say about that? Should we call up ol' Jackie D?"

The nickname was stupid, even juvenile, but the two of them had taken a jokey liking to it over the years.

"I should like to believe that, for the moment, Jacques Derrida's theoretical input would have very little to contribute to any potentially productive results of this conversation and, as such, I think it might be best for us to leave his hyper-stylized musings on the backburner for the moment, as it were, for our friend Mr. Derrida never writes of the body and, consequently, I might argue that he is utterly incapable of conceptualizing what might exist beyond the body, and I should also like to state that I can rather jovially do without his obsession with *différance*, puckish wordplay, and the like."

"Derrida's always already, like, asking the question before the question, don't you think?" Jem pressed.

"What you are suggesting, then, is that there exists a question that precedes your original query, that is to say, that there is an investigation predating the implications of one asking, 'What if I told you that there is a ghost living in my storage room?' which, I might add, is in itself a paradox, that is to say, the ghost as we understand it does not live, as it were, but occupies a space of nonliving life wherein the ghost does not inhabit our preconceptions of life as such."

"Wouldn't you say that the room itself is of little, uh, consequence?"

"I should like to question whether or not it can be argued as such and, moreover, how exactly we might decide to define the term *consequence* within this particular context."

"What if?" Jem said, not quite sure what he meant by it.

"I might be inclined to ask, 'What if what?' and, furthermore, I might be motivated to drain the remainder of this glass of scotch in a single gulp, as such," Raymond said, and did so presently.

"Okay," Jem said. "To rephrase: What if I simply, you know, told you that there's a ghost?"

"I should be inclined to ask what in the preternatural fuck you might be talking about, to put it rather crudely or, in the event that I had not yet consumed what some might consider a copious amount of fifteen-year single malt, I might politely inquire as to what it is, exactly, that you are attempting to address, as it were."

Jem rose from his seat and stood over Raymond with a wavering smile. "What if I told you that I knew for a goddamn fact that there's a ghost in this house? Huh?"

"I might be inclined to ask exactly where in the house you believe this ghost to be, or, perhaps, in the event that you had not originally specified the actual location of the ghost, I suppose I might first address the question on its own terms without considering the spatial specificities of this ghost's nonliving existence."

Jem thought that he might be getting somewhere, finally. "And what would you ask?"

"Well, first and foremost, as it were," Raymond said, "I might be inclined to turn to the original sources of our respective fascinations with phantoms, wraiths, or ghosts, so to speak."

"What?"

"Ah, I have been unclear, my dear friend, so if you will kindly allow me to top up, yes, four or five fingers should be splendid, that is just perfect, perhaps another finger or two, I think this glass is quite capable of containing a good seven fingers, which, in the case of a drink with such complex notes and such a delightful whisper of peat, as it were, would be irrefutably—"

"Ah-hem," Jem said, watching the majority of the bottle's contents make its way into Raymond's glass.

"Ah, yes, I have been deterred from the central focus of our discourse by what some might refer to as a problematically intense preoccupation with scotch, or, more broadly, with any sort of liquid that is aged, blended, distilled or, to put it rather crudely, alcoholised."

"What did you say about, uh, sources?"

"Ah yes," Raymond said. He glug-glug-glugged some whiskey, raising a meaty finger as he did so. "The sources that I refer to can be traced genealogically, perhaps as far back as to the Bible itself which, in our case, is probably most well understood in the King James version; however, what I am actually getting at, as it were, is a certain persuasive influence by practitioners of the Gothic tale, or, to be more specific, writers such as Joseph Sheridan Le Fanu, Matthew Gregory Lewis, Charles Robert Maturin, Ann Radcliffe, and Horace Walpole, to name only a very select few of the most culturally and historically prominent proponents of such a widespread and eventually ubiquitous fictional medium."

Jem tensed. Raymond had avoided the involvement of theoreticians, and here he was reducing the subject to a discussion of literature.

"What do these, uh, writers of fiction have to do with the, uh, assertion that there's a ghost living in my storage room?" he asked.

Raymond, now looking much like a grinning tomato, said, "I should like to believe that the breadth and history of logical and scientific evidence, as it were, as well as what some might call common sense, to put it rather crudely, points us in the direction of rationality which, ultimately, eschews what you apparently presuppose to be a plausible aspect of your waking reality and, as such, I am inclined to gesture to the fictitious influences of your literary research as possible impetuses for such a radically unfathomable suggestion."

The ghost was as real as the very fresh scars adorning Jem's bony ass. The suggestion that he'd imagined the whole thing was nothing short of maddening. "I still don't see how, uh, an overview of these, what's the word, these *canonized* Gothic writers is relevant at this moment, but, you know what, uh, I'll ask you something else instead—what do you think of parapsychology?"

Raymond huffed. "I do not, as it were, think of it a-tall."

"What I'm still wondering, then, is what you meant when you referred to relationships with rooms—what, uh, were you trying to get at there?"

"At this moment I feel it may be appropriate to recognize the fact that I am rather inebriated, as it were, drunk as a spotty skunk, fucked, to put it crudely, loaded, sloshed, soused, and, as such, I cannot at this time seem to recollect the particular instance in our exchange to which you refer."

"You said that you had different relationships with different rooms, uh, comparing the storage room there to this living room, uh, as an example—with that in mind, would you consider continuing our conversation in the storage room? You know, moseying on down there with the fifteen-year and polishing that puppy off?"

"In response to such an utterly befuddling suggestion, I might be inclined to admit that my head is currently spinning in a manner akin to your average carousel, as it were, and that my ass, my backside, my buttocks, my gluteus maximus, to put it rather medically, feels particularly comfortable and well supported in this lovely leather recliner, and consequently, I am openly and decidedly averse to the idea of relocation at this juncture."

As Raymond spoke, Jem thought he saw something stirring in the front hall. A whisper of movement. A glowing. And he knew, just knew, that the ghost had returned.

That the ghost had moved.

"Are you scared to go into that storage room?" Jem said. "You, uh, chicken?"

"I might be inclined to retort to such petulant juvenility with a liberal amount of animosity, that is to say, I might be inclined to advise you to go soak your head, as it were, suck an egg, or, to put it rather crudely, I might employ colloquialisms that suggest self-fornication, wherein the masturbatory action is reduced to a broader euphemism with profane and perhaps even aggressive connotations, inasmuch as the phrasing of the suggestion can effectively be summarized rather crudely as, Go *fuck yourself*."

Jem saw a blue and dimly luminous flickering, saw the shadow of something making its way closer. A smile pulled the corners of his mouth. "You're scared to go in there, aren't you?"

Raymond downed another third of the glass. How many fingers was that? Two? Three?

"The man that I am, that is to say the man who might be described as a scholar, an aesthete, a learned man, an academic, as it were..." the shape drew nearer, and Jem knew very well what it was, what *she* was "...might be inclined to take offense at this rather shrewd and antiquated demonstration of masculinity, machismo, phallogocentric musing, as it were..." and she was so close now that Jem could see her face, and his whiskey-drunk mind took intense pleasure in the fact "...and while the current bottle still remains unfinished, as such, the man that I am might be prone to..." But the shape kept moving, drifting through the couch, drifting *through* Raymond, casting a non-shadow on the hardwood as she moved slowly toward Jem.

"No," Jem said. "No."

Raymond cut his own ramblings short, his mouth a wet and silent hole in his crimson face; yes, he could see her too.

The ghost, the shape of a woman with a face of nightmares, drew back and plunged like an icy arrow into Jem's abdomen. He lurched up, like a pole-vaulter played in motion-lapse, and hurtled backward, crashing through the window and sailing through the backyard, landing with a splintering thump against the recently repainted fence.

Jem was dead.

Raymond poured the remainder of the bottle into his gaping mouth, not bothering to use his glass, and stared blankly into the space where the window had been mere moments ago. A lilting light, like floating bedsheets concealing a flashlight, sailed in his direction, and he made the only decision that a man like him could make:

First, he screamed; then he turned, and without further consideration for the theoretical, metaphysical, or epistemological implications of his experience, he ran.

Ran like hell without a destination in sight.

"Speaking of Ghosts" – Author Notes

PROBABLY MORE THAN any other piece in this collection, "Speaking of Ghosts" was explicitly influenced by a specific text. I had just read David Foster Wallace's *Brief Interviews with Hideous Men* (1999), and I wanted to reinterpret the modus operandi driving some of those stories. I set out to write a comically dialogue-driven, old-fashioned ghost tale, taking notes from Robert Aickman, Edgar Allan Poe, and even Charles Dickens' *A Christmas Carol* (1843). I was also thinking about some of the material in Robert Bloch's *Dragons and Nightmares* (1968).

"Speaking of Ghosts" is a pure exercise in containment, farce, and conversational circularity—Raymond was a lot of fun to write, in large part because of the performative intellectual gymnastics surrounding his generally basic ideas. I hope you laughed while reading it, because I laughed while writing it

LUCIO SCHLUTER

Originally published in *DarkFuse* (2017)

"DR. SCHLUTER'S WORK gives us subjects who are utterly *alive*, don't you think?" Larry asked. Before Maurice could affirm, Larry moved in closer, his wine glass sloshing mere inches from Maurice's newly tailored suit. "The subjects, though, are *in* the work."

These observations were hardly revelatory. Maurice could give Larry a generous pass, since Larry was an English professor, not an Art History scholar, but it was a generous pass indeed: the story of Lucio Schluter's work was renowned enough by this point to be considered public knowledge.

Schluter had impossibly, but successfully, managed to integrate elements of action figurine aesthetics into the rigor of classical nudist sculpture—scoff at this description you might, but Schluter's works were intensely gestural, physical, and yes, okay, Larry, they looked ineffably *real*. It was all in the vascular textures, the strained and somehow motioned musculature, and most undoubtedly in the faces. Maurice had read numerous essays on the eyes of Schluter's works, and some of the analyses were quite good, but none of them came close to translating the uncanniness of encounter. The first time Maurice had seen a Schluter in a museum he'd stared so long into its agonized visage that he'd actually started weeping, not crying softly but shaking with body-wracking sobs, emitting sounds so distressing that he was soon escorted away by security personnel.

To really *look* at one of Schluter's subjects was like seeing a reflection of yourself ten years from now, somehow locked in a stasis of fear and eternal nakedness. When it came down to it, Maurice felt that every one of Lucio's sculptures bespoke a distinct sense of unease, even horror.

That was just part of their beauty.

Larry was still espousing banalities. Maurice sipped more wine.

Even despite Larry's nattering and utter disregard for personal space, Maurice found himself enjoying this post-keynote reception. Maybe it was the six glasses of Cabernet talking. Maybe it was because Maurice had developed such intense admiration for Schluter's work.

Or maybe it was because he had the strangely distinct sense that, tonight, he would finally get to meet Schluter himself. Yes, that was probably what was keeping him in such agreeable spirits. For it was well known that the normally reclusive artist would be wining and dining with the faculty tonight and tonight only, before retreating to wherever it was he hailed from; in the age of the Internet, it was strongly speculated that Schluter hid somewhere in northern Canada, but nobody knew for sure.

Larry completed a sentence that he seemed to find very profound: "...don't you wonder?"

Maurice's eyes were wandering the banquet hall, scanning the hordes of faculty members and graduate students.

Scanning for Lucio Schluter.

"Well, don't you?" Larry spouted. He swayed in front of Maurice like a punching dummy, the corners of his mouth glistening with spit.

"Not really," Maurice said noncommittally. "Excuse me."

He touched Larry's shoulder and advanced through the sea of academics. He held his wine glass outward like a baton for crowd control, mumbling the obligatory string of *excuse me*'s as he proceeded. He was nearing the banquet's exit when, in the corner of his wine-fuzzy vision, he thought he saw the top of that famous bald head, gliding towards him like a shark fin through water.

Oh God, can it be Schluter himself? Maurice paused for a moment to collect himself, looking down at his shoes. *Of course, it must be. How many people are so absolutely tall and so absolutely bald?*

He didn't take the time to question his drunken half-logic. He drained the remainder of his drink, and he looked back up.

No Schluter head in sight; just like that, he'd vanished.

Surely he can't have gone far. Maurice stood on tiptoes, craning his neck.

He saw more than several bald heads, but none high enough to be Schluter's.

Have I lost him? He swore aloud, catching the attention of a nearby woman who looked utterly unassuming and put-together in an emerald gown. She gave him a look that was half disapproval and half confusion.

"Sorry," Maurice said, and lifted his empty glass.

The woman raised an eyebrow and turned away.

Thinking quite reasonably that Schluter might've simply paid a visit to the restroom, Maurice made a move to advance farther.

He squeezed through a trio of chattering men in tweed, catching a noseful of whiskey fumes before he made it to the other side. Emerging from the circle he saw Mathilde, the Art History department's new hire. Mathilde was grinning clownishly at Herman Funcke, the department head, who exploded periodically into fits of laughter that sounded more like the expulsions of a nasty chest cold.

Both Mathilde and Herman were friendly and agreeable people, no doubt, but hardly the sorts of individuals one wanted to get caught up with in the midst of an incomplete mission. They weren't socially handicapped to the same extent as, say...well, Larry, not quite, but with enough liquor in their systems Maurice had no doubt they could chat up a formidable and inescapable storm. After all, Mathilde had stopped him nearly a dozen times in the hall this week alone, stating with increasing urgency that they really *must* meet soon to discuss their Schluter papers-in-progress.

Maurice lowered his head as he pushed forward, searching desperately for a route that would put him out of Mathilde and Herman's eye-lines. He made it only a few steps before a voice hollered from behind. It was Larry, cutting through the clamor of the hall with unthinkable efficiency; he called both Maurice's given name and surname, his tone as clear as it was thunderous, drawing the attention of what felt like every other person in the room.

Including, of course, both Mathilde and Herman. They whipped their heads like actors reacting to some outrageous gag in a silent film, and they mouthed Maurice's name in unison. Without pause they swooped in, all sloppily wine-stained smiles, and Maurice grinned the grin of a man who has submitted to fate.

Goddammit, he thought. *No chance of meeting Schluter now.*

That sculpture from the museum raised its head mournfully in his mind, like a beautiful lost omen.

***

He'd tried his damnedest to shake them off. After five minutes of polite chit-chat, during which he shot frequent glances around the room in search of that notoriously hairless noggin, he confessed to Mathilde and Herman that he really *had* to use the restroom.

Futile. Herman's face was so purpled by now that one could only assume either asphyxiation or irreversible drunkenness; he was belligerently jolly, and so he wrapped a heavy arm around Maurice's throat and cried, "I'll come along!"

Mathilde hollered with delight at this before adding, "Oh what the hell! So will I!"

Every attempt to resume Maurice's hunt was met with similar resistance. The evening was filled with many Cabernet refills and evasive exchanges. By the time late evening became very early morning, he'd given up. When Mathilde and Herman had finally ambled out of the banquet to catch their cabs home, it was with weighted heart that Maurice stepped out after them.

He wandered the campus grounds, shivering quite miserably inside his blazer, craving a cigarette for the first time in what must've been decades. He felt so utterly destitute that, when a muscle-bound undergrad stomped past, taking swigs from a bottle of Bacardi, Maurice stopped him not to enforce the university's anti-drinking policies but to ask him if he might bum a smoke.

"Sure, bro," the young man said, ramming his free hand into his jeans pocket.

Maurice felt his face flushing with embarrassment. Pathetic. Lurking out here accepting a bent-up Pall Mall from this bulky delinquent.

He took the cigarette nonetheless and, when he raised his head to ask the young simpleton for a lighter, he saw it again, like a miracle—that unmistakably high, inimitably shaven skull, moving towards him down the path.

Maurice forgot the rum-swilling buffoon entirely. He stepped around the brute and strode confidently toward the silhouetted head, the unlit Pall Mall still jutting between his lips.

The moonlight shone upon Schluter's chiseled and expressive features; there was no denying it was him. Somehow, despite all odds, Maurice had managed to find him—and just when he'd given up looking.

Schluter moved like some timelessly cinematic enigma, emerging from the shadows with glasses glowing lunar blue.

Maurice stopped a few feet in front of the legend and tried to speak. He struggled to form a sentence and ended up producing a single word: "Doc—doctor—"

Schluter paused before him, sophisticated in forest-green turtleneck and fitted blazer, his face the textbook image of an influential man. His features crumpled into a lovely, avuncular smile, and he extended a hand toward Maurice. "To whom is the pleasure owed?"

"I—I...I'm a great admirer of your work, Doctor Schluter. Many essays. I've written them, I mean. Many essays about Doctor Lucio... I mean, about you, of course," Maurice stammered. Like a tickle, laughter ran suddenly up his throat before bursting involuntarily from his lips in a juvenile titter.

Somewhere down the path, the simian with the Pall Malls yelled a homophobic slur.

"Ha!" Lucio said, not unkindly. "Let's dispense with the 'doctor' business, yes? You look like you might like to light your cigarette."

Maurice realized with sinking embarrassment that, as he spoke, the cheap smoke was wagging, still unignited, in his mouth. "Yes," he said distantly.

"Good!" Lucio said. His enthusiasm was infectious. He spoke as if Maurice had just disclosed a marriage announcement. "Well then. I'm off to my friend Sheila's home. Very sexy woman, Sheila, partnered with an equally sexy man named Sven, a man with whom she shares a *very extraordinarily sexy* and unoccupied estate. In this estate, there is an available supply of whiskey, fine locally roasted coffee, and cheese, if you're into those sorts of indulgences. Since we've only just met, I hate to cut things so short. And I'm afraid I have no lighter on my person, but my car lighter is operational when last I checked."

"I—are you inviting me?"

Lucio threw his head back and expelled a chuckle toward the night sky.

Yes, it was as simple as that: Schluter was inviting Maurice.

***

Before Maurice knew it, he was slouched in a chaise lounge worth half his annual salary, swishing gorgeously amber scotch and casting his eyes around the opulent living room of Sheila and Sven Whoever the Hell.

By the time they had reached Lucio's vintage Lincoln earlier that morning, Maurice had decided the last thing he wanted was to smoke a cheap, stinky cigarette around a man of such high esteem. With a confident smirk, he'd tossed it in the gutter.

Schluter drove with ease and assurance, right hand maneuvering the steering wheel with a delicate touch, left hand providing hyperbolic gestures to accompany his winning anecdotes. Maurice smiled like a lovestruck schoolboy, asking questions in the few moments of pause that fell between Schluter's monologues.

When Schluter had pulled into the four-car driveway of that sharply designed modern estate, Maurice was feeling quite drunk. It wasn't just the wine, either. He was high on excitement, on admiration, and yes, maybe a little bit on infatuation, too.

The scotch was going down oh so smoothly, and it was with great reluctance that Maurice finally excused himself for a moment to use the restroom.

Schluter, looking huge and comfortable in a loveseat across the room, gestured with his hand and said, "Not a-tall. Let me top you up."

It wasn't until Maurice stood that he realized just how deeply inebriated he was. If it was anyone but Lucio Schluter offering, he might've turned down another glass. In this state of mind, though, Maurice wasn't about to do anything that might shorten the night's proceedings or, even worse, offend this ingenious and gracious man.

Maybe it was the alcohol that knocked him out, or maybe it was something Schluter had slipped into it. Whatever it was, Maurice spent his final able-bodied moments staring into the gold-ringed mirror of Sheila and Sven's main floor restroom, his urine splashing noisily in their clean ceramic toilet bowl.

He whistled Stravinsky's "Rite of Spring" as the water coursed from his body.

***

Maurice's awakening was quite unlike any other he'd experienced. His vision was sectioned into two dark-bordered ovals, as if each eye was contained within its own isolated limit of perception. His senses came half-realized and confused: foggy whiteness, antiseptic scents, a dim but ubiquitous pain.

Then, as if transmitted through a bad receiver, Schluter's voice: "...coming to your senses now..."

Maurice felt the powerful urge to speak, but his mouth wouldn't open. Likewise, when his brain ordered his body to move, his limbs, neck, and head remained inert.

Hefty fingers floated through the sea of blankness that yawned before Maurice. The fingers snapped twice in front of each eye, so close that Maurice could've counted the knuckles' golden hairs.

He tried to speak a second time. His mouth ignored him, again, and his brain screamed out with unassailable hysteria: *You've been drugged. No doubt about it—you've been drugged by Lucio Schluter.*

"Yes, this is all very puzzling, I'm sure..." Schluter's voice, floating wraith-like from somewhere to the left. "Oh, I imagine you'd prefer to look at me, wouldn't you?"

I'd prefer to shout at you. I'd prefer to hit you. I'd prefer to do something other than, what? Stand? Sit? Lie down? It dawned on Maurice now that he had no dimensional connection to this voided space—he might be suspended one hundred feet in the air from ceiling hooks, or he might be lying on his back in a hospital bed.

He heard the purring sound of an office chair gliding across the floor. He watched with infuriating paralysis as Schluter rolled before him, glasses gripped in one enormous hand. "Well then, very good. I can see signs of alertness. Let me cut to the chase. I've read all the work that you've produced on the topic of my art, and I could think of no better— or perhaps, no more *ironic* subject than you. I attended this tiny university event of yours with the express purpose of meeting you—I could see, from a distance, that *you* were seeking *me*. Rather charming, to be frank—like a pimply faced boy searching for his sweetheart at the prom." Schluter laughed, eyes cast ceiling-ward. Sweat beaded on the fleshy dome of his head, and he dabbed at it with a sleeve. "Yes, a sweetheart at the prom..."

Cut to the chase? None of this is adding up to much of anything. How about the fact that I can't seem to move, speak, do anything? My lovely genius Schluter, what is this all about...?

"Anyway, I had it all planned out quite meticulously, you see. The scotch you drank was spiked with extraordinarily strong sedatives. It might seem unfair, but so few of my subjects expressly *agree* to the terms—although, you'd be surprised to know that two *have*. Two have actually heard me out, listened to the terms, and *consented*. Given *express permission*." Schluter's eyes glazed. His face melted into a mask of sentimental recollection. Then, just as suddenly, he snapped out of it. He jerked his head, as if awakening from a deep and unplanned nap, and he clapped his meaty palms against his thighs. "Right then. Get to the point, Schluter. You, Maurice Brisseau, *are* a Schluter."

I am...you? Maurice felt the thought hang, suspended, in his mind. *What is this madness?*

"You must be getting awfully frustrated, unable to speak as you are. You'll need to get used to it, I'm afraid. Your lips are quite firmly sewn shut with a synthetic polymer suture—only the best, most surgically approved methods for my subjects... Yes, there's no doubt about that. One might adapt to muteness if one's other faculties remain intact, but this is where my work, if properly understood, would be considered controversial at best, and unethical at worst. You see, Maurice, you've been...adjusted." He blinked heavily, wiped fresh perspiration from his brow, and shook his head. "Your fingers, oddly enough, were the first point of contention. The tips have been trimmed off to fit the encasement. This next bit is generally the most shocking—your phallus and scrotum have been severed, I'm afraid—male genitals don't seem to fit properly into the moulds, and I've found that if I remove the...the loose ends, as it were...that the sculpting becomes that much more streamlined and efficient. Oh, the wounds have been cauterized, of course, and you're loaded up on so many superhuman painkillers that the sensations won't set in for quite a while still."

Maurice's mind screamed obscenity and horror. This reality couldn't be real. This was *not* something that could happen. Someone with such utterly sensitive vision would never, *could* never...

A look passed over Schluter's face, something like remorse. His eyebrows slanted and his mouth creased into a deep frown. "Yes, Maurice, all of my subjects do eventually die." And then, as if tauntingly, a tear scrolled a wet line down his cheek. He scrubbed it away with the same hastiness he kept dabbing off the sweat. "But *define* death for me, will you? I'm posing a hypothetical here, of course. I mean, there are metaphysical concerns...sure, everyone keeps railing on about the death of metaphysics itself, the post-human, the trans-human, the philosophy of fucking science. Well *I* say—Lucio Schluter, most *praised* and enigmatic artist in *the world* says—that my work is a radical metaphysics. A death of love. A process whereby subject literally *becomes* art in a way that has never been seen or even attempted." He stared at Maurice, mad blue eyes gazing from inside that wet and hairless head. "But back to pragmatics. Yes, you will die. And corpses smell, no doubt about that. The cadavers do put up a stink. And so, when enough time has passed, when your body has shut down from lack of water and nutrients and the like, I simply drill through..." He reached beside the office chair, realized that whatever he was looking for was not there, and raised a finger toward Maurice: *wait a minute.* He disappeared from Maurice's sectioned vision, and Maurice's mind continued screaming nonsense and unthinkable horror.

Schluter returned with a buzz drill and squeezed the trigger. It whirred noisily, and his body quaked with a mighty chuckle. "I excise the subjects—slowly, precisely, carefully—and I dispose of the remains." His face wrinkled into a smile that was somehow tragic. "A bathtub of corrosive acid. Of course, dear old Sheila and Sven might have an issue with this procedure if, my dear Maurice, Sheila and Sven existed. This is *my* working space, my mansion, and somehow it remains to this day largely undiscovered. And so, in one of your final waking days, let me give you the very least I can give." He turned around, set the buzz drill on the office chair, and disappeared somewhere into the recesses of this clinical and disturbingly blank space. "Let me give you your reflection!" he called.

The part of Maurice's mind that was a tumult of howling terror said, *No, don't ever show me that, I'd rather die; let me die believing in art that's truly sublime, and not cruel, violent, nihilistic.* Another part of his mind, which spoke in a chilling and paternal whisper, said, *You're going to die anyway, and the truth is already here. You cannot deny it when it's right here.* Then, a needling final thought, somehow even more horrible than all the others: *At least you've given something to your favorite artist.*

Maurice heard the squeaking of wheels and saw, sliding into his ocular prisons, the image of Schluter, towing behind himself a large rectangular mirror, and smiling like a child about to show Mommy his latest drawing.

Maurice waited for the mirror to turn and face him, and the moment he saw himself was the moment that he felt his soul, in one abyssal and hellish moment, wither and corrode. Just as his flesh would, when this was all said and done.

His mind screamed, but his sutured lips twitched noiselessly.

"Lucio Schluter" – Author Notes

"LUCIO SCHLUTER" SEES me mulling over Ligotti's terrifying explorations of mannequins and dolls, but this story is grounded in its own distinct world. I wanted to say something about power, academia, and art. In retrospect, I think I was also commenting on the limitations and dangers of hero worship: Maurice's undying, immovable admiration for Schluter leads to the most catastrophic end. Not only does the object of Maurice's worship let him down, but Schluter actually tortures and kills Maurice in the name of art (of course, Schluter's art would not even exist without mutilation and murder).

Under the pseudonym Rosamond Smith, Joyce Carol Oates wrote *Nemesis* (1990), a disturbing novel about abuse within academia—that book operates on a crushingly realist register, but I think some of its concerns worked its way into "Lucio Schluter," which directly announces itself as horror fiction. I suspect I was also unconsciously inspired by Kathe Koja's masterful *Skin* (1992), a psychological body horror novel set in the world of art.

FUSION

LIZ AWOKE TO the dull sting of something digging into her spine. First she tried to roll away, but there was only so much room. She swore, fumbled out of her sleeping bag, and slithered free. Crouching beneath the low tent ceiling, she found the culprit: a long, python-thick root bulging from the grass. It didn't take her long to spot the very knot that had been grinding into her back while she'd slept off the booze.

"How did we pitch the tent over this thing and not notice?" she asked her good friend and hungover tent-mate, Nicole.

Nicole responded with a half-conscious groan and flipped in her own sleeping bag, away from the commotion.

In sleep as in life. It was difficult enough to get Nicole to engage with her friends while her eyes were open—though Liz's atheist God knew she tried. Maybe she'd tried a little *too* hard last night. But she'd been wasted. They'd *all* been wasted. Yes, she'd said, "Nicole, you'll die alone if you don't learn to lighten the fuck up," and yes, she'd done so in a volume that verged on yelling, but she could always apologize when her friend woke up.

But you know damn well everyone only gets a limited supply of apologies, even from their best friends.

Liz shooed the thought away and gently kicked Nicole's shoulder. "Hey, I know you're mad at me...but we weren't even *drinking* yet when we put up the tent. How could we not *see* this thing?"

"Shut up and let me sleep," Nicole said.

"Bet you'll be insisting we head back home later today," Liz muttered, barely audible. "Give Nicky one night of fun and that's enough for a year..."

"What was that?"

Don't push it. Liz hesitated, then said, "Nothing. Go back to sleep."

Nicole could only seem to handle the smallest doses of social interaction before curling up in the foetal position and begging for release. It wasn't that Liz *minded*—Nicole identified proudly as an "introvert" (whatever the hell that meant)—but Liz thought her friend could really use some positive outside contact. Hell, as far as Liz was concerned, Nicole *needed* the support. Especially after the whole academia thing had fallen through. It wasn't often that one suffered the loss of a close aunt and was also turned down by one's dream PhD program in the same week. Aside from further academic pursuit, what was a biological sciences fanatic supposed to do with her life? For Nicole, knowledge was everything.

Liz got into a hoodie, unzipped the tent, and stepped out barefoot onto the dewy grass. While she'd been blessed with only the mildest of hangovers, her first thought upon emerging into the bright morning sunlight was, *Gimme some coffee.* Her second thought was, *Where the hell does that root lead?* She looked out toward the patch of aspens ringing their campsite and scratched her head. Thought number three emerged at the feel of her greasy hair: *I need a shower.* Scanning the ground, she saw that the weirdly grayish root rose at intervals from the grass, extending a long distance. Its bulbous knots reminded her of Granddad's arthritic knuckles. It was like no root she'd ever seen.

She heard footsteps moving toward her, and looked up to see Joyce approaching, a bottle of Wild Rose IPA in each hand.

Joyce wore the look of a woman entering a party, rather than a woman who had just slept one off. Her hair was neatly bundled on top of her head, her face cracked into an unreasonably buoyant smile.

"Already, Joyce? It's not even... What time *is* it?"

She'd forgotten to charge her phone before leaving, and consequently hadn't known the time since 3:30 this morning. That was when Sarah had proclaimed the ungodly hour and suggested they all finally get some sleep. It was not like they needed to worry about waking anyone up, because this was no public camping site. They'd arrived after driving off the beaten track for some unknown length of time, high on loud music and good conversation. When this seemingly abandoned green space had presented itself, they'd pulled in to set up camp. Because why the hell not?

"It's beer o'clock," Joyce said. "Shut up and drink."

"Well, this is your trip, I guess... Your trip, your rules." Liz took the Wild Rose, which was pleasantly cold against her palm, and she gulped some down. Wiping her lips with her wrist, she nodded at the treeless root and asked, "What's that, do you think?"

"Ummm...no glasses." Joyce shielded her eyes from the sun and squinted, hard. She shook her head. "Nah, can't see a damn thing. Hold up." She trudged back toward her tent, in which Sarah was probably as unwilling to move as Nicole.

Leave it to Joyce to keep spirits high. Maybe her friends were in varying states of despair, but that wouldn't stop her from holding them all to their word: this weekend would be the most fun and least sober camping excursion imaginable.

Liz crouched on her haunches to get a closer look at the root. Once she was near enough, she noticed that it was threaded with bulbous blue cords; they looked sort of like veins. And she also thought, for one brief instant, that she saw one of its knotty lumps expand and retract, like the belly of a breathing animal.

You're still drunk, she thought, swigging another mouthful of IPA.

A moment later, bespectacled Joyce came back and hunched down beside her. "Oh, shit... What the actual fuck?"

Liz laughed uneasily. "I know, right? What is it?"

"Oh man." Joyce leaned back. Her grin suggested she'd just been struck with one of her great-but-not-so-great Joyce thoughts. "Let's wake up Nicole. She studied biology or some shit, right?"

"Nicole is in full sleeping mode. We should probably leave it that way."

"What? Nonsense!"

Joyce got up to wake their sleeping friend, but Liz grabbed her arm.

"Joyce, I got a little bit...mean last night. Don't you remember?"

Joyce scanned her friend's face for a minute, her eyebrows bunched into a knot, then nodded sagely. "Guess you're right. Better let her sleep and talk things over later."

"Yeah, that's what I'm saying."

Joyce slugged back some beer. "Well, how about Sarah? Maybe she'll know what this is."

"I mean, we can always wait until she gets up herself—"

"Sarah!"

Joyce practically jogged back to her tent, yanking open the flap with an urgency that suggested she was about to report a terrorist attack. Liz heard Sarah mumble, "Gimme some goddamn aspirin," and smiled to herself. Tension aside, last night had mostly been fun, and much needed for all of them.

Moments later, Joyce re-emerged, tugging Sarah by the arm behind her. Unlike Joyce, Sarah looked nowhere near ready to crack open another one. She wore her sweater like a turtle shell; her small, mousy-haired head seemed to retract back into the folds.

Give it an hour and she'll be ready to get her drink on again, Liz thought faintly. *She'll remember that she just got laid off last week, and she'll go straight for the beer...*

Then, it happened again—only this time it was too pronounced to be shrugged off: two of the root's bulbs expanded simultaneously, like tree-bark balloons, and then retracted. As the knots sealed back to their normal sizes, they emitted puffs of greenish mist. Liz caught a noseful, and it was rancid—weirdly synthetic, like the scent of scorching rubber.

She coughed, brought a hand to her nostrils and backed away. "Shit!"

Joyce quickened her pace, dragging Sarah along.

"What?" Joyce called. "What happened?"

Liz swayed on her feet, feeling as if her hangover had just intensified tenfold. Her guts swam, sweat popping up along her brow. She opened her mouth, intending to answer her friend, but puke came out instead of words. It happened so fast, she had no time to prepare. The stream was thick, fast, and heavy. She got some on her toes, and some drops even deflected off the grass and splattered her pants.

Joyce jogged over and touched her back. "You okay, Liz? Why don't you go back to your tent and lie down? I'll get you some water."

Liz nodded woozily, grabbing hold of Joyce's shoulder to avoid toppling over. Her vision went shallow, then black, before it danced with wild blue-black speckles.

"Oh, damn," she said. "Joyce, I think I've inhaled something poisonous."

Slowly, incrementally, the speckles dwindled away, and she saw the fuzzy shape of Joyce's face floating mere inches from her own. Not much further back, Sarah leaned in too.

Liz thought she heard the word *doctor.* She thought she heard the words *head back to town.* But just as her vision started to regain its clarity, her hearing went dim. As a young girl, she'd once had an ear infection; it had started with an explosive popping sensation, followed by a sudden trickle of warm fluid. The sensation now was much different—it was almost as if there was a tiny vacuum inside her head, sucking away whatever anatomical features processed sound, bit by bit. Imploding rather than exploding.

She said, "I can't hear anything" (or hoped she did; she could no longer discern her own voice). She saw Joyce's mouth moving, but she couldn't lip-read the words because her friend was turned toward Sarah, who just kept staring at Liz like she was a deathbed patient.

Liz repeated herself—"I can't hear anything"—and then a pair of hands touched her shoulders from behind. Nicole had decided to wake up and join the party after all. Liz's knees went wobbly, and she sunk back down to her haunches. She could smell the barf on her toes, and she fought like hell to hold back another wave of nausea. Nicole crouched down in front of her, and Liz saw it happen, so quickly that it couldn't be stopped.

She yelled, "Nicole, run!" but there was no time.

One of those root-knuckles swelled (*it's not a root, you know damn well this is no root*), and then a vibrant puff of vapour gusted into Nicole's inquisitive, gaping face.

If her ears were still working, Liz thought she'd probably hear gagging and coughing and cursing and maybe even screaming. Instead, she only saw Nicole lurching forward like she was choking on an oversized bite of something thick, her tongue extended and her eyes watery. The knot ballooned again, then spat another cloud. This one was thicker and faster—Liz caught it in her nose again, and also in her mouth.

Fighting back the vomit was no longer a viable option. She smelled Nicole's puke first, and then she let loose. Painful retching; gut-twisting, throat-burning, hot and stinky and violent.

Joyce and Sarah turned to run. Somehow they had escaped this cloud.

That was when things got even weirder. The root (*not a root*) lifted itself up from the ground, spraying muddy clots of grass. Its underside was lined with thousands of twitching appendages. They looked like malformed mouse feet, their stubby toes clutching at the air as if searching for something to hold onto.

Liz fell backward and crab-walked away. Nicole, still hacking and gagging, crawled beside her, while Joyce and Sarah dove into their tent.

Jesus Christ, this is impossible...

The sentient root-thing excised itself fully from the earth, a wormy mud-flecked behemoth covered in sets of dumbly staring eyes. One of those tumorous-looking knots spurted another cloud, and Liz comprehended finally that the knots were swollen and misshaped mouths.

She yelled in horror and disbelief, the sound coming back silent. This hideous creature *could not be.*

Beside her, red-faced Nicole had risen and was now swaying on her feet, hands crossed over her throat in a gesture that said *I'm choking.* Liz had once taken a first aid course before working as a neighborhood babysitter at the age of thirteen, but in the midst of her stricken-deaf terror she didn't feel confident she'd know what to do.

Her mind flashed Sarah's face—even when Liz first met her at the age of fifteen, Sarah had already carried an air of assurance and success. Liz called her friend's name at the top of her lungs.

As she did, the horrific thing writhed toward her, its countless twitchy hand-feet skittering in unison. The mouths opened and closed repeatedly, as if expressing extreme excitement. Gaseous clouds puffed.

Like a fucked up steam engine.

Liz suddenly remembered that Joyce's car was parked nearby. They could carry Nicole inside, lock the doors, and speed off to the nearest hospital.

And how near is near, exactly? The whole point of this trip was to get as far away as possible... How can we expect anyone to find us when we don't even know where we are?

Liz's nasty inner pessimist went silent at the sight of Joyce and Sarah re-emerging from their tent, the former wielding an axe and the latter brandishing a can of bear spray like a handgun. Thank God Joyce had insisted on chopping their own firewood.

Joyce charged toward the shuffling, twitching, putrid-smelling monstrosity, lifting the axe over her head. Once the creature was within striking range, she brought the axe plunging down into one of its swollen mouth-knots. The beast's tail-body stiffened, like a cord pulled taut, and its many unblinking eyes widened. There was a brief delay, and then its punctured mouth exploded into a massive cloud of that noxious gas. Sarah covered her face with a forearm and retreated, but Joyce had no time. She caught the fumes full-on, her body lost for a second in the horrid greenness.

When the wind swept the fumes away, Liz's friend crumpled loosely to the ground, her face a mask of incomprehension.

"No—Joyce!" Liz yelled. "Sarah, get her keys! We need to drive to the hospital!"

This command seemed to drain Liz's body of its little remaining energy. Her deafness was suddenly replaced with a painfully shrill and persistent tone, and her sight blipped out again in a star-speckled haze. In her dizziness, her gaze drifted back to the spot where she'd vomited. And that was when she saw that the puddle of bile was moving. Roiling, stirring.

You're hallucinating. Just focus on getting to the car and—

Lying on her side, Joyce barfed a foamy geyser. There was no mistaking what Liz saw: an insectile shape, like some unholy centipede-maggot hybrid, emerging from the vomit and skittering back toward the hideous root-thing.

Liz traced its movement with her eyes and saw that the huge, sentient root was still moving, despite the axe buried in its flesh. It lurched, and it puffed. Lurch, puff, lurch, puff, lurch.

Sarah crept up behind it, keeping cautious distance.

As she snuck up, the barf-baptized baby skittered toward the beast. The spawn's mindless eyes glinted sunlight, fuzzy antennae twitching atop its head. More hideous offspring emerged from the other women's puddles of barf—what looked like dozens, even hundreds of them.

"Toss me Joyce's keys, Sarah!" Liz yelled, as Sarah stepped nearer to the beast.

When Sarah crouched down to reach into Joyce's pocket, the monster stopped in its tracks. Its vile younglings slithered up its body and onto its tube-shaped back.

Liz saw the rest happen as if in slow motion—Sarah yanked the keys from Joyce's pocket, but as she brought back her arm and flung them through the air, the creature opened its many mouths. A putrid wave of breath-gas clouded her, and she had no time to react.

The keys spun far and straight, landing directly in front of Liz, but Liz couldn't focus on them because she was too busy screaming, "Noooo, Sarah!"

Sarah went rigid, like she'd been spontaneously paralyzed. Her eyes rolled back to expose whites, and she fell forward.

Liz still couldn't hear properly over that whining frequency in her head, but she knew that if she could, she would've heard her unconscious friend's nose breaking against the ground.

One at a time, Liz thought, with panicked clarity. *Drag them into the car one at a time, and then get the ever-loving fuck out of here. Joyce refilled the tank not long ago.* Her eyes flashed crazy and unnatural patterns. *Think you're in any condition to drive?*

Didn't matter. She was the only hope they had.

Without further thought, she zig-zagged toward the vehicle. Somehow, the motion worsened her sight even more. Her sense of distance accordioned crazily, making the car look alternately close and far away. Eventually she made it, smacking face-first into the passenger window, the side mirror jabbing her stomach.

Ignoring the pain, she unlocked the door and swung it open. As she made her way around the vehicle to open the other doors, she kept her hand pressed against the metal. It helped quell the dizziness and nausea, but only a little. She turned to collect her friends, and she was immediately stunned by the spectacle she faced.

Her vision cleared, revealing the root-worm in grotesque detail. It now swarmed with its own puke-bathed offspring.

Liz had heard once that fire ants could collect themselves into cloud-like, synchronized formations in order to accomplish difficult tasks (*Thanks for that, Nicole*), and that was precisely what these alien creatures seemed to be doing. Their difficult task became clear as their countless wings buzzed into motion, flicking drops of vomit in their wake.

They were lifting Mama—or Papa; who knew how this thing's anatomy worked? As the miniscule beasts raised the root-thing into the air, Liz remembered another piece of Nicole-delivered trivia: ants could carry loads up to ten times their own weight. Working in cooperation with one another, these beastly babies also possessed unthinkable strength. Although the flesh of their gas-spouting parent obviously strained from the effort, the creature made its way into the hot summer air.

Liz shook her head and ran for Nicole, who was closest. She ignored the repulsive swarm as it soared off toward the treetops, carrying the giant beast.

Nicole's face was pale and unmoving, but Liz was relieved to find a pulse. She was not an athletic woman on the best of days, and it had been too long since she'd hit the gym, but adrenaline took charge. She tucked her hands under her friend's head and knees, grimaced, and pulled.

"I'm sorry, Nicky," she said. "I'm sorry for saying drunk, mean things last night."

Her back protested as she got to her feet, but she managed to hold onto Nicole as she hobbled over to the car. As soon as she dropped her friend into the passenger seat, her vision went speckly and dim again.

Perfect, she thought. *Right on time.*

And yet she couldn't really complain. Compared to her friends, she seemed to possess some kind of immunity to this thing's poison. Sure, her eyesight was going from bad to worse, and her hearing alternated between total deafness and a head-rattling ring, but at least she was still conscious.

She was halfway toward Sarah when she sensed it.

Something decidedly *not* Liz nuzzled its way into Liz's brain; strong, insistent, and hungry. She'd felt something like this when she'd smoked salvia her first and only time—mental drainage, followed by the feeling that her own self-control was spiraling down, down, down...into some black and unplumbed space.

The not-Liz presence spoke in a voice that seemed somehow to indicate fangs: *Share*, it said. *Combine.*

She cast her eyes back to the car, where Nicole sprawled prostrate. For the first time in her life, she looked at her friend and thought, *I want your arm to be my arm.* Only it wasn't Liz talking; it was Not-Liz, a vile and serpentine voice.

How'd you get in here? she asked her own brain. She had the terrifying sense that there were two figures enclosed within the gray matter filling her skull. One was Liz—scared, panicked, and guilty (*Will I ever get to apologize to Nicole...?*). The other had cruel and unthinkable motives; it stared into her consciousness with lizard eyes and said to itself, *I can use you.*

Liz collapsed into the grass beside Joyce's car, and Not-Liz lifted her arms to tug her body forward. Liz's sense of self faded slowly, until she heard only a litany of fiendish and hungry demands: *Share, combine, share, combine.*

What the fuck did it mean?

She reached Joyce and grabbed her calf.

But Liz's own arm, extended before her eyes, was not the arm that'd been attached to her body for as long as she'd known: instead, it was a shapeless, gooey pink rope of tissue—there was a suctioning, fingerless power at its end. As she clapped the appendage on Joyce's leg, she was stunned by its sticky strength.

That was the last sensation she experienced—a gluey, pulling sensation at the end of her Not-Liz arm, and the image of Joyce's leg-skin going loose and stringy before conjoining with her own flesh. Then the world went silent again, then dark, and she never awoke as Liz again.

***

Not-Liz stared up at the pastel sky with a greater scope of vision than she'd ever experienced. And her sight was not collected into one eye-line; it was divided into three separate pockets of perception. It made sense. Not-Liz's eyes were buried in the same mound of flesh as Not-Joyce's and Not-Sarah's. She registered this knowledge in a single, all-consuming instant.

The three friends had formed their own version of a sentient, fleshy root.

Time passed...who knew how long? Days? Weeks? Months? Not-Liz/Joyce/Sarah experienced time as a dim and vaguely hungry continuum, which alternated blandly between sunlight and moonlight. Their brain (or brains) spoke in humanless and relentless commands: *combine*, *share*, and a newly reappearing request—*create, create, create...*

NotLizJoyceSarah knew exactly what this request meant. When they finally saw a medic's age-lined face hovering over their body, they knew what to do.

They heard another medic or police officer or investigator speaking someplace behind this man, saying, "The woman in the car is comatose," but they cared nothing for such banal exchanges.

They focused only on the medic's nearing face, watching his dumb lips circle around the sentence, "What the hell is this?"

That was when they opened one of their own mouths, spouting a cloud of create-gas into the man's clueless visage.

They heard the other professional calling out, "Jerry!" before running toward his kneeling, heaving body.

Combine, they thought.

Create.

When professional number two reached Jerry, he also left his nostrils and mouth exposed to NotLizJoyceSarah's expulsions.

Just like the humans always did.

NotLizJoyceSarah gazed uncaringly at the morning sun and felt something like excitement.

"Fusion" – Author Notes

WHEN I SET out to write "Fusion," I was hoping to capture the particular, outdoorsy sense of mounting dread that Algernon Blackwood achieves in his novella *The Willows* (1907)...but the story had other intentions. This piece's dread pushed past its threshold, fast, until I realized I was dealing with a gruesome tale of body invasion. Some of the grotesquerie might stem from my unapologetic love for things like Stephen King's visceral, trippy alien novels, *The Tommyknockers* (1987) and *Dreamcatcher* (2001). H. P. Lovecraft's strange, otherworldly lifeforms are a strong point of reference, too, especially *At the Mountains of Madness* (1936). Although "Fusion" bears no clear resemblance to Harlan Ellison's writing, I was reading the collection *I Have No Mouth and I Must Scream* (1967) at the time that I wrote it.

I can clearly remember my writing soundtrack: the album *Posthuman*, by JK Flesh (2012).

REMEMBERING ABSENCE

Originally published in *Straylight Literary Arts Magazine* (2016)

DON'T ASK ME how long it's been since I saw myself die. I can't remember.

I *can* remember the pain, though: explosive, macrocosmic, a galaxy enclosed inside my head. And then there was a montage in my waning mind: looking down through my chubby toddler-fingers at the yellow kitchen linoleum of my parents' first house; a babysitter strolling beside me as I bicycled down Woodbriar Place; the electrifying first kiss shared with Emma Larson, in the patch of pine trees just beyond school grounds; and the moment I looked down into a coffin, at the embalmed, eerily doll-like face of my young cousin Jonah.

Then I was *behind* myself, behind my own body, watching it slump forward on the pavement. My slack face, no longer attached to my watching eyes, made a wet sound as it smacked the sidewalk.

I was no longer alive when I first saw my attacker, when he crouched over my limp body and shakily dropped his hammer in the gutter. His fingers trembled as he yanked my wallet from my pocket (*No bills in there,* I remembered blandly; the thought struck my mind like a dirty, unwanted urge). I saw my own hair glued to coagulating blood on the hammer's claw, glistening cold moonlight.

I looked up, across the street. Nothing had changed. My dead body was there in front of me, and nothing had changed. A light fizzled on the slushy platform of 8th Street station. A tweaked-out man trudged twitchily near Calgary's infamous "Crack Mac's," so named because the store's parking lot was a rumored hot-spot for crack deals.

How is it possible that I'm still thinking, when I can see my own brains sprayed across the ground? Frantic horror took hold, like the world's worst psychoactive high gone wrong: I could move, but I had no body. My unmoving, unbreathing form was, in fact, a hideous wreck before me. I'd just been killed: I was *there*, but I was also *here*.

My killer drew an audible intake of breath and said something that sounded like "Jesus Mary" before sprinting down 9th Street toward 6th Avenue, his ragged sneakers spraying snow.

I decided to pursue. It was instinct, I think, more than anything else. Running without feet, my own vision was like a movie's Steadicam shot. I moved steadily, smoothly, without the bumps and jolts that accompany physical motion. I got closer, and closer, and then closer still...

Until I passed through him. One moment I saw the back of his filthy parka filling my vision, and the next I was staring ahead at the empty street—until the man sped forward, gliding inside and out of my non-body in the space of a second.

I no longer existed.

***

This is the recollection that spins continuously, obsessively through my literally brainless mind. Not brainless as in stupid, but brainless as in a physical absence of cerebral lobes, all the mysteries of consciousness unchained from cortex containment. The loss of the body is a vexed and complex gift—or curse—of death, but the persistence of mind haunts me while I'm haunting you, haunting him, haunting her, haunting them. Haunting, haunting, haunting, and good God, I don't know why this trauma belongs to me.

Enough of the abstraction. Now, let me tell you what it's really like. Let me tell you, for instance, about the moment I was moving through a thicket of trees on the side of an inner-city highway. I assumed this area to be abandoned, and the wood-like scent of shedding leaves consumed me; yes, I can still register smell. I plunged into the thicket until the presence of vehicles was only a faint whooshing in the background. I wanted to close my eyes, but it quickly dawned on me that I could not, in fact, close eyes that were not there. And when I stared in reawakening horror across the thicket, the skeletal branches seemed like fingers pointing in eternal accusation at the space I could only pretend to fill. There was a gasping and a rustling and a half-dead moaning to my left, and I moved there to see a man, he was maybe fifty or maybe thirty, with a syringe full of cloudy brown liquid protruding from the puckered flesh of his arm, staring heavenward as foam filled his mouth and oozed down the rivets of his cracked and infected lips, and I watched first with terror and then with anticipation, with *eagerness* at the thought that maybe he was dying, that with his death came possibility: I could have contact with someone again, I could look to this man in his newfound and somehow tangible non-space and say, *Shhhh, don't worry, I'm here. You're here. We're here together.* But even as I watched the life rattle from his face, more skull than human visage, and even as I saw the rising-falling bubble at his lips go still and then retract into his gaping, unmoving mouth, I felt nothing change within the thicket. I circled the corpse that had moments ago been human, and I tried to will my thoughts into something he might hear: *I'm here. You're here. We're in this place together.*

Nothing changed. I hovered over that frail and lonely and unbreathing body until the sun dipped out of sight, and nothing changed.

And so the abstraction, when it comes down to it, counts for shit.

Sure, occasionally I think that I can *almost* conceptualize my own state of being, that I can maybe put my education's theoretical abstractions into this reality. But every time I think I might have reached a kind of peace, bolstered by the theories of some post-structuralist or mystic thinker, I'm locked with terror. It's static and alive, this terror, and it clenches me, restrains me into pockets of space, until I feel that I'm spiraling down, a slow drip into the molecular basis of the ground beneath me. I can *feel* my absence, soaking up the environment's energy: the cloud of steam from a nearby mouth, full of stress and antacids, or the exhaust of a passing vehicle filling me with poison. And in those moments my non-mind fills with the expectation to jolt awake, to learn that this is in fact the longest nightmare of my life, and that I'll emerge from it grasping at my own sweat-sheened skin, skin that will feel wet and cold and *there*. And then I look down, around, and up, and I'm reminded that I'm nothing...and again I'm spinning down, down, into the earth, into the smallest particles that comprise a fleck of dirt, and I feel the impossible horror coming back strong. The panic of a ghost is less noteworthy than the weight of a feather. My nothingness becomes a vacuum of terror and reawakened knowledge, and I can see that nobody will ever recognize my tortured face again. No one will look into the space that I once filled and say, "Are you doing okay?" or, "What's wrong?" or even, "Fuck off."

You'd think I would've adapted by now, but no—the anticipation of waking into a cozily material existence still plagues me. It damns me.

Now I'm left to wander the freewheeling, negligent oppression of Party Street on Party Night: 17th Avenue, Calgary, Alberta. I hear phrases charged with ideology and media and upbringings both shielded and tortured, I hear privilege or lack thereof, I hear alcohol, three beers deep, going home sober tonight, or the wet obscenity of too much Everclear, waning antidepressants, bodied voices and bodied histories.

Vague summer nightlight blankets the scene to illuminate my vacancy. It gets better in the most abysmal blackness, when physicality is only revealed by close proximity, split by winter plumes of living breath or the warm advancement of blooded summer bodies. Now I can see all those bodies rendered possible by biological universes left invisible for most of life: it's not until the body's machinery falters that we become aware of the machinery at all. I see the bodies and I audit sections of exchange, banal or profound, soppy tobacco-seeking mouths bantering loud and noiseless:

"Ohhhh shiiiiiiiiiit, no way, bro!"

"Do you want to head over to Ranchman's?"

"—and what's spicy to you is very mild to me, that's what I'm trying to tell you."

"Yo, do you have any weed left?"

"...I just wish she would answer, you know..."

"Where did you park? Is it over there or..."

"...shall we go buy some cigarettes?"

Bass poisoning and honeyed ballads wafting ghostlike through phrases untethered, no muscles gliding past patios and cab payments. I can move in, closer than any camera lens, closer than any microscope. Sometimes I playfully tell myself that I can *be* anyone. I'll see a group of men and women huddled outside, smoking cigarettes, hair catching snowflakes, and I'll drift until my vision is filled with someone's *inside*, until their space becomes mine. I can look down and see the interiors of their bodies, organs red and busy and alive, throbbing and pumping, working overtime to fight the cold and filter the liquor. And I'll be the provider of crack, or the provider of cash, and I'll dip into the alley, my eyesight full of churning innards and musculature and bone, and I'll be within the buyer when the first hit sinks in, when that body becomes torturously, gruesomely alive with the drug's warping properties. Sure, call it voyeurism, but it's voyeurism elevated to infinite possibilities: I can watch life itself at work. I can be a man. I can be a woman. I can be a child, or the shuddering homeless sleeping against dumpsters. I can kneel inches away from a bird and it won't flutter away in fright. The world is mine, but I have nothing.

Tonight is one of so many visits to our mutually familiar ground, Jonah, in which I hope for spectral revelation, impossible to envision, the dream of you seeing me seeing the collective them.

The dream of seeing.

Jonah. He's why I'm here, when it comes down to it. Because I just want to know. After it all crashed down like a house without foundation, after my dear cousin Jonah went missing and then turned up, skewered and mangled, and my own skull was cracked open like a coconut, brains spurting like so much wasted milk, I just want to find out where he is and what the hell happened to him.

Also, if I'm to be perfectly honest with myself, I absolutely, constantly yearn for just one more cigarette.

But ghosts, after all, cannot smoke.

***

Jonah was two grades ahead of me, and so we didn't speak on school grounds, an imperative put in place by the budding of social hierarchies. Jonah spent lunch period roaming the field with his two friends, Tom and Steve. I also made friends, or, more accurately, the ideas of friends, kids who exchanged not-so-discreet eyerolls at my all too knowing expense. I always spoke strangely and behaved strangely, strangely meaning that I occupied a social vacancy that nobody wanted to see filled. I would later learn in my mid-twenties that my first-grade teacher once spoke to my mother in private, strongly recommending that I be tested for ADHD. .

Once, when my class was asked to design paper beavers for the Canada Day school assembly, I watched my peers exhibit precise and meticulous use of glue guns and scissors, my palms scaled with drying adhesive, spirals of paper collecting at my feet, and I resigned to the fact that I was incapable of attending to such basic tasks, of summoning or feigning the confidence necessary to put raw materials to use, to shape something presentable and new.

I was always disoriented by the sense of existing in any space, the onslaughts of colour, all the noise and suggestion that was everyday life, and I would often scream until I couldn't breathe, cry until my head thrummed, feeling feral, feeling frantic, like an animal encroached on.

When you've come to the realization that you're probably, almost definitely, living out eternity, you tend to navigate the bitterest of autobiographical places. Just now I remember staying with Aunt Rita and Uncle Herb while Mom and Dad were on vacation, and while their son Jonah left the room to get a drink I plunged a nearby butter knife into the innards of his new GameCube. Why? Because I was jealous. I was destructive. Just as I was destructive when I first screamed, "*I hate you!*" at my flabbergasted mother, and I'm forced now to re-watch her face as it sinks and implodes in utter anguish. This is what it's like to be a ghost. Memories gush, pour, and wash in overwhelming, patternless patterns: like an unpredictable and endless nosebleed. Sometimes it clots, and sometimes it runs until you think the terror will snuff your ghostly self into nothing.

In the absence of body, thoughts acquire qualities seemingly more than real.

But it wasn't all bad; no, of course it wasn't all bad. When that lethal hammer's shadow clatters across my non-mind, I can always return to the glory of unadulterated nostalgia which, even in its immanence, sometimes brushes the lofty impossibilities of transcendence. My childhood was filled with the poetry of shelter, of love, of dizzying and overwhelming encounters with the new.

And so, when I want to hide from thoughts of Jonah's embalmer-recreated face, or the sight of that weapon beside my own unmoving shape; when I'm tempted to abandon my search and occupy what may be considered an approximation of heaven, I remember.

I remember the sound of the furnace as an aural distance from muted blizzards. I often curled like a cat on the heat register, and I spent hours reading old paperbacks by Stephen King and Kathe Koja, the smell of aged pages wafting into my nostrils.

I remember yellow, coughing afternoons, steaming mugs of lemon and honey. I'd pretend I was sick so that I could spend the day indoors, warm and quiet and alone.

I remember forbidden VHS tapes spurring my nights with welcomed nightmares. Mom and Dad returned the favors done by Aunt Rita and Uncle Herb; they'd let Jonah stay over and the two of us would rent videos with the most garish and menacing covers: we saw it all, from *Night of the Living Dead* to *Cannibal Holocaust* to *House of 1000 Corpses*.

I remember walks with Jonah, the awe of dripping green public parks rendered private in the event of too-rare rainstorms. The harder it rained, the more we wanted to step outside and melt time in the forest. We would talk about our families and our futures, and when we got older, we'd sneak the occasional cigarette, too. God, Jonah... I miss you so much.

I remember love in all its ambiguously shifting and mysterious forms. Sexual, familial, friendly and, even now, in the absence of body, love is still alive.

***

On the night I was killed, Jonah had already been dead for nearly three years. I was wasted on overpriced gin, which I drank alone long after my roommates Carissa and Meredith screamed, *"We're fucking leaving!"* into my ear. I pretended the sounds of the club had drowned them out, as I always did, and they pretended to believe I was soon going to hop off the booze train (for once) and follow them. The club was a blue-black ecosystem, undulating and chattering and pulsing all around me, charging my insides with the urge to take another shot. Or maybe that was all the Red Bull mixed drinks talking.

I made it to last call—some absurdly late hour for a Monday, especially when I had a 9 am lecture on Julia Kristeva to attend later that morning. But I was leaning dead-eyed against the bar, quiet and full of money, and so the bartenders didn't give me trouble. They kept the drinks coming, and I kept bleeding my chequing account.

I was sloppy drunk. Piss drunk. Wet-mouthed, red-faced, barely-capable-of-forming-a-sentence drunk. This was the effect I chased whenever I went for that first shot, pint, glass, whatever. If I was still able to register the world with some semblance of order by the end of the night, I simply hadn't had enough.

I passed through the waning crowd of toned bodies and stepped out into the parking lot. Snow crunched under my boots. I made my way to the train, chain-smoking Camels and fighting the urge to piss a river in every semi-discreet location that presented itself.

As I waited on the platform, I paid no mind to the trio of men standing a few meters away from me. Why would I?

It took nearly half an hour to realize that we were the only four people there. The transit-update sign kept flashing *TRAIN TIMES ARE CURRENTLY UNAVAILABLE. PLEASE SEE WEBSITE FOR DETAILS*, and I had to consult my phone for the time.

3:32 am. Yes, I remember that time very well, because it was the last hour and minute I saw in my life. I cursed and exited the platform, and I know now that one of those men followed me.

I drew and sparked my final Camel. The first drag resurfaced as a series of coughs, so violent that I almost tasted some of the night's tequila/beer/Jägermeister threatening to surface in the bottom of my throat.

One too many cigarettes tonight. I tossed it in the gutter and thought hazily, drunkenly, *Better try and get a cab.*

That was the moment, *Better try and get a cab*, when I reached again for my cellphone with a fumbling hand, and *WHAP*, my head, my skull, my *self* was cracked into pieces in the space of time it takes to wipe a stain from a tabletop, to blow your nose, to stomp and kill an ant.

They keep rushing back at me, the moments, instant by instant: a dreadfully recursive loop, paradoxical non-thinking thoughts.

Was it like that for you, Jonah? What was the last minute and hour that you lived? Whose face was the last you saw?

Maybe someday, somehow, in the absence of bodies, we'll meet. Maybe you'll be different from that man in the thicket. Somehow, I believe you will be. I believe that maybe we'll share these stories that no living ears can hear. Maybe I'll be able to replace that final, traumatizing image of your death-painted face with something warm, something affirming. That we'll find something other than this world.

Together.

Maybe, Jonah...maybe.

"Remembering Absence" – Author Notes

"REMEMBERING ABSENCE" CAME from the ambitious but obviously doomed idea of writing an entire long novel from a ghost's point of view (I'm sure it has been done before, but I couldn't seem to wrap my head around creating a protagonist with no agency). As I mention in my notes on "Long Man," the novel was structured as a road narrative, and it involved the protagonist's investigation into circumstances surrounding the death of his cousin, Jonah. To help make this work better as a standalone story, I removed all references to the Long Man and focused primarily on style. I wanted to capture the mournful, hallucinatory perspective of a ghost.

Plain and simple, this story arises from two main ingredients: a period of severe depression and a James Joyce seminar. Turns out I couldn't put down *Ulysses* (1922) without feeling completely intoxicated and attached—I really wanted to try my own hand at the kind of free-wheeling, interior style of narration threading through so many of that novel's amazing sequences. I also wanted to write something personal and cathartic. This is the result.

CRITICISM

INTRODUCTION: FILM TWITTER'S FAVORITE HORROR FILMS (2018 EDITION)

Originally published in *Cinematary* (2018)

IS IT NECESSARY to define the horror genre, or is it a genre whose definition has been built into our general consciousness? I turn often to Stephen King's statement in his 1985 study of horror cinema and fiction, *Danse Macabre*, that "horror simply *is*, exclusive of definition or rationalization." In some ways, King's open sentiment anticipates John Clute's argument in *The Darkening Garden: A Short Lexicon of Horror* (2006), that "since the beginning of the 1980s, it has become common to state not only that certain emotional responses are normally generated in the readers of horror texts, but also to claim that these responses are, in themselves, what actually define horror." To that end, one might argue that *Ernest Goes to School* (1994) could be labelled horror every bit as readily as *Cannibal Holocaust* (1980), given that a viewer experiences the affect denoted by the genre's name.

While King and Clute's statements speak to an artesian commonality imbedded within all horror films, I have come to grow increasingly suspicious of definitions that overstate the importance of the genre's self-announcing affect. Horror is distinct not only because of the subjective responses it incurs, but also because it stems from a history of recurring structures, motifs, images, and philosophical premises. This final category of philosophical inquiry or confrontation might sound counter-intuitive, given the genre's immediate and visceral nature. However, engagement with critical thought is, to me, fundamental to what the horror genre *is* and *does*. Consider Noël Carroll's argument in

The Philosophy of Horror: Or, Paradoxes of the Heart (1990), that the kinds of monstrosities found within the genre "are not only physically threatening," but "cognitively threatening [...] challenges to the foundations of a culture's way of thinking." To me, this is one of horror's most crucial tenets.

From a personal perspective, this does not mean I more highly value horror films that strive for didactic or overtly "cerebral" approaches; contrarily, I would argue that too many titles in our recent wave of "prestige" or so-called "post-horror" genre films crumble under extraordinarily simplistic ideas played for faux-profundity (I'm not naming names). I submit that the genre has at its very foundation always been built on philosophical disruption: at its most effective, horror destabilizes our customary ways of interpreting that which we take for granted in material and social reality. As such, the last thing the genre needs is to be "elevated." Horror should be combative, disturbing, rude, and antagonistic to popular belief. It should be impolite. It should be feared. Naturally, the genre should and will adjust and respond to contemporary concerns and anxieties, often in ways that are unconscious, coded, located below that which is immediately apparent.

To put it plainly, horror should fuck shit up.

MYTHIC CONDUITS FOR INTIMATE PAIN IN EDGAR G. ULMER'S *THE BLACK CAT*

Originally published in *Vague Visages* (2020)

THE TITLE CARD for Edgar G. Ulmer's *The Black Cat* (1934) declares that the film is "suggested by the immortal Edgar Allan Poe classic," an 1843 short story of the same name. While the film bears no immediate resemblance to Poe's story, the two pieces share intriguing thematic engagements: namely, the use of archetypal and mythological symbolism to contend with painfully intimate psychological experiences (addiction and madness in Poe's story, and psychological trauma in Ulmer's film). Poe's piece depicts a tormented, alcoholic protagonist who perceives a repeatedly re-emerging black cat as a manifestation of his awful misfortune. The story deploys unreliable narration to obfuscate connections between the title animal's supernatural influence and the main character's escalating acts of violence; it is tightly contained and populated by a small cast of characters, with almost all its action relegated to the protagonist and his cat, Pluto (named after the ruler of the underworld in Roman mythology).

By contrast, the protagonists of Ulmer's film are hapless newlyweds Peter (David Manners) and Joan (Julie Bishop), whose honeymoon plans are quickly upended by a chance encounter with Hungarian psychiatrist Dr. Vitus Werdegast (Bela Lugosi). After the couple is forced into sharing a train cabin with Werdegast, the trio shares a bus toward their respective destinations, but the vehicle crashes on a rain-slicked road, leaving them stranded. Werdegast then leads the couple to Austrian architect Hjalmar Poelzig (Boris Karloff)'s mansion, built upon the ruins of Fort Marmorus (a battle site that Poelzig commanded catastrophically during World War I). Poelzig's surrender of Marmorus to Russian forces left Werdegast to be taken captive as a prisoner at Kurgaal, separated for fifteen years from his wife and daughter (Karen senior and junior), during which time Werdegast accuses Poelzig of "stealing his wife." Joan is injured in the bus accident, and the couple is marooned at Poelzig's mansion without transport. The film quickly makes it clear that Peter and Joan are not the narrative's focus, but rather plot devices to protract the mounting tension between Werdegast and Poelzig. Given the presence of these innocent bystanders, Werdegast is not at liberty to immediately avenge his lost family and agency; as such, the first half of the film sees Werdegast and Poelzig forced to negotiate their conflicts under an air of false gentility. The film builds eventually toward a grisly showdown that takes place during a Satanic dark of the moon ritual conducted by Poelzig, at which point all false diplomacy dissolves into violence.

Although Poe's story employs its title animal more overtly for plot-related purposes than does Ulmer's film, the two share similarities in that black cats play key metaphoric and thematic roles in both. As mentioned above, Poe's story applies its focal animal as a symbol of addiction and madness, whereas in Ulmer's film, the cat acts as a cipher for Werdegast's psychological trauma. Consider an early scene wherein Poelzig's black cat enters a study and Werdegast cries out in horror, hurling an object across the room to kill the animal. This shocking scene foreshadows the film's brutal resolution, which sees Werdegast flay Poelzig alive (Lugosi performs this episode with a menacing grin, asking Poelzig outright if he has ever seen an animal skinned). These two moments centralize the cat as an embodiment of Werdegast's mental torment, the mythologized manifestation of evil he witnessed in the mechanized murder of World War I.

The film's mythological attributions to the animal connect to Poe's engagement with Roman mythology, emphasized when Werdegast refers to "certain ancient books" that describe the black cat as "the living embodiment of evil." Ulmer bolsters the cat's metaphoric role throughout the film, repeatedly depicting Poelzig wandering his mansion with the animal cradled in his arms. Playing a Satanic priest who houses himself in a Bauhaus mansion constructed on a site of recent atrocity, Karloff serves as an expressly religious symbol of evil. When Werdegast skins Poelzig alive, the film lays bare the two characters' archetypal statuses: the dark avenging angel Werdegast tears apart the physical symbol of his psychological trauma, the devilish Poelzig. In terms of mythic presence, Ulmer also maximizes on the status of his two stars— Dracula (Lugosi) and Frankenstein's monster (Karloff), onscreen together for the first time.

Although this reading might seem to suggest simplistic Manichean dualism, it is worth noting that the film carefully undoes good-evil binaries in nuanced ways. While *The Black Cat* undoubtedly draws on mythic and religious symbolism, specifically via engagements with Satanism, with the titular black cat, and with Poelzig's description of Werdegast as an "avenging angel," the film does not resign itself to baseline moralism. In a monologue scored by the haunting second movement of Beethoven's Symphony no. 7, Poelzig lays bare both characters' pain in the wake of their shared past. "You say your soul was killed and that you have been dead all these years," he presses Werdegast. "And what of me? Did we not both die here in Marmorus fifteen years ago? Are we any less victims of the war than those whose bodies were torn asunder? Are we not both the living dead? And now you come to me, playing at being an avenging angel, childishly thirsty for my blood. We understand each other too well. We know too much of life."

In its visceral dealings with the psychological aftermath of warfare, Ulmer's film bears as many similarities with Louis-Ferdinand Céline's *Journey to the End of the Night* (first published in 1932 and translated to English in 1934) as it does with Poe's story. Like Céline's novel, Ulmer's film observes the horrifying psychological consequences of warfare, using Werdegast as its catalyst. Subverting then-contemporary preconceptions of Lugosi's menacing onscreen presence (exemplified by *Dracula* [1931], *White Zombie* [1932], *Island of Lost Souls* [1932], and *Murders in the Rue Morgue* [1932], among others), *The Black Cat* draws on the actor's background in silent cinema to convey a man debilitated and maddened by psychological wounds. While the charming lead couple eases the audience into the plot, the film concerns itself primarily with Werdegast's voyage back to a site of trauma (Poelzig's manor). En route to this eerie location, the bus driver debriefs Peter and Joan on Fort Marmorus's grisly history: "The ravine down there was piled twelve-deep with dead and wounded," he tells them. "The little river below was swollen: a red, raging torrent of blood." During this monologue, Ulmer cuts to a close-up of Werdegast; possibly drawing on his own real-life experiences with combat in World War I, Lugosi expresses profound pain without speaking.

Poelzig's mansion thus develops an air of menace before the trio arrives. Ulmer employs ingenious set design to visualize this space, which is symbolically haunted by the ghosts of those who died on Fort Marmorus. The cold, angular rooms showcase an aesthetic that is equal parts art deco and Bauhaus, shot with Expressionist flair by cinematographer John J. Mescall. Drawing on World War I's nascent means of mechanized murder, the house's lower depths contain repurposed weapons from the battle that left Werdegast scarred and alone. In line with Gothic conventions, the atmospheric space is itself one of the film's key characters, powerfully representing the grotesquely false edifice of modernity that Poelzig has imposed on events too horrific to be swept aside.

While *The Black Cat* does not share many explicit connections with Edgar Allan Poe's 1843 story, both texts use archetypal symbolism to explore painfully intimate experiences (in Poe's case, addiction and mental disarray, and in Ulmer's case, psychological trauma). The honeymooning couple in Ulmer's film might serve as empathetic guides for the viewer, but at its center is Lugosi's Werdegast, hellbent on releasing his pain by destroying its human cipher, Karloff's Poelzig.

EXPERIMENTING WITH THE HORRIFIC: A REAPPRAISAL AND RETROSPECTIVE OF THE FILMS OF TOBE HOOPER

Originally published in *Bright Lights Film Journal* (2016)

TOBE HOOPER'S FINAL feature film, *Djinn* (2013), struggled to obtain wide release, and the limited reactions it received were largely dismissive. Unfortunately, this is a common response to much of Hooper's work; *The Texas Chain Saw Massacre* (1974) aside, the director's output has been frequently ignored, laughed aside, and scorned. Even his well-regarded *Poltergeist* (1982) has long suffered from untrue charges that its high-profile producer, Steven Spielberg, ghost-directed its majority. This phenomenon is not necessarily specific to Hooper. It is symptomatic of reception to horror auteurs at large, specifically those whose work saw infamy or controversy in the 1970s and '80s. John Carpenter, for example, commonly receives widespread accolades for the majority of his '70s and '80s output (especially *Halloween* [1978] and *The Thing* [1982]), but it is much harder to find praise for his equally interesting later works (such as *In the Mouth of Madness* [1994], *Village of the Damned* [1995], *Vampires* [1998], and *Ghosts of Mars* [2001]). The same might also be said for Dario Argento, George A. Romero, Stuart Gordon, or even Wes Craven (although *Scream* found great success in the '90s, you would be hard-pressed to find in-depth reappraisals of *My Soul to Take* [2010] or *Scream 4* [2011], both excellent films). My interest here, however, is not in the symptom: the auteurs I have mentioned are all responsible for unique filmographies, and to lump them together would be to deny them their singularity. While ageism certainly plays a role, and affects reception of aged filmmakers at large, what interests me in addressing this problem is the broader issue of genre reception. The "old masters" of non-genre cinema are not unanimously reduced to such temporally limited moments of celebration (taking the New Hollywood group as example, one thinks immediately of the accolades given to Steven Spielberg's *Lincoln* [2012] or Martin Scorsese's *The Wolf of Wall Street* [2013]). There is no doubt that context and individual directors present exceptions to this argument, but horror has consistently denied its celebrated auteurs the opportunity to branch out, expand, or diversify in their late careers.

This brings me back to the subject of this article, Tobe Hooper. Returning to *Djinn*, I see that film, like almost all of Hooper's works, as a remarkably stronger work than its reputation suggests. In some senses an old-fashioned domestic ghost story, it shows Hooper in typically precise form: actors' relationships to space, lighting, and cinematic perspective remain consistently compelling throughout. Its high quality is hardly a surprise. *Djinn* is yet another demonstration of Hooper's formal attentiveness, and of his unprecedented ability to rise above standard genre material. What I seek to do here, then, is not to provide a film-by-film rundown of an unheralded filmmaker's career. Instead, I aim to highlight and discuss specific works, with the intention of celebrating a creative voice that has been unfairly disregarded for far too long. What I have found in Hooper's work is not an explicit repetition of methods, but a provocative and developing philosophy that underpins formal mastery. Hooper's interest in horror articulates itself primarily in formal invention: How can the frame be used to incapacitate viewer expectations? How can the particulars of genre broaden our understanding of the moving image at large? His films incorporate points of view into these formal conceits (frequently specific to characters, but sometimes indicative of disturbing authorial intervention). What persists is the urge to make us see differently, to make us feel the familiar in unexpected ways. In this respect, the outlooks in *The Mangler* (1995) and *Mortuary* (2005) are every bit as sophisticated as that of *The Texas Chain Saw Massacre*, if not even more so. This is an auteur who grows, and who makes no apologies. To experience his work is to experience the recklessness of an artist who digs at the very roots of cinematic expression. With these observations in mind, I will look first at Hooper's avant-garde debut, *Eggshells* (1969), before turning my attention to two select films from each decade of his career.

Before landing the meager means to make *Eggshells*, Hooper had cut his teeth on documentaries and commercials, and demonstrated his avant-garde propensities with the playful short film *Heisters* (1964). His debut feature is characterized most notably by an infatuation with the new: the film is predominantly a technical exercise, abstract in its structure and imagery but sure-footed in its form. It wears its avant-garde ideals perhaps more brazenly than any of the director's later works. Through its psychotropic and free-floating gestures, it captures both the activities and spirit of hippie subculture; much of the film's runtime devotes itself to rambling and self-aggrandizing conversation, to the excitement of commune-living in all its sexual and psychedelic freedoms. Rather than presenting itself as an "ethnography" or an outsider's study, the film takes the very shape of its subjects' beliefs and worldviews. More than anything, its dedication to the aesthetics of a particular time and place recalls the 1960s works of Jonas Mekas (consider *Report from Millbrook* [1966], for example); at times, its depictions of psychoactive trips also bring to mind the early Stan Brakhage (specifically, spatially focused films such as *Cat's Cradle* [1959]). When Hooper deceives us through editing and sound design into believing that a man can swordfight with himself, he is celebrating the novelty of image and experience rather than judging the whacked-out hallucinations of drug users. This is a film about love: love for its subjects, love for their lives, and love for the form that can express that love.

"Love" might seem one of the least intuitive words to describe his follow-up, *The Texas Chain Saw Massacre*. While my primary intention with this article is to discuss Hooper's less celebrated works, I cannot help but bring this radical reframing of genre horror into the conversation. *Massacre* is nothing less than one of the game-changing entries of its genre, a film so committed and deeply felt that it alters the way we see horror. Again, Hooper channels his energies toward a very particular form, wherein immediacy and a kind of "realism" are achieved through deliberate styles of performance, photography, and editing. This form heightens the sense of association and empathy with the film's subjects: the victims suffer the brutal consequences of bad luck and naïveté, but so do their victimizers. The film attributes a democratic sense of "wrongness" to everything and everyone, so that horror stems more from a grotesque depiction of plans gone awry than it does from a tangible statement on morality. Case in point: "Leatherface" himself, a character who operates as much as an icon of innocence as he does as an icon of menace. The notion of a predatory killing machine terrorizing an innocent "final girl" is in no way established here, as some might claim. In fact, *Massacre* should not be viewed as a "slasher" by any standard definition. Instead, it is about two groups of people who perceive each other as utterly alien, whose chance collision results in a very stressful and violent scenario for everybody involved. To be sure, there is not a unilateral sense of "wrongdoing": Leatherface and his family are the first to inflict violence, and collectively they certainly convey no sense of conscience. But even so, this is not a film about "good" versus "evil": it is a film about a time and place, specifically the economically depressed, southern U.S. of the 1970s, and the possibility for slaughter lurking constantly beneath that cultural surface. The film's final image is one of the most ambiguous in American cinema: Leatherface dancing with his whirring chainsaw on an empty highway, his hulking body backlit by the beautiful, fiery pastels of a sunrise. *The Texas Chain Saw Massacre* charts a series of gruesome events within compressed space and time. The film scars with its irresolvable tensions.

It might seem intuitive to next discuss Hooper's 1979 TV adaptation of Stephen King's *'Salem's Lot* (1975), a reasonably well-respected picture that showcases many of the auteur's most interesting tendencies. However, I find myself drawn more to the unusual textures and tonalities of *Eaten Alive* (1976), which acts in many ways as a reframing or even a deconstruction of *Massacre*. *Eaten Alive*'s proceedings trap our focus inside a murky, swamp-moated hotel in rural Texas. The establishment is run by a psychopathic shut-in (Neville Brand), who slaughters his clients with a scythe and feeds their bodies to an alligator. Unlike *Massacre*, *Eaten Alive* subverts any standard notion of cinematic "realism," opting instead for an oneiric tone that calls active attention to its own artificiality. Reports suggest that actor Brand spent much of the shoot drunk and delirious, and the film itself incorporates his performance's energy: the atmosphere is oppressively affected by red gel lighting, incessant fog, and a droning score that melts into the sound design. The film feels wasted, washed-up, and angry, belligerent in its unwillingness to provide what audiences might expect. Like *Massacre*, it positions itself in a state of pure ambivalence: there are no empathetic protagonists to speak of, and the outbursts of violence quickly lose traction in the film's soupy, hyper-stylized fever dream. It is an easy film to describe in terms of plot, but nearly impossible to describe in terms of affect.

Moving on to the 1980s, it becomes even more difficult to limit myself to two titles. Of course, one might expect a discussion of the previously mentioned *Poltergeist*; it is likely, too, that many might choose to focus on *The Funhouse* (1981), a carnival-set reinterpretation of *Massacre* that also satisfies the genre-codified demands of the "slasher." These are both excellent films, and worthy of discussion, but I lend my focus here instead to *Lifeforce* (1985) and *The Texas Chainsaw Massacre 2* (1986), two of Hooper's most audacious and bizarre works. It is also worth noting that *Lifeforce* might be the director's most romantic film, rooted as it is in the passion and eroticism of vampire narratives established most famously by Joseph Sheridan Le Fanu's 1872 novella *Carmilla* and Bram Stoker's 1897 novel *Dracula*. Vaulting haplessly between various narrative structures and genre expectations, *Lifeforce* contains at its core Colonel Tom Carlsen (Steve Railsback)'s deep longing for an inhumanly beautiful space vampire (Mathilda May). This vampire spends most of the film wandering nude through London spaces, disempowering men with her physical beauty and pinning the film's sensibility in a palpable, unflinching (hetero)sexuality. Everything in *Lifeforce* oscillates between extremes of bloodlust and erotic lust, with physical connections between the vampire and her various prey beginning with arousal and ending with the men's gruesomely shriveled, lifeless bodies. The film's tactile and intimate sensuality is offset by its grandly theatrical gestures: its widescreen compositions recall the great Richard Fleischer, who also infused genre material with poetic grandiosity (consider, for example, *Soylent Green* [1973] and *Red Sonja* [1985]).

The Texas Chainsaw Massacre 2 (1986) eases nicely into conversation with *Lifeforce* (and all the other preceding titles) in that it resists audience expectations and designs itself primarily around powerfully radical form. When we look forward a few decades at the horror madhouses of director Rob Zombie (especially *House of 1000 Corpses* [2003] and *The Devil's Rejects* [2005]), it is crucial to acknowledge their antecedent in *Massacre 2*. The *Massacre* sequel locates meaning in direct opposition to its predecessor: surface grimness is replaced here with unapologetic gallows humour, "realism" is replaced with carnivalesque celebration of cinematic sets and expressions, and even the first film's final shot is reversed in deliberate and meaningful ways. The film's philosophy can best be expressed through the final siege on the Sawyers' subterranean dwelling, conducted with gusto by Lieutenant "Lefty" Enright (Dennis Hopper). The scene sees Hopper channeling his most anarchic performance energy, chain-sawing the foundations of the otherworldly Sawyer home while chanting, "Bring it all down!" Hooper loudly calls the first film's fictional armature to attention, stripping it back and reconfiguring it into a totally new shape. Potential for vegan and anti-capitalist critique remains: an early scene sees the Sawyer family winning one of many local chili contests, their secret being that they feed the ground-up flesh of their victims to the judges. Hooper's sequel celebrates a larger budget and bigger production possibilities than its predecessor, and the director makes us aware that he has repackaged his fiction in discomforting ways. It is impossible to ignore the connections between carnage and commerce, but in what ways might that unspoken connection be subverted? The final shot sees Vanita "Stretch" Brock (Caroline Williams) spinning atop a precipice with a chainsaw wielded over her head, screaming in a combination of victory and horror. The predecessor's ambivalence remains, but the subject has necessarily shifted.

This brings me to the 1990s, possibly the director's least commonly celebrated creative period. To begin, I turn my attention to *Spontaneous Combustion* (1990). In terms of reputation, it is worth recognizing that the great Japanese filmmaker Kiyoshi Kurosawa recently compiled a list of his favorite films for *LaCinetek*, and that he included *Spontaneous Combustion* among his chosen titles. The choice makes sense: like Kurosawa's *Cure* (1997), *Pulse* (2001), and *Retribution* (2006), *Spontaneous Combustion* stages its horror within the structures of human drama, while also lending sustained attention to the affective possibilities of spaces. Also, like many of Kurosawa's works, *Spontaneous Combustion* concerns itself with the dreadful re-emergence of the past, focusing especially on the individual and internal. Protagonist Sam (played with great exuberance by Brad Dourif) discovers that his parents were transformed by experiments involving atomic weapons, and he sees his life traumatically shaped by this discovery. In confronting his own pyrokinetic abilities, Sam finds terror rather than emancipation. The film stages a consistent visualization of Sam's psychology through space; for example, after Sam suffers an explosive episode set off by his own anger, Hooper frames him against a multitude of his own reflections. His reaction multiplied by bathroom mirrors, Sam's sweating face refracts from various angles while his girlfriend Lisa (Cynthia Bain) stares in shock and fear. The film's interest in drama does not stifle Hooper's aptitude for cinematic excess, though: Dourif's broad and hectic performance is complemented by the sets' unusual palettes, layouts, and lighting schemes. The potential for "standard" genre fare buckles under the director's avant-garde impulses, resulting again in a film that feels extraordinarily instinctive and singular.

Taking into consideration this concept of avant-garde aesthetic sensibilities, *The Mangler* presents a new peak in Hooper's oeuvre. Adapted from Stephen King's short story of the same title, *The Mangler* heightens *Spontaneous Combustion*'s complicated content-form interplay and ultimately stands out as Hooper's most outlandish work. This is the moment when the director's interpretation of genre goes full circle, bringing its author to the same openly experimental space that launched his career in *Eggshells*. *The Mangler* showcases a more mature, sophisticated, and focused artist, though, wearing crazed aspirations in every scene like a badge of honor. However, the film does not simply revel in formal excess; rather, it finds the potential for serious and damning social allegory in its source text. Most of the horror stems from horrifically gory factory accidents, and its sympathies are clear: the narrative sees oppressed factory laborers (mostly women) forced to work in brutal, unsafe conditions. These women live under the constant threat of "the machine," represented not only by the titular "mangler" (a possessed folding machine that gnaws body parts and disposes of human life with all-too-frequent abandon), but also by the factory manager (played with sickening conviction by Robert Englund as a machine-human hybrid). In its visceral interpretation of King's mechanophobia, the film opts for dreamlike visual strokes: the sets are vast, their sharply angular shapes emphasized through camera placement and brazen lighting schemes. It's a nightmare bathed in primary colours, smoky haze, and uniformly bizarre performances. Through incorporating the angry energy of a young Stephen King, Hooper finds in *The Mangler* an opportunity to sharpen the mania of *Spontaneous Combustion*. The result is one of the unsung masterpieces of horror cinema, every bit as striking and fully formed as *The Texas Chain Saw Massacre*.

After *The Mangler*'s mad experimentation, it would seem that Hooper's form could not possibly reach greater heights. In looking at his 2000s work, it is interesting to see the filmmaker in a self-aware "old master" stage, dialing back his aesthetic excess while still pushing further his cinematic philosophies. While *Toolbox Murders* (2004) is a remake of Dennis Donnelly's 1978 film, the result is undoubtedly a piece of Hooper's very personal career-long visions and concerns. Staging its horror within the confines of an apartment complex, the film moves spatially downward to the building's depths, finding in its killer a deformed and depraved outcast who has hidden beneath the feet of his victimized tenants. Like the monstrous killer in *The Funhouse* and the Sawyer family in *Massacre 2*, this predator is rendered horrific by virtue of his nearly inhuman appearance and animal-like aversion to light and personal interaction. By staging another iteration of this familiar narrative within the context of an existing filmic plot, Hooper again draws our attention to the fictional surface (and production environment) of his work. *Toolbox Murders* incorporates gloomy, textural details into its proceedings, characterizing protagonist Nell Barrows (Angela Bettis)'s day-to-day life with a sensory unease that builds toward its brutal climax. The film necessarily locks itself within these particulars: the sense of the space, the mounting dread that can be contained within a set of walls, the possibility of horror that exists in domestic settings. It is a technical exercise in reinterpretation, one that waives the possibility of repetition in favor of reinvention. It is a new masterpiece, unmistakably Hooper but fresh in its feelings and formal intuitions.

Last, I move on to the woefully underappreciated *Mortuary*, possibly Hooper's most punishingly grimy horror film since the first *Massacre*. The yellow-brown tones of *Toolbox Murders* darken into the sickly, sludgy browns of this film's central home. Appropriate, considering that the domestic and the morbid blend inextricably together: the plot sees mother Leslie (Denise Crosby) and son Jonathan (Dan Byrd) moving residence into the title mortuary. Hooper stages meal preparation and embalming in unnervingly close proximity, lighting the house with a queasy pallor and imbuing the sense of death into nearly every scene. This being a Hooper film, the horror runs deeper than expected: even this grotesque, sickly brown space has secrets, previously unplumbed and grim. Bobby Fowler, a physically deformed outcast, lurks in the hellish tunnels beneath the home. The difference between this film and the similarly plotted earlier Hooper output is that, here, there is never any sense of reprieve or distance from the genre's fate of death and decay: the film itself is made of this stuff, mucky and wet and full of mortal reminders. It might be the filmmaker's very darkest, even if it resolves with fiendishly simple plot contrivance and a bout of computer-generated artifice. *Mortuary* is to *Toolbox Murders* what *The Mangler* is to *Spontaneous Combustion*: an even more radical expansion of ideas and aesthetic fixations.

What I have sought to do here is identify thematic and formal through-lines in Tobe Hooper's oeuvre by placing emphasis on specific works. All the titles mentioned here warrant sustained and focused analysis, but I aim to celebrate an entire filmography, and the contributions of an auteur at large. Tobe Hooper is nothing less than one of the horror genre's most radical contributors. His films tell us that horror and experimentation need not be separated; an artist can change, and an artist can revisit without repeating. Thanks to Hooper, the genre is now much broader and more open to future possibilities.

TOBE HOOPER'S *THE TEXAS CHAIN SAW MASSACRE* OFFERS A CLOSE-UP LOOK AT COSMIC PESSIMISM

Originally published in *Vague Visages* (2020)

TOBE HOOPER'S *The Texas Chain Saw Massacre* (1974) is entrenched in mid-seventies American iconography and milieus: haunted by post-Vietnam War disillusionment and fatigue, it quivers with the trauma of a nation staring at its reflection and seeing the likes of Ed Gein and Charles Manson. These national anxieties bristle on the peripheries of a simple plot, which sees siblings Franklin and Sally Hardesty traveling with three friends to visit their grandfather's grave in Texas. When the group takes an ill-advised detour, they soon become prey to the cannibalistic, sadistic Sawyer family, and the film descends into a relentless, hopeless fight for survival.

Within its tight, historically specific construction, which is visceral and close-up in terms of narrative, aesthetics, and sensibility, *Chain Saw* gestures to ideas that transcend sociopolitical specifics. Indeed, this film, which at its basest level portrays two very different groups of people brutally colliding over the course of one very bad night, functions as an expression of cosmic pessimism. By orienting its characters within an indifferent world governed by contingency and disorder, the film highlights its deeply anti-anthropocentric ideas—most notably and most bluntly, that *we are not special*—and these ideas are further exemplified by its graphic, disturbing allusions to the atrocities of the meat industry. It fixes an unblinking stare on the violence that humans inflict on both human and nonhuman animals, reminding us of our fallibility and inconsequentiality. Unthinkable things happen to us without reason or consequence, our capitalist social structures cultivate our resentments toward one another, and we inhabit a society designed to swallow us whole.

This bleak philosophy emphasizes the absurd cruelty in privileging human well-being over the rights of nonhuman animals. The film is unforgiving in its deployment of images to illustrate this point: taxidermy hybrids of human and nonhuman animals, piles of bones from indeterminate origins, methods of slaughter normally reserved for enslaved cattle now inflicted on our hapless protagonists. Hooper deftly applies visual language to convey the Sawyers' cannibalistic practices and indifference to humanist ideals; art director Robert Burns brilliantly designs the family's house with grotesque detail, turning it into a madhouse of grisly signifiers. Rather than offering narrative exposition to detail this clan's practices, Hooper allows their environment and actions to convey the necessary information. Within this space, the protagonists quickly devolve into engines of survival instinct. Dialogue and reason disintegrate in the film's final act, which is scored prominently by screams, cackles, and the ceaseless buzz of Leatherface's chainsaw. This devolution serves the film's overarching thesis of cosmic pessimism: despite its implicitly vegan and animal abolitionist politics, *Texas Chain Saw* ultimately finds a void in its search for morality and reason.

The underlying thread of cosmic pessimism is further visualized by the film's powerful use of rack focus, which repeatedly sees human characters pictorially dissolve into the sun, the moon, and on one occasion, a swarm of insects. This visual upending of scale works to diminish the human characters as puppets within an indifferent universe, subservient to a star's subsistence. This imagistic design gestures to the terrifying concerns with physics and universal disorder found within the fiction and philosophy of H. P. Lovecraft (cosmic pessimism's great, hopelessly paranoid godfather). While it would be a stretch to compare *Texas Chain Saw*'s plot to Lovecraft's trademark, sci-fi inflected horror narratives, the terror of an indifferent cosmos figures large in both. Under its brutal dissembling of anthropocentrism and customary moral divides, *The Texas Chain Saw Massacre* points to the terror of a harsh and uncaring universe.

M. NIGHT SHYAMALAN'S TERROR TRILOGY: *SIGNS, THE VILLAGE,* AND *THE HAPPENING*

Originally published in *Bright Lights Film Journal* (2016)

M. NIGHT SHYAMALAN'S oeuvre organizes conveniently into thematic groupings: first, the optimistic religious questioning of *Praying with Anger* (1992) and *Wide Awake* (1998); then the dark, interior revelations of *The Sixth Sense* (1999) and *Unbreakable* (2000); and most recently, the big-budget experimentation of *The Last Airbender* (2010) and *After Earth* (2013). Of interest here is the fact that in 2008, the filmmaker rounded out a thematic trilogy with the release of *The Happening*. That cycle, starting with *Signs* (2002) and *The Village* (2004), is comprised of three genre-codified studies of post-9/11 paranoia and trauma in distinctly American milieus; in fact, to make the link even more apparent, all three films station the bulk of their narratives within rural Pennsylvanian settings. Furthermore, each film finds an emotional center of gravity within distinctly familial interactions, and another point of connection presents itself in the fact that cinematographer Tak Fujimoto lensed the trilogy's bookends. To my knowledge, the clear connection between these films has not yet been explicitly identified or studied at length. While not as distinctly pessimistic as, say, John Carpenter's Apocalypse Trilogy (comprised of *The Thing* [1982], *Prince of Darkness* [1987], and *In the Mouth of Madness* [1994]), Shyamalan's three films portray an imbalanced and endangered world; they engage to varying degrees with the imagery and anxiety surrounding terrorist attacks in the wake of September 11, 2001, while also sharing formal conceits and signatures. By putting the three films into conversation with each other, I have identified a unified schematic logic. What I have found is a decidedly downward trajectory; each successive film presents a worldview less reassuring than the one preceding it.

The similarities between *Signs* and *The Village* are most readily apparent, while *The Happening* is less obviously connected, and acts as the trilogy's counterpoint. To begin, it is worth noting that the first two films openly evoke the compositional classicism and formal rigor of Shyamalan's oft-cited idols Steven Spielberg and Alfred Hitchcock. *Signs*, for example, employs long takes, static camerawork, and meticulous sound design to emphasize the stillness of its rural Pennsylvania setting and to further underline its moments of shock. This aesthetic style inverts the schema at work in Spielberg's *Close Encounters of the Third Kind* (1977) or *E. T. The Extra-Terrestrial* (1982), wherein alien visitors provide the protagonists with reprieve from the banality of daily suburban life. Also, in true Hitchcockian fashion, *Signs* pits the viewer's awareness of threat against the obliviousness of its characters; case in point, the scene in which Morgan Hess (Rory Culkin) faces the camera, unaware of an alien's arm slipping into frame behind his neck. *Psycho* (1960) serves as perhaps the most infamous example of this technique, when we see the shadow of a murderous Norman Bates through the shower curtain before Marion Crane (Janet Leigh) has the chance to defend herself. *The Village* also employs this strategy, most blatantly when its visually impaired protagonist Ivy Elizabeth Walker (Bryce Dallas Howard) stumbles her way through the eerie forest ringing her community. For much of this sequence the camera maintains obstructively close proximity to Ivy, forcing the viewer to empathize with her disability. However, when the frame opens itself up, we see one of the creepily enigmatic creatures waiting among the trees. Shyamalan employs this technique to maximize on visceral scenes of suspense, but it also bolsters the films' thematic concerns. Both films present characters stunted by fear and trauma, their viewpoints marred by deep-set anxiety; in *Signs*, the Hess family mourns the unexpected death of protagonist Graham's wife, which destabilized their foundation of faith. Additionally, the film's first two acts depict their encounters with aliens in shocking, disorienting images of fragmentation: a leg slipping back into the shadowy crops, a hand creeping unexpectedly from underneath a doorway. Shyamalan fosters viewer sympathy toward his characters as their insular lives appear to be cracking at the seams. Likewise, *The*

Village depicts a community that has willingly blinded itself to the external world, emphasized powerfully by the affective Hitchcockian rhythms.

The formal similarities between *Signs* and *The Village* are manifold, not least in their visual composure and restraint. When considering their aesthetic styles in conjunction with their religiosity, it's difficult to ignore their shared allegiances to the films of Carl Th. Dreyer. Specifically, the familial trauma and faith-related struggles of *Signs* recall *Ordet* (1952), while *The Village*'s paranoia-induced isolation indirectly invokes the 17th-century witch hunt at the center of *Day of Wrath* (1947). Indeed, *Signs* culminates explicitly in religious symbolism, in that the monstrous threats are warded off by the baptismal weapon of water. Fitting, then, that the film's final scene reveals protagonist Graham Hess (Mel Gibson) reclaiming his religious identity as a Christian reverend. *The Village* culminates similarly in a scene of absolute revelation; Ivy breaks free of her community's surveillance and faces a world-shattering truth when she confronts the gatekeeper of her manufactured reality (played quite fittingly by the author of the film himself). Taking these endings into consideration, it is worth noting that while Shyamalan is infamous (and sometimes mocked) for his twist endings, these films use the plot technique as a form of catharsis for both character and viewer. When both knowledge and "awakening" (to employ a religiously laden word) are withheld for a sustained period, especially within the context of genre horror, anxiety peaks and eventually climaxes. Shyamalan punctuates these crescendos with moments of absolute realization: in *Signs*, the realization is that the very act of believing can still change the world, and in *The Village*, it is that the truth (no matter how damning or shocking) can be uncovered, even in the face of complex governmental control.

The Happening presents an intriguing divergence in its religious undercurrents, in that its lead character Elliott Moore (Mark Wahlberg) invests his faith in science; in fact, the film itself incorporates "objective" knowledge-systems into its emotional gradient. Case in point: a scene that depicts Elliott's best friend Julian (John Leguizamo) challenging a horrified young woman with a math puzzle to distract her from the image of recent suicides hanging from the trees around their car. In more direct relation to *The Happening*'s thematic predecessors, Elliott's trajectory serves in some ways as an inverse to Graham's or Ivy's. While those two characters obtain newfound belief in the aftermath of their experiences, Elliott's contained scientific worldview gradually crumbles in the face of horrific disaster. Thus, *The Happening*'s primary character arc offers one of many counterpoints to the previous entries; to begin, *The Happening* differs from its predecessors in visual terms. While *Signs* and *The Village* function as eerily placid, almost contemplative thrillers, *The Happening* operates largely through motion (particularly in terms of plot). This difference is nowhere more apparent than in each of the films' opening shots: both *Signs* and *The Village* situate viewer perspective immediately, with the former's shot framing the Hesses' yard through a window, and the latter viewing a funeral over a crowd of villagers' heads. In both cases, our eye-line is dictated and contained by the camera's location. By contrast, *The Happening*'s opening shot brings us uneasily close to the ground, following a dog as it trots beside its owner's legs. Where are we? Why is this dog's face the first we see? *The Happening*'s "uneasiness" arises also from performance style. Shyamalan's direction here incites performances that recall B-movie overreaction, both comical and uncanny in their weirdness. These stylistic shifts register in line with the film's thematic concerns: unlike the evil figures in *Signs* and *The Village*, the threat in *The Happening* cannot be demarcated—it is transient, practically invisible, and almost certainly indifferent to human morality. The danger cannot be indicated as something coming from "over there," but instead manifests itself as the very air we breathe, the trees that surround us, the grass beneath our feet.

While *The Happening* undoubtedly addresses environmentalist anxieties of an exploited world striking back, it also welcomes several other interpretive approaches. Specifically, it addresses the trilogy's preceding entries' recurrent engagements with the issue of terrorism, a tricky subtextual zeitgeist. In *Signs*, Shyamalan echoes the fear of then-contemporary American families by focusing on the Hesses' collective obsession with the television set, which acts as their information (and affect) delivery system. In 2002, American moviegoing audiences could all too easily remember the sense of watching the 9/11 terrorist attacks play out repeatedly on their own TV sets, a documentation of horror both incomprehensible and undeniably real. *Signs* employs genre to engage with this particular cultural moment, in the sense that "aliens" are literally that which is other, unknown, elsewhere; in the context of horror cinema, this translates often to that which is terrifying. Not to mention, the film makes explicit the sense of "the real" as played out on television—in the first hazy reveal of an alien invader, a newscaster's voice informs viewers that "what [they] are about to see is real." In connection, *The Village* portrays a community so wracked with collective trauma that it systematically generates fear to keep its inhabitants contained. This power-sanctioned process involves an almost absurd network of performativity, in which the village's occupants construct a reawakened 19th-century past to do away with the dreadful present.

The Happening also portrays characters who learn of terrible forces through limited and omnipresent sources: the first half of the film is riddled with confused news reports transmitted by television and radio, half-understood murmurings of "terrorism" with no locus or origin. So too does it relate to *The Village* in its engagements with the past: not only does *The Happening* resurrect the sensibilities of '50s and '60s genre movies like Don Siegel's *Invasion of the Body Snatchers* (1956), Hitchcock's *The Birds* (1963), and George A. Romero's *Night of the Living Dead* (1968), but it also finds its central group moving further and further away from the solace of contemporary communication technologies. Motorized vehicles become an inviable source of transportation, televisions and radios retreat into the background, mobile phones slowly fade from the onscreen proceedings. This notion plays out most evidently in the film's climax, when the central characters are stowed away in a radically isolated farmhouse, disconnected from the outside world. All this is not to mention protagonist Elliott's wide-eyed, dopey childishness, which recalls the kind of absurdly idyllic Americana that we see defaced in genre ancestors such as Jack Arnold's *Tarantula* (1955), *The Incredible Shrinking Man* (1957), and *Monster on the Campus* (1958). Wahlberg plays this character as a man continually out of sync with his time and surroundings; his off-kilter line delivery falls somewhere between the otherworldly inhabitants of David Lynch's *Twin Peaks* and the kind of doe-eyed purity one might expect from James Stewart in a Frank Capra film.

Yes, these films differ in their deliveries and permutations; however, what stands out is a consistent thematic thread, which evolves and expands from entry to entry. The question, then, is what the trilogy's "evolution" suggests. At the end of *Signs*, the protagonist finds renewed faith in a Christian God. At the end of *The Village*, the heroine discovers a truth that is both world-shattering and emancipatory. *The Happening*, however, ends with a baffled news report that simply labels the source of mass casualty as an "act of nature"; not long after, we learn that the horror has not been quashed. Before the credits have rolled, we discover that the threat (whatever it is) has moved on from the U.S.A. to claim more victims in France. Shyamalan's Terror Trilogy offers three variations on a theme, with each entry descending further into uncertainty and doubt; the cost of discovery magnifies more with every film. If this is where revelation finally takes us, do we really want to know "the truth"?

THE GREASE-PAINTED CORPSE OF AMERICANA: REVISITING ROB ZOMBIE'S *HOUSE OF 1000 CORPSES* AND *THE DEVIL'S REJECTS*

Originally published in *HorrorNews.net* (2019)

IN A 2012 interview with *The News & Observer*, Alice Cooper says, "Rob Zombie and I are basically best friends, because he totally gets that horror and comedy are in bed together." Certainly, the uneasy connection between humour and revulsion informs Rob Zombie's first two films, *House of 1000 Corpses* (2003) and its sequel *The Devil's Rejects* (2005). However, rather than opting for straightforward comedy-horror hybridity, both films carry out a deconstructive and tonally destabilizing exploration of Americana in its bawdiest, goriest, and most outrageous forms. With a musical background in '80s New York noise giving way to industrialized hillbilly psychedelia, Zombie established himself as part-time creative renegade, part-time purveyor of America's darkest famous iconography.

The musician's directorial debut *House of 1000 Corpses* uses overt pastiche to its advantage. It draws broadly from the plot structures of Tobe Hooper's *Texas Chain Saw Massacre* films, riffs on vaudeville performer and filmmaker Tod Browning's sensibility, and names its murderous Firefly family members after various Groucho Marx characters. The film moves beyond the confines of specific pop cultural references to visualize parallels between broader American traditions:

vaudeville, the traveling carnival, and of course the mythology surrounding "celebrity" serial killers. *House* delivers its acrid vision of white Americana in a mode showcasing Zombie's background in music video direction. Its scenes are replete with bold primary color filters, rack zooms, hyper-stylized lighting, and constant slippages between various film stocks (16mm, 35mm, and even occasionally videotape).

This formal bombast undergirds a bare-bones narrative. *House* follows a group of urban friends traveling together in hopes of finding material for a planned book on bizarre American roadside attractions. They end up stopping at clown-faced Captain Spaulding (Sid Haig)'s Museum of Monsters and Madmen; in one of the film's most vividly disturbing sequences, Spaulding guides the would-be protagonist friends through his Museum ride, which displays gruesome animatronic dioramas devoted to America's most infamous serial murderers. Before long, the urban friends are lured to the Fireflys' otherworldly home, which resembles an Ed Wood soundstage reimagined for an alternate-universe episode of *MTV Cribs*, marinated in primary-colored light and detailed with otherworldly production design. The friends are trapped and subjected to torture through a litany of means, which intensifies in both scope and theatricality as the film charges toward its climax.

House's dramatic tension is simple, pitting visibly upper-class, white non-heroes against white "hillbilly" butchers, who want nothing to do with their visitors' pseudo-anthropological condescension. Crucially, Zombie offers no redeeming characteristics to his victims but graces the Firefly killers with burlesque charisma and anarchic energy. The writer-director uses affective disjunction and constant images of exaggerated Americana not to moralize, but rather to simply represent a hyper-cinematic, genre-codified vision of specific national identities. Spaulding himself acts as an amalgam of cinematic and national reference points, donning a star-spangled top hat in the tradition of Uncle Sam, boasting an arm tattoo of John Wayne and knuckle tattoos reading *Love* and *Hate* in a nod to Robert Mitchum's predatorial character from Charles Laughton's *The Night of the Hunter* (1955).

It is important to recognize that *House of 1000 Corpses* emerges in the wake of Wes Craven's *Scream* (1996) and its slew of hip, postmodern teen horror followers (from *I Know What You Did Last Summer* [1997] to *Urban Legend* [1998] to *Final Destination* [2000]). Much like his musical mentor Alice Cooper, who darkly reinterpreted Beatles and Yardbirds song structures to terrorize a hippie generation gone sour, Zombie invokes postmodern self-awareness while re-orienting the horror genre in its embodied, visceral, and sociopolitical roots. *Corpses* openly accepts its own referentiality and genre-play while also bombarding its viewers with extreme, culturally specific images of debasement and mutilation. "*This* is Americana," screams *House of 1000 Corpses*, opening space for the more concentrated efforts of its sequel, *The Devil's Rejects*.

It is worth noting that Rob Zombie's cinema is not a project of finger-wagging miserablism. If anything, Zombie's work is situated within a space of ambivalence. Nowhere is this made clearer than in his bleak post-Western, *The Devil's Rejects*, which offers a sun-baked vision of corrosive colonial America even as it basks in the textures, attitudes, and milieus of its genre origins (Western films, of course, but also exploitation movies, video nasties, and rock and roll). If *Corpses* turns its familiar narrative structure into an exercise in vaudevillian horror deconstruction, then *Rejects* turns Western conventions against themselves to undo customary ideas surrounding ethical binarity. The film pits ruthless, psychopathic Sherriff Wydell (played with aggressive gusto by William Forsythe) against the Fireflys in a blood-soaked game of cat and bigger cat.

The Devil's Rejects boasts a radically different aesthetic from its predecessor, with cinematographer Phil Parmet's 16mm photography explicitly evoking '70s grindhouse cinema. Film grain dances over sweaty close-ups and punishingly dry panoramas, incessant sunlight serving as a counterpoint to *House*'s neon-soaked nightscapes. The plot begins with a police battalion surrounding the Fireflys' home, a siege planned by Wydell, who invokes the ominous rhetoric of an Old Testament God ("It's time for us to do what the Good Lord would refer to as a cleansing of the wicked," he growls before ordering his troops to open fire). A brutal gunfight ensues between the cops and the Fireflys, sending Otis and Baby (Bill Moseley and Sheri Moon Zombie) fleeing while Mama (Leslie Easterbrook) is taken hostage. The plot tracks Wydell's pursuit of the Fireflys across bleak desert landscapes, punctuated by moments of intense violence perpetrated by both hunter and hunted.

Where *House* practically scoffs at the notion of morality, *Rejects* positions itself closer to questions of genre-defined ethics. Wydell views his pursuit of the Fireflys as a mission ordained by God. By contrast, Otis towers over one of his victims and proclaims, "I am the devil, and

I'm here to do the devil's work" (a direct quote lifted from real-life Manson Family member Charles "Tex" Watson).

The film positions its characters as ciphers of good and evil through such explicitly religious invocations, but Zombie is no Manichean thinker. Case in point: *Rejects* pivots around two central torture sequences, one in which the Fireflys terrorize and sexually humiliate an innocent family inside a motel room, and another near the conclusion in which Wydell plays vigilante and performs pseudo-crucifixions on the serial murderers. Here, Zombie further erodes genre-defined expectations surrounding "self" and "other," offering instead a vision of the Western as ferocious diagnosis: in *Rejects*, colonial America is an ambivalent space of relentless, almost unilateral violence and cruelty.

The film climaxes with the Fireflys driving across a deserted U.S. highway toward a police-barricaded border, soundtracked by the majority of Lynyrd Skynyrd's American rock classic, "Free Bird." The scene culminates with an extended slow-motion shootout between Fireflys and cops, the serial murdering family's Cadillac surging into a torrent of gore and ammunition. Always conscious of his cinematic lineage, Zombie gestures here to hyper-violent New Hollywood classics *Bonnie and Clyde* (1967) and *The Wild Bunch* (1969).

Calling attention to its own cinematic artifice through ironically nostalgic flashbacks of the Firefly family frolicking outside their home, this climax deconstructs ciphers of American "freedom" (the Fireflys) and "justice" (Wydell and company). Both groups collide in an operatic, almost celebratory display of brutality, one of the most baroque snapshots of Americana in 21st century cinema.

DIARY OF THE DEAD AND GEORGE A. ROMERO'S FORMAL SELF-AWARENESS

Originally published in *The Film Stage* (2017)

SPANNING HALF A century and six films, George A. Romero's *Dead* series could reasonably be labeled the most ambitious single-auteur franchise in horror cinema. Beginning with *Night of the Living Dead* (1968), this sequence is linked by various uses of zombie uprisings as vessels for sociopolitical critique. *Night* found as its inspiration Richard Matheson's classic 1954 novel *I Am Legend*, a sci-fi horror tale that places its isolated protagonist within an apocalyptic world of humans-turned-vampires; surely, Matheson's text posits an early sketch for the contemporary zombie, and Romero's film cements that concept by replacing the novel's creatures with reanimated corpses. Before *Night of the Living Dead*, the zombies of horror cinema aligned more directly with an origin in voodoo ritualism. Consider, for example, Victor Halperin's *White Zombie* (1932) and Jacques Tourneur's *I Walked with a Zombie* (1943), a model Wes Craven later revisited in *The Serpent and the Rainbow* (1988).

Night of the Living Dead's notoriety stems not only from its genre-related development; it also stands as a tentpole achievement of independent filmmaking, boasting rich black-and-white cinematography, a calculated development of tension, and insights into the angst of its contemporary zeitgeist, particularly ongoing battles for civil rights and protests of the Vietnam war. Romero's political intuition carries through *Dawn of the Dead* (1978)'s critique of then-burgeoning rampant consumerism, *Day of the Dead* (1985)'s thoughts on militarism and scientific ethics, and *Land of the Dead* (2005)'s proto-Occupy evaluation of late capitalism's monstrous wealth inequality.

Enter 2007's *Diary of the Dead*, a film as deeply political as its predecessors, but characterized by a uniquely pronounced formal self-awareness. After *Land* saw major studio development under the banner of Universal Pictures, *Diary* finds Romero re-evaluating the kind of micro-budget conditions that produced *Night of the Living Dead*. It calls attention to the sensibilities that have overwhelmingly haunted mainstream horror since the release of two genre-shaking titles in the late 1990s: Wes Craven's *Scream* (1996) and Daniel Myrick and Eduardo Sánchez's *The Blair Witch Project* (1999). Romero taps into the postmodern autocritique of the former, and the subjective "found footage" aesthetic of the latter. It is worth noting that 2007 sees a general resurgence of the found-footage genre, bolstered most loudly by the premiere of *Paranormal Activity*, as well as Spain's highly regarded *[REC]*. But as a rigorous self-evaluation and confrontational engagement with contemporary technology, *Diary* stands out. Romero's film is forward-thinking genre cinema, as opposed to a work of simple reaction like *Paranormal Activity*, which mostly recycles the *Blair Witch* model.

Indeed, an accurate description for *Diary of the Dead* is less "found footage" and more "mock documentary." The film's voiceover alleges that it has been edited by Debra (Michelle Morgan) from various sources, including footage shot by her boyfriend, Jason (Joshua Close). The "documentary" also includes coverage from surveillance cameras, along with additional footage from Debra and Jason's film-school classmates. Romero regularly calls attention to his own film's fictitiousness. Debra's opening narration lays bare the film's methods of production: "The film was shot with a Panasonic HDX-900 and an HBX-200," she says. "I did the final cut on Jason's laptop. I've added music occasionally for effect, hoping to scare you." Shortly after this reflexive admission, *Diary* sees Jason guiding the production of a mummy-themed horror film; in true post-*Scream* fashion, the scene incorporates Tracy's (Amy Lalonde) incisive critiques of generic sexism: "Can somebody please explain to me why girls in scary movies always have to, like, fall down and lose their shoes and shit?" she asks in exasperation. "It's totally lame. And why do we always have to get our dresses torn off?" Romero furthers this self-awareness when a climactic scene mirrors the droll opening: now, the mummy-costumed boy chasing Tracy really does mean to hurt her, and she voluntarily disposes of her shoes before her dress is torn.

What sets *Diary* apart is not simply its self-acknowledgment as mock documentary, but its sustained and attentive scrutiny of itself as a cinematic object. It also conducts a genuinely complex study of information overload in the age of digital technology. Romero gets away with skillful editing and composition by attributing his subjects with backgrounds in film education. In providing this character information, Romero also justifies his work's incorporation of highly stylized montages, which consist of overlaid newscast footage and narrations alongside Debra's sharply political commentary. The formal self-awareness plays out even more powerfully in an emphasis on individual images: multiple scenes find subjects recording each other on handheld cameras, so that the audience is watching itself watching. Romero, highly critical of digital media's fallibility, mirrors these images with one striking shot that finds the camera pointed similarly into the barrel of a National Guard member's rifle. This explicit visual metaphor speaks to the film's questions about the merits (or lack thereof) of documenting violence—"There will always be people like you," film professor Andrew Maxwell tells Jason, "wanting to document, wanting to record some sort of diary."

Yes, Romero is aware of the pun on "shot" that goes along with recording brutal imagery, and he makes his autocritique clear. Romero has no apparent interest in subtlety, stationing himself instead within the territory of direct confrontation. This is a film of unavoidable conflicts, rendered even more indelible through its horrific imagery. One especially disturbing episode finds Debra revisiting her suburban home to find her undead mother feasting on her father's flesh, before being attacked by her young brother. The paradoxically "sophisticated" and "feral" Maxwell dispenses with the boy using a bow and arrow. Indeed, as the oldest major character in the film, Maxwell might well be Romero's stand-in—erudite, pessimistic, and wryly humorous, he acts as a guardian and lovably cynical overseer of the young adults' journey. One telling scene shows Maxwell discovering a first edition of Charles Dickens's *A Tale of Two Cities* (1859) and quoting without an apparent sense of irony: "It was the best of times, it was the worst of times."

Upon finding his vision newly rejuvenated by digital technology, Romero might admit that, in some sense, this is "the best of times." In offering perhaps his bleakest worldview to date, with a final line that asks, "Are we worth saving?" he might be just as quick to state that this is "the worst of times." A decade later, it has perhaps become tiresome to belabor the dire political state of our world. But it is fascinating to ponder whether a 2017 *Dead* entry would still allow for a belief that this contemporary moment is the best of times.

RE-FEAR: *HALLOWEEN* (2007) / *HALLOWEEN II* (2009) BY ROB ZOMBIE (WITH NADINE SMITH)

Originally published in *Cinematary* (2018)

Nadine Smith: So I suppose we should probably begin by breaking down our own personal relationships to the *Halloween* franchise; to say the least, I think that most people's feelings about Rob Zombie's reinterpretation of the Myers saga are colored by their connection to the other films. Though I'll always be a freak for Freddy Krueger at heart, I do find Myers to be one of the more compelling brand-name slashers, but it's only been recently that I've really come around to the series at all. I've always liked Carpenter, but when first viewing *Halloween* several years ago, I felt a little underwhelmed. My taste has changed quite a bit in the years since, so I anticipated that I'd love *Halloween* upon re-watch, and I did. I had a similar experience with James Cameron's *The Terminator*: both movies were too "simple" for me as a young cinephile, but as I get older, simplicity reveals itself as the central virtue of both works. Carpenter's *Halloween* is much like Michael Myers himself: an engine that can't be stopped. It just goes and goes and goes.

As far as the other sequels are concerned, I like Rick Rosenthal's *Halloween II* well enough, I don't care much for *Season of the Witch*, *The Return of Michael Myers* is solid lazy Sunday viewing, and I thought the David Gordon Green remake was unfortunately rather abysmal. I still haven't made it through *Revenge*, *Curse*, *H20*, or *Resurrection*, though I plan on it soon. Unlike a lot of people, I actually don't mind how the sequels (at least thus far) extend the Myers mythology. What makes Myers interesting to me is his essential blankness, how hollow he is, but I don't think filling in some of the margins necessarily makes him less interesting. He works for me as evil incarnate on two legs, but his emptiness promises a certain potential for malleability, which is why I'm open to other interpretations. How are things between you and Michael Myers, Mike?

Mike Thorn: John Carpenter might be my favorite American horror auteur to come out of the late-twentieth century, but while I love and respect *Halloween* (1978) a great deal, it has never been one of my top favorites of his (I'm drawn much more toward *Prince of Darkness* [1987], *The Thing* [1982], *Christine* [1983], *In the Mouth of Madness* [1994] and *Ghosts of Mars* [2001], to name a few). Your description of both the film and Michael Myers as "an engine" is absolutely on point, and I think the entire piece works as a kind of vessel for Carpenter to develop many of his formalist ideas. I especially love the way the film uses "space" not only architecturally and compositionally, but also conceptually—it's deliberately designed around the placement and duration of pauses and lulls, maybe one of the best visual illustrations of Carpenter's rhythmic intuitions (which, of course, show very clearly in his work as a musical composer).

I like almost all the sequels, especially *Season of the Witch*, which offers compelling possibilities for an auteur-driven series revolving around the theme of Halloween rather than the character of Michael Myers. *Halloween II* (1981) is an efficient slasher film; I enjoy the fourth, fifth and sixth entries, which owe most of their humble effects to Donald Pleasence's presence; *H20*, possibly my least favorite, plays to me as a pretty vacant and cynical cash-in on the meta-sensibilities made popular by Wes Craven and Kevin Williamson in the late-nineties; *Halloween: Resurrection* is dumb and a little boring, but not insufferable; and David Gordon Green's newest reboot is incredibly muddled, made up of lots of incompatible parts (some of which are intriguing, many of which are not).

Rob Zombie's two films might be my favorite works under the *Halloween* banner, and I have no issue viewing them as entirely separate entities from Carpenter's original. I think they work together to form a very complex and thoughtful exegesis on American serial killer mythologies, with the first film primarily exploring social, familial, and institutional systems while the sequel delves into the intricate and vexing connections between violence and un- (or sub) consciousness. I think these films' thematic concerns speak clearly to Rob Zombie's career-long interests (as a filmmaker, musician, and visual artist), not only in terms of serial killer narratives and Americana, but also in their empathetic views toward societal "others," which suggest Zombie's allegiance to the Universal monster films released in the 1930s and 1940s.

How do you feel about reading Rob Zombie's *Halloween* films in relation to their auteur's body of work, rather than in relation to the Michael Myers saga? What is gained and/or lost?

Nadine: I think I'd rank *Halloween* a little higher in Carpenter's filmography than you would, but I agree that its appeal is largely a formalist one, in that it's basically an endless narrative labyrinth that allows Carpenter to show off his stuff. Any "faithful" sequel or remake would need someone behind the camera with an equal understanding of space, which David Gordon Green doesn't really have. Rob Zombie does have some mighty impressive formal chops, but I totally agree it makes more sense to read the *Halloween* remake and its sequel in line with his filmography more than the rest of the actual franchise. Carpenter drew us a blank outline; Zombie merely fills it in. If there is any real connection between the two films, it's that both are unimaginable without the specific visions of their respective auteurs.

You do a very astute job outlining what is uniquely Zombie about these two movies. Though perhaps more restrained than *House of 1000 Corpses* or *The Devil's Rejects*, there's still a strong element of "hillbilly horror" to these films. Laurie Strode leads a fairly stable suburban existence in Carpenter's original, but Zombie throws all that out—the Myers family is poor, dysfunctional, and abusive, with a strong stench of "white trash." The milieu we're thrown in could not be more different from the Haddonfield of 1978.

What I think Zombie adds most is a sense of specificity. The 1978 *Halloween* may be set in a specific place with specific people, but its uniqueness stems from its ordinariness. Michael is, of course, The Shape: an outline of a human being, a vague apparition, a face in the window. He is whatever we want him to be. I almost feel like the Carpenter *Halloween* is more akin to something like Alan Clarke's *Elephant*, a structuralist experiment set in a world where people are only capable of relating to each other through brutal violence, than the slashers that followed suit. In Zombie's world, Michael Myers is Michael Myers. The first forty minutes or so of the director's cut of Zombie's *Halloween* color in his childhood, which is relegated to a point-of-view prologue in the original. Even more specifically, it is not just about Myers' childhood, but the intensive therapy he undergoes and his relationship with Dr. Loomis. I'm often resistant to this kind of mythologizing, but in *Halloween*, it works. For Zombie, Michael's "origin" story isn't one of beginning or birth, but of devolution and death. What we witness is not so much an origin as a decline. This is the hollowing out of a human being, a transformation from Person to Shape. Daeg Ferch is perfect as an abused and androgynous child who has an obvious sweetness despite the torment heaped upon him, but his environment and the circumstances of his existence—as well as the carceral system he is thrown away in—push him into non-existence. He wants and is made to want to die but he is not allowed to physically die, so he is killed and kills himself emotionally, becoming something much more machine-like, acting only on empty instinct and pure drive.

Mike: Yes, this reading is on point. *Halloween*'s depiction of Michael's destructive ideations provides the foundation for *Halloween II*'s focus: the unconscious. Michael's arc is indeed a kind of dissolve, but it is worth noting that while Zombie is attuned to the role of parental and institutional failings, he never presents us with a purely cherubic child whose violence is attributable solely to external factors; when we first see young Myers, he's donning a plastic clown mask and blasting Kiss's "God of Thunder," playing a kind of little God as he prepares to kill his pet mouse. This film's depiction of violent individuals is complicated from the outset, giving us a character whose eventual outcome is the result of "a perfect storm of internal and external factors" (to paraphrase Zombie's Loomis). That is, we see seeds of psychopathy which Zombie wisely chooses not to locate—both films explore tenets of Jungian and (early) Freudian understandings of trauma, but we are not provided with easy resolution through a single "scene" whereby Michael is "made" a monster. Much like Alan Clarke's *Elephant* and Gus Van Sant's film of the same name, Rob Zombie's *Halloween* understands the fundamentally inexplicable nature of violence. At the same time, though, the film is sympathetic to Michael and recognizes the factors that play into his formation (the socializing of oppressive gender norms, domestic abuse, etc.). At the risk of oversimplifying, I see a remarkably interesting relationship between the two halves of Zombie's first *Halloween* film: the first half is concerned primarily with theory (contemplating the nature of violence and our relationship to slasher "icons" like Michael Myers), while the second is a study in cinematic practice (with one distinct formalist [Zombie] re-evaluating and reframing the content made famous by another [Carpenter]).

To return to this idea of Michael's "dissolve" into the unconscious, *Halloween II* is deeply committed to the study of psychological states and spaces. By the end of *Halloween*, Michael's self has been utterly fragmented and dislocated (and Zombie visualizes this through the archetypal masks lining Myers's cell's walls—here, it's hard to ignore the role of masks in Jung's understanding of individual personae). In *Halloween II*, Myers removes himself from embodied "reality" to find a strange kind of solace in a liminal dream-space; by contrast, his estranged sister (the traumatized Laurie) sees her psychological interiority as a labyrinthine hell—all agonizing flashbacks and dead ends (very few films capture the exhausting process of intensive therapy as well as this one). Perhaps this sequel's most brazen moves are its forays into the territory of shared unconscious. Not only does it deal overtly with ciphers of "universal" symbolism (the mask, the white horse, the watchful mother figure), but it also suggests a disturbing psychic chain between Michael, Laurie, and Samuel Loomis. The first *Halloween* directly poses questions about the social variables inherent to violence, and its sequel makes a brilliant choice by not answering any of those questions. Structured around the quasi-abstract slippages between different characters' psychic states, it expresses horror as pure violence and affect.

Nadine: Your description of the first half of *Halloween* as being the theory to the second half's practice—a metaphor I really love—could be extended a bit further to explain the relationship between that film and its sequel. Zombie's first film is a bit like his master's thesis: he does his duty and acknowledges the debt he owes to his cinematic ancestors, but he articulates something unique in his own voice. The second *Halloween* is his dissertation: balls to the wall, throwing out the rule book, asserting his own authorship. There's something almost Borgesian to how Zombie imagines Laurie's mental state as a kind of shifting labyrinth, with Michael the minotaur in the middle.

The first Halloween ends with Laurie screaming into oblivion while razor-blade cuts shock us out of reality, which inevitably recalls the various screams of *Twin Peaks'* Laura Palmer, but the second movie is a vicious unmasking of American iconography that brings Lynch to mind even more. Like Lynch, there's horror, more disturbing than almost anything else in American cinema, but there's also a great deal of empathy. Michael may be motivated by drive alone, but Rob Zombie feels for him more than any other director who has ever handled the series; Myers may be a shape now, but as the first film clearly shows, he still retains something of his humanity.

It's particularly moving to me that Zombie defines Myers' humanity most through his relationship to his mother, played by Zombie's wife, Sheri Moon Zombie, who appears to Michael multiple times in *Halloween II* as a ghostly figure accompanied by a white horse. Sheri Moon Zombie gives an achingly good performance in *Halloween* as Michael's struggling sex worker mother, but she's only in the first forty minutes of the film. There's a lot of love every time she's on screen, but Zombie feels a little less interested in everything that doesn't have to do with her (as do I). However, her spirit appears throughout *Halloween II*, so that same affection is woven into the entire film. That said, it's still a vicious movie; the film's opening, which reimagines and condenses the hospital sequence from Rick Rosenthal's *Halloween* sequel, is maybe one of the single most visceral scenes in any horror movie. I feel Laurie's bones crunch as she tries to evade Michael's endless pursuit on broken legs. I think the emphasis you put on affect is key, Mike, because this is a very affective movie from all sides, as intense as it is tender.

Mike: You've nicely unpacked the role of emotionality in these films' approaches to violence. Zombie directs and shoots the most graphic sequences with a queasy kind of intimacy; maybe the most noteworthy aspect of these films' onscreen brutality is that they so frequently invest time in the aftermath. Of course, we've talked about the fundamental role of trauma in *Halloween II*, both thematically and narratively, but the film also places emphasis on the incomprehensible, impossible-to-process sensation of shock immediately following loss. Consider the moment when Sherriff Brackett comes home to find his murdered daughter, Annie. Critical language escapes me: this is simply one of the most painful and profoundly upsetting scenes I've ever seen in a horror film.

As you've pointed out, it's crucial to acknowledge that Zombie also feels for Michael Myers. However, unlike, say, Jason Voorhees in some of the *Friday the 13th* sequels, Myers does not function simply as a catalyst for the audience's most fucked up and antisocial desires. I find it useful to turn again to some of the Universal monster films that Zombie has cited as formative: even if these frames of reference are dramatically abstracted, Zombie's Myers draws from traits in Lon Chaney Jr.'s Larry Talbot in *The Wolf Man* (1941) and Boris Karloff's monster from *Frankenstein* (1931). These characters possess a kind of monstrosity that's socially condemned, deeply rooted, and self-corroding (we've discussed Michael Myers' desire to die in Zombie's *Halloween* films, and it's worth noting that both *Frankenstein Meets the Wolf Man* [1943] and *House of Dracula* [1945] portray the Wolf Man as an openly suicidal and self-hating character).

To me, Rob Zombie's *Halloween* films form one of the more distinctive and complicated statements in contemporary American horror cinema. It is important to recognize that they're engaging with a pre-existing franchise, but they speak very specifically to one auteur's career-long aesthetic, formal and cultural interests. They have so much to say about otherness, monstrosity, violence, trauma, family, cultural mythology, social institutions, psychology, and maybe most fundamentally, despair. That they never once veer into didacticism or simplistic conclusion-making is no small miracle.

Nadine Smith is a writer, DJ, and co-host of the podcasts *Hotbox the Cinema* and *Cinematary*. Her work has appeared in publications like *The New York Times Magazine*, *Pitchfork*, *The Outline*, *Bandcamp Daily*, *Hyperallergic*, and *The Nashville Scene*.

HOSTEL: PART II AND THE MONSTER OF NEOLIBERAL LATE-CAPITALISM

Originally published in *The Film Stage* (2017)

THE TORTURE SCENES in writer-director Eli Roth's *Hostel* (2005) openly evoke the 2003 Abu Ghraib photographs, which depict United States military and Central Intelligence Agency personnel subjecting Iraqi prisoners to acts of profound cruelty and abuse. The film also addresses post-9/11 U.S.A.'s widespread xenophobia and confusion under an incompetent, hyper-conservative administration while satirizing upper-class masculinist group dynamics.

Shortly after *Hostel* enjoyed overwhelming mainstream success, David Edelstein published "Now Playing at Your Local Multiplex: Torture Porn" for *New York Magazine*, an article that haphazardly leveled unilateral arguments against the wave of brutal films flooding the American mainstream—including *Hostel*, but also works like Greg Mclean's *Wolf Creek* (2005), Rob Zombie's *The Devil's Rejects*, and the *Saw* franchise.

This incendiary context set the stage for Roth's *Hostel: Part II* (2007), which acts both as an inversion and political expansion of its predecessor. Where *Hostel* offers a glib satire of homosocial desire among hyper-masculine males, the sequel focuses on a trio of young women. If *Hostel* reacts to the Abu Ghraib photographs by leveling a critique against unchecked Western military imperialism, *Part II* specifically condemns rampant late-capitalist neoliberalism. In 2007, the sequel's political resonance was lost amidst blanket arguments against "torture porn" (a term that Edelstein's article leaves unfortunately broad and open-ended); in 2017, its nastily incisive observations remain too relevant to be brushed aside.

But Roth's films are not simply exercises in pessimistic wallowing. Following in the tradition of its predecessor, *Hostel: Part II* amplifies its horrifying political insights with dark humor. It uses these most emotionally charged of genres, horror and comedy, to attribute its subject matter with physical reaction, seeking visceral impact above all else. If subtlety is what you seek, Roth is probably not the filmmaker for you—here's a film that uses castration to symbolize resistance against violent masculinity; that shows human bodies turned into consumable and disposable objects in order to illustrate capitalism's brutal exploitation of animals and people alike. Unlike the first entry, *Part II*'s point-of-view is not restricted to the victims. Instead, the film is divided into two plot lines—the first sees the aforementioned group of women vacationing in a small Slovakian village, and the second follows two wealthy, white American businessmen who win a bid to "purchase" the unknowing women for torture and murder.

By extending its narrative reach to include the Hostel "clients" as well as its prisoners, *Part II* deepens its moral and political insights. The audience is asked not only to empathize with the victims, but also to recognize its own spectatorship and complicity. This broadened perspective also substantiates Roth's sustained homage to Italian horror auteur Sergio Martino; like Martino's excellent *Torso* (1973), *Hostel: Part II* oscillates visually and narratively between different subjective positions to disturb the viewer and to complicate their political assumptions. *Part II* makes its connection to *Torso* blatantly clear, going so far as to play an early scene as a direct reversal of *Torso*'s introduction. Where Martino's film begins with an inquiry into the objectification of women in art history, Roth's stages a nude male model for the leading trio of women to sketch. Edwige Fenech, Martino's career-long collaborator, plays the art instructor; "Hands on your pencils, boys," she says, when female model Axelle (Vera Jordanova) takes the male's place.

This genre-specific self-awareness supports a political commentary. Following in the tradition of Martino's masterpiece, *Hostel: Part II* does not use horror as an escape from reality but rather as a means of confronting it. In 2017, this method of genre filmmaking remains generally unpopular. With some exceptions, most contemporary, mainstream American horror (e.g. the *Paranormal Activity* and *Conjuring* franchises) continues following a trend of old-school paranormal superstition. By comparison, combative genre cinema such as *Hostel: Part II* urges American audiences to reflect on horrific sociopolitical realities. In 2017, its plot holds truer than ever—with boorish, chauvinist tycoon Donald Trump now serving as president of the U.S.A., capitalist enterprise and political leadership are more explicitly linked than ever. In 2007, Roth already saw the scariest machinations of neoliberal capitalism at work.

While addressing lofty political through-lines, *Part II* also boasts more formal flourishes than its predecessor. This sequel offsets its Martino references with coyly Gothic imagery: one scene finds a client lying within a ring of candles, scything her suspended, nude young victim before bathing in her blood, Elizabeth Báthory style. *Part II* also maximizes on architecture and locales, using them as defamiliarizing spaces rather than geographical markers. Scenes in misty Slovakian spas play out as placeless, sensual daydreams, and an anachronistic music festival echoes the first film's visual allusions to the Minotaur myth. Specific Slovakian characteristics are largely left in the background because, like its predecessor, this film is much more about its protagonists' perceptions of Europe than about Europe itself. Whitney (Bijou Phillips), one of the focal vacationers, demonstrates this point-of-view: she conflates Bosnia with Slovakia, and calls local Miroslav (Stanislav Ianevski) "Borat." (Fittingly, comedian Sacha Baron Cohen uses the titular *Borat* of his 2006 satirical mockumentary to tease out evidence of widespread American ignorance.)

Yes, there is plenty of humor in *Hostel: Part II*, but it never allows us to forget its primary vocation: fear. In the tradition of pure horror cinema, it denies us a happy ending. While the third act briefly hints at simplistic moralizing, it quickly steers away from that course. Ultimately, its resolution arises bluntly from financial negotiation, and it concludes with a gang of street children playing soccer with a decapitated head. Some of the victims may get out alive, but what good is survival if it only results from torturing the torturers? In 2007, the film's box-office earnings and critical reception suggested a pale and unsuccessful sequel. A decade later, *Hostel: Part II* stands out as one of the most urgent, combative, and complicated American horror movies of its time.

THE MANY PECULIAR VIRTUES OF WES CRAVEN'S *MY SOUL TO TAKE*

Originally published in *Vague Visages* (2017)

CONVERSATIONS AROUND Wes Craven's decades-long career often boil the filmmaker's cinematic contributions down to a trifecta of tent-pole achievements—first came *The Last House on the Left* (1972), a customarily described "exploitation" film inspired by Ingmar Bergman's *The Virgin Spring* (1960); next, Craven revolutionized the horror genre with his surrealist slasher *A Nightmare on Elm Street* (1984), a tonally adventurous work that evokes the likes of Luis Buñuel and Jean Cocteau; finally, the director upended conventions with the postmodern *Scream* (1996), whose credit is owed in no small part to Kevin Williamson's extraordinarily reflexive and meta-cinematic script. Some might also attribute *The Hills Have Eyes* (1977) with the status of "classic" genre fare, although it owes a large part of its style and sensibility to Tobe Hooper's masterful *The Texas Chain Saw Massacre* (1974).

This characterizing of Craven's career is problematic, not because it is "untrue," but because it is woefully incomplete. Out of the three films listed above, only one (*A Nightmare on Elm Street*) ranks among the most idiosyncratic and challenging titles in the director's prolific career. While *The Last House on the Left* is a demanding and ably directed work, it shows its director in noticeably developing form. Still, its influence is clear, with traces of its sensibility showing through in later '70s works as varied as the aforementioned *Massacre*, John Carpenter's *Assault on Precinct 13* (1976), and Meir Zarchi's *I Spit on Your Grave* (1978). Likewise, *Scream* shows Craven in remarkably assured mode, and deserves commendation for its influence (which, in 2017, still lingers);

however, the film is debatably a less complex and rigorously designed comment on meta-horror than the ambitious *New Nightmare* (1994).

Further, this recurrent emphasis on only three titles discourages closer analysis of the twenty-five years of work that followed *Scream*. Key among the later films of Wes Craven's oeuvre is the peculiar and allegedly semi-autobiographical *My Soul to Take* (2010). This film, widely dismissed by critics and audiences upon release, stands out as one of its director's boldest, most sensitive, and most authentically *singular* works.

Set in a small town called Riverton, *My Soul to Take* begins with a condensed backstory for its central local legend: constructing insidiously concise scenes, Craven takes us into the tormented inner world of serial killer Abel Plenkov (Raul Esparza), who murders his wife before he is unsuccessfully thwarted by law enforcement agents. The introductory flashback plays out as a film within the film, leaving off with the reveal that Plenkov disappeared en route to the hospital after he was shot by a police officer. The film's primary plot follows seven Riverton teens who were born on the night that Plenkov purportedly died, all of whom Plenkov vowed to come back and murder. Surely enough, Plenkov (or some sadistic imitator) returns sixteen years later to hunt and slaughter these teens; Craven often directs the murder sequences in a manner akin to his friend and colleague Sean S. Cunningham's *Friday the 13th* (1980), especially during one chase that pits the killer against a young man and woman in the woods. This is one of the film's many references to familiar genre iconography and imagery; the Riverton seven recalls the "lucky seven" of Stephen King's classic novel, *It* (1986), while the returned Plenkov dons a Slipknot-like mask that recalls the early-2000s meeting point between exploitation horror and nü metal (consider titles as varied as *Resident Evil* [2002], *Queen of the Damned* [2002], and *Freddy vs. Jason* [2003]).

Anchoring *My Soul to Take*'s narrative is protagonist Bug (Max Thieriot), a maladjusted and ostracized teen who suffers from migraines and recurrent nightmares. Aided by his shifty and abused best friend Alex (John Magaro), Bug navigates the daily hells of teenage life (hormones, bullying, social structures) while also attending to the mystery of maybe-Plenkov's return. That the horror/mystery of the killer sometimes moves to the narrative backburner in lieu of Bug's day-to-day tribulations speaks to this film's interests; in a truly outstanding way, Craven uses tonal disorientation (through bizarre dialogue and performances, highly stylized editing, and a manipulated color palette) to capture the haywire inner world of adolescence. In doing so, he highlights the ways that the horror genre speaks particularly to "the outsider" or "the excluded"; rather than acting as a routine or generic exercise, My Soul to Take explores the dark and unpleasant corners of its own psychology, bringing its protagonist intimately close to the very horror at its center. In this way, it performs the double duty of calling into question Bug's "innocence" while also shaping a powerfully unique correspondence between genre and subject.

Taking all of this thematic work into consideration, it is worth noting that Soul was Craven's first original screenplay since New Nightmare; also worth noting is that, due to the auteur's death in August 2015, it was the last film in which he took on the dual role of writer and director, and was in fact the second last film he ever made (his final release was Scream 4 [2011]). With all this in mind, Soul shows Craven in thematically reflective mode, returning to undercurrents that typify his most famous films while also boasting a formal and tonal bombast unseen since his borderline experimental horror-comedy, Shocker (1989).

It is probably this unexpected dissonance that can be most readily blamed for the largely merciless reaction to My Soul to Take—that is, one sees within it the adolescent slasher conventions of Nightmare and Scream, but Soul re-evaluates those pictures' material in a completely new framework (especially considering the nuanced genre-protagonist interaction described above). However, while Soul's muted palette and Twin Peaks-esque tonality set it apart from these two works, it is worth considering whether Nightmare and Scream are as "conventional" as popular memory would suggest. Scream radically rethinks generic conventions of "authenticity," even calling out the presence of its director in an introductory reference to the Nightmare series. Likewise, Elm Street reframes conceptions of stable "reality" and reliable point of view, organizing its narrative into the structure of a nightmare without end.

Where My Soul to Take differs most starkly from these classic works is in its emotional gradient. That is, both Nightmare and Scream find Craven in obstructive mode, wherein he foregrounds the armature of cinematic language itself. This is not to say that these films bypass any interest in character, but rather that their formal characteristics do not work toward a statement on empathy in the same way as in My Soul to

Take. Soul's empathy becomes problematized and, in fact, deeply challenging when the film reaches the point at which its tortured young protagonist's perception becomes questionable. Fascinating to note that two other high-profile American auteurs, John Carpenter and Martin Scorsese, explored such similar territory with their own horror films that same year (with *The Ward* and *Shutter Island*, respectively).

Not only does Wes Craven's picture stage a fascinatingly nuanced study of "the outsider" (with non-judgmental awareness of the violence that can result from processes of marginalization), but he also fills the story with wonderfully idiosyncratic details. A birdwatcher himself, the auteur steeps his screenplay in the symbolism and mythology surrounding the California condor; he stages an ambiguous performance of identity-shifting in a high school hallway, with Bug and Alex mirroring each other's movements; he incorporates Bug's unusual knack for spontaneously imitating the voices and attitudes of others, a bizarrely unexplained plot element that speaks to the film's larger suggestions of psychic connectivity.

One gets the sense in watching *My Soul to Take* that it rewards multiple attentive viewings; it deserves recognition for its ambition and unique perspective alone. As the second to last film in one of the greatest American horror filmmakers' careers, it is an extraordinary example of artistic self-reflection and development. For this critic's money, it might very well be the highest accomplishment in Craven's career.

MOMENTS OF REVELATION IN MARTIN SCORSESE'S *SHUTTER ISLAND* AND *SILENCE*

Originally published in *Vague Visages* (2017)

ASSESSED ON ITS own terms, Martin Scorsese's *Silence* (2016) is a daunting piece; released after two and a half decades of staggered development, it might reasonably be considered the most "definitive" title in its director's oeuvre. Incorporating many of Scorsese's career-long questions regarding Christianity, violence, and self, *Silence* feels deeply cumulative. For this reason, it is worth contextualizing its lofty philosophical and formal concepts alongside previous Scorsese films. In "Holy Men, Holy Losers: Scorsese, *Silence* and the Mystery of Faith," Bilge Ebiri has already written insightfully on the movie's connections to its auteur's most openly faith-based works, *The Last Temptation of Christ* (1988) and *Kundun* (1997); and Scorsese alludes in interviews to its connections with *Bringing Out the Dead* (1999). These points of reference are key, and it is also worth reflecting on *Silence* both as a standalone title, and as an adaptation of Shūsaku Endō's excellent novel (originally published in Japanese in 1966, first published in English in 1969). However, after much reflection, I find myself most fascinated by the ways in which *Silence* engages with *Shutter Island* (2010), another literary adaptation (Dennis Lehane's source novel was published in 2003). To be sure, these two films share no immediately apparent characteristics. *Silence* shows Scorsese in a patiently disciplined mode, echoing the visual focus of Kenji Mizoguchi and Robert Bresson rather than embracing his increasingly maximalist form (his exuberant visual style develops noticeably around *Life Lessons* [1989], but stands out especially in the period connecting 1995's *Casino* to 2013's *The Wolf of Wall Street*). Indeed, *Shutter Island* fits the maximalist label, conveying its protagonist's fragmented point of view through energetic camerawork, confrontational music cues, and fierce editing. At first glance, then, *Silence* and *Shutter Island* might present Scorsese in starkly opposing positions: a deliberate and formally meditative study of faith, versus an aggressive exploration of Gothic iconography and violence's psychological tolls.

However, an analysis of these two films' endpoints reveals an intriguing connection. Specifically, consider the scene in *Silence* that finds Father Rodrigues (Andrew Garfield) finally meeting Father Ferreira (Liam Neeson). Put into conversation with Teddy Daniels's (Leonardo DiCaprio) encounter with Dr. Cawley (Ben Kingsley) at the top of a mysterious lighthouse, the scene develops deeper meaning and implication. Indeed, both narratives reveal surprising commonalities when comparing these two scenes. *Silence* reinterprets the search for "lost soul" Kurtz as depicted in Joseph Conrad's *Heart of Darkness*, while *Shutter Island* employs the dark soul-searching of Gothic horror to unleash a "return of the repressed." Rather than finding conspiratorial horrors at the top of the lighthouse, Teddy is forced instead to confront his own unspeakable acts of violence: after discovering that his wife had drowned their three children, he shot and killed her.

Both Rodrigues and Daniels exhibit the intent to maintain their worldviews: Rodrigues commits to the preservation of his Christianity, refusing to apostatize no matter what the consequences. If he must be tortured, or even watch others being tortured and murdered, then such is the mysterious will of God. Daniels, conversely, commits to the unconscious fantasy of undergoing an investigation at Ashecliffe Hospital for the criminally insane. He perceives himself as the steadfast and rational detective, navigating an environment of ubiquitous threat and madness. More explicitly complicit in violence than Rodrigues, he suffers migraines throughout the film, tormented by horrific flashbacks of his participation in the Dachau liberation reprisals. Both men conduct searches with external objectives (Rodrigues must confront the apostatized Ferreira, while Daniels must expose the labyrinthine conspiracy of Ashecliffe Hospital); however, both men's destinations unfold into processes of internal re-evaluation. Finally, though, both protagonists choose to revert to their original ways of navigating the world. Although they are faced with debilitating arguments against their perspectives, they choose to maintain their internal status quos. That both films inflect these choices with the impact of revelation links them further.

More specifically, *Silence* pits Rodrigues against Ferreira in an extended conversation, whereby Ferreira insists that to apostatize is to mitigate, and in fact to prevent, the unnecessary violence enacted by Japanese landowners against Christian peasants. The conversation unfolds to suggest that Rodrigues's refusal to apostatize is ultimately an act of self-deception; the Japanese people do not perceive his Christian faith through his own religious ontology, but through a cultural reinterpretation more akin to Buddhism. These people are not dying for a Christian God, but for a misreading of Rodrigues's faith. Thus, it might be said that they are dying for Rodrigues. Rodrigues reacts to this information with anger and resistance, ultimately accusing Ferreira that he is irreconcilably lost to the Church. However, after further violent coercion by the landowners' forces, Rodrigues apostatizes in a gesture of mercy for the tortured Christian peasants. Importantly, though, the film's profound final shot shows Rodrigues's dead hands wrapped around a Christian cross. Although it eventually became a secret, he maintained his faith until the end.

Conversely, *Shutter Island*'s climactic lighthouse scene finds Dr. Cawley forcing Teddy Daniels to relive his memory of murdering his wife. The truth is that there is no conspiracy going on at Ashecliffe Hospital, and that he is in fact the missing patient he has spent the film's entirety pursuing. Like Rodrigues, Daniels reacts first with fury and defense; Cawley must be participating in some elaborate and mysterious plot, he insists. However, the film finds Teddy finally confessing to the murder of his wife before he radically reinterprets that confession. Like Rodrigues in *Silence*, Teddy shows us in *Shutter Island*'s final scene that he intends to hold onto his worldview; while it may keep him imprisoned, he has weighed out the costs versus benefits and decided on the importance of denial. The film's telling last lines substantiate his decision; "Which would be worse—to live as a monster, or to die as a good man?" He chooses the latter, preferring to live out a performative role as a "good man," a dutiful agent of the law, rather than to eke out his existence with the knowledge that he murdered his own wife. To be sure, *Shutter Island* lends itself to multiple interpretations, even leaving open the possibility that Ashecliffe Hospital is in fact an elaborately designed system of psychological control.

However, played in conversation with *Silence*, the film substantiates an artistic recurrence in Martin Scorsese's body of work. What is the cost to oneself of living by a system of belief? How does one balance one's commitment to an ontology within a world of incompatible ideals and perspectives? Finally, one finds in *Silence* yet another reflection on that haunting question that closes *Shutter Island*: Which *would* be worse? To live as a monster, or to die as a good person? Further, how does one approach the notion of "truth" in a world that provides no stable definition?

THE DIGITAL PERVERSE: DARIO ARGENTO'S *DRACULA 3D*

Originally published in *Vague Visages* (2018)

DRACULA 3D (2012) is certainly an anomaly in Dario Argento's cinematic DNA, and I understand the popular impulse to write it off as "incoherent," but I am not personally willing to leave it there. If the director's pre-*Suspiria* (1977) output can be read non-pejoratively as a series of formal trial runs, and his five-film sequence from *Suspiria* to *Opera* (1987) comprises a kind of fully realized auteurist vision, then where does that leave his late career? I really do not think I have figured out Argento's 1990-2009 modus operandi (although I really admire its results)—it seems that the late 20th and early 21st century mostly sees Argento probing, revisiting, and teasing out past obsessions rather than advancing a concise new "agenda." With that in mind, *Dracula* appears to stand entirely on its own.

Above all, this film showcases a director actively, recklessly searching for new means of expression: his public insistence that the film be shot in 3D is crucial. So too is its release date worth noting, since it premiered only three years after the 2009 release of James Cameron's *Avatar*, which was hailed at the time as a true benchmark in cinematic development: consider A.O. Scott's rather baffling comparison between Cameron's film and D. W. Griffith's *The Birth of a Nation* (1915). The superficial similarities between Cameron and Argento's films are next to none, but it is useful to recognize both auteurs' uses of 3D technology for their respective narratives. If nothing else, the comparison begins to illuminate some of *Dracula*'s perverse logic.

James Cameron has acknowledged that *Avatar* pulls from familiar plot designs, patterns, and iconography to create a guiding light for the audience through radically new visual terrain. So too has he recognized his own dream-states as the source for many of the film's vibrant images. Argento is, of course, no stranger to the oneiric himself, considering that Thomas De Quincey's opium dreams broadly provide the framework for his Three Mothers trilogy (*Suspiria*, *Inferno* [1980] and *Mother of Tears* [2007]). Much like Cameron's *Avatar*, *Dracula* illustrates a means of subordinating narrative to visual exploration (it is key, then, that Argento uses a plot as familiar and often-adapted as Bram Stoker's 1897 novel).

Diametrically opposed to the science-fiction-meets-fantasy-mysticism of Cameron's bioluminescent Pandora, Argento's *Dracula* imagines digital cinema's most sacrilegious, filthy possibilities. Where Cameron dreams, Argento goes back to that space that has outlined so much of his logic-dismantling filmography—the space of the nightmare.

When recalling the extravagant camera movements that persist through many of Argento's earlier films, *Dracula*'s primarily classicist, tableaux-based mode seems almost restrained. However, the auteur mines his first 3D nightmare not for variations on a familiar style, but rather for an as-yet-unprecedented sample of the digital perverse. One might turn to the genre's previous 21st century forays into 3D technology as counterarguments (like, for example, Patrick Lussier's 2009 *My Bloody Valentine* remake). But Lussier, whose resumé is notably filled with several editing credits for Wes Craven's films, directs his slasher update as a mostly straightforward throwback exercise. He makes use of the third dimension only occasionally as a playful device rather than as a grammatical foundation.

By comparison, Argento uses 3D versions of classical compositions as the basis for some of the most flagrant and confrontational artifice in his career—CGI animals burst into pockets of high-key lighting while the auteur paints the frame's corners with deep black shadow. Typically for this director, the actors perform the role of moving pieces in a stylistic exercise rather than as character-devoted sources for audience empathy. So much of Argento's focus on the 3D technology comes through in the use of light—*Dracula* is really about depth of field and guiding eye-lines within a novel dimensional range. The filmmaker finds in this new tool a means of further interrogating career-long fixations—*Dracula* is almost hysterical in its imagistic devotion to sexual lust, animal/human relations, blood, and the fallibility of the body.

And, like almost everything else in the auteur's filmography, this work resists rational systems of evaluation and explanation. Argento even defiles Stoker's narrative rigor, repurposing the source material as a foundation for his cinema of images rather than as a consistent plot blueprint. Critics condemned the director for "failing" to adhere to his text of choice, but why should we assume that it was ever his intention to undergo a "faithful" adaptation in the first place? This filmmaker's oeuvre has never been a showcase of "good taste" or conventional demonstrations in character/story development, so why should we expect him to play by the rules now?

LESS HUMAN THAN HUMAN: A DECADE OF ROB ZOMBIE

Originally published by *In Review Online* (2019)

EVER SINCE HIS 2003 debut *House of 1000 Corpses*, Rob Zombie has used cinema to engage the paradox of counter-cultural extremity and populism. Raised as a child of the seventies who saw violent episodes unfold in his family's traveling carnival, Zombie built up an eclectic resource of reference points (not only through the carnie world, but also through a vast array of pop cultural phenomena—everything from Tod Browning to ABBA to Black Sabbath to Evel Knievel to Steven Spielberg). These tensions sit at the foundation of his entire creative output, beginning with his original band White Zombie: originally a ragged art-rock outfit defined by DIY punk ethos and psychedelic horror imagery, the band later transitioned to cleaner, industrial-tinged groove metal that lifted as much from stadium acts like Alice Cooper and Kiss as it did from its underground roots. As a filmmaker, the musician began developing his aesthetic style by directing music videos for White Zombie, and then for his solo outings from the late nineties onward. His videos often filter a range of horror influences (most notably German Expressionism and the Universal monster cycle of the thirties and forties) through the color-soaked postmodernism typical of peak MTV.

As a filmmaker, Zombie became an involuntary key player in the oft-derided "torture porn" subgenre of the mid-2000s, which, despite outrage from the popular critical establishment, saw big box office success in the likes of James Wan's *Saw* (2004), Eli Roth's *Hostel*, and Zombie's own *The Devil's Rejects* (2005). By the end of the decade, the Weinstein Company saw enough financial potential in the director to hire him for a reimagining of the then-exhausted *Halloween* franchise.

Zombie took the opportunity to radically remake John Carpenter's classic 1978 film, reinventing the soulless stalker Michael Myers as the by-product of sociocultural and psychological factors central to middle-class, suburban American life. Despite its abrasive depictions of violence and its demanding scope, the film became an enormous box office success (one of the biggest in the Weinstein Company's history). When Zombie was rehired to direct a sequel, he doubled down on his esoteric preoccupations; *Halloween II* (2009) further advanced its predecessor's psychoanalytic undercurrents within a feature-length meditation on intergenerational trauma. While the film was critically reviled and enjoyed significantly less financial success than *Halloween* (2007), it served as another demonstration of Zombie's unmistakable point of view.

What makes Zombie such a vital American artist is his troubled relationship to the culture he depicts and inhabits. While Zombie's films are intoxicated by the aesthetics of genre cinema, renegade carnies, heavy metal, and Americana, they ultimately offer a portrait of decay and human failure. No doubt informed by the director's commitment to animal rights and veganism, these films directly dismantle the myth of human exceptionalism; there is no space for unchecked solipsism and escapism in Zombie's cinema. His work engages constantly with the conflicted relationship between glorification and disdain, fixating on the impact and aftermath of physical violence, but not without also reveling in the base, triune brain pleasures therein. Much like his musical output, the director's films pair dissonant affects (humour and horror, arousal and disgust), laying bare the ways in which his culture's fetishes are infected with sick contradictions.

Nowhere is this fixation clearer than in *The Lords of Salem*, Zombie's first release of the 2010s. Set in Salem, Massachusetts, the film revolves around radio DJ Heidi (Sheri Moon Zombie), a recovering drug addict who receives a mysterious record from a group who call themselves The Lords. Heidi becomes obsessed with the record's powerful sonic effects, which lead her to psychically confront local and familial legacies of witchcraft and persecution. The film presents the most dramatic shift in Zombie's filmography to date, turning to more conceptually and visually abstract expressions of anti-humanism than any of the director's previous works. As Zombie's first film to be shot digitally, it maximizes on crisp widescreen compositions that emphasize Heidi's fraught relationship with her memories and environment. Ultimately, the film presents an ambivalent celebration of nihilism. Subordinate to forces both supernatural and natural (specifically addiction), Heidi finally submits and embraces her demons. *The Lords of Salem* thus speaks to a long-standing tradition in the American Gothic, upending the tenets of Renaissance humanism through a heroine who is irreparably damaged and powerless to both internal and external forces. Given Zombie's penchant for compelling contradictions, this conclusion plays out as a disorienting triumph, scored by The Velvet Underground & Nico's "All Tomorrow's Parties."

Four years after *The Lords of Salem*'s release, Zombie presents another pessimistic portrait of Americana in *31* (2016). Following the doomed development of a '70s hockey drama called *Broad Street Bullies*, Zombie turned to crowdfunding to pad his next micro-budget, closed-concept horror film. *31* stands as the director's most powerful allegory for factory farming and the unstable foundation of human exceptionalism, pitting the kidnapped members of a traveling carnival against hired killers dressed as clowns. Forced to participate in a game of cat-and-mouse in a locked warehouse for the amusement of omniscient aristocrats donning powdered wigs, these characters stumble through their dimly lit environments and engage in hopeless bouts of physical combat with their hunters. The concept is a devilishly simple homage to Ernest B. Schoedsack and Irving Pichel's *The Most Dangerous Game* (1932), which was itself a pre-code explication of humankind's innate animality. *31* frames its captive carnies as stand-ins for animals raised for slaughter in hellish environments—one scene depicts these characters accidentally eating the flesh of their dead friend after mistaking his flesh for that of a nonhuman animal's. The film's structural simplicity bolsters its critique, which offers a microcosmic view of late-capitalist America and the incumbent atrocity it wreaks on human and nonhuman animals alike.

After *31* was released, Zombie saw the death of another passion project in *Raised Eyebrows*. For this film, Zombie connected with *Love & Mercy* co-writer Oren Moverman to adapt Steve Stoliar's book of the same name, which documents the tragic final chapters of comic Groucho Marx's life. Zombie described his vision for *Raised Eyebrows* as bearing some similarities to Billy Wilder's *Sunset Boulevard* (1950) and Tim Burton's *Ed Wood* (1994). Eventually, logistical and financial obstacles prevented the film from moving ahead, and Zombie finally conceded to make *3 from Hell* (2019), a sequel to his most successful film, *The Devil's Rejects* (2005). Complicated by the unexpectedly quickening illness of star Sid Haig, the film underwent last-minute rewrites less than a week before production began. The film unmistakably bears its limitations and obstacles, lacking some of the conviction undergirding the director's best work.

Much like its predecessor, *3 from Hell* presents a postmodern treatise on genre, hybridizing horror with mockumentary, Western, and comedy conventions. *3 from Hell* pays tribute most blatantly to Sam Peckinpah's *The Wild Bunch* (1969), but it also nods to screwball comedy, toying with America's serial killer fixation through scenarios that play like Preston Sturges or Howard Hawks pushed beyond moral limits. *3 from Hell* differs from *The Devil's Rejects* most notably in formal terms; where *Rejects* benefited from a larger scale production and the distinct texture of its 16mm cinematography, *3 from Hell* has a rushed visual quality, exemplified by its low-budget digital approach and a heavy reliance on CGI. Nevertheless, it showcases a filmmaker with a distinct point of view who, despite significant budget and schedule constraints, pushes fervently against the self-centered simplicity of contemporary genre cinema. In an era that foregrounds self-aggrandizing moralism and reactionary appeals to humanist potential, Rob Zombie's cinema offers an importantly disruptive point of view.

JAMES BENNING'S *STEMPLE PASS*: MINIMALIST HORROR FOR TRUMP'S AMERICA

Originally published in *Vague Visages* (2016)

ALTHOUGH PRESIDENT-ELECT Donald Trump has not yet been sworn into office, the term "Trump's America" has already become a usual suspect in film criticism. Indeed, it is difficult to avoid reflecting on this seismic political event when assessing contemporary American films. Recently, I have found myself thinking back to James Benning's *Stemple Pass* (2012) (released, incidentally, midway through Barack Obama's eight-year presidency). Benning's film deals with distinctly American subject matter, and those sociopolitical fixations warrant close analysis. Said fixations include the obsessive lust for "returning to the past," an intensifying fear of the outsider, and the tenuous connection between the human and the nonhuman (this last topic underpins issues like factory farming and capital expansion resulting in ecological catastrophe).

I caution against referring to *Stemple Pass* simply as a work of "non-narrative" cinema, because its progression is so rigorously and specifically designed. The film is comprised of four static shots with virtually identical framing, the sequences divided by a progressing change in season. Benning shoots the film on HD digital video, capturing minute changes in weather with crystalline detail while always maintaining focus on the film's main "subject": a precise reconstruction of the cabin that once housed infamous "Unabomber" Ted Kaczynski. The seasonal sections are couched with minutes-long stretches of natural ambient noise, which Benning interrupts with readings from Kaczynski's diaries, recited in voiceover narration.

The film plays almost like a work of genre horror, charting as it does the descent of one man's mental state: Kaczynski begins with banal recollections of his day-to-day routines while living in the wild, before eventually going on to boast about deliberately injuring nearby motorists and eventually mailing explosives to major tech firms. The film's serenity moves slowly from hypnotizing to dread-inducing, trapping the viewer within the confines of an unmoving image and the words of a mentally unfurling individual. This affect is magnified by the tension between claustrophobia and openness: although the film is built of wide, "open" repetitions of its image, the generally unchanging frame also keeps the viewer's focus "trapped."

Benning incorporates elements of ominous foreshadowing as early as the film's first season (spring). He slowly reads Kaczynski's graphic description of preparing a porcupine for eating, during which he repeatedly recalls dealing with the animal's blood clots and internal organs. This scene immediately undoes Kaczynski's own perception of his living space as purely picturesque and Edenic. While the Unabomber perceives the intrusion of vehicular noise and technology as a "fall" from his private grace, he himself enacts violence on his surroundings that are unfit for his delusional pre-lapsarian (or "pre-fall") worldview. This delusion eerily predicts the kind of logic motivating many Trump voters, who perceive their notoriously corrupt and corporatist leader as a "voice of the people" when in fact he is the embodiment of their oppression. So too does Kaczynski's yearning for a "return" to a utopic past reflect the empty logic of Trump's campaign slogan, "Make America Great Again." As with the American past implied by Trump's slogan, the past idealized by Kaczynski is one rooted in violent exceptionalism and xenophobia.

And it is the issue of exceptionalism that both connects and divides the philosophy of Kaczynski and Trump. Kaczynski perceives himself as exceptional enough that his worldview warrants brutal action, but he also views himself to be "one" with his natural environment. He employs this self-defying logic to justify the fact that he regularly kills and eats animals for survival, but he doesn't consider the ways in which he impedes on the space and rights of other human and nonhuman animals. Trump's campaign, however, operates on the basis of human exceptionalism, which posits that the natural environment is subordinate to human (and more specifically corporate) interest.

Again, it is this violent foundation of exceptionalism which links Trump most clearly to Kaczynski, and to the themes of *Stemple Pass*: just as Trump's campaign promises mass deportation and the construction of a wall around national borders, so too does Kaczynski pride himself on his insular world. Like Trump, Kaczynski emphasizes the importance of shutting out unwanted outsiders, and of proving his own exceptionalism. If the cost is violence, then so be it. For such a quiet film (what many would describe as "minimalist cinema"), *Stemple Pass* speaks with more volume and terror than many contemporary horror films. Played in 2016, it's eerily prophetic.

THE HORROR OF A NATION'S DESPAIR: ROB ZOMBIE'S *31*

Originally published in *Bright Lights Film Journal* (2016)

ROB ZOMBIE'S *31* (2016) comes from a place of rage. Press interviews surrounding Zombie's previous film, *The Lords of Salem* (2012), found the director vowing to take a break from the horror genre. Since that time, he has described two passion projects in troubled development: *Broad Street Bullies*, which would follow the Philadelphia Flyers hockey team in the 1970s, and a biopic of Groucho Marx, tentatively titled *Raised Eyebrows*, which Zombie says would take cues from Billy Wilder's *Sunset Blvd.* (1950) while emphasizing the later stages of the comic's life. If the press is to be trusted, Zombie's progress on *Bullies* has been delayed indefinitely due to rights complications, and *Raised Eyebrows* is still in early development.

Enter *31*, a partially crowdfunded horror film that submits completely to its genre's darkest impulses. The plot is diabolically simple—Halloween, 1976: a group of RV-traveling carnies are ambushed on the road. The survivors wake up inside a vast, labyrinthine warehouse, where they are subjected to a sadistic game: they must spend the next twelve hours trying to survive the pursuit of murderous clowns. This game, called 31, is organized by a seemingly omniscient trio of people who wear powdered wigs and an air of parodied antiquity, led by Malcolm McDowell as Father Napoleon-Horatio-Silas Murder.

Intriguingly, the film instantly establishes a confrontational relationship with its audience, wherein its own narrative logic and reliability are called into question. For example, we never learn how these three aristocrats can witness the proceedings that we, the audience, see. When Father Murder and his associates muse and bet about the possibilities of the film's protagonists surviving, it seems that Zombie is commenting on the flippant attitude of critical and popular audiences toward violence. The aristocrats' powdered wigs and 18th-century attire convey an image of propriety, which is viciously and thoroughly undercut by their gleeful organization of the film's proceedings. Nobody is safe from this film's scrutiny; even society's politest, most well-adorned members reveal hideous potential through Zombie's lens.

Zombie makes such direct confrontation with the audience clear in the opening shot: a long black-and-white take of Doom-Head (Richard Brake), the film's most vile and dangerous clown, delivering a monologue that prepares us for the film's moral abyss. "I am not here to elicit an amused response," Doom-Head spits, staring us (the audience) directly in the eyes. It seems that Zombie, forced into returning to his genre-specific origins, has committed completely to the black hole at the center of this film. This is more of what the audience wants: the kind of ethically ambivalent savagery that characterized his first two films, *House of 1000 Corpses* (2003) and *The Devil's Rejects* (2005)—but he is not going to succumb. He is not going to make this fun for us. No, this is a film about literally and figuratively godless spaces, where unthinkable atrocities go unreported and incite the amusement of the sociopathic and faceless elite.

To be sure, the film concerns itself overtly with the imagery of Hell itself: when one of the carnies, Charly (Sheri Moon Zombie), hides inside a filthy bathroom, she sees the word *HELL* scrawled in muck on the stall doors. Not to mention, when the captives first awaken, the camera frames the phrase *"There ain't no God in here"* written on the side of a concrete pillar. (There is recent evidence that this may be a trend in mainstream American horror: consider *Don't Breathe* [2016], wherein the blind veteran who rapes and kills uses the invocation of a missing God to justify committing as much violence as he pleases.) *31*'s eerily godlike spectators might actually be the film's devils, overseeing the events of their own privately sanctioned underworld. This notion is visualized through the film's interest in marionettes; *31* reminded me repeatedly of the philosophy and fiction of Thomas Ligotti, who sees horror's true face in the possibility of indifferent cosmic puppeteers. These characters are explicitly identified as subservient to the wills of their author; autonomy means nothing, individuality means less.

This is no *Lords of Salem*, though; Zombie does not totally give in to his most abstract impulses. Instead, he returns to many of the thematic concerns of his pre-2012 works: most clearly, this aligns with *House of 1000 Corpses* and his *Halloween* films (2007 and 2009) in its setting—Halloween night in the 1970s, somewhere in the U.S.A. And like those previous films, this is very much about the U.S.A., about the ongoing and worsening hangover that followed the death of the hippie movement in the 1970s. This is the U.S.A. of Charles Manson, Jeffrey Dahmer, Richard Ramirez, and of course John Wayne Gacy. Much like the serial-killer-themed amusement park ride in *House of 1000 Corpses*, *31* is a fast and hyper-sensory excursion into a nation's sickest and bleakest fixations.

As a work of visual art, it is a grotesquely pronounced masterwork: gone is the classical composure of *Salem*. Here, scenes of violence see the camera jittering like a frightened animal; the lens crawls over the actors' sweaty and panic-stricken faces with claustrophobic closeness. Unusual use of focus sends giant bokeh drifting near characters' heads, like colorful omens of death. The editing often recalls the frenetic mania of *Corpses*, with one scene splicing disturbingly aggressive sex against images of F. W. Murnau's *Nosferatu* (1922). The digital evocation of 16mm grit effectively captures the sensory discomfort: this is a wet, grimy, and thoroughly unnerving experience.

The final scene recalls the infamous conclusion of *The Devil's Rejects*, in which the focal serial killer family charges their car headlong into a police blockade to the blaring soundtrack of Lynyrd Skynyrd's "Free Bird." *31* concludes with yet another image of a seemingly endless American highway, scoring provided by Aerosmith's anthemic "Dream On." The film's survivors stare each other down with weapons prepared: one with switchblades, the other with fists. We know who's going to make it out of this alive, and the answer leaves us feeling hopeless and drained. If you want optimism and fun, look elsewhere. If you are prepared to listen to one long scream into the bowels of a nation's despair, look no further than Rob Zombie's newest masterpiece.

"NO DESIRE IF IT'S NOT FORBIDDEN": DREAD, EROTICISM, AND TEXT MESSAGING IN *PERSONAL SHOPPER*

Originally published in *Seventh Row* (2017)

THE MESSAGE COMES from an unknown number: "I know you." As Maureen (Kristen Stewart) goes through Paris transit security, the messenger continues: "And you know me... You're off to London." When Maureen responds with her own text, demanding that the messenger reveal her or his identity, the answer is teasingly ambiguous: "Have a guess."

So begins *Personal Shopper* (2016)'s twenty-minute centerpiece: while commuting from Paris to London and back, Maureen engages in a series of uneasy SMS exchanges with this mysterious, ghost-like texter. Writer-director Olivier Assayas shoots this sequence from Maureen's perspective, often framing and editing in a quick shot-reverse shot style that gives equal space to the messages and Maureen's reactions. By maintaining our intimate proximity with Maureen, Assayas achieves central focus on her affective responses.

Early in the conversation, Maureen considers asking the anonymous texter whether he or she is the ghost of her deceased brother, Lewis. She starts to misspell the name, reconsiders, and then sends the request, waiting with bated breath. There is no immediate response, and Maureen puts her phone away. When she returns to the conversation, the messages are threatening and sexually forthcoming in equal measure: "I want you," writes the messenger. "I want you and I will have you."

Eventually, the persistent messages motivate Maureen to transgress; she tries on her boss Kyra's (Nora von Waldstätten) dress (something she is forbidden to do) and reports back to the mysterious texter: "I did it." The messenger's response: "You're scared."

That the mysterious texter may be Maureen's brother complicates the sequence, initially reducing the sense of threat. The mere possibility that Lewis may be on the other end of this dialogue consequently allows Maureen to develop a fast intimacy with the texter. This problematizes the sequence: if the messenger is not in fact Lewis, then Maureen's vulnerable emotional state has been exploited for unknown ends (is there a voyeuristic ghost manipulating her in order to watch her get undressed?). Alternately, if the messenger *is* Lewis, then Maureen's erotic transgression bears incestuous implications.

This long and tonally complex sequence is bookmarked by the film's most openly supernatural images. In the scene before Maureen receives her first message, a threatening spectre corners her inside Lewis's dark, abandoned house, spewing ectoplasm in her direction. Shortly after the central SMS sequence culminates in sexual release, that same ghost materializes in a corner of Kyra's bedroom. If it is not Lewis, then the messenger might well be the still-living human suspect at the center of the film's murder-mystery, but it might just as well be a cyber-connected spirit with a perverse fixation on Maureen.

In *Personal Shopper*, Olivier Assayas and his close collaborator Kristen Stewart provide two iterations of the ghost story: Maureen's attempts to contact Lewis, having made an oath that whoever died first would send a sign; and Maureen's SMS exchange with an anonymous texter, potentially from the beyond. Texting provides the medium for the film's most overtly horror-driven sequence, characterized by unease, fear, tension, and eroticism.

The messenger's disembodiment heightens Maureen's transgression: her eroticized act may or *may not* have an audience. The possible presence of an audience elevates the risk and therefore intensifies the excitement as well. Whether through physical absence left behind by death, or corporeal spaces afforded by technological communication, the film closely follows Maureen's navigations through the unresponsive, the invisible, the unknown.

Assayas repeatedly shows communication through digital technology as resulting in both presence and absence. Through Skype, Maureen has emotionally distant conversations with her boyfriend. On her iPhone, she watches videos about deceased symbolist painter Hilma af Klint. Maureen's boyfriend and, less literally, the deceased Klint are "present" only in that they can be seen through a screen.

Because a text message's author could be anyone and anywhere, the messages are scary—especially when their content emphasizes their surveillance-like nature with an erotic bent: "I'm watching you" and "I'm in London." This pushes Maureen to respond in kind, agreeing to the unknown messenger's request to go to a hotel room. She arrives at the desk in a trench coat, heels, and one of Kyra's dresses, as though for a sexual assignation. When she makes her way into the room, she takes a selfie in the hotel mirror, posing and holding the dress tightly against her body. The entire scene bears all the tropes of a meeting for an illicit affair, minus the physical presence of a partner. Indeed, the figure's very existence as a corporeal being remains uncertain.

By using technology, particularly text messages, as a source of terror that morphs into eroticism, *Personal Shopper* situates itself knowingly and brazenly within horror traditions. Kiyoshi Kurosawa's *Pulse* (2001) also foregrounds then-contemporary technological advances (the relatively early Internet) to highlight both its dramatic concerns and its horror. Similarly, many horror films have incorporated phones into their terrifying sequences: *Black Christmas* (Bob Clark, 1974), *A Nightmare on Elm Street* (Wes Craven, 1984), and *Ringu* (Hideo Nakata, 1998) are some of the most famous examples. Perhaps most strikingly similar to *Personal Shopper* is the opening of Wes Craven's *Scream* (1996), in which an unknown caller asks Casey Becker (Drew Barrymore) if she likes scary movies. Similarly, in *Personal Shopper*, the ominous unknown messenger says, "Tell me something you find unsettling," to which Maureen responds, "Horror movies."

Traditionally, horror movies feature links between eroticism and fear—specifically, between death and carnal "release." For example, the *Friday the 13th* (1980-2009) series boasts multiple sequences that cut between the advancing Jason Voorhees and various camp counselors as they get undressed and get it on. As the counselors' sexual energy builds, Voorhees draws closer—often, the characters' orgasms are either punctuated or cut off by the killer's phallic machete. Killers like Voorhees emerge from the dark at inopportune moments to brutally extinguish their victims for their transgressions, sometimes purported to forward a conservative ideological agenda, whereby transgressors (especially teenagers engaging in premarital sex) are punished for their "impurity."

Personal Shopper subverts this genre tradition in part because the messenger is not evidently corporeal. Rather than maintaining a purely threatening position, the messenger's "absence" allows the film to foreground Maureen's psychological interiority rather than her instinctive, panicked reactions. Unlike the killers in the aforementioned films, *Personal Shopper*'s unknown messenger possesses no "voice"; a long series of text messages are its only trace. The film emphasizes its threatening figure's physical ambiguity: when Maureen sends a text message asking, "R u a man or woman?", the messenger responds, "What difference does it make?" When Maureen questions whether the messenger is alive or dead, she receives no answer. The text messaging sequence acts not only as an exercise in suspense, but also as an extension of Maureen's character arc: her struggle to contend with absences, with non-responses, with vacancies.

Perhaps because of the messenger's lack of corporeality, the SMS becomes a motivator for Maureen's self-actualization. The messenger ("predator") and Maureen ("prey") exchange most of their messages as Maureen moves through daylit public spaces, which further sets the sequence apart from horror tropes (when the messenger asks Maureen why she is afraid of horror movies, she replies, "A woman runs from a killer and hides"). The texting sequence culminates with Maureen facing her fears to achieve arousal. As a personal shopper, she spends her days collecting pieces for her boss, Kyra. She often catches herself eyeing the pieces longingly: because Kyra forbids it, what she wants most is to try the clothes on herself. At the texter's urging, Maureen slips into Kyra's house and dresses herself in the woman's clothing. She informs the texter of her transgression, which establishes a form of complicity, and then she masturbates on Kyra's bed. As she had earlier explained to the unknown figure: "No desire if it's not forbidden." Maureen's arousal is possibly motivated by the fact that she now has a "spectator," even if that spectator remains contained within her phone. Deviating from the majority of the texting sequence's visual approach, this scene places us, the viewers, in a position to observe Maureen rather than see through her perspective. Assayas positions the camera outside the closet where Maureen is dressing; we are exiled to the bedroom and watching from a distance. Maureen completes the outfit offscreen, so that when she re-enters the frame wearing Kyra's harness and dress, it plays as a reveal. The shot pans away and fades to black when Maureen masturbates, providing her with the privacy that would not necessarily be afforded in a lurid slasher. That her erotic transgression does not end in violence speaks to the ways in which *Personal Shopper* breaks the horror-specific bind between brutality and sexual "misdeed."

Maureen never verifies for certain whether Lewis has responded to her calls, nor does the film unequivocally reveal the mysterious messenger's identity. Instead, *Personal Shopper* closes fittingly on a close-up of Stewart's pained and expressive face as she implores Lewis one last time. She pauses, and the screen fades not to black but to white, the absence of all colour. This is a crucial visual metaphor: the film itself leaves us with absence above all else. The final scene suggests that absence is grief's most exacting and excruciating toll: an absence of explanation, reason, and voice—an absence of presence. By drawing from horror conventions, Assayas and Stewart draw our attention to absence as a filmic device, emphasizing the texter's non-corporeality as a catalyst for both eroticism and fear. In this final scene, fear lingers in the silence and pain of grief.

GENRE TRAUMA IN M. NIGHT SHYAMALAN'S *SPLIT*

Originally published in *MUBI Notebook* (2017)

FROM *THE SIXTH SENSE* (1999) onward, writer-director M. Night Shyamalan has been popularly and critically typecast as the champion of "plot twists." This label probably plays into the unusually intensive scrutiny undergone by his films. Specifically, the scrutiny likely stems from Shyamalan's tendency to design narratives around the selective doling out of information, which lends itself to unusually plot-focused viewing. There is something to be said for the fact that a plot twist, on some level, deceives its viewers, leading them to believe something before abruptly unfurling that belief. Reviewing his latest film, *Split*, I would like to mostly dispense with this emphasis on "twists." By stressing one specific element of Shyamalan's storytelling process, one runs the risk of neglecting to address his commitment to storytelling itself. That is, it is worth noting that Shyamalan sees cathartic possibilities (often profoundly affirming ones) embedded in the very notion of story. Take, for example, *The Sixth Sense*—the film does not "work" simply because it effectively "dupes" its viewers; rather, its "twist" operates as a psychological and emotional revelation that completes the film's thematic thrust. Repeat viewings reveal a profound sadness within the film, seeing as it gives us a child whose only friend is a ghost, and a man so absent in his marriage that he has come to haunt rather than embody.

Certainly, Shyamalan's career-long focus on narrative makes its way into *Split*, which is perhaps his most confrontational and ambitious work to date. At first glance, the plot appears almost deviously simple. Within ten minutes, the film shows Kevin (James McAvoy) kidnapping three young women (Claire, played by Haley Lu Richardson; Marcia, played by

Jessica Sula; and outsider Casey, played by Anya Taylor-Joy). The story's schematic is laid out quickly: these women want to escape, and Kevin wants to keep them contained for initially unknown reasons. As the plot continues, it gradually reveals background information pertaining both to Kevin and Casey, centralizing their roles. Details surrounding Kevin, who suffers from DID (Dissociative Identity Disorder), unfold largely through therapy sessions conducted by Dr. Karen Fletcher (Betty Buckley). Occasionally, the film veers into asides with Fletcher to substantiate the possibility that Kevin's ominous twenty-fourth personality, "the beast," might reveal itself at any moment. Casey is also afforded background information through flashbacks, which come to reveal a traumatic childhood episode that has contributed to her status as a social outsider.

Playing out this story, *Split* explores possibilities inherent to the narrative design of "psychological horror," studying the ways in which that genre's patterns offer insights into human behavior. In doing so, the film also undoes assumptions about "normal" versus "abnormal" psychology, devoting much of its runtime to an assessment of what makes one "different," and how society's practices of marginalization cause immense damage. These questions work themselves out through the methodical exploration of Kevin, but also through the devastating revelations pertaining to Casey. Most interesting, perhaps, is the way in which *Split* concerns itself with the notion of victimhood as characterized and typified by standard predator-prey horror film scenarios.

The film initially appears to pit antagonist Kevin against protagonist Casey and friends. Such a set-up neatly organizes moral commitments, thus situating a potentially problematic division of mental disability versus mental well-being. However, as the narrative proceeds, it reveals trauma itself as the antagonist; said trauma finds its vessel in violence perpetrated by adults against children. We learn that Casey is also probably suffering from PTSD (Post Traumatic Stress Disorder), and her eventual confrontation with Kevin plays out as devastating reconciliation rather than suspenseful combat. The execution of this resolution is maybe the truest revelation, or "twist," in the film, subverting as it does the customary Manichean commitments of standard genre fare. It is interesting to note that this emphasis on childhood trauma reveals a career-long focus for Shyamalan; looking back, I can identify the same thematic undercurrent in *The Sixth Sense*, *Unbreakable* (2000), *Signs*

(2002), *The Village* (2004), *After Earth* (2013), and *The Visit* (2015). *Split*'s primary concern, then, is not the connection from "Event A" to "Event B" (although Shyamalan demonstrates a keen attentiveness to narrative craft); rather, the film focuses on the ways that genre can contend with painful material and offer affirming reinterpretations of tropes.

The film certainly encourages a study of the relationship between affect and storytelling, but also stunning are Shyamalan's faculties as a visual director. Seeing as he commits to these complex valences of violence and trauma, it is fascinating to note how *Split* deals with confined spaces. Although sympathy takes center-stage, the film does not betray its genre trappings: rather, *Split* acts as a disciplined exercise in Hitchcockian technique. Tension plays out often in spatial relations between the young women and the door leading to their potential escape, with Kevin's multiple personas positioned strategically elsewhere within the frame or scene. Indeed, the staging works toward maintaining suspense, but the film also conveys a lot of its psychological and thematic meaning through lighting, camera placement, precisely timed cuts, and some of the most careful *mise en scène* in the director's career. While Shyamalan has consistently demonstrated such aesthetic focus, it is worth noting that after *The Visit*, *Split* is the director's second collaboration with producer Jason Blum, who specializes in low-budget, mainstream horror; both *The Visit* and *Split* find the auteur working on a smaller scale, which is especially notable after his two consecutive special effects epics (*The Last Airbender* and *After Earth*). Indeed, *Split* finds Shyamalan in a formally invigorated mode, likely due in no small part to his collaborations with a younger crew (take, for example, director of photography Mike Gioulakis, who has shot recent independent productions such as David Robert Mitchell's *It Follows* and Mike Ott's *Lake Los Angeles*).

Considering both the narrative subversion and visual acuteness detailed above, the film's climactic scene warrants discussion: the sequence finds Kevin (now embodying his "beast" persona) scuttling spider-like through a dimly lit tunnel toward Casey. The scene incorporates the horror genre's visual language—Kevin has already committed acts of violence, and he smashes lightbulbs as he advances on his prey. Both the increasing darkness and the intercut close-ups of Casey's terrified face work toward a mounting sense of dread. Worth noting here is that throughout the film, Kevin has coerced his three captors to remove their garments, piece by piece. Initially, this appears to be Shyamalan's confrontation with the horror genre's clichéd "unclothing" of female victims; until this moment, the director's confrontation wavers between exploitation (even despite subversive intent, he is still gazing at young women's bodies) and coy self-awareness. However, in the episode at hand, those exploitative possibilities disappear given the narrative significance of being "revealed." That is, the pursued woman experiences her revelation and a forced contact with her own trauma at the exact moment that her shirt is torn, revealing her abuse-induced scars. So too does Kevin appear shirtless here, his naked body scarred and painfully dehumanized. Shyamalan pits these two characters on opposite ends of jail cell-like bars, shooting the man in close-up as he pushes through like an animal uncaged. This scene delves into the impact of trauma, depicting two similarly wounded and socially ostracized people. The imagery finds them connected metaphorically but divided physically by acts of violence.

The fact that this scene affords both pursuer and pursued with such empathy speaks to Shyamalan's proclivity for human drama, and to his genuine respect for genre. This is a rare picture, working both as a tightly designed work of horror while also causing its audience to reconsider customary notions of victimization. And yes, there is a sort of twist ending to finish it all off, which is appropriately surprising. I do not want to reduce this singular auteur to one element of storytelling, though; M. Night Shyamalan is one of the most consistently interesting auteurs in contemporary American cinema. *Split* is further evidence.

ACKNOWLEDGMENTS

DARKEST HOURS would not exist without all the magazine, anthology, and website editors who gave space to my fiction and criticism. Thanks to those folks.

Thanks to Christopher Payne, Scarlett R. Algee, and Sean Leonard at JournalStone for giving the book a new home, and for allowing me to flesh it out into something bigger and better.

Thanks to my agent, Stacey Kondla, who is always patient, wise, and encouraging.

Thanks to Randy Nikkel Schroeder, who taught me so much about craft and publishing in an undergraduate Directed Writings course. Thanks to Kit Dobson for allowing me to write an undergraduate honours thesis on Stephen King's *It*, thereby giving my dark fixations room to flourish. Thanks to Anthony Camara for his supervision of my master's thesis on John Carpenter's *Prince of Darkness*.

Thanks to Tom Hubschmid, Dan Thorn, Tomas Boudreau, and Syd Peacock for offering helpful notes on some of these stories' early drafts. Your feedback was invaluable.

Thanks to all the amazing folks who offered blurbs and praise. Your support means the world.

Thanks to Sadie Hartmann for being an early believer in my work, and for writing the reissue's thoughtful foreword.

Thanks to my family. Thanks to my friends. I wrote most of this book over the course of two tumultuous years, and you were always around.

And to all those who read, review, and spread the word: I wouldn't be here without you. Thank you, always.

ABOUT THE AUTHOR

(*Author photo by Robert Boschman*)

MIKE THORN is the author of the novel *Shelter for the Damned*. His second short story collection, *Peel Back and See*, is coming soon from JournalStone. His fiction has appeared in numerous magazines, anthologies, and podcasts, including *Vastarien*, *Dark Moon Digest*, *The NoSleep Podcast*, *Tales to Terrify*, and *Prairie Gothic*. His film criticism has been published in *MUBI Notebook*, *The Film Stage*, *Seventh Row*, *In Review Online*, and *Vague Visages*. He completed his M.A. with a major in English literature at the University of Calgary, where he wrote a thesis on epistemophobia in John Carpenter's *Prince of Darkness*. Connect with him on Twitter (@MikeThornWrites) and visit his website: mikethornwrites.com.

CPSIA information can be obtained
at www.ICGtesting.com
Printed in the USA
LVHW040919020621
689130LV00004B/270